Was it murder...
or a trick of light?

"An investigation that goes down some
very dark alleys...Hypnotic."
—*The New York Times Book Review*

continued . . .

Berkley Books by David Hunt

THE MAGICIAN'S TALE
TRICK OF LIGHT

TRICK

OF

LIGHT

David Hunt

B

BERKLEY BOOKS, NEW YORK

This is a work of fiction. The events described here are imaginary. The settings and characters are fictitious, even when a real name may be used. They are not intended to represent specific places or persons, or, even when a real name is used, to suggest that the events described actually occurred.

TRICK OF LIGHT

A Berkley Book / published by arrangement with the author

PRINTING HISTORY
G. P. Putnam's Sons edition / September 1998
Berkley edition / September 1999

The Penguin Putnam Inc. World Wide Web site address is
http://penguinputnam.com

ISBN: 0-425-17035-7

BERKLEY®
Berkley Books are published by The Berkley Publishing Group, a division of Penguin Putnam Inc., 375 Hudson Street, New York, New York 10014. BERKLEY and the "B" logo are trademarks belonging to Penguin Putnam Inc.

PRINTED IN THE UNITED STATES OF AMERICA

10 9 8 7 6 5 4 3 2 1

EROTIC GUNS

Among the rarest classes of firearm collectors are those who specialize in guns engraved with erotic motifs. On such weapons one will find lecherous satyrs, noblewomen in abandon, concupiscent couples, even relations beween humans and primates— scenes, in short, which encompass the full range of the artist's imagination.

I am given to understand that the fascination for collectors lies in the juxtaposition, that it is the contiguity of obscenity and weaponry, of the hunt and the debauch, in short the pure and blatant eroticism of violence, that is at the root of this outré brand of connoisseurship.

O. WELD HOPKINS

Gun Collectors and Their Quirks

(privately published, Gates Mills, 1949)

1
THE
CAMERA

I'm standing by the seawall just inside the entrance to San Francisco Bay, near the old Fort Point Coast Guard station, long since relegated to other use.

It's past midnight. The sea fog clings to the water like black smoke. There's little wind. No breakers splash against the wall. Bells ring gently on the buoys, and foghorns moan from ships entering the Bay. My friend Joel Glickman stands beside me. We listen to the mournful symphony, just the two of us alone, waiting for something to happen . . . we know not what.

I'm wearing a black sweatshirt, black jeans, black high-top sneakers, and have two black Contax cameras strung around my neck. Joel too is dressed dark, head to foot. We're here on a tip he received by phone this afternoon from an anonymous source who spoke swiftly, then hung up. This informant, Joel tells me, had a thick Chinese accent. Joel didn't recognize his voice and thinks the accent was phony.

"Like he was doing an imitation of one of those just-off-the-boat Chinese waiters," Joel says. "But he spoke clearly so I'd be sure to get the message." Joel offers an imitation of the imitation: " 'Wait tonigh' Presidio near ol' Coas' Guar' station. Sometin' velly interestin' gonna happen down there.' "

"Which means he knows you're working on a series about crime on the waterfront."

"Not uncommon knowledge," Joel says.

"Which means this could be a setup."

"Yeah, I suppose." He shrugs. "I doubt it though."

Well, thanks, Joel, I think. *Thanks for inviting me to the ambush.*

Joel titters. "Not scared, are you, kiddo?"

"Me?" I ask with mock surprise.

Joel gives me a brotherly pat on the shoulder. He's fifteen years older than me, nine inches taller. "No, not you. You're an Amazon warrior. No one messes with Kay Farrow if he knows what's good for him. Mess with her you're likely to get a kick in the butt." He smiles at me. "That *is* what you do in aikido class, isn't it?"

"Sure, Joel—we just kick ass."

Which, of course, is *not at all* what we do in aikido class, but such banter is typical of the way we've been carrying on this evening, waiting here in the open air with nothing better to do than practice ironic ripostes. Joel's a Pulitzer Prize–winning investigative reporter for the alternative weekly *Bay Area News.* I'm a former *News* colleague turned fine-art photographer. Whenever he needs pictures he gives me a call, and because I enjoy his company, I usually tag along.

"It's always the same on stakeouts," he says.

"What's that?"

"The way you stand and wiggle your toes. Or sit on your ass till some part of you gets tingly and falls asleep. You munch potato chips or chew gum and make tough-guy/tough-girl talk with your partner. You bitch and moan and glance at your watch. Most times nothing happens.

When something does, you usually miss it since you've fallen off to sleep."

"A real dog's life."

"You got it, kiddo."

He's fifty-one, gray-haired, gray-bearded, wears granny glasses and is thin as a rail. A former hippie who came out here for the Summer of Love in 1967, he's become a famous Bay Area personality by virtue of a string of news exclusives sniffed out by a prying instinct not to be denied.

Lightly he touches my arm. "Something's coming in."

I gaze across the water. The Golden Gate Bridge looms above; not much traffic on it at one A.M. this warm April night. But from this angle its architecture, the powerful arrangement of its girders and cables, moves me. It was here that Hitchcock shot the scene in *Vertigo* in which Kim Novak jumps into the Bay.

The fog has thinned. I hear water lapping against the seawall, then the low-pitched moan of a powerful foghorn, so low and deep its vibrations resound within my ears. The fog parts a little more; then something massive blocks my view of the north tower of the bridge. I make out lights, then the prow of an enormous ship.

"Supertanker," Joel says. "Down from Alaska. You know how dangerous it is to come in here in heavy night fog?"

I have no idea, wait for him to explain as I watch the huge ship slip silently into the Bay.

"I've been talking to the bar pilots. Great guys. They meet the big ships twelve miles out, climb on board, take control. They know these waters cold. Often on a long sea voyage the greatest peril's in the last hundred yards. A full tanker like that—if it hits a shoal the ecology of the Bay could be ruined. Look at that thing: ten stories high, two football fields long, forty million tons of crude in her hold. Boat like that, she goes a mile before you can bring her to a stop. She's not what we're waiting for though. Tankers come in here all the time." Joel glances at his watch. "Must be something else, like somebody's going to dump something illegally, commit an environmental crime."

"What about that?" I point to a small boat trailing the supertanker.

Joel stares at the vessel, dwarfed to insignificance by the tanker, which is heading now toward the oil wharfs of Richmond. The small boat is turning. It looks like a fishing boat, and now it's heading straight toward us.

"Look!"

Joel points to a man swinging a lantern from the end of the abandoned Coast Guard pier a hundred yards to our right.

"This is it. Haul ass, kiddo," he says, trotting toward the beach.

I race to keep up with him. The fishing boat's rapidly closing in.

"I don't think we're being too smart," I tell him when I catch up.

He nods. "If they're smuggling we're going to be toast."

He pulls me down behind one of the pilings that support the rotting pier where it crosses the beach. My nostrils fill with the rich aroma of seaweed, mollusks, wet black sand.

"Of course they're smuggling, Joel. Let's get out of here."

But Joel wants to stay. He's waited half the night for this; moreover, his tip is proving out.

"Sure, go," he says. "Just leave me a camera, okay?"

Like, right, I'm really going to do that.

Better two pieces of toast than one, I think.

We crouch down, then watch as the fishing boat swoops in. A man jumps onto the pier while another on board throws him a line. Within a minute they have the vessel secure.

"Came in right behind the tanker so she wouldn't be spotted. Pretty smart," Joel whispers.

We can hear the men talking. They're speaking Chinese. I pick up on a few words and their sense of urgency: *Move fast, do what we've come to do, get out quick.*

We watch as a stream of human beings, men, women and children, emerge from the hold, line up on deck, then, prodded by the crew, leap to the pier.

"It's not drugs they're smuggling, it's people," Joel says, "probably from Fujian province. That's where most Chinese illegals come from these days."

I watch amazed as the stream of human cargo continues to emerge, twenty . . . thirty . . . forty Chinese souls . . . and still they keep coming. I can't imagine how so many people could have been packed into so small a boat. Sixty . . . seventy . . . the stream continues—old men with wispy beards, young mothers with mewing infants in their arms, boys and girls with identical bowl-style haircuts—clinging to one another in what I assume are familial groups.

"I count over a hundred," Joel whispers. "Must've been packed in like sardines."

Lots of shouting now. The crew members are impatient. People hesitant to jump are prodded till they do. Old women are pushed. Two young girls are dragged out of the hold, heaved toward the outstretched arms of relatives already on the pier.

As the last illegals jump and the crew prepares to cast off, the man who swung the lantern leads the horde toward us on the beach. Just then a ragtag armada of vehicles appears out of the fog—jalopies, pickups, campers and panel trucks, even an old hearse from one of the traditional funeral parlors in Chinatown.

"This is incredible! Gotta get pictures!" Joel says.

He's right, this is a great scene. But what's going to happen when I stand up and start firing off my strobe? Will this army of illegals smash my camera? Beat me up? A lot of hopes and dreams are at stake tonight. After a cruel voyage these people have arrived at the promised land, huddled masses yearning to breathe free. So who am I to stand up and take their pictures at the illegal golden door?

Daring myself to take the risk, I rise and start to shoot. Perhaps my size makes me appear nonthreatening; I'm all of five two, 114 pounds. Whatever the cause, the illegals grin at me as they pass; some even wave. They wear identical dark cheap-fabric tracksuits with racing stripes down the legs. Their vessel has already disappeared into the fog. It will sneak back out to open sea as stealthily as it snuck in. Meantime, drivers of the vehicles are ordering them aboard for the final leg to town.

I lose track of Joel as I follow the illegals to the cars. Then I spot him talking to one of the drivers. The young man looks frightened. Joel, intent on his story, won't let him go. I don't blame him. It's a terrific story. I've heard of illegals landing from small boats on beaches south of the city, but never anything so bold, so organized or on such a scale as this—a vessel, with over a hundred aboard, actually swooping into San Francisco Bay, landing at a U.S. government–owned pier, met by a convoy that will transport its passengers to Chinatown, where they will merge in the clogged streets and disappear.

Suddenly—a whine in the air, a sound of meshing gears! A helicopter appears out of the gloom. It drops from the sky, hovers just above us, rotor wings whirling, beating aside the mist. A powerful searchlight shines down, creating a column of swirling dust. The light cuts through the fog, harshly probing, prying, pinning us where we stand.

I no longer need my strobe. The brilliant raw cone of light creates fantastic highlights and shadows on the ground.

A disembodied voice issues from the craft.

"ATTENTION! THIS IS THE UNITED STATES COAST GUARD. YOU ARE UNDER ARREST! LIE FACEDOWN ON THE GROUND, LEGS SPREAD, ARMS APART. REPEAT: YOU ARE UNDER ARREST!"

But the illegals don't comprehend. Terrified, they scurry, seeking escape from the storm of sound and light.

I switch on my motor-drive, fire off my camera as they scatter. *Whap!whap!whap!whap!whap!* I want to catch their confusion and panic as they attempt to flee this new tyranny bearing down upon them from the sky.

At the sound of sirens, the drivers desert their vehicles, join the illegals in frenzied attempts at flight. *Whap! whap! whap!* My motor-drive hums. Caught up in the hysteria, I fire away, picking out figures in midflight, freezing them against the nightscape. I'm excited, know I'm getting great stuff. I shoot by instinct, and when the roll is finished, bring up my spare camera and continue firing with that.

Joel's at my side. "Go for it, kiddo!"

Oh, I go for it! Swept up, feeling the rush, I strive to merge with the action. Finally, both my cameras out of film, I pause briefly to reload.

Sirens scream! Brakes squeal! Patrol cars screech in! Uniformed people leap out. Suddenly the area's crawling with cops, customs officers, assorted Feds and Coast Guard personnel, rushing to cut off escape.

But there's no way they can contain this multitude of desperate illegals, now widely scattered across the terrain. Only young mothers and the elderly remain riveted to the beach, eyes enlarged by terror. The rest are scrambling over fences, then dashing off in different directions, defying the shrill whistles and shouted commands.

Joel and I surrender to a freckle-faced MP. Though he totes a submachine gun, he's as frightened as any refugee. He takes us to his commander, who sniffs disdainfully at our press credentials. Then Joel is recognized by a senior immigration official, a man he interviewed just a week ago.

"How'd you hear about this?" the official demands.

"Tip," Joel says. "Same as you, right?"

The man grins. Plump, middle-aged, sporting a buzz cut and brush mustache, he wears a vinyl jacket with *I.N.S.* stenciled in block letters on the back.

Since we're accredited, can't be held or expelled, he beckons us aside for an impromptu briefing.

"It's like this," Buzz Cut says. "These human cargo smugglers get cockier by the week, but this is the first time they've dared enter the Bay. Next thing you know, they'll be landing illegals at high noon on Fisherman's Wharf."

He gestures toward the women and elders being marched to a police van.

"Look at 'em! Those folks are going back to China to spread the word getting here isn't enough. Doesn't matter what the smugglers promise you, you don't get a free ride just for scrambling up the beach. We catch you, we ship you back—that's the message tonight."

The meanness of the guy turns me off. I let him preen, take his picture, then wander off to cover the roundup.

Night's my time, when my vision's at its best. Being a complete achromat means I lack cone function in my eyes, and am thus completely color-blind. But for me color blindness is more an aesthetic issue than a problem. The other symptoms of achromatopsia—poor visual acuity and photophobia—are serious. Like most achromats, I don't see well, and can be snow-blinded when bright light saturates the rods in my eyes. During daylight hours I try to control this problem with extremely dark red wraparound shades. At night my rod function, which is normal, takes over, and then, perhaps because of my keen hearing and sensitivity in matters of sight, I see better than most vision-normals.

The illegals, routed and with no knowledge of the terrain, have been drawn to the wooded hills of the Presidio where pines and brush offer natural shelter. I follow their pursuers, purposeful men and women wielding radios and high-beam lanterns, as they try to cut off a quarry that has nothing to lose but its dreams.

I want to use my camera to capture the awful thrill of this manhunt, this game of stalkers and prey. The odds are skewed so sorely in favor of the trackers that I find my neutrality bent as well. It's the illegals I root for, not my fellow salt-of-the-earth Americans; after all, I saw the dreams dancing in their eyes.

I pick out one law enforcer, a strapping blond cop in his twenties, six feet two, purposeful eyes, scowl of determination on his face. I follow him. It takes him a while to notice me.

"Hey, who're you?" he demands, as we pant together up a bluff toward the woods.

"News photographer. Mind if I tag along?"

He looks me over. "Just doin' my job, ma'am. Don't mess with me, I won't mess with you."

Fair enough.

He turns back to the chase. He and his fellow hunters have the advantage; they're organized, know the Presidio well, while the illegals don't know it at all.

I catch sight of a pair of male refugees in the woods, poised, trying to decide which way to run. My blond companion spots them too, pins them with his flashlight, pulls out his side arm, charges forward ordering them to halt.

They stare at him, baffled. Suddenly all the pep goes out of them. *Whap!whap!whap!* I strive to catch the moment—the gloating triumph of the cop, the cornered looks on the illegals, grimaces of defeat. I document the cuffing and then the prodding as their captor marches them back down to the beach. I haven't the heart to follow them.

Standing there on the bluff, looking around for something else to shoot, I hear a moan. Turning, I notice movement in a nearby clump of bushes. Moving closer to investigate, I come upon another cowering figure, this one a young Chinese woman who looks to be no older than seventeen.

Her hair's bowl-cut, she's wearing the same dark cheap fabric tracksuit as the others, but there's something distinctive about her—her oversize almond-shaped eyes. They're much larger than normal Asian eyes, and since she's weeping, they endow her face with a particular pathos.

In an instant my heart goes out to her. Rather than photograph her and risk revealing her position with my strobe, I kneel beside her to try to give her comfort.

She speaks barely ten words of English: "please,"

"thanks you," "yes," "no," "me," "you" and the one that strikes at me most poignantly, "mercy."

"Please mercy please," she moans.

No way can I resist an entreaty like that. I take her face in my hands, wipe away her tears, gently stroke her hair, tell her she'll be all right, then pull out my wallet, extract a twenty-dollar bill and press it into her hand.

She gazes at me, querying expression on her face. I pull off my black sweatshirt and indicate to her that she should put it on. After she does I point the way to the nearest exit from the Presidio. She nods to show me she understands.

"Go," I tell her. "Go on! Scoot!"

She takes several steps, then turns, meeting my eyes once again.

"Thanks you," she whispers.

"Yes, yes. Now go!" I implore her, gesturing for her to run. She smiles, then dashes off into the woods.

God, I hope you make it!

Back on the beach I find Joel still interviewing his friend from I.N.S.

"Okay, we got a tip," Buzz Cut admits. "So we went to level-A alert and watched our radars. Soon as that boat turned up, we had her in view. Once she unloaded, we flew in."

"What's happening with the boat?"

"Coast Guard's tracking her. When she connects with the mother ship, they'll seize them both."

"Tell me something," Joel says. "You do a pretty good Chinese accent, right?"

Buzz Cut cups his ear.

"It was you called me, wasn't it, passed the tip?"

Buzz Cut smirks. "Still don't get it, do you, Joel? We don't like the press."

To show our appreciation, we hang around till just before dawn, watching the illegals as they're brought in, made to squat on the ground, hands cuffed behind their backs with plastic strips. Under the harsh lamps of the squad cars, they appear a forlorn bunch.

"Aren't you cold?" Joel asks. "What happened to your sweatshirt?"

I tell him I gave it to a refugee.

"That's beautiful," he says. "I wish I could do stuff like that. Unfortunately I have this block about getting involved. You know, 'stay out of the story'—the hard-ass journalist's code."

He looks around. "A scene like this is sadder than what happens down on the Mexican border. There it's: 'If we don't make it today, we'll try again tomorrow.' But for these people there won't be a second chance. Too long a distance, too high a cost."

"They can ask for political asylum, can't they, Joel?"

"They can ask, but they probably won't get. Truth is they come over for economic reasons, not to escape political persecution. And they won't be persecuted on their return either . . . as the Chinese consul will testify at their hearing."

"So the only winners are the smugglers."

"That's about right. The price is around thirty grand per head, life savings up front, remainder plus unconscionable interest to be paid out of earnings once you're here. Essentially this means years of indentured servitude working in restaurants and garment sweatshops. The guys who drove the cars and the ones on the boats—they're poor slobs too. It's the Chinatown fat-cat gangsters, the Wo Hop To boys, who get rich off of this."

It's so depressing we decide to leave, especially now that just about everyone who disembarked the little boat has been caught. The joint interception operation has been a success, signified by the self-congratulatory way Buzz Cut and the other big shots are now strutting about.

In Joel's car, driving out of the Presidio, I assure him I got terrific stuff.

"It's a good story," he says. "Something bothers me

though. Who tipped us off—me and the Feds? Why'd he
do it? Why'd he want those people rounded up? Believe
me, Kay, it wasn't some patriot all upset over illegal immigration. Someone was trying to hurt somebody. Who?
Why? That's the story I want."

Joel's been driving the same battered VW Beetle for
years. It bears the usual radical/funny Bay Area bumper
stickers, old UCal parking permits, a mess of sneakers and
pop bottles on the floor in back, a photo of Joel's Swedish
ice-goddess girlfriend, Kirstin, taped to the steering wheel.
A recent addition, a pair of their love child's baby shoes,
swings from the rearview mirror.

We head over to an all-night diner on Lombard. Though
it's not yet six A.M., the place is filled with bedraggled cab-
bies and burly teamsters sipping fastidiously ordered coffee preparations—double espressos, cappuccinos, caffe
mochas and macchiatos. We take a booth, order lattes,
stare at one another, exhale.

"How's little Roland?" I ask.

Joel grins. "Totally lovable."

Joel's such a pussy cat! I've seen him at the Marina
Safeway, the kid swaddled in his backpack like a papoose,
while he and Kirstin fill their grocery cart with baby food
and Pampers.

"How's your girl-boxer thing going?" he asks.

He's talking about my current photographic project—
hanging around gyms, shooting young female fighters. I
like the kids, their commitment and discipline. My shots
look good, I've caught the energy and the sweat. Just one
problem—the pictures aren't leading me anywhere.

"Actually I'm floundering," I tell him. "I've lost my
way."

"Stick with me, kiddo," he says, "you'll find it again.
There's a big book in the waterfront, the whole Bay situation. Incredible beauty, incredible pollution. Bridge-
jumpers, floaters, smugglers, corruption—you name it, it's
out there."

I shrug.

"Meantime are you really going for your black belt?" he asks.

I nod. "*Shodan* is what we call it. When I started with aikido I never thought I'd get this far. I thought if I could just half the stuff those black belts do, I'd be satisfied. Well, somehow, after six years, I seem to have picked up a technique or two. Sensei Rita says it'd be a shame not to try and go all the way."

He nods, though I doubt he has much sympathy. He detests sports, even pretends not to know the names of Bay Area pro teams. For years he's ribbed me about my devotion to martial arts. Still, he respects commitment, so perhaps on some level he does understand. Also, I think he relishes the notion that someday, when we're in a tight spot, little me, his dewy-eyed former protégé, will protect him from a beating.

After coffee, he drops me in front of my building at the crest of Russian Hill.

"Thanks for an exciting evening," I tell him. "I'll drop off prints for you this afternoon."

He busses my cheek. "You were great, Kay. Took guts to stand up back there."

The light's flashing on my answering machine. I ignore it, go to the window, look out upon the city as it's touched by first light. There is a loneliness I feel as the sun comes up, a sorrow I can't quite define. Knowing that soon the light will be overpowering, I turn away from the window, undress, shower and then, in a robe, go to my answering machine to check my messages.

There's only one, from David Yamada. The message is neutral enough: "Please call me, Kay, when you get in." But there's something intense in his tone that causes me to worry.

Since I barely know David, I know his message must

concern Maddy, my photography coach, mentor and guru, the guiding female light in my life since my mother killed herself when I was twenty-one. Now I'm worried that something's happened to her. I can't think of any other reason for David to call.

Though it's not yet seven A.M., I phone him back. He picks up on the first ring.

"Oh, Kay—I've got sad news. Better sit down," he says.

I remain on my feet. "Maddy?"

"I'm so sorry to have to tell you this, Kay. She passed away last night. I just don't know any other way to say it."

Maddy dead! She's been in fragile health the last few years, but still I can't believe it. I saw her just two days ago, visited her in her flat in the Marina. She went over my proof sheets; then we gabbed as usual about photography, people, life.

"Oh, my God!" I drop the phone, stoop to pick it up. "What happened, David? Was it a stroke?"

"No . . . something else."

"What?"

He doesn't answer.

"For God's sakes, David—what happened?"

"Seems she was killed in a hit-and-run."

Jesus! The news slams into my stomach like a blow. Hit-and-run! That doesn't seem possible. She rarely went out in daytime, let alone at night. She lived in one of the safest neighborhoods in the city. How could such a thing happen?

I sit down, take several long deep breaths, feel tears pulsing from my eyes.

"Listen," he says, "there're a lot of people I've got to call, people in the East, Europe too. But I want you to know I tried you first, called you soon as I heard."

"I was out all night shooting."

"She would have loved that, Kay. You know she would. I'll call you back later, we'll talk some more. Is that all right?"

"Yeah . . ."

"You're okay?"

"I'll manage, David. Talk to you later."

After I hang up I stare out the window. The fog has lifted, the city is resplendent—glittering, white, cubic city of towers and hills. The light, growing intense, forces me to blink. I go to the windows, draw the drapes, allow my eyes to rest. Brilliant San Francisco days, so glorious for others, are painful for me. I like the city best when it's enveloped in fog, swaddled in mystery and mist.

I sit again, visualize Maddy as she appeared two days ago, her body so frail, her eyes brilliant as lasers. "Eyes that should be registered as dangerous weapons," an interviewer once wrote. In fact, I think, Maddy truly *was* her eyes, not just because they were so prominent, but on account of the way she employed them in her work. Her eyes defined her. Her work was about seeing, unmasking, looking through surfaces, penetrating to hidden cores. If photography, like all visual art, is about the artist's vision, then Maddy's art cut deep.

I pick up the phone, dial David again, apologize for interrupting him, tell him I must know more before I try to sleep.

He tells me there'll be a graveside service day after tomorrow. People will be flying in from L.A. and New York. Maddy will be buried beside Harry Yamada, David's father, in the Japanese cemetery in Colma.

"She wanted that," David tells me. "She left a letter, mentioned you in it, Kay, wanted you to have all her cameras."

Now I can't hold back my tears.

"But that's great!" David tries to reassure me. "You were her favorite student. What better way to pass on the baton?"

He tells me her archive, prints and negatives, will go to the San Francisco Museum of Modern Art. He can't, however, tell me much about the hit-and-run. Just that Maddy was run down by a motorcyclist in the Mission district sometime after midnight. The police, finding David's name in her purse, called him to ID her body.

"What was she doing there, David?"

"I can't figure it out."

"Did she have friends in the Mission?"

He doesn't think so, but isn't sure. Then, when he tells me where the accident took place, on Capp near Twenty-fourth, I'm even more confused. I've shot film near there, covered the narcotics and prostitution scene, know it as one of the roughest areas of the city.

"Could she have been out shooting?" I ask, knowing full well that three years ago she told everyone she was giving up photography to devote herself full-time to her students and to organizing her archive.

"Hard to believe," David says. "She turned sixty-eight in February, was barely well enough to walk to the store, let alone shoot on the street. No camera was found, and since the cops found her purse with money inside, I think they'd have found her camera too if she'd been carrying one."

"But she must have been doing something?"

"Beats me," he says.

After we say goodbye, I know I must try and get some sleep. I pull the bedroom drapes, then, just before slipping into bed, gaze at a print Maddy gave me that hangs on the opposite wall.

It's from the series of astonishing photographs she took for *Life* during the Vietnam War. The contrast is extreme, the blacks inky and rich, the scene set in the highlands under brooding failing light. It's a simple picture really: a group of five GIs, cold, grizzled and dirty, crouching by a small fire, holding their hands above the flames for warmth. It speaks eloquently of misery, mud, filth and chill, days spent beneath drab skies in close proximity to death. The most important aspect of the picture is the connection Maddy makes with the soldiers' eyes. All five gaze straight at her in a manner that seems to reach beyond her lens. It's the famous haunted "thousand-yard stare" of combat soldiers — eyes that have witnessed unspeakable horror.

It's certainly not a cheery picture for a bedroom, not one a decorator would choose. But I love it, it moves me, not only because I find it profound but because of what it tells me about the photographer—that she saw deeply and clearly, with strong emotion but without a scintilla of sentimentality. It reminds me that Maddy was a great photojournalist, gives me a standard to aspire to. And now that she's gone I know that every time I look at it I'll see what she once saw through those remarkable eyes.

I wake up a little after noon, rested if not refreshed. The bed is redolent of sandalwood soap, the scent of my occasional lover, Dr. Sasha Patel. For a moment I wonder why I've slept so late, then recall last night's adventure and the terrible news that hit me when I got home.

Maddy gone.

A surge of sadness fills me. I'm tempted to close my eyes, go back to sleep. But that isn't my way. Instead I get up, splash water on my face, pull on a T-shirt and jeans, then go into my darkroom to process the rolls I shot last night.

There's something soothing about darkroom work, the quiet solitude, the routine. The light's dim, which calms my eyes. I even like the smell of the photochemicals, no doubt an acquired taste. Negative images fascinate me, the reversal of tones, seeing dark objects as light and light as dark. Best of all I love the magic of the process, seeing images emerge where none were visible before.

My pictures of the illegals are as strong as I'd hoped. I believe I've caught their cheer as they came ashore, their terror beneath the chopper, desperation as they fled, dejection when they were caught. I think about what Maddy will say, her criticisms as she holds my proof sheets in her hands. Then, remembering she's gone, I grasp the magnitude of my loss.

I'll have to become my own critic now.

Rapidly I machine-dry the proofs, clean up my darkroom, place the dry prints in an envelope, phone for a taxi, grab my gym bag, then go downstairs to wait.

I drop the proof sheets for Joel at the *News* offices in SoMa, then circle back to the corner of Lombard and Octavia, where there's a storefront Cambodian restaurant.

Marina Aikido's on the second floor. The sensei here is a kick-ass former Marine—Rita Reese, lean, tall, black, hair braided into cornrows, white plastic clacker beads secured to the braids. No inscrutable koans from her. She's not one of your mystical Northern Californian types. She's deceptively casual, a down-to-earth martial artist. But just try sneaking up on her. Her awareness is superhuman!

The dojo's austere. The mat is white. On one wall, the *kamiza,* there's a photograph of Morihei Ueshiba, founder of aikido, while the opposite wall is lined with mirrors. Wooden swords and assorted stabbing and striking weapons are arranged aesthetically in a rack. A vase on a low table displays a budding cherry branch.

When I come in, early arrivals are already warming up. I go to the changing room, put on my *ki,* join them on the mat, start my breathing and stretching routines. Just as class is to begin, Rita emerges from her office, sleek in her black floor-length *hakama* skirt. When and if I achieve my *shodan,* I shall wear a *hakama* too.

I recall the night, six years ago, when I first came here with a friend. We were training in karate, but curious to see what aikido was about. Amazed by what I witnessed, I decided to give up karate and train here, and have been coming three times a week ever since.

For me aikido seems just so . . . right. For one thing it's a defensive art. We don't kick, nor do we strike very much; rather we wheel, blend and throw. The techniques are difficult, requiring great concentration, the art's physically, mentally and spiritually demanding. But the end result's extremely beautiful—balletic, clean, composed of quick breathtaking moves combined in a seemingly effortless flow.

It's the purity of aikido that I love, also something curious that transforms me whenever I train. Although the dojo is well lit and thus should be hard on my eyes, here my poor vision seems to abate. In practice I become acutely aware of everything around me, sensing, feeling, achieving a state that calms my soul.

This afternoon my workout partner is Tom, a student at U.C. Tall, shaggy-haired, he has a gentle manner—fitting, I think, since I can use some gentleness today. We train well together, practice wrist-holds, throws and falls, blend in whirlpools of energy. By the end of class, sweaty and slightly sore, I feel I've been through a clarifying experience.

Usually after class, several of us walk over to Chestnut Street for coffee. Today, when Tom asks me to join in, I gently decline. Instead I walk on to Maddy's building on Alhambra, following a route I've taken many times. It was my habit to drop in on her at least once a week after class, carrying my proof sheets in my gym bag.

I stand outside the 1930s period structure of stucco and embedded beams, gazing up at her windows on the second floor. Even wearing my heaviest wraparound shades, I can scarcely bear the glitter of the light bouncing off the walls. Still, I can see that the blinds are open. Always, when Maddy knew I was coming, she would thoughtfully close them in advance.

Saturday afternoon: The sky's overcast when I reach the Japanese cemetery. Maddy, of course, wasn't Japanese, she was born and brought up in Wyoming, one grandfather a Wind River Shoshone. But when she married Harry Yamada she became fascinated with Japanese-American culture. The beautiful heart-wrenching book they created on the memories of Nisei herded off to internment camps—her pictures, his text—undoubtedly influenced the passage of the 1988 Civil Liberties Act that finally granted reparations to internees.

The cemetery is austere, smelling faintly of pine. I enter through a wooden portal, find myself in a kind of garden in which stone markers are sunk to the level of the earth amidst a variety of mosses clinging to randomly placed rocks.

A group is gathered at the grave site. I recognize several famous photographers: Ernest Caprio, Jerry Rosen from New York, landscapist Donatella Bruce from Santa Fe.

But it's the photojournalists, masters of black-and-white photography, who are Maddy's real colleagues: Lloyd Summer-Jones, now in his eighties—in 1944 he photographed the liberation of the German death camps; David Hirsch, famous for his prison photographs, so filled with rage and despair; Anna Lars Stapleton, whose brilliant coverage of fighting in Bosnia reminded people of Maddy's coverage of the Vietnam War.

Bay Area arts leaders are also present: curators, teachers, dealers, as well as not so famous people—Maddy's haircutter, her housekeeper, neighbors, friends. There are people I don't recognize too, including a small handsome woman with silver bangs who, weeping copiously, stands apart.

I stand with her other students, the four of us who went to her for private coaching. We listen, awestruck, as Lloyd Summer-Jones, leonine, voice tremulous, gives the formal eulogy.

"Maddy was a great observer of life, also a great participant. Never one to hide behind the camera, she engaged herself with the great issues of her time. When Harry Bridges rallied the San Francisco longshoremen, Maddy stood among them in the crowd. Soon as she got to Vietnam she demanded to go to where the fighting was. There she slept in trenches and suffered the hardships of the men she'd come to photograph. When, in 1968, protestors were attacked by the Chicago police, she was on the next plane to join and document them on the barricades. The same thing during the race riots in Watts, the Yom Kippur War, the rebellion in Eritrea. Funny thing—though she was honored many times, she never hung her awards on her walls. Rather she kept them in her closet in a tattered old box. 'It's the pictures,' she said, 'that are important. They're the best reward you ever get.'"

Summer-Jones pauses. His cheeks, I note, are streaked with tears. "Oh, Maddy," he says, "hard to believe you're gone, old girl. The world's going to be a different place without you and your gorgeous melt-you-down eyes."

The ceremony is swift. A Shinto priest says a few words; then a Japanese flutist plays as the casket is lowered into the ground.

After most everyone else leaves, we, her students, stand around. We speak quietly of her death, the bizarre way she was killed, speculate about what she was doing in such a place at such an hour.

Jim Lovell is certain she was shooting film. He was a self-taught street photographer who used to hang around Washington Square selling his pictures for twenty dollars apiece out of a portfolio propped against a park bench. One day Maddy walked by, looked at his stuff, bought several prints. Later, when he asked if she would coach him, she agreed. Since he couldn't afford her fees, she accepted payment in photographs, one per session. That was the kind of open, available person she was.

"She sure wasn't up there buying burritos," Jim says. Looking at him in his old ill-fitting suit, I realize this is the first time I've seen him freshly shaved.

"I don't think she was shooting," Lacy Harper says. She appears completely stricken. Formerly Maddy's darkroom assistant, she's become a successful portraitist under Maddy's tutelage. "A year ago I had this idea that we should do a double portrait. She told me she'd stopped taking pictures and that was that. She refused even to touch the camera. She was adamant."

"The cops didn't find a camera," I remind them.

"Someone could have stolen it."

"They found her purse with money inside."

"Maybe she fell on her purse but her camera fell loose."

"Could be the motorcyclist took it," Kevin Wang says. He's the youngest among us, a gifted graduate of the San Francisco Art Institute specializing in candid shots taken in smoky light on the streets of Chinatown. "Say he came back, saw what he'd done, spotted the camera, scooped it up. Or say she took his picture just before he hit her—he'd have to retrieve her camera to protect himself."

"Speculative bullshit," Jim says. And of course, he's right. We stand awhile in silence.

Then someone asks: "What was she doing there?"

There's no explaining it. We knew Maddy as a teacher, a coach, but have no knowledge of what she did when we weren't around.

The others drift off, but I stay on. Finally David and I are the only ones left. The cemetery workers have finished filling in the grave. David clutches one of Maddy's old self-portraits to his chest.

It's time to leave. As we walk to David's car a flock of crows breaks from the branches of an exquisitely formed Monterey cypress.

I turn to David.

"Summer-Jones was right," I tell him. "Without her the world won't be the same."

I **want the hurt to go away . . . but** it won't. Three days after Maddy's burial, I'm burning with fury. Hit-and-run! Only a coward abandons an old woman to die on the street.

Early in the evening I take a bus up to Mission Street and Seventeenth, the heart of Hispanic San Francisco, the crossroads where our Latin citizens shop and meet. Mexicans, Cubans, Colombians, Salvadorans, Peruvians, Nicaraguans . . . each group has its own enclave nearby, its street murals, coffeehouses, bars and restaurants.

The Mission district is studded with labor union offices, all-night groceries, open-air fruit stands, storefront theaters, alternative galleries, radical newsstands, Santeria churches, as well as a tortilla factory, an anarchist meeting hall and a cooperative women-owned erotic boutique.

Stores here don't close till late. I walk past a left-wing bookshop filled with serious-looking people browsing beneath a huge poster of Lenin. Spotting a florist's, I enter, then purchase a bouquet of somber irises.

The stretch of Capp between Sixteenth and Twentieth streets, called "Capp Corridor," is notorious for its bottom-of-the-barrel prostitution scene. I did a photo story here once when I worked at the *News,* didn't see any beauties, down-on-their-luck actresses or adventurous literary Stanford grad-student types seeking material to deploy in their novellas and poems. Rather I found scarred old-timers and grungy disheveled "rock whores," so called because they work for the price of a rock of crack cocaine or a hit of meth.

Turning into Capp, I feel myself tense up. The trick, I know, is to walk with purpose lest I attract the notice of johns cruising in pickups and cars.

This is a tough area. Rapes and beatings are common, and there're ten to twelve unsolved homicides a year— Capp Corridor being a natural habitat for psychotics in search of prey. Joel Glickman told me of still another threat—rumors that the local homeowners association, upset by the effects of the prostitution scene upon property values, regularly pays Mission Street toughs to terrorize the women in hope of driving them away.

After crossing the intersection with Twentieth, I relax. Here Capp becomes a quiet, normal, working-class residential street, the buildings abutting one another, some with small, home-based businesses located on lower floors. There are groceries, nail salons and bars at the intersections. There's even an occasional church. At the corner of Twenty-fourth I pause beneath a streetlamp. Spotting a woman hauling bags of trash from her stoop down to the street, I approach, ask if she can tell me where the hit-and-run accident took place.

"The señora?" she asks. She's middle-aged, speaks with a Mexican accent. She looks deeply into my eyes.

I nod.

"There," she says, rapidly crossing herself, then pointing toward a pool of darkness down the block on the other side. Feeling unsteady, I nod, thank her and move toward the site.

Immediately I spot several packets of flowers lying together beside the curb. Their modesty endows them with special poignancy. There's wax residue too, where people have placed memorial candles. I lay my flowers beside the others, step back, spend a few seconds taking in the scene. Then, as in aikido class, I center myself and peer about.

This block, I realize at once, is not as I'd imagined. I thought it would be busy, active with street life; in fact, it's extremely quiet. Small apartment buildings, subdivided wooden houses, one-family residences. Cars are parked along the street, spaces left between to allow access to garages.

This is not, I understand, a spot where one would stand waiting to photograph a street scene. Rather it's a place one might walk by to or from somewhere else. I ask myself: What was Maddy doing off the sidewalk? Was she trying to cross the street in the middle of the block?

I stand back from the curb, turn and examine the house directly behind. Nothing special about it, just a nondescript wooden home in need of paint. I peer back across the street. If Maddy stepped off the curb here to cross, then what might she have been crossing to?

I pick out three buildings: an ordinary four-story stucco apartment house, molded escutcheon above the door, and two wooden Edwardians on either side, one well kept, the other kept not so well. I peer at the windows of the apartment building. Through several I see the flicker of TVs.

But suppose Maddy wasn't crossing the street here, rather had just crossed, reached this side, when she was hit?

I pivot to look again at the house in need of paint, catching, as I do, a movement in a window as if someone looking out has quickly pulled a drape.

Nothing strange about that. Rather, I realize, it's me, a stranger standing here in the dark, who is out of place.

The woman who pointed out the spot is still watching me from her stoop. Deciding I'd like to speak with her again, I cross Capp as I imagine Maddy may have done.

It's so quiet I can't imagine that the sound of an approaching motorcycle wouldn't have alerted her.

The woman doesn't smile as I approach; neither does she grimace or retreat. Rather she stands her ground, forcing me to stop three steps below.

"Do you know which way the motorcycle came?" I ask.

She shrugs. "I did not see it happen."

"Did you hear anything?"

"I already talked to the cops."

"I'm not a cop." Again she stares into my eyes. "The old woman who was killed—she was like a mother to me."

She nods slightly to show understanding, crosses herself again. "My own mother died last year," she says.

I feel she would like to be kind, but is uncomfortable speaking with me here.

"Thanks for showing me the place," I tell her. "I left some flowers."

She gives me another searching look. "I did too," she says, then turns and retreats into her house.

Feeling something behind me as I head back toward Mission Street, I quickly turn. Again I see a glimmer in the same window across the street, a quick furtive movement. I think: *They're watching me, everyone on the block. They know something's wrong with what happened here. Now they're wondering if I am part of it.*

Detective Kostas Kremezi boasts that he wears two hats.

"Night Investigations and Crime Response—I work both units," he says proudly.

"Does that mean you work night and day?" I ask.

He shows me a crooked grin. "I'll tell you this, I work damn hard," he says.

It's ten A.M. We're sitting in his cubicle on the fifth floor of the Hall of Justice, a huge structure on Bryant

Street, a rabbit warren of bureaus and corridors. In theory everything pertaining to criminal justice in San Francisco is handled out of here—police administration, investigations, prosecutions, bookings, jailings and trials.

Kremezi's a husky, swarthy, mustachioed Greek-American with canny noncommittal eyes. I figure him for early forties. After numerous shufflings and unsatisfactory encounters around the Hall, I've finally landed at his desk, the correct place, he's just assured me, to discuss the investigation of the hit-and-run death of Amanda Yamada.

Except, it turns out, he won't discuss it, though he's quite willing to hear what I have to say. It's police policy, he tells me, not to talk about ongoing investigations. But in a case such as this, in which the victim was fairly prominent, it's also policy to reassure friends and relatives of the deceased that everything possible is being done.

"I went by there last night," I tell him. "A woman told me the cops had been around."

"SOP with hit-and-runs. We always canvass the neighborhood."

"Find out anything?"

"Not much." Kremezi speaks in the manner of a man weighing his words.

"Just what's that supposed to mean?"

"Look, Ms. Farrow, no one saw it happen, therefore no ID on the motorcycle or the driver. Yes, people heard the accident, but by the time they looked out it was over and the vehicle was gone. Still, there're a lot of good citizens over there. Right away we got five, six calls. An ambulance arrived in under four minutes. Sadly too late. Your friend was DOA."

"What was she doing there?"

Kremezi shrugs. "No one including her stepson seems to know."

"You called it an accident."

"Some reason you think it wasn't?"

Now it's my turn to shrug.

"Trying to tell me something?" he asks.

"You sure as hell aren't telling me anything."

"I explained—"

"Yeah, you did."

We stare at one another, each of us bristling. It's Kremezi who breaks the silence.

"Why are you so confrontational, Ms. Farrow?"

"Why are you withholding information, Detective Kremezi?"

He bites his lip, ponders. "All right," he says. "Since you're so keen for answers, here's a little hypothetical for you, something to mull over just before you go to sleep."

He tilts back his chair till it touches the wall behind.

"Let's say there's this elderly individual in frail health, and he, or she as the case may be, is run down at a time and in a place when and where by all rights this person oughtn't to be. No one sees anything. The driver gets away clean. When the cops and medics arrive, they find neighbors out on the street shaking their heads and more or less securing the scene. There's this odd mood, least that's the way it seems to one of the investigators. Like the neighbors want to protect this old person, make sure the body isn't messed with, that nothing belonging to this person is stolen or moved. But they don't know the victim—least that's what they say. Never seen him or her before. Got no idea who he or she is. But the way they're standing there— it's like they're real upset, that he/she's not a stranger, that he/she's . . . well, like one of their own, if you get what I mean. It's strange, this feeling a cop might get . . . and . . . well, that's the odd thing, in fact the *only* thing about this . . . er . . . hypothetical case."

During his recitation, Kremezi has looked past me at the wall. Now he resettles his chair and meets my eyes.

"Fleeing the scene—it's run-of-the-mill these days. So many hit-and-runs you can barely keep up with 'em, and without any evidence—an eyewitness statement, a piece of

the vehicle, a smudge of paint, something, anything—
there's really no place to start. So you just keep the case in
the back of your mind, hoping sooner or later something'll
turn up. Often nothing does. So what're you going to do? An
odd feeling at the scene that the neighbors' denials didn't
quite ring true—that's not enough to put in the legwork . . .
there being only so many hours in the day"—he smiles—
"and the night."

I stare at him, trying to glean his message. I receive little encouragement.

"Like I said, Ms. Farrow, it's a hypothetical. What more
can I tell you?" He rises to signal our meeting is over. He
smiles weakly, extends his hand. "Nice meeting you. Sorry
for your loss."

David Yamada, like his father, is a CalTech graduate and engineer. Four years ago he started a business
designing and building ingenious, expensive, high-tech
kaleidoscopes. With his instruments, viewers can mix
light of different hues, creating shapes which are then
multiplied with mirrors into pleasing designs. Since I
don't see colors, a portion of the effect of these devices is
lost on me, but even within a range of grays I find the
resulting images intriguing.

David has never married, goes through girlfriends too
fast, can rightly be described as a "ladies' man." His features are Japanese; his accent is pure American. He was
nine when his mother died, twelve when his father, Harry
Yamada, married Maddy. She mothered him through his
teens, was immensely proud of him. To all appearances
they were devoted.

An hour ago he called to make sure I was home, so he
could drop off Maddy's cameras. I offered to pick them up
at her flat, but he said the load was too heavy and it would
make more sense for him to drop them off.

Now I'm waiting for him outside my building, thinking

about my visit to the accident scene last night and my meeting with Detective Kremezi this morning. Something about the behavior of people on the block didn't seem right to us both. When Kremezi as much as said he couldn't justify following up on his hunch, was he, I wonder, handing me the cudgel?

A cable car passes, tourists clinging to its sides. I hear the conductor announce the next stop: "Lombard at Hyde, crookedest street in the world, they say."

Three cars behind I spot David's Saab. He waves, pulls into a loading space in front of my door, gets out, embraces me. His cheek smells faintly of aftershave.

"You're not going to believe this," he says, moving to the rear of his car, unlocking the trunk, raising it with a flourish. I peer in. The entire space is stuffed with wine cartons. He opens the flaps of one to expose its contents. I see a bunch of old Nikon bodies nestled vertically in the wine bottle compartments.

"Cameras and lenses . . . and more cameras and more lenses," he says. "I don't think she ever threw one away. There's another one filled with cameras, two more of lenses and accessories."

I'm overwhelmed. "What am I going to do with them?"

"Beats me, Kay."

I pick out one of the Nikons, an F-model, one she may actually have used in Vietnam. I smile. The camera's battered and the brass shows through the coating. Amateurs like to keep their equipment nice; pros, particularly photojournalists, work theirs hard. I set the shutter speed to 125/sec, cock the shutter, trip it. The mirror clanks loud; the shutter speed sounds right. I think: *Of course it works—if it didn't she wouldn't have kept it.*

I turn to David. "What if I donate them to the Art Institute to be loaned to photography students?"

"Great idea," he says.

We haul the boxes into my building, load them into the elevator, take them up to the ninth floor. After we've got them neatly stacked in my front hall, I offer him a glass of Chardonnay.

He takes it, sips, walks to my living room window.

"You've got the best view in the city, Kay. Maddy said so and she was right."

"She was only up here once. I showed her my darkroom."

He turns. "There's a load of darkroom stuff in her storeroom. I'd like to sell it. I don't know where to begin."

I suggest he call me next week, I'll meet him at Maddy's, we'll go over everything, I'll help him sort it out. We stand looking at one another. The moment feels awkward. I realize this is probably the first time we've been alone together, and that though Maddy was like a mother to us both, we have little else in common.

"I was over at the Hall of Justice this morning," I tell him. "I spoke with Kremezi. I hope you don't mind."

He gazes at me.

"My dad was a cop for nearly twenty years," I add. "I know a lot about cops, good and bad. I went over there to see what's going on, make sure her case is in good hands."

"Is it?"

"I think so. Kremezi seemed an okay guy."

He turns again to the window. "I thought he acted pretty detached."

"Cops are like that, David—trained to keep their distance. He says he doesn't have anyplace to start. No leads, since no one saw it happen."

"Yeah . . ."

When David turns back to me I detect disturbance in his eyes.

"Would it bother you if I kept after him?" I ask.

"Do you want to?"

I nod. "Yeah, I do. My dad's still in touch with lots of cops. He can pass the word. And my friend Joel, he's an investigative journalist—if I ask him he'll keep on top of it. When the press shows interest in an investigation, S.F.P.D. tends not to let it fade."

David stares at me, whether with gratitude or irritation I can't be sure.

"It's not like I'm looking for revenge," he says.

"Of course not, though I'm sure you'd like to see some justice. I guess what I really want to know is what she was doing there."

He shakes his head. "I don't understand it."

"Neither do I," I tell him. "And I want to. I really do."

This morning I decide to take a close look at Maddy's cameras. I pull the boxes into the living room, sit among them, open them up, spread everything on the rug.

Lots of Nikons, the tough reflex camera she preferred, and a good selection of Nikon lenses, most in the wide-angle category—24mm, 28mm, 35mm—since Maddy liked working close. I also find six Leica range-finder models, including an old screw mount, again with an array of wide-angle lenses. One camera particularly stands out, a fairly unblemished Leica M6 mounted with a 135mm lens, an oddity since the camera is relatively unscathed and the telephoto is attached.

I pick it up, examine it. It has a databack, a documentation device that inscribes the date and time of exposures directly on the negative. Just as I'm about to open it, I notice a curious thing: the camera is loaded, the shutter dial showing that the roll inside has reached frame 22.

A camera isn't like a gun in the sense that there's a test to show whether it's been freshly fired. Still, if you work a lot with cameras, it's possible to acquire a sixth sense about them. Maybe it's just a matter of dust on the viewfinder and lens, skin oil on the shutter and grip. Whatever, I start getting a definite feeling about this particular M6—that it has been recently used, and thus the film inside wasn't left in by mistake but because it had yet to be shot out.

I take it into the darkroom, carefully rewind the film, open the camera and remove the roll: Kodak Tri-X with a year to go before expiration. Suddenly I feel a chill. Maddy, it's clear, has recently worked with this camera, which puts the lie to her declaration that she hadn't picked up a camera in years.

My hands are steady as I process the negative, transferring it first, in total darkness, to a developing tank. From this point the process is mechanical. The moment I'm certain the images are fixed, I unravel the strip, hang it up, examine it wet.

I'm used to reading negatives, but this one's got me stumped. I can't make out a thing. Oh, there're images, the film's been exposed, but all I can detect are occasional dabs of light amidst pools of darkness, nothing I can properly define.

I cut the long negative into six-frame strips, arrange them in a proofer, expose a proof sheet, process the paper and look again. Doing so, it strikes me there's something ironic in this, a reversal of roles—me the student examining the proof sheet of my teacher, trying to see what she was after, just the way she used to look at mine.

I still can't make out anything intelligible, anything that looks real. Could the pictures be abstract, extreme close-ups of textured surfaces? Could they have been shot deliberately out of focus?

I dismiss both possibilities. Abstraction was against everything Maddy stood for; razor-sharp focus was her pride. I recall her admonition: "I like to see the pores on their faces, the grooves on their palms." Her pictures were famous for their stamp-minted crystalline quality. That was her trademark, along with the concentrated density of her images.

So, I ask myself, could such a strong-willed artist radically change her style late in her career? What's on this strip of film? Was she merely testing the camera mechanism, the lens?

I study the databack information. The dates inscribed on all the frames are either March 3 or 4. I check my calendar; March 3 was a Wednesday, six weeks before the Wednesday when Maddy was killed. The times on the frames range from shortly before ten P.M. to a little after one A.M.—night shots, which may explain the large dark patches in the proof sheet frames. Such a span of time, three hours long, suggests a session of work.

Clearly there's something on these strips I'm not seeing. To reveal the content I must blow them up. A photographic session occurring six weeks before her death which ended at nearly the same hour she was killed—that work product *has* to be examined.

My first prints don't tell me much. The resolution isn't good. Despite the excellent Leitz lens on the camera, the images are grainy and unclear.

However, after working awhile with several of the negatives, I begin to detect a pattern: a consistent uneven black latticework imposed upon the images which tells me they've been taken from the same position off a tripod. Since Maddy preferred to shoot handheld, this consistency of position suggests a new approach.

Working up more prints, then looking deeper, I discover a second pattern, this one less evident: a consistent obfuscation in the upper right and lower center of the images, telling me there was something between Maddy's camera and her subject which partially blocked the light. Since whatever it was is out of focus, it's barely discernible, but being familiar with the effect, I recognize the cloudiness that appears in pictures shot through soiled glass.

Now I've got it! She was shooting through a dirty window, focusing upon action on the other side. The fuzzy latticework that seems imposed upon the images is probably an out-of-focus unevenly painted window frame.

Forget the foreground—it only confuses you. Concentrate on the background. Try and decode what's behind the glass.

Now, with a clear objective in mind, I get down to serious labor. I start blowing up the frames, larger and larger, ignoring the latticework, trying to resolve detail out of the blocks of nebulous gray light in between.

I realize, after a time, that I may have improperly developed the roll, that most likely Maddy exposed it at double or even triple the normal rating while I developed it straight. I had no reason to do otherwise; there was no notation on the cassette. Also, no reason there should have been. Since the roll wasn't shot out, Maddy didn't have the opportunity to mark it for special development.

No matter. Examining the negative strips on my light table, I feel there's enough in them to provide me with readable images. By burning in the light grainy areas within the window frame, I should be able to produce intelligible pictures.

I start concentrating on the dark gray areas, using all my darkroom tricks to resolve them. I employ filters, then a stronger than normal solution of Dektol. I even heat some up and rub it into the exposed paper. Little by little I come up with patterns suggesting human beings—a partial cascade of hair, an image of fingers and half a hand, the tubular shaft of a thigh, the round of a shoulder, the hollow of a navel, a shape that could possibly be a nipple, field after field of unclad and undifferentiated flesh.

Then, in the ninth frame, I discern a shape that tells me I've not just been imagining all of this: the profile of a nude woman from her waist to her neck, nipple, breast, arm and belly defined. The image, though grainy and soft, is nonetheless unmistakable: a human being, an incomplete nude, perhaps visible only because of the particular angle at which she's standing relative to an unseen source of light, and the fact that, at the moment she was photographed, she was standing in front of something dark.

I start working with this frame, exposing and developing enlargements at different densities. My problem is that the more closely I define the female, the more I cast the object behind her into shadow. Finally, I map out a complex printing plan, highlighting areas to be dodged, shading in areas to be burned, then set to work.

I blow my first three attempts, discarding the sheets without bothering to develop them. My fourth try, though awkward and poorly resolved, at least proves to me the job can be done. It takes six more tries before I obtain a satisfactory print. When I do I'm well rewarded. What I took to be a murky contrasting field behind the woman turns out, upon close inspection, to be a second person, a male, dressed in very dark clothes. I'm able to make out the buttons on his jacket, the diagonals of his lapels, can even see his hand overlying the stomach of the woman, a watch on a metal strap dangling from his wrist.

At four P.M., I stumble out of my darkroom, disoriented and dizzy. I've spent, I realize, nearly eight uninterrupted hours inside, a marathon considering the level of my concentration.

Seeking nourishment, I wander into my kitchen, find an apple, skin it, cut it into slices, embellish the slices with thin slices of cheese, devour it at the counter standing up.

I know I can't go back into the darkroom today; my mental energy's too depleted. What I need now is exercise, a hard clarifying workout at the dojo, where the concentration is of a different stripe, not of the mind but of the body.

Usually I wait till dark to take aikido class, but today I feel desperate. Something's been revealed to me. I've turned nonsense into pictures. But though I've resolved some images, I'm haunted by the question: What do they mean?

Most particularly I want to understand why Maddy felt a need to capture them, a need so strong it compelled her to take up her camera once again, then shoot under terrible conditions, in poor light, through filthy glass. Maddy was a pro, her mind was sharp, she knew exactly what she was doing. Which means she had to know that whatever results she obtained could not possibly meet her standards.

"Use your camera to face your demons, Kay!" she used to tell me. "Shoot what you fear!"

What, I wonder, were *Maddy's* demons? What was it *she* feared and thus felt compelled to shoot?

Pain, Kay, can be your most important teacher."

Thus speaks Rita, at Marina Aikido, as I gingerly lift myself off the mat onto which she has just flung me with transcendent, indeed ineffable grace.

To fling and to be flung, to learn to give up our fear of falling and to feel the joy of flying—such is aikido training . . . and both activities require finesse. What can be most beautiful in aikido can also be painful. I know Rita never intends to hurt us, except, possibly, when she feels doing so will be to our benefit.

I look into her eyes. We stand facing one another on the mat. Other members of the class sit in the *seiza* position, watching us, trying to divine the lesson.

I am the *uke,* the attacker. Rita is the *nage,* the thrower. It is she who is applying techniques. It is I who am being vanquished by them.

It's five P.M. The sky outside is bright, but for me the light in the dojo is tolerable. I don't wear shades on the mat; to do so would be dangerous. But here, even in daytime, my visual acuity improves and my photophobia recedes. I can't explain it. It's one of the mysteries of the martial arts experience. Rita says it's the result of the inner clarity that aikido instills.

I breathe deeply. Rita does the same. The air in the dojo always smells good to me, though others, outsiders, might find it overly pungent. The scent here is slightly sour, composed of human sweat, the fabric of our practice uniforms, the material of the mat, the solution with which the floor and walls are cleaned, all suspended in the sweet San Francisco breeze that flows in through the open windows and skylight.

I breathe deeply again, then suddenly rush at Rita full force. I intend to bash her with a head strike, but she's too quick for me, too formidable. At the last moment she moves, perhaps only a few inches, enough so she can deflect my attack, take hold of my wrist, twist it in such a way that I swirl with her as she turns, blend with her, become subject to her control, then go flying through the air to land again upon the mat with a mighty thud.

"See what I did?" Rita asks the class. She nods to Ralph, recently relocated from Seattle, a young, lithe, eager, well-practiced black belt new to our dojo.

"You threw her away," he says.

Rita smiles. "Is that what I did?"

Someone else suggests that she shed me.

" 'Shed'—I like that better than 'throw away.' Anyone else?"

"I felt you maybe kind of . . . abandoned her."

"Abandoned? Really?" Rita turns to me. "Tell us, Kay—did it feel like that to you?"

"Not at all," I say. "I never felt abandoned. Or thrown away. Shed perhaps, but only at the end. The good part was when we were in touch. Then I felt lifted, like I could fly."

"And you did," Ralph adds.

The class titters.

"I lost my feet."

"There you are!" Rita says. "She lost her feet. And it wasn't so bad, was it, Kay?"

"It actually felt good."

"That's because we blended. My feet became your feet—until I let you go. That's sometimes the sadness of it, I think, the melancholy of our techniques—that after a second or two we must let one another go. Yet . . . let go we must."

She has something there, something I feel but can't properly explain. I wasn't thrown away, or shed. I was, I now realize, guided, then let go. The best parts of class are these times when Rita departs from technical instruction, speaking instead of feelings, delving into the mysteries of our mysterious shared beautiful/violent art.

Our eyes meet. We bow to one another. She motions to Ralph to join her on the floor. I take his place among the others, join my breathing to theirs. Sometimes everyone in the dojo seems to breathe together. At such times I feel joined to a marvelous cosmic process that extends far beyond my body.

When Ralph attacks, Rita applies the same technique she applied to me. He flies well, better than me, I think, certainly lands with more poise, springs up with a smile. Seeing the throw like this, from outside, gives me insight into what I felt, my ecstasy in giving up control to the powerful one who could make me fly.

After class, in the changing room, I mop my body with a towel. No showers here, just a pair of sinks. Marina Aikido is clean, provides good space, but isn't luxurious.

On my way out, Rita spots me passing her office, gestures for me to come in. For the past month we've been discussing whether I should try for my black belt at the end of the summer when the next ranking tests will take place. In principle I've agreed, though without a formal commitment.

"You were good today," she says. "I felt the flow. You blended really well."

"Not as well as Ralph, I'm afraid."

"Actually better," she says. "I mean it, Kay. Don't sell yourself short. You were good."

Suddenly I feel moisture pulsing to my eyes. I squint so as not to let it show. What Rita has said is the very sort of thing Maddy would say whenever I felt discouraged about my work. Not surprising since Maddy was also a coach, though in an entirely different field. Still, to receive strong encouragement from a woman who does not readily dispense it is to be reminded that though I have incurred a major loss, I have not been cast out on my own.

"*I* know you're ready to go for your *shodan*," she says. "The question is—do *you* know it?"

"Oh, I *know* it," I tell her, feeling a fresh surge of confidence. "You're right, I was good today. Thanks for reminding me."

Rita grins. "My pleasure, girlfriend."

Dr. Sasha Patel is an emergency room resident at St. Francis Memorial Hospital. He also has the dreamiest, most beautiful eyes I have ever seen. Born in London of Gujrati parents, he came to America to study medicine. He keeps a small apartment on Jones Street to which he has graciously given me a key.

We both understand the rules. I'm to call first to be sure he's home and not ministering to one of his numerous nurse girlfriends. "I'd give them all up for you if you'd have me, Kay," he's told me several times, with his trademark blend of irony and sincerity. "But you won't, will you?"

"Sure . . . sometime," I tell him. "You know I like you, Sasha."

" 'Sometime' just won't do it for me, Kay. Because what I feel for you is more than just liking."

I understand, but there's nothing I can do about that. As fond as I am of him, and appreciative of his adoration, I cannot oblige; thus we have worked out our arrangement. Each of us is always there for the other when needed, which is not to say simply for sex. Also for cuddling, kissing, holding one another, talking, advising—all the lovely things one enjoys doing with a lover whether occasional or not.

Tonight I call, ask if I may visit and, receiving his consent, let myself in. The grinning satyr is waiting for me, reclining in his living room on what he calls his "love seat," the only light issuing from embers smoldering in the fireplace a few feet away.

Coolly, without rising, he offers me a drink. Just as coolly I decline. Our eyes meet; then I rush to him, pull open his heavy silk brocade robe, press my face against his dusky skin and breathe in his inimitable scent.

"Sasha!"

"Kay! Kay! Kay!"

He wraps me in his arms, kisses my hair.

Moments later we're making love on the carpet before the fire—violent, thrashing love. I want him to take me passionately, even harshly, and so he does, but with the underlying sweetness that is his gift. Reveling in our sensuality, I lose myself, forget who I am, forget everything except that I am a woman rutting like a teen, crying out, gasping, grasping at the flesh of this marvelous man with deep liquid eyes who knows so well how to pleasure me.

Later, in Sasha's bed, we fit together like spoons, enveloped in the aroma of our lovemaking. He lies behind me, strong arms wrapping me, palms cupping my breasts. I press my face down against his dusky hand, breathe in the scent of his skin, a scent composed of sandalwood, wind, sand and ancient stone temples. I feel his breath against my ear, the occasional brush of his closely shaven cheeks. When I lie very still I can feel the beating of his heart as he presses his chest against my spine.

I adjust myself slightly against him, wishing to strengthen the moist bond by which we're fused. I want to create a seal through which our shared heat will flow, mine warming him, his warming me.

He whispers into my ear: "You make me so happy." He kisses the hollow at the back of my neck.

I smile; I am happy too.

At dawn I slip away, quietly so as not to awaken him. But when I turn for a final look from the bedroom door, I spot him watching me.

"I love you, Kay," he murmurs.

I throw him a kiss. Then, walking down the stairs, I try not to wonder why he must always remind me of what he feels and I, sadly, do not.

At seven in the morning the telephone rings. I'm sipping coffee. It's Joel, excited.

"Have you seen the *News*?" he asks. When I tell him I haven't: "Rush out to your local newsstand, kiddo. Go! Go now!"

Seems one of my photographs of the illegals adorns the front page full bleed, with a double page of photos inside.

"You're the toast of San Francisco," he tells me. "You own this town today."

"Ergo the world?" I ask. "Funny, Joel, I don't feel any different, just like my old self—if you want to know."

"You'll get over it. You'll be flying high and mighty pretty soon. It always happens. First they play humble, then the pride starts to build. Success breeds arrogance. Huge success breeds huge arrogance. Glickman's Law. It never fails."

Soon as we hang up, I pull on clothes, rush down to the corner of Union and Hyde. The *News* box is filled with freshly delivered copies. I pull out one, gaze at my work.

I'm enormously pleased. My pictures look terrific, my byline's as large as Joel's, and his text, written in his special style (not bleeding heart, just coolly told so the story truly rends), makes a perfect complement.

Walking home, I practice holding my head higher than usual, cultivating a prideful tilt. Maddy, I know, would be proud, and since she's no longer here, I must feel the pride myself.

Nine A.M., I'm back in the darkroom, Maddy's strips of negative neatly laid out on my light box, fresh chemistry in my trays. Today, I'm determined, I will crack the secret of the roll I found inside her Leica.

Right away I spot images which escaped me yesterday. Perhaps it's because I'm looking with a fresh eye, or having decoded frame 9, I now know what I'm looking for. Also, using a magnifying glass to inspect the negatives, I eliminate the pervasive grain that appeared in my enlargements.

Quickly I make a decision: I'll print out each frame in a uniform four-by-five size, and rather than trying to reveal content via complicated dodging and burning, I'll print straight exposing for bare flesh.

It takes me little more than an hour to do this. Once I achieve a rhythm, the prints come fast. When I'm finished I pin them up wet to the cork wall.

Nude females interacting with dressed males—now, suddenly, I see them everywhere. Not whole, of course, but bits and pieces here and there. Something odd too, I notice—though it's sometimes difficult to tell, the women all seem to be Asian while the men all seem to be white. What, if anything, I ask myself, does that mean?

Maddy, I note from the databank information, shot in short bursts, with ten- or fifteen-minute intervals between. Since she was shooting with a long lens through a window from a position higher than her subject, her angle of vision was extremely limited.

I close my eyes, try to imagine the physical situation: Maddy, standing in a darkened room, peering through her camera locked into position on a tripod. Her lens is pointed through the window aimed at still another lower window that's unwashed and closed. The action she's trying to record takes place in the room on the other side of that second window, where there's also a dim source of light. Every once in a while, when the people in that room drift into sight, she starts taking pictures. As soon as they leave frame, she stops, poised to resume when they reappear.

Two rooms, two windows in between, surreptitious photographs taken in one of action taking place in the other. For all I know, the window in the room from which Maddy shoots is also closed so as not to reveal her presence. These, I realize, are the kind of pictures a blackmailer might take, or a cop on a stakeout: surveillance photos of people who have no inkling they can be seen; photos which document illicit activity; photos which, if they were known to exist, might put the photographer in jeopardy; photos, moreover, which the photographer has gone to great pains to take—locating the site, finding a surveillance position, setting up, patiently waiting for something to shoot. Difficult to imagine a sixty-eight-year-old woman in poor health doing all this, unless the content was enormously important to her.

So what is going on? An orgy? I stifle a yawn. Hard to imagine anyone getting excited about one of those these days . . . certainly not here in San Francisco. The lounge of a house of prostitution catering to Caucasian men who like Asian women? No, it's got to be more than that, something that justified her effort.

I think a moment, pick up the phone, dial David Yamada.

"Hi, it's Kay. I've been looking over the cameras. Did you box them, or were they already packed?"

"No," he says, "they were all over the place. I gathered them, then packed them up in cartons."

"Remember one that looked fairly new?"

"The Leica?"

"Where'd you find it?"

"Gee, I don't remember. It was just sitting out somewhere, maybe in the bedroom." A pause. "Something wrong?"

"Uh-uh, just curious, David. Listen, if you want to go over her darkroom stuff, I'm free this afternoon."

I spend the rest of the morning designing a flyer. I choose a photo I took of Maddy three years back, before she became ill, one in which she smiles broadly and her powerful eyes flash merriment. I center this picture at the top of an ordinary sheet of paper, then rough out a text:

DID YOU SEE THIS WOMAN?

On April 15, at approximately 1:30 A.M., the woman pictured above was killed near the corner of Capp and 24th by a hit-and-run motorcyclist. Her name was Amanda Yamada, "Maddy" to her friends. She lived in the Marina, was 68 years old, not in good health, yet in full command of her faculties.

We, her family and friends, are confused about her presence so far from home at such an hour of the night. We are asking anyone who might have seen her to please let us know. Nothing, of course, can bring our loved one back, but it would help those of us who mourn her if we could understand what she was doing that night, whether visiting friends, wandering the streets, perhaps even taking photographs.

Any assistance will be greatly appreciated. Please be assured your privacy will be respected. Thank you.

Friends and Family
of Maddy Yamada

Arriving at Maddy's building at three P.M., I spot David's Saab parked in front. I ring, he buzzes back, not the quick short response I'm used to, but one unfamiliarly long. On the second floor I find the door to the flat wide open.

"I'm in back. Be right out," David calls.

I enter. Inside, the blinds are up, the living and dining

rooms flooded with dazzling San Francisco light. For a moment I'm snow-blinded, the rods in my eyes saturated by the brilliance. I shut down, put on my dark red wrap-around shades, wait until I regain my vision, then peer about.

Already the flat looks different. The numerous framed photographs which used to cover the walls have all been taken down. The Persian rug in the living room has been rolled, and the couch where Maddy and I used to sit has been pushed against the wall.

David comes in. "She had so much stuff," he says. "You wouldn't believe it, Kay—boxes and boxes of photos, diaries, letters. Organized too. The other night I found a file of letters from my dad. I was here till two in the morning reading them. Fascinating stuff. She led such a rich, full life. That's what strikes me—how rich it was."

He tells me the Museum of Modern Art people are coming on Monday to pack up and cart out her archive: negative and proof sheet files, plus most of the paperwork with the exception of a few personal items David's decided to hold back.

"That way it'll be available to scholars and biographers. It's what she wanted. I hope I'm doing the right thing."

I assure him that he is. I ask if I can take a look around before we start.

"Sure, take your time. I'll be down in her storeroom. Come find me when you're ready."

I'm thrilled to be alone, able to do certain things without having to explain what I'm up to. As soon as he leaves I start my search, moving from room to room, methodically checking the windows, looking for possible camera positions and views of windows in buildings nearby. I don't believe Maddy took those pictures from her flat, but I want to make sure before searching elsewhere.

The front rooms and kitchen are familiar to me. From these the views of surrounding buildings are incompatible with the shots, much too far away. Judging by the images and the lens Maddy used, I've estimated the space between the two windows at no greater than twenty-five feet.

The back rooms tell a different story. The two bedrooms look across a shallow garden into the back rooms of the building just behind. It's an apartment house much like Maddy's—four stories, Deco period, typical of Marina district architecture. I raise my Contax, study each window across the way. All are clean, the frames neatly outlined, the distances and angle of vision incorrect.

No, Maddy—you didn't shoot from here.

I find David in the basement storeroom surrounded by cartons of darkroom gear. We go through it—used trays, beakers, drying racks, thermometers, most of it fairly worthless. The easels and scopes have value, as does the big enlarger, a Beseler 4x5 with motor control. The best items are the Leica Focomat enlarger and the superb Leitz and Rodenstock enlarger lenses. All together, as used goods, they may be worth two thousand dollars.

I turn to David, make a suggestion. "Why not do what I'm doing with the cameras, give it all to the Art Institute? I went there. So did Kevin Wang. They'd love to have this stuff and I know the kids there would use it well."

While he mulls this over, I note that one of Maddy's Rodenstocks is a 75mm, more appropriate for medium-format work than for enlarging 35mm film. That and the big Beseler enlarger suggest Maddy worked at least occasionally with medium-format film. This is something I didn't know, and I recall there were no medium-format models among her cameras.

"Okay," David says, "it goes to the Art Institute." He asks me to transmit the gift and arrange the pickup.

Before I leave I show him the mock-up of my flyer. He inspects it carefully.

"I don't want to hand these out without your blessing," I explain.

"Nothing here about ID'ing the driver," he points out.

I explain I don't want to get into that, believing the matter is best left to the police. The issue, I tell him, is what Maddy was doing there that night and whether she'd been seen around the neighborhood before.

He looks at me, nods. "Sure," he says, "go ahead."

I meet his eyes. There's something subdued about his approval, telling me it's barely meant.

Saturday afternoon: I pick up my flyers from the 24-Hour Printer, take the Van Ness bus to the Mission, get off at Twenty-fourth, walk over to Capp, start distribution.

As I go about my work, I imagine how I appear to today's lookout on the block: a small dark-haired woman in her thirties, wraparounds concealing her eyes, camera around her neck, methodically working her way house to house leaving flyers under every door.

When I finish the block, I work my way east, then west on Twenty-fourth, then paper the Capp Street blocks north and south of where Maddy was hit. After a brief time-out for Cuban coffee on Valencia, I return to the original block on Capp to place flyers beneath the windshield wipers of parked cars.

Walking back to Mission to catch my bus, I spot the same middle-aged Mexican woman who showed me the accident site. She's dressed in a nurse's uniform, walking toward Capp on the other side of the street. I cross, then run to overtake her. Evidently she hears me, for she abruptly turns around.

"Oh, it's you," she says, when I take off my wraps.

"Sorry. I didn't mean to scare you."

She studies me. "Why are you blinking?"

"Photophobia," I tell her. "My eyes are sensitive to bright light."

I replace my shades, we stare at one another, then I hand her a flyer.

"I just finished leaving these," I say.

She looks at me, then the flyer. I watch her as she reads it. When she's finished she hands it back.

"You'll find one under your door," I tell her.

"Thank you," she says.

"I hope you can help me. Please think about it."

She looks searchingly at me, then turns and continues on her way.

Tonight, feeling lonely at nine o'clock, I decide to walk in the city. I grab my Contax and descend Russian Hill to North Beach. Quickly I lose myself in the crowds on Columbus, moving past coffeehouses, hair salons, pizza parlors and boutiques.

Around Broadway there's a tame little commercial sex district, a dozen or so strip joints where sexy young women stand beneath bawdy marquees hawking the shows and assorted iniquitous wares to passersby.

I stop at a newsstand. Nothing sinister about this area, rather something almost sweet. The girls, leashed to their doorways by short lengths of velvet rope, act as human gateposts.

"Hey! Sailors!" The leggy blonde in front of the True Love Saloon beckons to a threesome of uniformed youths.

"Will we really find 'true love'?" one of them asks.

The woman grins. "Maybe not *true* love," she says, "but for sure . . . naughty girls for naughty boys!"

The sailors decline, but a balding middle-aged man in a business suit slinks inside. Just as he passes the gatepost girl, she pats him sweetly on his pate.

I browse in City Lights Bookstore, scan memoirs of the Beat period, finally purchase a French photography magazine. I carry it next door to the Vesuvio Cafe, order an espresso, then study a glossy fetishistic photo taken in an ornate dining room. A slick-haired muscular female in off-the-shoulder gown and glistening boots inspects a table set luxuriously for dinner while a submissive uniformed maid awaits her approval.

Back on the street, I turn up Broadway to Chinatown. As I walk up the block the scent in the air changes—from espresso and pizza to tea and roasting pork. On Stockton the crowds carry me along, past seafood restaurants, dim sum parlors, all-night trinket shops. Suddenly my pager beeps. I check the tiny screen, recognize Joel's cell phone number.

I call him back from the corner of Stockton and Clay. He tells me he's on Market in his car heading for the waterfront. He's just received another tip. Do I want to join him and photograph the fun?

"Of course! But I've only got one camera with me and no strobe."

"That'll have to do," Joel says. "Meet you at Clay and Kearny in say . . . six minutes."

Suddenly I'm hyped, can feel the adrenaline coursing. I toss the French magazine into a trash barrel, stop at a novelty store, purchase half a dozen rolls of film. Seconds after I reach the designated corner, Joel shows up in his VW. He pulls to the curb and I jump in.

"Fasten your seat belt, kiddo," he says, goosing the gas. We take off fast, tires squealing. A minute later we're on the Embarcadero, the girders of the Bay Bridge looming above.

"Where're we going?"

"China Basin."

"What's over there?"

"That's what we're going to find out."

As we follow the Embarcadero south, he explains.

"Tip came maybe fifteen minutes ago. Same guy as the other night, same phony Chinese accent. 'Velly goody stolly, Mista Glick-man. You do goody job, so here another goody stolly for you.' The guy says go to the end of El Dorado Alley near Pier sixty-four, wait there, 'maybe sometin' interestin' gonna happen.' Then . . . click! He's off the line. I punch in call-return, but no ring. Like he's got that feature blocked."

"So we're going on this guy's say-so?"

"His last tip panned out pretty well."

"Suppose that was bait. Be a good way to sucker you in."

"Me? Why bother?"

"You don't have enemies, Joel?"

"I've got tons."

"So?"

"So someone wants to get me, all he's gotta do is wait in front of my house. Every morning six A.M. I step out on my porch to get my newspapers. I stretch, then bend, making a perfect target. That's his time to take his shot."

It's spooky on Sixteenth—no traffic, poor lighting, block after block of windowless flat-roofed warehouses. Just before Third there's a late-night jazz club, a row of parked cars in front. Joel slows, then works his way through the labyrinth of narrow streets that lead to the China Basin waterfront. He finds El Dorado, drives down to the dead end, cuts the engine.

I peer around. We're in a lonely place. No residential or commercial buildings, just a burned-out structure to our right. Straight ahead, perhaps a hundred yards to the east, a couple of huge cargo vessels are tied up at piers. There're bright lights over there, the kind they use when loading ships at night. The lights are harsh, hurt my eyes. I turn back to Joel.

"Which one's Pier sixty-four?"

He points to the left. He's alert now, edgy.

"I don't like it here."

"Neither do I, kiddo. If we were on China Basin Street we'd be closer to the water and we could drive out either way. From here we gotta hike to the water and there's only one way out."

"Kinda like we're in a box."

"That bothers me." He pauses. "Unless—"

"What?"

"It's safer over here."

"Safer from what?"

"Whatever's going to happen."

"Which is?"

"No way to know that yet."

Jesus, Joel! Spare me, please!

"I'm getting out," I announce, opening the door.

"Wouldn't do that, kiddo."

"Why not?" I aim my camera toward the water.

"Just wouldn't, that's all. Sit tight awhile. See what happens."

I laugh. "Next thing you'll be telling me to keep my powder dry." I aim at the ships, check focus.

Joel starts to grin. The explosion cuts him off. Even as I'm blinded, I shoot by instinct.

"Down! Head down!" he yells, yanking me back into the car, pushing me into the space beneath the dash, a space into which I can't possibly fit. The roar is huge. My ears go deaf. Then it feels as if the car is actually lifted off the street. I feel the weight of Joel's body crushing me down, my camera biting into my breasts. There's a great rush of air; then, as suddenly as it began, the world becomes quiet once again.

I take a deep breath. Something nauseous and acrid enters my lungs.

"Let me up, Joel! I can't breathe."

I'm grateful when he takes the pressure off my back. I shake my head to clear it, sit up and look ahead. The vessel that was docked at Pier 64 is engulfed in flames and there's a terrible chemical smell in the air.

"Jesus!"

"The ship blew up," Joel says. "Incredible! There was this huge fireball. Then . . . BOOM!" He looks at me. "You okay?"

I nod, touch my camera. "I think I got it."

We get out of the car, start across a rubble-strewn field toward the pier. I'm a little dizzy, hate the smell in the air, am fearful of more explosions, but plod on, seeking a clear field of view. When I find one, stop and look, I feel myself drawn in. I forget about Joel, move closer. I know what I'm looking for—people to give scale to the fire. But I don't see anyone, and then it occurs to me that the explosion was so powerful anyone on or near that ship was knocked down or blown to bits.

Sirens in the distance. The hook and ladder companies are on their way. A fire like this will burn for hours and there'll be no exclusive film; in minutes the waterfront will be crawling with press. Still I advance toward the flames.

"Get close as you can before you shoot," Maddy always said.

The air's unbreathable, the heat sears my face; still I continue to work. I'm seeking a strong encapsulating image that will say more than merely *Fire!* It's people I need, and since the only people around are firefighters, I concentrate on them.

There's one who catches my eye, a young guy with classical features, a warrior's eyes, an athlete's noble brow. When I approach, he turns.

"Real dangerous here!" he yells above the roar. "Better stand off!"

"Look, I got my job," I tell him. "Let me tag along."

He looks at me. "Trying to be the brave reporter-girl, are you?"

"That's me!" I yell.

"Sure, girlie, tag along." He grins. "I like your spunk."

He turns his back, making it impossible to shoot his face. I track him to the dock. Out on the water, I see three fireboats, water guns blazing, working the burning ship.

"Hey, Mr. Fireman Man!" I yell. "What's the cargo aboard this tub?" He ignores me. "Smells awful!"

Just then there's a secondary explosion on the ship. He crouches, half turns. That's the moment that I shoot. *Whap!whap!* The agony contorting his face is just about perfect.

"Wow, you look great!" I tell him.

He stares at me, crazed. "This isn't a movie, lady. We're fighting a real fire here."

Whap!whap!

"Gotcha! Thanks!" Then I back off from the flames.

Joel finds me in the tangle of fire trucks on China Basin Street, tells me the toll so far is one dead, thirteen injured, and that it looks as though a bomb went off, igniting the ship's fuel tanks.

"A few hours earlier," he says, "it would have been much worse. They'd just finished unloading her. She was carrying anhydrous ammonia. When that stuff hits water you get a cloud of toxic gas, the kind that explodes your larynx and scorches your lungs."

"What's going on, Joel?"

He shakes his head. "Two tips, same source, both dead-on accurate. The first about illegals, the second about a bomb. What's the connection and why the tip-off? I don't get it." Again he shakes his head. "I'm being used, kiddo, and I don't know why. That worries me a lot."

It worries me too.

We hang around. Unlike the scene at the Presidio, there're no law enforcers strutting here tonight, just weary firefighters and arson investigators, sweaty paramedics and hollow-eyed cops. When I tell Joel I'm afraid the bad air's going to make me faint, he escorts me back to his car. On the way home, at my request he stops on the Embarcadero, lets me out. I go to the seawall, breathe deeply, trying to clear my lungs. He joins me. We stand together facing the water, inhaling, exhaling, taking in the fresh thick salty air. When, at last, we feel cleansed, we sit side by side on the seawall, staring at the skyline of Oakland sparkling across the Bay.

"Usually, when you get a tip," Joel says, "it's about something that's already happened. Like, 'Check out the basement,' 'So-and-so did it,' 'Rumor on the street is such and such.' This is different. These tips are about events that haven't happened yet. So I wonder—what kind of person knows when a boatload of illegals is coming in and that a bomb's going to go off . . . can even tell me where to park so I won't get hurt? Someone obviously wired into the waterfront. But I think it's more. When someone can predict the future like that, it's a signal he controls the events he predicts." He turns to me. "Power, kiddo—I think that's the message here."

It's been three days since I papered Capp Street; so far no messages on my machine. Deciding to cover the block again, I return with a fresh sheaf of flyers. When I get there, the first thing I observe is that all my posted flyers have been torn off the telephone poles.

Fine, I think, *that's just fine.*

I set to work with hammer and tacks, vigorously restoring my notices. Then I work the block, up one side, down the other, slipping my flyers alternately beneath windshield wipers and front doors. When I'm finished, I stand, hands on hips, surveying the street, displaying my determination to whomever may be peering out. I'll keep coming back, I promise silently, until I get results . . . and if that means standing on the corner handing off flyers to passersby, that's what I'll do.

My action portraits of the handsome fireman are intense and my accidental shot of the fireball is as strong a disaster image as I've ever shot. Carla Dean, *News* picture editor, phones to tell me she's thrilled. The shot's exclusive, no one else caught the fireball, she wants to run it on the front page full bleed.

"It's Pulitzer caliber," she says.

"Wow, I don't get that," I tell her. "I was just fooling around when suddenly the thing went off. I wasn't even looking through the finder. I barely had time to trip the shutter before Joel tried to stuff me into a space you couldn't stuff a hat."

She laughs. "Trying to save a freelancer—sounds like Joel." Then she turns serious. "It's a good story, Kay. Only problem—since you were there and ready to shoot when it happened, you're going to be questioned about, like, 'How come you knew?' "

My hand shakes as I put down the phone. It never occurred to me the picture could get me in trouble, that I'd have to explain how I happened to be at the right place at the right time: "Tell us, Ms. Farrow, do you make a habit of hanging around piers waiting for explosions, or were you there because you knew one was going to go off? In which case wouldn't it have been prudent to inform the authorities? A man was killed, you know."

Jesus!

At one A.M. the phone rings.

"Hello?" I hear heavy breathing at the other end. "Hello?" I say again.

"Yeah, you the cunt leaving paper up and down Capp?" The voice is gruff, the tone mean.

Normally I'd hang up, and if he called again, unplug the phone. Tonight I decide to stay connected.

"Hey! Hear what I'm saying, bitch?"

I don't say a word.

"Whatsamatta? You some kind of fuckin' freak or something?"

It would be so easy to tell him which one of us is the freak, but instead I bite my lip.

"Listen up good. Don't come around with that shit again. Show your face around here you're gonna get hurt. Got it, cunt?"

He waits a beat, then hangs up.

Calmly I replace the headset. Probably just a secret admirer, I decide.

I'm back on Capp at seven A.M., my intention to catch the residents as they leave for work. Walking the block, I don't see a single one of my flyers—not on the telephone poles, the windshields of parked cars, even discarded on the street.

I post myself at the exact spot where Maddy was run down. As pedestrians pass I offer them my flyer. A few accept, the rest walk by, some gazing at me curiously, most avoiding my eyes. I detect no particular hostility, certainly nothing to equal the venom of my anonymous caller. One high school boy accepts a flyer, then says, "Have a good day." That cheers me, proving kindness still exists among the young.

Two hours pass. People come and go, exit buildings, get into cars, drive off. My feet start to hurt. Tired of standing in one place, I walk down to the corner, reposition myself beside a stop sign. Here, whenever I try to hand off a flyer, the driver waves me away.

By nine-thirty I'm filled with compassion for all the

street people whose handouts I've shrugged off through the years—earnest Scientologists, creepy Jehovah's Witnesses, pathetic oldsters wearing sandwich boards trying to lure me into cheap eateries. It's a lousy job, handing stuff out. Rejection is the norm. After a certain number of snubs you start to offer in a manner that tells passersby you expect to be rebuffed.

By ten o'clock my pride is pretty much worn down. I walk the block, repaper the poles and cars, slip flyers again beneath doors. This is it, I tell myself, as I finish up. This'll be my last shot. I've made my point, shown my contempt for my anonymous caller and his threat. If the people here are too mean-spirited to help, there's nothing more I can do.

My answering machine's blinking when I get home. Immediately I play the message. I recognize the voice from nearly the first word. It's the Mexican woman, the nurse who lives on the corner of Capp and Twenty-fourth.

"I saw you on the street this morning," she says. "I believe you are sincere. I have something to tell you, not too much, but we must meet someplace where we won't be seen. Please wait for me at five this afternoon inside Mission Dolores Basilica. Sit on the left side. I will find you." Pause. "My name is Maria Quintana."

I spend the day in anticipation. At two I walk over to Marina Aikido to train. I return home, shower, then go out with my camera. The sunlight's too bright. I can barely stand it even wearing my heaviest shades. At four-thirty I stop at a pay phone and call a cab. I instruct the driver to take me to Mission Dolores.

The original adobe mission chapel is small, elegant, austere. Built in 1782, it's the oldest building in San Francisco. The basilica next door, constructed in 1913 in the style called churrigueresque, is huge, exuberant. It's here, in the flamboyant chapel, that I genuflect, then take a seat in a pew eight rows back from the main altar.

Five P.M.: Incense fills the air. A mass is scheduled to begin in half an hour. A concerned-looking priest hurriedly crosses the nave. Another slips into a confessional, then turns on the light to signal he's open for business. Three confession boxes are now in use. Elderly women in black, assembled close by, patiently wait their turns.

This is a Hispanic church, different from the Irish Catholic churches I attended in my youth. Here the lighting level is low, a comfort to my eyes, the smell is of incense and damp stone, and the statues are brooding and mysterious, with an emphasis on startled eyes and the pain and bloody wounds of martyrs.

I'm lost in these thoughts when I feel a presence at my side. I turn to find Maria Quintana, bowed head wrapped in black scarf, nurse's uniform concealed by black raincoat, knees firm on the kneeling bench. Hearing her start to mutter a prayer, I kneel and mutter a half-forgotten one of my own.

We sit in silence side by side. The pews are filling. The organist is playing. Mass will soon begin. I wait for her signal. Are we going to have to sit through the entire mass before we speak?

At 5:28, as people swarm in, she rises and moves to the side aisle. I follow her up the transept to the door that leads to the cemetery garden of the old mission. Silently she leads me past the gravestones of forty-niners and early Franciscan friars, across ground where thousands of nameless Costanoan Indians are buried, until we reach a small hedged area surrounded by rosebushes near the statue of the great Franciscan Junipero Serra.

Here, where the light is soft, she turns to me at last, meets my eyes and, for the first time since we met, greets me with a smile.

"Thanks for calling me," I tell her. "I was about to give up."

"I kept hoping someone would contact you. When I saw you this morning, I understood no one had."

"That's why you decided to call?"

She nods. "I could not bear to watch you standing there so patiently where she fell. If no one else would speak with you I knew my duty, that it would have to be me."

Her face seems pretty to me now. When she smiles a network of crinkles appears on either side of her eyes and a dimple deepens in her chin. But it's her voice that compels me—throaty, accented, resonant with compassion.

"Did you see my friend before?" I ask.

"Oh, yes," she says, "several times, always at night, but not usually on our block. She was more often on Cypress, the next street over. But people on Capp also noticed her. It was her eyes and the camera that made her stand out. Where we live people do not walk with cameras on the street. I believe she and you are the only two I have seen. That is how I knew you were connected."

I'm stunned. "When you say you saw her several times, how often do you mean?"

She thinks a moment. "Perhaps ten times, maybe more."

"When was the first time? Do you remember?"

"Yes," she says. "I thought about it this morning. It was in January, I am sure. I remember because I was surprised. It was raining, I was putting out my trash, when I saw her walking in the rain up the block."

"Others saw her too?"

"Oh, yes. People mentioned it, the old Anglo lady with the extraordinary eyes—what was she doing, why had she come?"

"Did anyone know?"

"Not at first."

"Then—?"

"There were rumors. She was crazy, a *gringa loca*." Maria Quintana lowers her eyes. "I am sorry, but that is what people said."

"Why do you think nobody called?"

"They were afraid. They did not wish to become involved. I did not either, but now—" She shrugs. "This morning when I saw you I knew I had to speak."

I gaze into her eyes. "What was she doing there?"

"No one knows. But she had a room, a little room she rented on Cypress Street. When we saw her, I think, she was coming or going from that house."

Maddy rented a room!

"Do you know the address?"

"I am not sure."

"You could find out?"

Her eyes turn cautious.

"I am sorry but I do not wish to ask. To do so is to invite trouble," she says. "People are afraid to speak about it now that she was killed."

"Did you see her killed?"

She shakes her head. "I only heard the sound."

"Others heard it too?"

"Everyone."

"Yet no one saw it?"

"I believe some did, but they do not wish to speak of it. It was a very bad thing. Everyone felt that way. They felt badly that it could happen to such a nice person and so close to where we live."

"It wasn't an accident, was it?"

She shakes her head. "I do not know."

"If it wasn't an accident, Maria, people wouldn't be afraid to speak. Even if you didn't see it, I wish you'd tell me what you think."

She shakes her head again, yet her eyes stay locked to mine. It's then that I understand she will only speak of things she has seen.

"Thanks for what you've told me," I tell her. "The rest I'll have to find out on my own." I pause. "First, I need to find the rented room. I'll make up more flyers, leave them on Cypress under all the doors. Maybe then someone will call, tell me which house."

"Please do not leave more paper," she says. Her eyes are disturbed. "That is why I called you, so you would not leave more. The neighbors do not like it. It makes them afraid."

It's my turn to shrug. "I must find her room."

Maria stares at me, then looks down. "Try the green door," she whispers. "But I did not tell you this. I did not tell you anything."

I nod. She embraces me, kisses me on both cheeks.

"Thank you, Maria."

"It is nothing," she says, slipping away.

I watch as she moves through the garden cemetery, then reenters the basilica by the side door. I check my watch. The mass must be nearly over. Too late for her to take communion, but still time to catch the benediction. Making my way out directly to the street, I feel no sorrow for my own lost faith. It's the dojo, with its stringent values and discipline, that is my temple now.

This morning the *News* is out, my fireball picture is smeared all over town. I know I should be happy about it, but I feel detached, as if someone else took the shot and it has nothing to do with me.

As expected, Joel's article is brilliant. He writes of "a recent surge of unrest on the San Francisco waterfront, a feeling held by many that the traditional balance here is on the verge of collapse." He writes that his sources—tugboat captains, bar pilots, assorted old salts—"are unwilling to name names or cite specific incidents, but most agree that the current mood is troubled. Too many unexplained events, such as the recent explosion of a just-emptied ammonia tanker, point to a struggle over territory and control. As one knowledgeable source put it (on condition he not be named): 'There's always been struggle here, ever since the Gold Rush days. In recent years things have stabilized, contending forces have struck a balance. Now that time of tranquillity may be over.' No one knows quite

why, or who is responsible. But about one thing there's little disagreement—a new era of turmoil has begun."

It's early evening. Sasha, off duty tonight, is
doing me a great favor, driving me up and down the eight
narrow two-block-long alleys that run from Twenty-fourth
to Twenty-sixth in the Mission.

We weave first through the botanical series, alleys
named Poplar, Orange, Osage, Lilac and Cypress, followed by two named for classical authors, Virgil and
Horace, followed in turn by Lucky Street—which, if not
named with ambivalence at its inception, is surely an
ironic designation today.

It's Cypress, of course, that's the focus of my interest.
But rather than linger here and attract attention, I've
asked Sasha to give me a proper tour of the entire back
street network. I want to get a feel for it, the kind of people who reside here. Although I've lived in San Francisco
all my life, I've never passed through these alleyways
before.

Each block has its own character. One is fronted by
buildings sporting gaudy murals, another is lined with
garages, nothing else. There are clusters of garbage cans,
back doors, rear cottages, fenced-in garden plots. On Lilac
Alley we spot a warning painted on a wall: "Yo! Slime
Boy! Next time I see your ass you're gonna get a blast of
hot lead! No kiddin!"

Cypress is no better or worse than the others. A green
door, of course, is not something I'd recognize, so Sasha
kindly points it out as we pass. I memorize its position,
then quickly appraise the buildings across the way. The
alley's too narrow and the light too dim for me to get a fix
on the upper windows. When I ask Sasha to circle the
block, he shakes his head.

"I don't think we should. If we come through again,
we'll be noticed," he says.

We compromise—we'll take a half-hour time-out at the Cuban Cafe on Valencia, then make a second pass.

Over double espressos, when he asks what I intend, I tell him truthfully I have no idea.

"You can try and find out who lives there," he says, "then phone them up. Or come by in the morning and present yourself, though I don't recommend that."

"What then?"

"Maybe you should write a letter."

"And if no one answers?"

He shrugs. "You've got a problem," he agrees.

Back in the car, I tell him of my decision. "I'm going to knock on that door now, tonight."

"And if whoever lives there refuses to let you in?"

"I'll improvise," I tell him.

He drives me back down Cypress, finds a place to wait where he won't block the alley.

"Whatever response you get, friendly or unfriendly, promise me you'll come back in ten minutes?"

I agree.

"If you don't, I'm coming in after you." He kisses me. "Good luck."

It's with some dread that I approach the green door—which appears nearly black to me. Outwardly I'm calm, inside I'm worried. It's been forty-eight hours since I've been warned off, thirty-six since I feigned bravery by handing out flyers on the next street. Surely the people who live around here know all about my quest. If Maddy rented a room, why didn't someone respond?

The door's set in a solid wooden wall. I don't see a buzzer, so I knock. Nothing. I wait twenty seconds, then knock again with greater force. Again no response, so I step back into the alley and look up. I make out dim light in a window on the second floor. It could be a night-light or a lamp left on to scare off prospecting burglars. I return to the door, work up my nerve, this time bang on it hard. Then, noticing a light switch set in the frame, I rapidly switch it on and off. It's then that I start hearing noises behind the door. A moment later a short elderly Chinese woman with a Mao-era haircut opens up and stares quizzically at my face.

"Hello," I say to her. She continues to stare, waiting for me to explain myself. "I'm a friend of Maddy's." I hand her my flyer. She looks at the picture, then down at my camera. She smiles in recognition. "I understand she rented a room here." Her smile broadens; she nods, gestures me inside. I get the feeling she's expecting me.

I follow her down a dim corridor. There's a sour smell of soy sauce, cooking oil, cabbage. She leads me through a kitchen where a teenage Chinese girl is studying at a table beneath a fluorescent light. As we pass through the room the girl does not look up.

We cross a small sitting room, furnished with a huge TV and austere unpadded wooden Chinese-style chairs. An old Chinese man is dozing in an overstuffed chair. The TV is on, set to the Chinese cable channel with the volume turned completely off.

Exiting this room, we arrive at a set of stairs. The old woman, who has yet to address me or mutter a single word, removes a large ring of keys from a hook on the wall, leads me up to the second floor, then down a hallway back toward Cypress Alley.

Here, to the right of the window I noticed when I looked up from the street, we face another staircase, steeper and narrower than the first. She climbs, I follow, arriving at what I take to be the attic floor. Facing us, in a cul-de-sac, are three closed doors, one in the center, the others angled at ninety degrees on either side. Employing one of her keys, she unlocks the center door, turns to me, gestures for me to enter. I hesitate. Sasha is waiting down in the alley. If I don't return soon, he'll come barging in. I turn back to the woman. Again she nods. Cautiously I push the door open with my foot. It's then, catching a faint aroma of photochemicals, that I know I've found Maddy's lair.

There's no light inside, but my night vision's superb; it takes me but a moment to comprehend the space. The room's small, the floor's bare, the ceiling's slanted, there's a sink on one wall and a dormer window with drawn shade on the wall opposite the door. In the center of the room, halfway to the window, stands a tripod topped by a magnificent camera, a Pentax 6×7, mounted with a telephoto lens. The camera, pointing slightly downward, is aimed at the blacked-out window. On a table beside the sink there's a developing tank, bottles of chemicals, a light box, a thermometer, a pair of scissors, a magnifying glass, glassine envelopes and a file box for negatives. Above the table two rolls of developed 120mm negative, weight clips attached, hang from a wire drying line.

I move to the window, then turn back to the woman. My body's trembling. I feel sweat forming in my armpits. She gazes at me, eyes intent. I make a gesture toward the shade. She nods. I tug it gently, then release it, allowing it to roll just halfway up.

At once I feel I've been here before. The window glass behind is unwashed . . . as I knew it would be. I step back behind the Pentax, peer through the viewfinder. The lens, as expected, is focused on a plane behind a window in the rear of an apartment building across the alley. I recognize the same soft edges of the window grid and window frame from the film I found in Maddy's Leica.

I turn back to the woman, but she's no longer there. Then I hear Sasha's voice below. I rush down the two flights to find him standing in the kitchen with the woman and the teenage girl. Sasha and the girl are vigorously gesticulating at one another. Seeing me, Sasha smiles.

"I decided to come looking for you," he says. "Interesting there're all deaf-mutes here."

I stare at him.

"You didn't know?"

"I had no idea. Though, come to think of it, this lady didn't say a word."

"That's why there's no doorbell. You switch a light on and off to signal you're at the door. The young lady here is Esther Chen. The older woman, her grandmother, is Grace Wong. Esther signs in American, so she's been interpreting for us." He grins. "Didn't know I could sign, did you?"

I shake my head. In fact, I'm astonished. "You have so many talents, Sasha."

He asks if I've found what I was looking for.

"Oh, I did! It's all in a little room upstairs—camera, tripod, exposed film, the view through the window, everything."

"I'm happy for you, Kay. I really am."

At my suggestion, he'll stay down here and interview Grace while I return upstairs. I want him to find out, with Esther's help, how Maddy came to rent the room.

On my way back up I pause on the second-floor landing to gaze at the apartment building across the way. It's then that I realize it's the rear of a building I've passed many times on Capp, the four-story stucco apartment house with molded escutcheon above the door that stands directly across from the spot where Maddy was run down.

Back in the little room I'm struck by the fact that not only did she take photographs here, it was also here that she processed them. No sign, however, that she tried to make prints. For a photographer of her experience, inspection of her developed negatives would be enough.

I pull the window shade, turn on Maddy's light box, pick up her magnifying glass, examine frames from the first of the two hanging rolls. The pictures are similar to shots I found in her Leica, but better, clearer, easier to decode. I carefully cut the two rolls into three-frame strips, pack the strips in glassine envelopes, add them to the file box, then carry it back downstairs.

I rejoin Sasha, Esther and Grace at the kitchen table. Mr. Wong, in the adjacent room, continues to snooze in front of the silent TV.

"Here's the story," Sasha tells me. "One morning three months ago, an elderly woman with sharp penetrating eyes appeared at the door. Luckily Grace's niece, who has normal speech and hearing, was here to interpret. Through the niece the lady asked whether it would be possible to rent a room on a monthly basis facing the street. She told Grace she wanted a quiet place to work, preferably on an upper floor where she wouldn't interfere with family activities. She said she would only use it sporadically and at night. As that didn't seem like much of an intrusion and Grace could use the money, she agreed. A deal was struck. Maddy would pay two hundred dollars per month.

"The next time she came, she brought a heavy suitcase. And she kept her word, she came only occasionally and always at night. Grace doesn't remember which nights, but she does recall that sometimes a week or two would pass between visits. Maddy always paid her rent in cash, and whenever she came she brought a modest gift, usually a sweet of some sort or a bag of fruit. She usually stayed until one or two in the morning, though sometimes she stayed till dawn. The last time she came was the same evening she was killed.

"Grace heard about the accident the following morning from another Chinese neighbor down the block. It turns out there are several disabled Chinese families on Cypress, placed here by social workers who visit regularly to assist. Grace was saddened by the news. She liked Maddy very much. She didn't know who to contact or who she should return Maddy's things to. Since most of the people on Capp are Hispanic, and since neither she nor her husband can hear or speak, they have virtually no contact with their neighbors. Thus she knew nothing of your flyers. Had she received one, she assures me, she'd have immediately recognized Maddy's picture. Meantime she's been waiting for someone to come around and claim Maddy's possessions. This evening, when you showed up, camera around your neck, she knew immediately you were the one."

Both Grace and Esther watch me closely, nodding as Sasha speaks. When he's finished they both turn to me and nod with vigor, as if to confirm that all he has conveyed to me is true.

It's then, simultaneous with their nods, that an idea springs full-born in my brain. I turn to Sasha.

"Please tell them I'd like to continue to rent the room and to come here as Maddy did from time to time at night."

Sasha looks at me. "You're sure that's what you want?"

I tell him I do, it's the only way I'll understand what's been going on.

I watch as he and Esther sign, then Esther signs to Grace in Chinese. When Grace understands what I want she gives me a curious look. Then she signs back to Esther, who conveys her response to Sasha in American Sign.

"Yes, you may continue to rent the room," he translates. "Grace also wants you to know the rent's been paid through the end of the month."

2
THE
WINDOW

*T*onight, gazing out my window, the city appears so serene I almost doubt my knowledge that it roils with passions. It's a pretty town, San Francisco; visitors are much taken by it — the whiteness, clarity of light, sweetness of air, majesty of bridges, romance of ravishing hills and tranquil Bay. All these give it the quality of an unreal place, a diorama, a stage set. But this beauty is fragile; San Francisco, built upon fault lines, can be shaken to rubble in seconds. Thrashed by vicious storms or enmeshed in suffocating fog, it can turn nasty, irascible, depressing. Ultimately, as those of us who live here know, it's a real city inhabited by real people . . . and people here are as capable of cruelty as people anywhere on earth.

Tonight such thoughts swirl in my brain. I've spent the day in the darkroom working with the film I found in Maddy's hideaway, trying to make sense out of the images . . . with no success. Though they're clearer, more legible than the earlier material, I find nothing more than flashes of female nudity amidst males who appear fully dressed.

Over and over I ask myself: *What was she trying to photograph?* The clear exposition she was seeking did not, as far as I can see, materialize. Her pictures tell me about the passion of her search, but not what she was searching for.

I drop in on Sasha. As usual, making love we roll off his love seat onto the living room rug as the embers in his fireplace break, producing sparks. Afterwards he retreats to his kitchen. Moments later I hear the throb and hiss of his espresso maker, an old-fashioned machine, the kind you find in North Beach cafes—sculptural, with the mechanism exposed, all knobs and valves and gleaming metal.

He returns with two demitasse cups filled with steaming coffee, which emit an aroma so enticing it makes me weak in the knees.

As we sip I tell him about my problem with Maddy's last photographs, this sense I have that there's something hidden in the images.

He offers me a square of bittersweet chocolate. "Ever heard of David Bohm?" he asks.

I shake my head.

"He was a physicist. In his final years, he became a kind of mystic. Born and educated here in the States, he joined Einstein's circle, then, during the McCarthy period, moved to Britain, where I met him not long before he died. He was a great thinker, his ideas cut deep . . . yet throughout his life he sought ever deeper theories to explain the universe. One such theory he called 'implicate order,' a hidden order enfolded in the visible surface that we know. According to Bohm, the implicate order lies beneath the visible order and gives rise to it. It is out of it that the universe we observe has sprung. It's the implicate order that I want to tell you about, not the theory, which is complex and difficult to explain, but an image that inspired it, which, I think, is relevant to what you're looking for."

He has my attention now, knows it too, has gotten it the way he often does, speaking of something apparently unrelated to my concern, sneaking up on me until, suddenly, he connects it to an event or motif in my life.

"Yes, tell me, Sasha . . . please."

He shows me his deep, liquid dreamboat eyes. "The way Bohm used to tell it, he was half dozing one night, half watching TV, one of those science shows the BBC does so well, when he was struck by an experiment being demonstrated on the screen. In this experiment a quantity of glycerine was suspended between two glass cylinders. A drop of black ink was added. Then, as the outer cylinder was slowly rotated, the ink drop was spun thinner and thinner into a thread until finally it disappeared. The ink was still in the glycerine, you understand—it just couldn't be seen. But then, when the outer cylinder was slowly rotated again, this time in reverse, the thread reappeared, becoming thicker and thicker, finally collapsing back into the original drop of ink."

I like visualizing this. "It must have seemed like magic."

"Yes," he says, "which, of course, is why the TV scientist used it—to catch the viewers' interest. It caught Bohm's interest too. Then, because he was a genius, he took it another step, using it as the starting point for a theory. Think of the ink drop, Kay, as the explicate order, matter which we can see. The invisible thread of ink enfolded in the glycerine—think of that as the implicate order yet to be exposed or understood."

"You're saying I should imagine Maddy's pictures as a kind of glycerine with ink hidden inside . . . and now I must reveal the hidden pattern."

"That's it," he says.

"Yes, I see. But how do I do it?"

He smiles. "Just turn the cylinder—metaphorically, of

course. Turn it slowly in reverse and then perhaps the secret structure will be revealed."

Tonight I dream of a drama taking place upon a stage. The theater in which I sit is pitch-black. At first I can see nothing, only hear faint sounds as the actors prowl, indecipherable whispers as they speak. Ever so slowly, the stage lights come on, barely bright enough to reveal shadows, windows, doors, the outlines of the set, the dark shrouded forms of the actors. I peer into this dim light, struggling to see. Though my night vision and hearing are good, I feel as if I'm blind and deaf. I can't understand the drama taking place before me. Frustrated, desperate to know what's happening, I cry out: "Speak louder so I can hear! Pour on more light so I can see!" No one pays attention. If anything, the light level drops and the actors whisper even more softly. Then, suddenly, knowing what I must do, I leave my seat, approach the stage, leap onto it and enter into the play myself.

Photography can be thought of in numerous ways—in terms of f-stops and shutter speeds, film types and lenses, composition, content, print quality and a hundred ways more. But in the end—this was Maddy's primary lesson—photography is about the photographer's vision, her way of seeing.

"Always ask yourself," she would say, " 'What am I seeing?' and then, 'How can I convey it in the strongest possible way?' " When she found fault with work, she'd say: "I don't feel anything here, I can't see what you were looking at."

To take pictures without encapsulating one's feelings— that, in Maddy's view, was a sin. "Nice snapshots," she'd declare, dismissing uninteresting work. Then: "Did you bring me any photographs today?"

She could be tough. A weak student might wither before her gaze. But Maddy didn't coach weak students. When she took you on she was telling you that she knew you were strong.

She'd say: "You can photograph anything you like. I never quarrel over content. But the intensity of your vision—that's fair game." Also: "My job is to help you see what you have seen, in your own way, the strongest way for you. All I ask is that every time you take a picture, you invest yourself completely. To do less is to cheat the art."

This morning I think about this as I examine her shots once again, seeking the implicate order, the hidden order enfolded within them. Maddy was brilliant. She didn't take empty pictures. She knew what she was doing and didn't waste time. I can't imagine her taking shot after shot, each of them equally meaningless.

So, I decide, there must be something embedded in these shots, something which, perhaps on account of some weakness within myself, I fail or am unwilling to see.

At noon I take a bus to the new Main Library at Civic Center, passing through Polk Gulch en route. Two years ago I did a lot of picture taking here, documenting the lives of male hustlers. Tim, the one I liked most, became my friend. Later he was brutally killed. I made a book out of his story, published last fall, *Exposures*. If it hadn't been for Maddy's guidance, I doubt I would have finished it.

On the bus I think about color blindness. Could the hidden order in Maddy's pictures be invisible to me because I'm unable to distinguish its color? Maddy, of course, shot in black and white, so that doesn't make sense . . . unless she saw something in color with her naked eye which she then shot in black and white simply out of habit.

At the library, in the open stacks, I find a copy of David Bohm's *Wholeness and the Implicate Order*. I take it to a table, open it, start to read. The text is difficult. My mind wanders as I skip over material about problems in quantum physics. But then, when I come upon a reference to photography, I sit up, alert.

Bohm is describing his theory in terms of the differences between photography and holography, suggesting that a photograph is analogous to the explicate order, while a hologram is analogous to the implicate.

With a lens, he points out, one captures and replicates on film the same spatial relationships that exist in the scene being photographed. For example, if there's a bird in the upper right corner of the viewfinder frame, it will be in the upper right corner of the negative that light reflected off the bird will fall.

A hologram, however, is different, a three-dimensional representation in which it's possible to examine the scene from different points of view. In a hologram, created by lasers and without a lens, light reflected by the entire scene is embedded, in the form of an interference pattern, in every single portion of the picture. Thus even the tiniest part of a hologram will contain light reflected by the bird, the bird-light being enfolded within light reflected by everything else.

The implication is clear: if the implicate order, the secret, is enfolded within every part of a hologram, then it should be possible to explicate it from every part as well. But, I'm quick to recall, Maddy didn't leave behind any holograms. She left only photographs.

So, I think, standing in the doorway of Main Library, *I'm back just where I started.*

Or am I? I wonder, as I put on wraps, then cross sunstruck Civic Center Plaza to the bus stop on Van Ness.

I take the bus as far as Mission and Twenty-fourth, then walk over to Capp. Instead of lingering in my usual manner, I walk straight to the front of 4106, the apartment building that backs on Cypress Alley. I enter the lobby as if I know the place, and immediately inspect the building register. Opposite a series of doorbells I find a list of names embossed on plastic strips, the embossing executed in various sizes and styles, suggesting different durations of residency.

The apartment I'm interested in is on the second floor, but the numbers on the register don't give a hint as to location. Second-floor apartments here aren't labeled in the usual way: 2-A, 2-B, 2-C and so on. Rather the apartments are numbered sequentially 1 to 11, suggesting a lack of symmetry upstairs.

Since I don't want to be caught snooping around, I rapidly photograph the register.

I call Joel from a grocery on the corner of Twenty-fifth, reach him on his cell phone, which he always carries in a holster suspended from his belt. When he answers he informs me he's munching a hot dog at a waterfront dive in Oakland, the Chile Pepper Lounge.

"I keep waiting for a new tip, kiddo. Or at least a compliment on our explosion story. I know it's coming, just don't know when. This guy, whoever he is, has got me upset. Kirstin says I'm acting like a loony tune."

I ask him how I can get hold of the floor plan of a residential building.

"What kind?" he asks.

"Multidwelling. Rental."

"Easy," he says. "Building Inspection Department, Records Management Division. They'll let you look at plans, and if you pay a little something, make you a copy to take home." He pauses. "Wanna tell me what this is about?"

"Not just yet."

"Whenever, kiddo. I'll be here when you need me. Always remember that."

"I will, Joel. Thanks."

The Building Inspection Department, I discover, is on Mission near Civic Center, an easy stop on my way home. Even as I enter I catch the aroma of city bureaucracy—boredom, indifference, low morale, starchy food and lousy coffee all suspended in poorly recycled air.

I fill out a form, then spend twenty minutes in line before a counter presided over by a huge black woman sporting a dashiki and the kind of huge Afro white folks used to think connoted militancy.

When, finally, I reach the head of the line, she takes my form without bothering to look up. Failing to find fault with my application, she smiles broadly, hits the form with several stamps, then demands fifteen dollars, cash or personal check accompanied by California ID. After I pay, she glances quickly at my face.

"Here's your receipt, sweet pea. Come back in two days. Pick up your paperwork at window six."

Walking home, I ponder the implicate order—that which is implicit yet hidden from view. At Larkin and Greenwich I climb the steep steps that lead to the Greenwich Street cul-de-sac. From here I enter Sterling Park, the beautiful wooded area honoring the early-twentieth-century San Francisco poet George Sterling, which covers a block on the south peak of Russian Hill.

The failing light is comfortable for me now. It also endows the park, filled with mature specimens of Monterey cypress and pine, with the shadowy feeling of an ancient wood. There's lots of deep shade and strange thick low-lying trees which undulate like giant serpents along the ground.

Nobody's around, the park is empty. I go to a bench, sit and contemplate the view. The Marin Headlands are etched by the late-afternoon sun. The Golden Gate Bridge, so mighty close up, from here looks almost like a toy.

How, I ask myself, can I account for Maddy's meaningless shots, which look more like failed surveillance photos than the work of an important artist/photographer?

Suppose I've been looking at her pictures too closely, searching out details when the message is in the overall effect? Suppose Maddy wasn't trying to photograph specific action, rather was trying to capture something deeper such as a feeling or a mood?

In that case the hidden order in her pictures would be the very thing she emphasized in her tutorials: the photographer's struggle to instill emotion in her work. If so, then in a metaphorical sense, as Sasha put it, her photographs *would* resemble holograms.

These thoughts excite me so much I dash out of the park, past the tennis courts, the rosebushes on Hyde, dart into my building, impatiently ride the elevator to my floor, fumble with my keys, open my door, then rush immediately into my office, where I've pinned up prints of the medium-format shots I found in Maddy's lair.

This time, rather than inspecting each print closely, I stand back and examine them as a group.

What's there? What's the feeling? What was she trying to convey?

It's then, that moment, in the very act of posing the question, that the answer comes to me with striking clarity. Menace, depravity, even evil—*that's* what's in her pictures, *that's* what they're all about.

Thursday, midmorning, apartment floor plans in hand, I take the Sacramento Street bus up to the Richmond, get off at Arguello, then walk to City Stone Ground, my dad's bread bakery on Clement.

I can smell the bread even from the street, the same fabulous mouthwatering aroma that permeated our house when I was young, when bread making was my father's hobby.

"Hey, darlin'!" he says, spotting me as I walk in. "What a grand surprise!"

As always when I appear, he grins with pleasure, then scoops me up in his mighty arms. Though the bread making is finished for the day, he's still in his baking whites and floppy hat, his bare forearms and cheeks spotted here and there with flour.

He kisses the top of my head, then sets me down. He's a big blocky guy, his hair's a shaggy mop of soft gray locks, he has the grooved, weathered face of a man who's spent years living in the open, riding beneath the sun, sleeping beneath the stars. In fact, he walked a policeman's beat until he was forty, when, under pressure to resign, he decided to embrace his dream—open a bakery where he would make great-tasting honest loaves of bread with perfect shattering crusts.

He's been successful. His *pain au levain* is coveted. He sells most of his production to restaurants; the remainder, reserved for walk-ins, is inevitably sold out by noon. He adores his work, the sorcery of it, making something wondrous out of the simplest things—water, flour, yeast, salt and heat.

He leads me into his small office off the baking floor, glassed in so he can watch his Russian émigré staff at work. His desk's covered with heaps of receipts, letters, undeposited checks, telephone message slips, unwashed coffee mugs, even crumbs from the morning's sample loaves.

"What brings you here, darlin'?" he asks, merriment in his eyes. "You don't like going out in daylight, so I know you didn't just drop by."

He nods; he remembers. He was always a good father, happy to play with me at the odd times dictated by my achromatopsia, taking me on moonlight walks, to the beach at sunset, understanding my love of and comfort in the night. He told me bedtime stories too, stories about a little girl who couldn't see colors but could see things other normal-sighted girls couldn't—could read through color disguises, discern peripheral threats, whose night vision was so keen she would lead her friends on exciting nocturnal adventures. In his stories the heroine's apparent weakness always became her strength, and though she often had to struggle to accomplish simple tasks, her bravery, intelligence and special vision enabled her to perform great deeds, proving herself to those who'd earlier mocked her for her malady.

They were tomboyish tales; Dad wasn't good at spinning yarns about girls in pretty dresses who played with dolls and sported curly locks. I'm sure his bedtime stories helped form my character. I know my mother disapproved, believing they encouraged my willfulness.

"Well," Dad says, eyeing my floor plans, "let's see what you got."

I unroll the plan of the second floor of the Capp Street building, show him the apartment that backs on Cypress Alley.

"I want to know who rents this space," I tell him. "Then I want to know all about him."

"Him?"

"Him, her, whoever. Look, it's apartment 5. Carroll's the name beside the lobby buzzer. I checked the phone book. There're lots of Carrolls, none with a listed address at 4106 Capp. Of course a lot of people, me included, don't list their address, and there're plenty with unlisted phones. Anyhow, I thought maybe you can get Rusty to help."

"Sure, I can ask him, darlin'. But you're gonna have to tell me a little first."

He listens intently, gazing into my eyes, as I describe how I found Maddy's spy room in the deaf Chinese couple's house on Cypress, why I'm certain she rented it because she'd targeted the apartment across the way, and how the photographs she took convey a mood of menace, but say virtually nothing about why she was interested.

"Why not take this to Kremezi?" he asks.

"Because it doesn't really mean anything, does it, Dad?"

He ponders. "I was a street cop, not a detective, but I guess if I was working a hit-and-run and someone brought me this, I probably wouldn't put much legwork into it." He looks at me. "What do you intend to do?"

I shrug. "Don't know yet. I'm taking it one step at a time. Right now all I want is to find out why Maddy was so interested in that apartment."

He nods, but I can tell he's skeptical, knows that I think there's a connection between Maddy's spying and her death and that it's my intention to link them up. On the other hand, I can tell, he likes the notion that I'm not the type to leave a mystery unsolved, perhaps because it reminds him of the brave little color-blind girl in the stories he used to regale me with before I went to sleep.

"Gimme a couple days," he says. "I'll check with Rusty, see what he can turn up. But"—he raises his finger—"one condition."

"Yes?"

"You don't use what I get for you to do something stupid, like spy on people who may be dealing drugs."

"Is that what you think's going on over there?"

"Maybe, maybe not. I just don't want you getting hurt, darlin'. So promise me?"

"Sure, Dad—nothing stupid, I promise."

I'm sitting in the attic room on a simple bentwood chair, peering out the window. There're no lights on or any signs of life in the apartment across the way. I sit frozen in the cane seat, stiff and awkward, feeling as if I don't really belong here, am an intruder in someone else's space. It's not the apartment across Cypress, the object of my scrutiny, that gives me this feeling; it's this room, Maddy's lair, her spy nest. There were confidential aspects to her life which I am here to probe. She's gone, no longer able to defend her privacy. I'm here to learn her secrets, and though I don't yet know what they are, I'm certain that when I've uncovered them I will view her differently than before.

After fifteen minutes, my eyes fully adjusted, my night vision acute, I study the little room.

The tripod and big Pentax dominate the space. On my first visit, I immediately fixed on them, then on the processing tank and accessories laid out on the worktable beside the sink. Now, prowling the room, I come across other mementoes of Maddy's visits: her empty suitcase in the closet, along with a belted black raincoat and umbrella; a neatly folded ski sweater stored in a dresser drawer along with a pencil-beam flashlight. I remember this sweater, recall her wearing it when I came to her flat for tutorials. Holding it up, I discover a pocket-size spiral-bound notebook hidden within its folds.

Greatly excited, I flip through the pages. About half of them contain writing. On some I find only a word or two, on others brief notes scrawled in haste.

There's mundane stuff such as shopping lists (inevitably including yogurt and fruit), and reminders about her tutorials. I find a note referring to David Yamada: "DAVID RE CELL PHONE / EMERGENCIES? / PICKUP TIMES / SCHEDULE?" I even find a note about me: "TELL K. RE HER BOXERS / GET UNDER THEIR FEET."

A good idea! I'd have tried it if she'd suggested it. She never did. I think she realized I was on the verge of giving up the project and for that reason didn't push her ideas.

"DUEL / CHECK FILES" seems like a reminder to look through her negative files. But what does "duel" mean? Or is the word actually "dual"?

Some of her notes are illegible. Probably she scribbled them while sitting in the dark waiting to view some action across the way.

There're also a couple notes written clearly enough, whose meaning I can't decipher. On three different pages she repeats the same two words: "THE GUN." The third time she underlines the words twice. On another page she writes: "THE GUN / FIND THE GUN / WHERE'S THE GUN?" In each instance the word "gun" is circled.

Feeling dizzy, I put the notebook down, go to the sink, splash water on my face, then lie down on the daybed near the door. I can feel my heart throbbing in my chest, sweat breaking out on my forehead.

Why? Is it the notebook? What does the notebook tell me?

Nothing, I decide . . . nothing that I can understand.

That, I realize, is the problem—that the deeper I look into things, the less sense they seem to make. An important photographer has been killed—my teacher, role model and heroine. In her last months her behavior was strange and out of character. She started shooting film after she told everyone she'd given up active photography. She rented an attic room in a private house in a very bad neighborhood overlooking the back windows of an apartment. She wrote cryptic notes to herself in a notebook she concealed in the folds of a sweater. And then, one night, she was run down by a motorcyclist in front of the building she was spying on.

It's the same enigma I've been grappling with for two full weeks, slightly embellished by my discovery of the notebook. But just as at each earlier discovery (the film in the Leica, the rental of the attic room), the basic impasse remains: I'm no closer to discovering what she was doing.

Weary of the whole business, I close my eyes, hoping to regain calm in a meditative state. Instead, I fall asleep, awakening after just an hour, seized by a notion that perhaps there is something revealing in the notebook.

Maddy's note about David: if they discussed her getting a cell phone for emergencies, and if her reference to a pickup schedule alluded to his transporting her to and/or from the Wongs', then David's professed ignorance about her presence in the Mission was a lie.

Again I fall asleep. Waking just before dawn, I check the windows across the alley. Nothing. I steal downstairs, past the Wongs' open bedroom door, let myself out, walk rapidly to Twenty-fourth, then over to Mission Street, where I call a cab.

Taking a tip from Maddy's notes, I decide a beeper's too passive, that it's time to graduate to a cell phone. If I'm going to spend time around Capp and Cypress, I may need a way to summon help.

I shower, change, put on shades, then go out into the blazing morning light. I don't particularly want to face the sun, but feel the need to talk with David Yamada face-to-face.

His company, Kaleidoscopics, is situated in a cavernous brick building on Second Street, in the heart of the funky district around South Park which the press has dubbed "Multimedia Gulch."

There're hundreds of cyber-oriented companies here, some large, most small, a few just one- or two-person shops. The list of tenants in David's lobby tells the story: BrainTools, Pixel People, GenXTronics, Ballz-Gamez, Web-Fleet . . . The lofts above, formerly occupied by coffee packers, are filled now with hip computer nerds—CD-ROM creators, game and web page designers, cyberartists, cyberanimators, people who write about people who are cool-wired, hard-wired, hot-wired, or just write code.

Kaleidoscopics is on the seventh floor. The receptionist, a pretty Asian girl, buff and decked out in SoMa grunge, is playing a video game at her desk. I stand patiently before her. It takes her a while to notice.

"David? Sure, he's back in the shop." She gestures with her thumb. "Want some latte? I'm about to order up."

I tell her no thanks, saunter toward the rear of the loft. A sad-eyed cocker spaniel, leashed to a radiator pipe, is peering at something in the gloom. I follow the dog's line of sight, spot some kind of horn-backed creature crawling among the bicycles stacked against the wall.

"Hey, there's a reptile back here," I tell the girl.

"That's Joe. He won't bother you. He's an iguana, so, like, he likes to roam."

Figuring that explains it, I walk farther, finally find David by the back wall sitting at a computer workstation. Nearby, two employees, perched on stools before a bench, are busy assembling kaleidoscopes.

"Hi, Kay! Take a look," David says, inviting me to peek at his screen. I lean forward, see a nine-pointed symmetrical chakra image slowly changing the way it would if one were rotating a manual kaleidoscope.

"Now watch," he says, punching at his keyboard.

Suddenly the changing process speeds up. David enters more data. The speed increases. He types more. The process becomes overwhelming. Then, when he types again, the image explodes, the pieces finally settling into what appears to be a pile of broken glass at the bottom of the screen.

"Nice, huh?" he says. "You start out warm, get hot, then hotter, you start doing all this crazy stuff, then . . . release."

"Cybersex, David—is that what you're up to?"

The assemblers titter. David looks embarrassed.

"I think it's an exciting work of cyberart," he says.

I'm sure it is. I'm also sure it looks a lot better in color. Although I don't see colors, I have a sense of how they can enrich an image. My mother, who was a middle school music teacher, used to explain colors to me in terms of the harmonics of different instruments: the "golden" sound of the clarinets, the "crimson" of the flutes, the "maroon" of the cellos. All through school my art teachers told me how colors convey emotion. Monet, Renoir, van Gogh, Cézanne—each had his special palette. Literature too is filled with color analogues—Walt Whitman's greens, Conrad's blues, Hemingway's earth tones, the moody ochers in the poems of Edgar Allan Poe. And of course, I know colors from everyday speech: "He's a yellow belly." "She's green with envy." "He makes me see red." "Tonight I'm feeling blue."

Since there's no privacy in the loft, David suggests we adjourn to a cafe. He chooses one right on South Park, where the decor consists of innards of old computers and discarded keyboards embedded in the walls.

As soon as we sit down, I cut short the small talk.

"Did Maddy ever mention getting a cell phone?"

He nods. "She wanted one. I ordered it for her. She was killed before it arrived."

"You drove her over to the Mission and picked her up there, didn't you?"

He stares, stunned.

"Come on, David. The house with the green door on Cypress Alley. You know the one."

"Why are you asking me this?" he demands.

"How many times did you take her there?"

"You're not answering my question."

"Hey! You're not answering mine."

He turns away, can't look me in the eye. Though angry, I speak as gently as I can.

"You knew she was going there. You even knew the house. You knew she was taking pictures. Why did you lie about it, David? Tell me. *Why?*"

"You came all the way over here to corner me?"

"What should I have done? Taken the matter to Kremezi?"

"I feel like I'm being interrogated."

"Good! That's how I want you to feel."

"For God's sake, Kay! I didn't *do* anything."

"I didn't say you did. But you didn't share with me. And worse, you lied."

"Okay!" He turns back to me. "You're right, I didn't share. I drove her over to the Mission a couple of times."

"How many?" I ask sharply.

"I don't remember. Maybe six or seven."

"That's more than 'a couple.' "

"Where do you get the right to question me like this?"

Embarrassed at being caught in a lie, he's doing the human thing, lashing back. *Fine,* I think. In fact, I decide, I'll pour on a little more contempt since anger seems to open him up.

"You're fudging your answers," I tell him. "Why not give it to me straight?"

"I want to. I'm trying . . ."

"I want the story. Nothing more or less."

"There isn't any *story,* Kay. She asked me to drive her a few times. I did. She didn't tell me why and I didn't ask. Twice too she had me pick her up."

"How did she get home the other times?"

"Probably took taxis. I don't know."

"What about the night she was killed?"

"What about it?"

"You drove her that night too, didn't you?"

Again he looks away. For me that's as good as a confession.

"Look, it's all right," I tell him, softening my tone. "You're not responsible for the hit-and-run. If you hadn't driven her, she'd have gone some other way. She was a strong woman, David—I think the strongest I ever knew. When she made up her mind to do something, she did it. She had tremendous will. No one, especially you, her loyal stepson, could stand in her way."

There're tears in his eyes now. I take his hand. "Is this why you lied—because you felt guilty? Afraid people would blame you?" He nods. "No one's going to blame you, David. Least of all me. You'd do anything for her.

She knew that. That doesn't make you responsible. You're *not* responsible. You must believe that or you'll go on feeling bad."

He's gazing at me now. "I'm sorry I lied to you. I feel like such an asshole."

I squeeze his hand. "I want you to tell me everything you know. Things she said, even if they seem unimportant. Her attitude in the car. Was she eager? Determined? Nervous? And on the way home the two times you picked her up, how did she act then? There were just two times, weren't there, David? Or could there have been more?"

Asking these questions I've no particular goal in mind other than to accumulate information. But by being specific, I hope to get him talking. And, it seems, having prevaricated before, he's eager now to tell me all he knows.

Maddy was brooding—that much he knew. She was generally a cheerful sort . . . though, like anyone, she had her moods, what David's father used to call her "brown studies." Still, he had a definite sense the last few months that she was brooding over something, turning it over and over in her mind.

She seemed distracted in a way he hadn't observed before. At first he thought it was her illness. She'd gone to a cardiologist the preceding autumn, learned she had coronary artery disease and wasn't a good candidate for bypass surgery. But even if surgery were possible, he doubted she'd have allowed it. She had too great a need to keep control.

But then he realized it wasn't ill health distracting her, it was something else. He knew better than to ask; experience had taught him that the initiative for such a conversation had to come from her.

However, she did give a reason for her requests for lifts. She said she'd recently encountered an old friend named Bea whom she hadn't seen in years. They'd run into one another by chance, renewed their friendship. Would David mind driving her up to the Mission where Bea lived, and where she and Bea had agreed to meet for dinner?

He was delighted. He'd do anything to help her, all the more because it was so rare for her to ask for help. The first time, she had him drop her off at Mission and Twenty-fourth in front of a bookstore, where, she told him, she and Bea would meet, go to a restaurant, possibly take in a movie; then Bea would send her home in a cab.

David didn't question any of this; no reason that he should. He was so thrilled she was interested in going out it didn't occur to him to question her story.

The first time he dropped her, he suggested he wait so he could meet Bea too. She told him not to bother, Bea was shy and often late; she'd amuse herself browsing in the store until her friend arrived.

This was the routine: he'd pick her up early in the evening, drop her in front of the bookstore. After the first time, she told him it was easier to spend the night at Bea's, so he needn't call later to make sure she'd gotten home.

Only slowly did it dawn on him that these evenings allegedly spent with Bea might be a subterfuge for something else. There was an eager, almost voracious quality about her in the car which reminded him of the way she used to act years before when preparing to go out on a shoot. It was the same hunger, he felt, the same desire to capture and bring home coveted images. He remembered it well from his youth—the glint in her eyes, the glow in her cheeks, the way she actually seemed to vibrate with awareness. And though she was a lot older now and also ill, he felt the same vibrancy in her as she sat beside him in the car.

His father, Harry Yamada, had once made reference to that quality: "With a camera in your hands, Maddy, you remind me of a hunter with a gun." Maddy had immediately corrected him: "How 'bout a huntress with a bow and arrow? Maddy the Huntress." Then she'd laughed.

There were only two times that she asked David to

retrieve her. On both occasions they made the arrangement in advance. Would he be so kind as to pick her up in front of the bookstore at eight A.M.? She didn't give an explanation, didn't bother to mention the ever elusive Bea, whose existence, by this time, he'd begun seriously to doubt. She just made her request, then thanked him for helping her out.

Both times there was a noticeable change in her, a mood quite different from the eager huntress quality she'd discharged when he dropped her off. Both times she was monosyllabic, appeared depleted and fatigued. This too he recognized, for this was the way she'd acted in the early days on those rare occasions when she returned from a shoot without the images she had sought.

He understood then that she was shooting film. And though he was worried for her, mystified by her secretiveness and her bogus explanations, he was also gratified. Though evidently she was not bringing home the goods, the chase itself, it seemed to him, was giving renewed purpose to her life.

Never, during any of these forays, did he see a camera or roll of film in her hands. All drop-offs and pickups were made at the bookstore on Mission. He knew nothing of Cypress Alley or of a house with a green door.

What he did know was that whatever had been troubling her was now being worked out in some private way. His only concern was that she be happy and fulfilled. In this latest quest there was, he felt, the possibility of fulfillment. In the face of that, her secrecy, the nature and details of the project, the issue of Bea, all seemed beside the point.

David and I leave the cybercafe to take a turn around South Park. Though the light is brilliant, forcing me to shield my eyes, I still enjoy the stroll. The elongated oval of the park is elegant. Trees are in full bloom. Half-nude sunbathers sprawl upon the grass. Young toilers from

Multimedia Gulch sit on benches working at laptops propped open on their knees.

David gestures expansively to indicate the neighborhood.

"You know what they say about this place, Kay? That it's like Florence at the start of the Renaissance, a community of artists bursting with creativity, each striving to outdo the next."

He may have a point. I certainly sense the energy. The differences, of course, are that now the medium is electronic rather than paint or fresco or marble, and that while the Florentine artists strove for fame and glory, contemporary cyberartists hope to make their fortunes by taking their software companies public, then cashing out.

I have specific questions for David. The first is about what Maddy called "the gun."

He shakes his head. "She really hated guns," he says, "which is why she corrected my father. A huntress with a bow and arrow was fine, a hunter with a gun was not."

David's right about her dislike of guns. A lot of Maddy's work can be interpreted as antigun: her war photos of soldiers, weapons in hand; her numerous shots of angry cops with guns. It's as if, in these pictures, she's saying that guns corrupt, bringing misery and grief to those who hold and use them.

"I still don't understand why you lied," I tell him. "You could have said she had a friend named Bea and was probably visiting her."

"I lied because I knew she'd lied to me."

"Do you think she was killed deliberately?"

"You mean like by a mugger who panicked after he ran her down?"

"No, I mean singled out, killed because of what she was trying to shoot."

He shakes his head. "I can't imagine it. I don't believe she had an enemy in the world. And always, when she took pictures, she was totally up-front."

"You went through her papers. Did you find anything that might relate to this?"

He hesitates a moment. "There were some letters from a woman way back when. She signed herself Bea."

"So Bea *did* exist. But didn't you just say you thought she didn't?"

"What I meant was I didn't believe Maddy was seeing her, or that this Bea, whoever she is, had anything to do with her visits to the Mission."

Maybe David's right, maybe Maddy just pulled an old name out of her memory, then spun a fib around it.

"A final question—did she tell you why she wanted a cell phone?"

"She said so she could call me to come and fetch her." David's eyes start tearing up. "It came the day after she was killed. I still have it. The number's active—I had to sign her up for a year. It's no use to me, I already have one. I suppose, since she died, I could turn it back into the company, make some kind of a deal. But for some reason, I don't know why, I just don't have the heart."

Maybe, I think, he's hoping it will ring, and she'll be at the other end.

"Transfer it to me. I'll reimburse you and take over the contract. What d'you say?"

"Gee, Kay." He nods. "I think that'd be great."

There's still something wrong with his tale, I think, as we walk back to Kaleidoscopics, something false in his offered reason for lying about Maddy's forays to Kremezi and to me. But though I'm not convinced he's told all he knows, I'm certain I won't get more out of him today.

Back in the loft, he hands over Maddy's cell phone, shows me how to use it. To test it I call Joel, who picks up on the first ring. He tells me he's in San Pablo checking on an oil spill. I give him my new number.

"Now you're ready for the twenty-first century," he says.

"What I'm ready for," I tell him, "is to take urgent calls from you in the middle of the night."

It's time to go. David hugs me. "Thanks for understand-ing."

As I head for the door, Joe, the house iguana, scam-pers across my path. The pretty Asian girl at the desk, engrossed in her video game, doesn't look up as I depart.

It's only in the elevator, on my way back down to the street, that I realize how weird our conversation was. At the start, David wanted to know why I was asking him questions and how I knew he'd chauffeured Maddy to the Mission. But once I started pressing him, he didn't ask again.

Why not? Wasn't he curious?

David, I decide, played some role in the implicate order of Maddy's final days, a role I've yet to comprehend.

My new regime: spend nights in the attic room on Cypress Street; taxi back to Russian Hill at dawn; sleep until two P.M.; eat breakfast; attend four P.M. aikido class; return home, prepare and eat dinner . . . then take the bus back to Cypress, where, again, I spend the night.

It's a weird existence, and I think the weirdest part is that after six nights, I've yet to see a single thing in the apartment across the alley—not a person, a movement, a flash of light.

Dad calls, says his old partner, Rusty Quinn, is with him at the bakery.

"We got goodies for you, darlin'. Come on up. Rusty went all out for you, as you'll see."

I take a bus up to the Richmond, find Dad and Rusty lounging around Dad's office telling old-cop war stories. They look relaxed.

Dad adores Rusty. The feeling I think is mutual. They

worked the Chinatown bunco squad together for five years, bonding closely as two Irish guys would do in such a situation. Over those years Dad learned a smattering of Cantonese; Rusty learned to speak it well from his numerous Chinese girlfriends. Now he's married to a pretty Chinese girl, Soo-Lin, former nightclub singer and exotic dancer, and they have three gorgeous kids.

After Dad hugs me, Rusty hugs me too. He's a short stocky guy, almost squat, with blocky football player's shoulders. His Irish eyes dance with merriment as he appraises me. The strong cologne he wears reminds me of my mother's funeral: I recall smelling it on him when he hugged me that damp and sorrowful day.

Rusty, due to retire from S.F.P.D. this summer, is getting involved, he tells me, in an import-export venture. "You know, mainland bric-a-brac," he says. "It's mostly junk, but I love it. So I figure other folks'll love it too."

"Well," I ask him, after the hugging and exclamations over what a fine woman I've grown up to be, "what've you got for me, Rusty?"

He smiles. "Always the bottom line, eh, Kay?"

"One of the names Rusty came up with sounds familiar," Dad says. "But I can't place it."

"What're the names?" I ask.

Rusty tells me apartment 5 at 4106 Capp is not rented out. According to the resident manager, it's kept tenant-free by the property-owner company for occasional use by friends and associates. The company is the CFJ Realty Corporation, a firm with numerous holdings, commercial and residential, in numerous San Francisco neighborhoods. CFJ is named for the last initials of its three principals: J. Ramsey Carson, Chaplin D. Fontaine and Orrin R. Jennett.

"Good research," I tell him. "So who's this Mr. Carroll with his name beside the bell?"

"That's the interesting part," Rusty says. "When I couldn't match him to anyone at CFJ Realty, I decided to check with the utility companies."

"Smart move," Dad says. "Rusty would've made a fine detective."

Rusty demurs. "Too much office work. Like your dad here, I liked the street." He pauses. "Anyway, I found out there's no phone currently connected in the apartment, which seemed odd and made me mildly curious. So then I checked with PG&E. Bingo! The electricity account's listed under the name of one Vincent Carroll, with a post office box address up north in Mendocino County."

Dad nods solemnly. I know why he finds that interesting. Mendocino's the principal marijuana-farming district in California, which strengthens his theory that there's drug activity taking place in the apartment.

"Is it Carroll's name that's familiar?" I ask.

"Uh-uh, Ramsey Carson's," Dad says. "I've heard of him someplace or maybe read about him in the papers. When I remember I'll let you know."

"Don't know what you're after, Kay," Rusty says. "But whatever it is, keep on it. You need any more help, don't hesitate to ask. I'll always be there for you."

"Oh, she'll keep on it," Dad says. "Kay doesn't give up. Never has."

"Kind of girl I like," Rusty says.

But then, when I leave, I wonder why, with Dad always trying to dampen my investigative enthusiasms, Rusty was so encouraging.

Tonight, sitting here in the dark studying the streaked window across the way, I'm as bored and fatigued as I've been all week. I can't read because a reading lamp will reveal me, and if I pull the shade, I won't be able to keep watch. Now I understand why cops view surveillance work as hard duty, and why those who engage in it tend to get fat. Boredom, I've discovered, increases hunger. It takes all my willpower to keep from devouring my entire store of snacks. Luckily, I brought only apples and wafers, not pizza, potato chips or any of those other starchy goodies cops like so much.

There are times, I know, when I doze off in my chair. Then suddenly my head will slump to my chest and wake me up. It's not a pleasant awakening, more like the way one wakes on an airplane during an overseas trip, stiff, groggy and annoyed, as opposed to the sublime experience of waking up on a feather bed beside one's lover because his hand has gently grazed one's breast or a moonbeam has lightly danced across one's eyes.

I've tried various methods of staying awake, such as listening through earphones to taped books and music. But then, after the novel or music's finished, I fall asleep. It's the tedium that's so tiring, also the darkness and quiet. I think I understand now why convicts, kept in solitary, sleep twelve to fourteen hours a day.

Suddenly I'm jarred from one of my semisleep states by the appearance of light in the apartment window. I crane forward, heart pounding. *Something's happening!* I check my watch. Eleven-thirty. But then after a few minutes the light goes off.

Someone was there. Now perhaps he or she's in another room. Trembling, I wait, eyes fixed upon the dirty glass, hoping he/she will enter again—even, hopefully, appear.

Maybe they're sitting in darkness watching me?

No, that's paranoid! I can't possibly be seen. There's barely any ambient light in the alley. And if the people across the way are concerned about being watched, all they have to do is cover their windows and black me out.

I never considered cleaning the windows here for the same reason, I'm sure, Maddy never did—fear of signaling that the apparently uninhabited room on the top floor is now in use.

I catch some light again, dimmer this time, yet filling the window with a subtle glow. Perhaps someone over there has opened a door, allowing light to seep into the room.

I'm alert now, vibrating with awareness, the way David described Maddy when she was about to go on a shoot. It's similar to the hyperaware state Rita works to instill in us in aikido class, except, she teaches, for martial arts reasons, it's often better to appear sleepy to one's opponent.

I move my chair a little closer to the window. Maddy's tripod-mounted Pentax looms just above my head. She was clever with the Pentax, covering the shiny metal parts with matte black tape so they wouldn't reflect and give her away.

The glow in the room across the alley becomes more intense, as if someone has turned on a lamp. Then I detect rapid changes in the lighting level as if someone is moving between the light source and the window.

I squint to sharpen my vision, ready to fasten on the first person to show himself. I also want to gain a feeling for the space. Since Maddy shot with a telephoto, she didn't pick up anything except people in an extremely narrow plane just behind the window.

I make out a chair and what might be a portion of a bed. I'm also pretty sure that there's an open closet on the opposite wall, which could account for the changing light values in the background: flashes created by someone shoving hangers aside or pulling out a garment.

A woman steps into frame. Naked, back to the window, she stands before the closet as if contemplating what to wear. Movement, more flashes, then a tall dark-figured person appears near the window, blocking out the woman and half my view.

Waiting for this person to move, I have a sense it's a man. Maybe it's the line of his shoulders, or the fact that all the clothed figures in Maddy's photos appeared to be male.

He moves toward the woman, stands beside her, touches her. Then I see another male-female pair facing them. The woman could be Asian, I think. I blink several times. I don't understand why people would stand inside a closet looking out.

The first couple, the one with their backs to me, move slightly, at which point I catch a similar movement in the other pair. Are they dancing? They seem to mimic one another. Then I get it: it's the same couple, the man touching the woman, regarding themselves in a full-length mirror.

So now I know the room's probably a bedroom with a closet and mirror on the inside of the closet door. A Caucasian man and an Asian woman are in the room. The woman is naked. The man is caressing her. Perhaps they're lovers. Perhaps he's whispering to her, telling her how beautiful and seductive she is.

A perfectly innocent scene. Nothing sinister about it. So why did Maddy work to instill such a strong sense of menace?

The man moves toward the window, then turns his back, again partially blocking my view. I catch glimpses of the woman as she approaches him. Then she disappears.

Impossible! She was there a moment ago. She must be standing directly in front of him, out of my line of sight. Suddenly I catch a flash from the mirror—something moving near his waist. It's her head, I think, bobbing rhythmically, one of his hands controlling her, grasping her hair, while the other strokes her cheek.

She's on her knees performing oral sex—that's the only explanation. Nothing shocking about that . . . except there's an element of force suggested by their pose which doesn't sit well with me. And there's something else. I keep catching flashes of movement in the mirror that don't coincide with the motions of the couple in the center of the room.

Suddenly I understand. There're other people watching. The couple—the man dressed and dominant, the woman naked and on her knees—are performing for a group. There's some sort of sex party going on.

This revelation, which I feel I should have grasped when the couple first appeared, throws the scene into another category: exhibitionism and scopophilia in the room, while I, hidden here across the alley, am no longer merely a watcher, am now a voyeur.

I don't like this role, am disgusted to find myself playing it, so much so that now I must force myself to continue watching. It's one thing to scrutinize an intimate scene through a viewfinder, another to observe it with the naked eye. I'm not sure why this should be so, except that, camera in hand, I may allow myself the title of artist. But here, now, I can't convince myself I'm anything but a female Peeping Tom.

So . . . there they are, a woman giving a man head in a demeaning way while others stand around and watch. And yet there's more, another level of activity, which I can barely make out, something so curious, out of the ordinary, as to nearly defy belief.

Again I blink. To be sure I'm seeing what I think I'm seeing, to make certain my color blindness isn't deceiving me, I turn my head to the side to utilize my good peripheral vision . . . and still I can't be sure. It's that damn mirror that could be distorting things, or the dirty window glass in my room or theirs. It could also be my imagination, overstimulated by the empty hours I've spent waiting here. Probably, I think, it's just a trick of light. For what I believe I see (though I cannot be sure) is that the naked woman on her knees is not actually performing oral sex upon the standing dark-suited man, rather she's sucking on the shiny metal barrel of a handgun he's forcing deep into her throat.

One-thirty in the morning: The lights have finally gone out across the way. No more movement over there, no more activity. Everything's as it was before.

Except for me. I'm different. My eyes are sore from gazing so long and my mind's a whirlpool of half-resolved images. I'm reminded of my dream, the one in which I could barely see or hear the play. Tonight I felt the same frustration: my angle of vision was too narrow, my view clouded by two layers of dirty glass, the light was too dim to properly illuminate the scene and I couldn't hear a single word.

There's also something else—my terror of guns, which goes back to my mother's suicide. She used my father's spare service revolver, thrust it into her mouth, then pulled the trigger while lying on their bed with her head hanging upside down over the foot end. I've feared and hated guns ever since, refused to touch them, recoiled whenever I've seen them, even when secured in the holster of a friendly cop.

So I wonder: Was it some kind of mirage, a trick of light, or did I actually see it? And if so, is that what Maddy, who also hated guns, saw as well?

The ink drop may not be whole as yet, but threads of ink, previously unseen within the glycerine, are starting to appear. Meantime, the play I've constructed out of the bits that reached me is turning rapidly into a Grand Guignol.

Two A.M.: No point hanging around. Clearly the evening's festivities are over. I use my new cell phone to call a taxi, then go downstairs. Hearing deep rhythmic breathing as I pass the Wongs' bedroom door, I tiptoe so as not to wake them up.

After letting myself out, securing the green door behind me, I pause. Is it really wise to walk to Mission Street? I could have arranged for the cab to meet me here, but didn't want to attract attention. Now I must walk three blocks in a bad neighborhood at night.

I stand still, listen, can hear nothing but the sound of occasional distant traffic. I start to walk . . . then freeze.

Varoom!varoom! The deep growl of a motorcycle rends the air. It's not close, perhaps a block away, but it's loud, it pulsates and it's closing fast. Scared, I slip into a narrow space between the back wall of the Wongs' house and the neighboring garage, pressing my back against the concrete.

The motorcycle doesn't sound as if it's moving, rather as if its driver is gunning his engine while standing still near the corner of Cypress and Twenty-fifth. Then he takes off. I hear him circle the block. He roars down Capp, pausing this time at the other end of the alley, the intersection with Twenty-fourth.

I peer out. I hear him, but can't see him; he must be just out of sight. I get out my key to the green door, prepare to quickly reenter the house. But then, just as I'm about to step into the alley, I hear the noise louder than before.

Varoom!varoom!

I withdraw again, then cautiously peek out. He's dead center now at the end of the alley, gunning his engine with such ferocity that the machine rises on its rear wheel like a sharply reined-in horse.

The roar's enormous. He wants to attract attention. Impossible to make him out. Dressed totally in black, he wears a black helmet with visor that completely covers his face.

Varoom!varoom!

Front wheel back on the pavement, the machine lurches forward, blasting straight down the center of Cypress like a rocket. I shrink back, press my body hard into my little niche. He streaks by so fast I catch nothing of him but a blur. After he's gone I feel the rush of air, inhale the sharp gasoline smell of his exhaust. He thunders to the end of the block, then, with a squealing of tires, turns the corner and roars off.

I remain still. Before stepping out again, I want to be sure he's not coming back. To my surprise no one appears in any of the windows or leans out to see what's going on. The alley seems even quieter than before, as if terrorized to silence by the display of power.

Finally, convinced he's gone, I jog all the way to Mission Street, where I find my taxi hovering before the bookstore where David used to drop Maddy off. The driver, a black guy in his fifties, is annoyed at being delayed.

"Round here I don't wait for fares," he tells me. "Next time best git here first."

Ten A.M.: The telephone rings. I clutch for the receiver, bring it to my ear.

"Hello?"

"It is Maria Quintana."

"Yes, Maria. Good morning."

"Maybe not so good," she whispers.

I sit up. "What's wrong?"

"You must not come anymore."

"I don't understand—"

"I cannot speak now. I am at work. Please meet me this evening at Mission Dolores. Wait in the garden at six-thirty. Will you come? Please. This is important."

I tell her I'll be there.

"Thanks to God," she says.

At noon I call Joel, find him in his office at the *News*. He's in a cheery mood.

"Hey, kiddo! What can I do for you today?"

I tell him I've got a hypothetical question. "Suppose you can see people but can't hear what they're saying—is there a way you can snoop?"

"Listen in on them?"

"Something like that."

"You into some kind of heavy shit?"

"Can it be done?"

"Of course it can. Ever see *The Conversation*?"

He reminds me of the movie, set in San Francisco, in which an obsessed audio expert uses exotic equipment to bug the conversation of a couple as they walk around crowded Union Square at noon.

"Shotgun and parabolic mikes, sound filters, stuff like that. And remember, the movie was made back in the seventies. There's far better, smaller equipment today. You can probably buy it under the counter at one of those counterspy shops, but you won't know how to use it and it'll cost you a bundle. Another approach is to hire a surveillance expert. There're a couple good ones around. They generally work for attorneys and charge accordingly, and because they're legit, they won't do anything illegal. The sleazy types who'll do an illegal tap or plant an illegal bug will charge you even more. So unless you've got a lot of money, your best bet is just get close and use your ears."

"You wouldn't be trying to discourage me, Joel?"

"I'd certainly discourage you from committing an unlawful act. Electronic eavesdropping can land you in jail, which isn't to say it isn't done. But it's not something to fool around with unless you know what you're doing and unless there's a hell of a lot at stake."

"You've never done it?"

"Oh, I've been tempted. But you know me, kiddo—I'm from the hard-ass school. Some of my tabloid colleagues aren't so scrupulous. But when they play those kinds of games they insulate themselves real good."

"How?"

"Like, say, hire a sleazy private eye, tell him what they want without asking how he's going to go about it. It's understood the guy'll use a bug, but that never comes up in the conversation . . . which is also being recorded, by the way. They're paying for a result. It's up to the sleaze to get it."

"Now I *am* discouraged."

"Good. You won't do anything stupid."

"Like—?"

"Like put on a disguise, try and talk your way in someplace, then plant a miniature transmitter."

"Why's that stupid?"

"Because you'll probably get caught. Because the person you're bugging will probably have the room swept. Because the bug'll have a serial number and be traceable back to you. Because it's Nancy Drew time. Because life isn't like the movies." He pauses. "I wish you'd tell me what you're up to."

"I will . . . one of these days."

Hurt that I'm holding back, he cuts our conversation short. "Yeah, I'll look forward to that."

Walking to Marina Aikido, I ask myself whether I have the nerve to do what Joel's just told me I shouldn't. Yes, I decide, I most certainly have the nerve, but not the necessary stupidity or money. In fact, I make my small living from royalties on my books and sales of prints through my gallery, which I supplement with savings accumulated when I did advertising and fashion work, before I turned full-time to art photography.

After class, Rita calls me aside. She asks: "How 'bout a commitment on the *shodan* exam?"

"Please," I ask her, "give me a little more time. I'm distracted right now. When I go for it I want to concentrate a hundred percent."

"More like a hundred and ten," she says. "Okay, we'll wait awhile. But not too long, girlfriend. Remember, when your time comes, you seize it." She grins. "'Course I wouldn't want to intimidate you . . . or anything like that."

Having watched others face their moments of truth, I know exactly what she means. To prepare for the *shodan* is to be highly intimidated, by one's sensei of course, but also, ultimately, by oneself.

Standing still in the darkening cemetery garden of Mission Dolores, I listen to the final minutes of the evening mass. The chanting and music spill out of the basilica, rebound off the stone compound walls, disperse in the open air, otherworldly sounds of mystery and yearning.

Maria Quintana, dressed in black, floats toward me out of the shadows. It's only when she's close that I make out the deep crease of concern between her eyes.

"You must not go back," she says, voice clear, decisive. "It is dangerous now. For you and also for others."

"How do you know—"

"That you have been going there? Everyone knows. The whole neighborhood."

"But—"

"Do you think you can stand for hours on the street handing out pieces of paper and then go night after night to the same house and people will not recognize you, will not know that you are there? Do you suppose that when you pause before a door, then peer around to see if anyone can see you, there are not a hundred pairs of eyes watching your every move?"

"You're embarrassing me, Maria."

"I do not wish to embarrass you. I only wish for you to stay away."

"I'm sorry, I can't, I'm not finished yet."

"What is this 'finished'? Is to be finished to be killed?"

There's an edge to her, a belligerence she hasn't shown before.

"The motorcyclist—who is he?"

She stares hard at me. "Promise me you will stay away."

"The motorcyclist, Maria—I need to know."

She continues to gaze.

"He's the one, isn't he—the same one who ran down my friend?"

"I know nothing of this man," she says, biting off the word.

"You've seen him before."

"He showed himself to you. Is that not enough?"

I meet her eyes. Is she saying last night's appearance was for my benefit?

"Did he also show himself to her?" I ask.

She turns away as if stunned. For a moment she holds

her composure, then starts to weep. I move toward her, reach for her hand, lead her to a stone bench. We sit in the darkness. As she continues to sob I place my arm about her, hold her shoulder lightly, feel her convulse.

"I am so sorry," she says. "I feel so badly about everything."

"You didn't do anything wrong," I assure her.

"I should not have told you about the room."

"I'm very glad you did."

"I should have known that you would go there. They control the neighborhood, you see. They know everything. Now they have warned you. You must not go back. They will not give a second warning. Next time they will kill you too."

"Who are 'they,' Maria?"

It takes her a while to get the story out. The neighborhood, she tells me, is controlled by drug dealers. They operate out of several houses, one of which is in the middle of the Capp/Twenty-fourth Street block. Security is tight. Couriers turn up at odd hours to deliver money and pick up drugs. A freelance enforcer patrols by motorcycle. In return for the silence of neighbors, he keeps the neighborhood safe. There's no crime within a three-block radius, and the pushers and prostitutes who roam freely on lower Capp never venture above Twenty-third.

When she's finished, I'm left with a strange thought: that the person who killed Maddy and the people Maddy was watching may not be the same.

"The group that uses the second-floor apartment at 4106—what do you know about them?"

"Only that they come on Wednesdays twice a month, spend a few hours, then leave."

"Are they connected to the drug people?"

She shrugs. "They dress differently, act differently, come and go in different cars."

"And the drug dealers don't mind them?"

She shrugs again. "Well, they do not walk about the street with a camera," she says.

"Is that why the enforcer killed my friend?"

Maria shifts her eyes. "She crouched on the street at night, hiding behind cars," she says. "Of course people felt threatened. The motorcycle man ran by her several times, but still she stayed. Though your friend was old and weak, she was not afraid. It would have been better if she had taken his warning."

Not afraid: Maria's right about that. With a camera in her hand, Maddy was fearless. I think of her, frail in her illness, crouching behind a car across the street from 4106 Capp, watching the front entrance, waiting for someone to come out. How awkward, uncomfortable, even painful it must have been for her, yet she wanted their pictures so much she was happy to endure the pain.

"You will stay away now—yes?" Maria asks. Night has cloaked the garden cemetery. Her eyes glow in the darkness.

"I don't know," I tell her truthfully. "You've given me a lot to think about."

She closes her eyes, crosses herself. She doesn't believe I'll stay away.

When she's gone, I walk out to Dolores Street. From in front of the basilica, I call Kremezi on my cell phone.

"Been expecting to hear from you," he says. "You seem to know powerful people." He pauses to let his irritation sink in. "What I got to tell you is I got nothing new to tell you."

"You're saying you don't know anything about drug dealers operating on the block and their motorcyclist enforcer?"

"Where'd you get this?" he asks sharply. When I tell him I have an informant, he chuckles again: "Seems I figured you right."

"Just how did you figure me, Detective?"

"As a lady who wouldn't let go."

A lady! "So now that you know the story, what're you going to do about it?"

"Look into it. Meantime, I suggest you back off."

"Funny the way everyone's issuing me warnings these days."

"Why don't you knock that chip off your shoulder, Ms. Farrow? You did your part. Now let me do mine."

Tonight, I decide, I won't go over to Cypress, and not just because I've been warned off. Now that I've learned the people who use the apartment at 4106 Capp apparently do so on alternate Wednesdays, it's not worth my time to sit in the dark staring at a blank window till they return.

It feels good to be free of my night regime, yet I'm left feeling empty too. After living off the tension of the enterprise for a week, it's a letdown to have nothing to do.

Still, I decide, it will be good to rest my eyes. Next time I peer into that window, I want to be absolutely certain about what I see.

THE GUN / *FIND THE GUN/WHERE'S THE GUN?*

Maddy's peculiar notation haunts my mind. I spend the morning examining all the photographs she took through the window, searching her negatives for glimmers of metal—gun barrels, hammers, triggers, anything that might have caught the light and gleamed.

I start seeing guns everywhere. I'm amazed. It's as if every vague and grainy highlight in the film is actually a part of a gun.

Am I imagining them? Where did they come from? How come I didn't see them before?

I peer closely with my naked eye, then with a magnify-

ing glass. Guns . . . guns . . . guns! *What is going on here?
Is this what she was shooting—sex with guns?*

I take an early-evening aikido class. Rita has us practice
randori, dealing with multiple attackers. I dutifully play
the part of attacker, waiting patiently for my turn to be the
nage. When it comes I truly revel in the role, twirling,
whirling, applying techniques, throwing opponents right
and left, moving beyond exhaustion into a pure state of
exhilaration and empowerment.

At the end of class Rita sums up, referring to the nearly
supernatural abilities of Morihei Ueshiba, founder of
aikido.

"O-Sensei would turn his back on his attackers," she
tells us. "Then when they got to where he'd been they were
surprised—he wasn't there."

At which I think: *Maybe he wasn't there. And maybe
the guns aren't in Maddy's pictures either.*

Four-thirty A.M.: The telephone rings. It's Joel. He's
just received a tip from his informant with the phony Chinese accent. He'll be by to pick me up in twenty minutes.

"Load up your cameras, kiddo. And don't bother making coffee—we'll pick some up along the way."

Outside the air's chilly, cold sea fog swirling up Russian Hill. As I wait for Joel my cameras feel like dead
weight. I adjust the collar of my black leather jacket, then
rub my hands together for warmth. A minute later Joel
pulls up, I hop in, he U-turns, then tears back down Hyde
toward Market.

"Where're we going?"

Joel mimics his informant: " 'You go Tan-Hing Enterprises, 2221 Alameda. Velly interestin' storage facility
there. Enjoy. Bye-bye.' "

"That's it?"

Joel nods. "I especially appreciated his 'enjoy.' Like we're going to get a really tasty meal."

We rush past St. Francis Memorial, where Sasha works in the ER, then cruise down the hill through the western tip of the Tenderloin. At the intersection with O'Farrell we just miss sideswiping a shivering transvestite prostitute who lurches at us out of the gloom. Joel pulls over at Ellis, where there's an Arab-owned all-night deli. While he goes inside to purchase carryout coffee, I study the old apartment house across the street. Called the Ben-Hur, its facade is decorated with embedded terra-cotta Roman chariots.

Alameda is situated in the South of Market decorator and design district, a neighborhood of antique dealers and wholesale furniture showrooms. Number 2221 turns out to be an enormous old stand-alone brick warehouse, the kind that can be extremely dangerous in a serious earthquake, when thirty seconds of vigorous trembling can shake the mortar loose and collapse the structure into a heap of bricks.

Here, in the SoMa flatland, there's no fog, but because it's an industrial area, the street lighting's dim and spare. Joel circles the building searching for an entrance. There are several huge wooden doors; all appear well secured. Then, as we pass the enclosed loading area in the back, I notice a tear in the chain-link fence.

I tell Joel to stop, let me out.

"I'll slip through, see if there's a way in from the loading dock."

"Be careful, kiddo. There could be a night watchman, even a dog. Any trouble, run like hell."

I hadn't considered the possibility of a dog. Making my way toward the barrier, I quiver at the thought of being pursued by some drooling Doberman. Passing through the fence, I note the tear looks fresh. When I reach the loading dock, I turn back toward Joel, take confidence in the fact that he's watching me from the car. Once I mount the concrete stairs I'll be out of his sight line. I wave to him, then climb.

There're two big loading doors, both firmly shut, plus a normal-size door for pedestrians. I try it. Locked. I'm about to return to the car when I'm surprised by a mechanical sound. I step to the side and watch transfixed as the left loading door slowly rolls up, revealing a freight elevator, empty, rickety, without a ceiling, descending, then stopping with a shudder flush with the concrete loading-dock floor.

It takes a while for the sounds of the mechanism to subside. When everything's quiet I call out.

"Hello! Anyone there?" My words echo up the shaft.

Someone has sent the elevator down. Now it waits, lit by a single bare bulb, beckoning me to enter and take a ride.

I scurry down the stairs, gesture to Joel. When he reaches me, I lead him to the loading dock. He gazes at the open elevator cab, the size of my bedroom.

"Kind of inviting, isn't it?" He gestures like a courtier. "After you, kiddo."

From inside, the empty elevator seems even bigger. I go to the control panel.

"Which floor?"

Joel shrugs. "I suppose we should start at the top, work our way down. But first let's wait a minute or two, see if anything happens."

We wait a minute or two. I'm about to push the button for five, when suddenly the horizontal doors of the cab start to close. When I glance over at Joel, he shrugs again.

"Let's see where it takes us," he says.

The doors shut and latch, the elevator jerks. Sounds of cables straining over rusty pulleys as we rise. I'm uncomfortable with the notion of being guided by unseen persons, but Joel acts as if he expected this—we'd arrive, find a rip in the fence, find an empty elevator which would mysteriously appear, then take us to our destination.

At the third floor the elevator jerks to a stop. The doors open, the mechanism quiets, we step out, find ourselves in a huge loft dimly lit by widely spaced dangling low-wattage bulbs. The loft is divided into storage cages surrounded by steel fencing.

Each cage has a steel gate and above it the lessee's name: South Asia Antiquities, Rakoubian Carpet Company, Evelyn Perry Designs, "La Belle France." Through the fencing we can see stored merchandise: chairs, tables, chandeliers, vases, andirons, sculptures, hookahs, stone heads of Asian deities, rolled Oriental rugs.

There's a list of lessees and a floor plan posted on a pillar. Tan-Hing Enterprises is at the end of Corridor C. Making our way beneath the free-hanging bulbs, we pass Urban Solutions, The Swiss Loft, Treasures of the Souks, Tran Van Minh Ceramic Arts—I feel as though I'm striding through a mall of Aladdin's caves.

Halfway down the aisle the cages give way to storage rooms with solid walls which render the stored items invisible. At the door to Tan-Hing Enterprises we pause to listen. There's a gurgling sound within.

"Running water," Joel whispers. "I wonder—" He pushes lightly on the door. Neither of us is surprised when it swings open.

We find ourselves in an anteroom. The air's warm, fetid, and there's an odor of something organic. Following the running water sound, Joel moves to an inner door. The moment he opens it, the smell grows strong, a pungent tropical-jungle aroma carrying a hint of rot.

We peer inside. The room's lined with aquaria, lit from behind, filled with schools of darting tropical fish and bubbles gurgling out of tubes.

Joel sniffs. "Tropical fish don't smell like this. There's gotta be something else."

I point to a small half-door beneath one of the aquarium stands that looks like it might lead to a utility closet. Joel gets down on his hands and knees, crawls beneath the aquarium.

"Smell's getting stronger." He pulls the door open, reels back. "Jesus!"

I crawl in after him. The odor in the next room is over-powering and the sounds are strange, sharp low-pitched grunts followed by hissing. I recoil, not knowing what living things surround us. Joel, always the "intrepid reporter," stands, stumbles, finds a light switch, flicks it on.

The source of the hissing is soon revealed. A deep crate covered with chicken wire contains a dozen strange turtle-like creatures, the smallest ten inches in diameter, several half again as large. Swiveling eyes in gnomish heads, darting in and out of hard dome shells, seek a way out of the crate.

Joel studies them. "Radiated tortoises," he says, "probably smuggled from Madagascar via Ceylon. Collectors love 'em for the designs on their backs. On the animal black market these'll fetch five to ten grand a piece."

I stare at the largest of the creatures. The top of its shell is beautiful, like a work of intricate marquetry. The shell also has a radiant quality as if lit from within.

"What're the colors, Joel?"

"Black, brown, amber."

Though to me all the tones read dark, the contrasts are defined. I wonder what kind of extravagant environment these creatures come from where such designs would serve as camouflage.

"Look over here." Joel's standing at a table across the room. On it is a cage divided into two compartments. In each there's a large coiled snake.

"Australian pythons," he says. "Like chameleons, they change color to blend in. These babies'll run you twenty grand apiece." He leads me to another table supporting more cages, these containing strange scaly horned creatures with flat unblinking eyes. "Don't know what these are called. Point is, we're in black-market animal country. God knows where they keep the cockatoos." He checks his watch. "Almost dawn. There's probably going to be a raid. I'm sure that's why we were tipped. Better start taking pictures, kiddo—before the Fish and Wildlife folks get here and all hell starts breaking loose."

While Joel looks around for more animals, I set to work documenting the setup: the sign for Tan-Hing Enterprises out front, the first room filled with tropical fish, the crawl-through into the second room, then shots of the illegally imported endangered creatures.

In addition to the radiated tortoises, pythons and lizards, there are other species secreted in cage boxes: tree boas, anacondas, teju lizards and a huge and, according to Joel, particularly venomous snake, an Australian taipan.

This, of course, is not fine-art photography; it's journeyman's work, which is fine by me. I become so immersed I'm able to put aside my fear of snakes and my revulsion at the sickening odor that pervades the room. The coverage becomes a project: How can I best convey the meanness of the people involved—those who stole these creatures from their habitats, those who cruelly imprison them and, worst of all, the collectors on whose account the heinous racket endures?

There's no way, I decide, except to shoot straight with the strobe, to take deadpan documentary photographs. No cute close-ups of the animals to show their exotic beauty, rather medium-distance shots that will emphasize their desperation in confinement.

I become so engrossed I forget about Joel. When finally I turn to look for him, he's no longer there. I take a couple more shots, then crawl back out through the low door.

He's not in the aquarium room. Since I know he wouldn't abandon me, I grab my stuff and retreat to the corridor. No sign of him. I start to worry. Where could he have gone? Then I remember: someone, using some kind of remote control, sent the elevator down to us. Finding that person, a possible lead to his informant, would be more important to Joel than documenting conditions at Tan-Hing.

I jog back down Corridor C, past the closed storage areas and cages. The freight elevator's gone. A quick glance up and down the shaft: I spot it on the ground floor. I push the call button, but the machinery doesn't respond.

"Joel!"

I call out, then listen as my voice echoes through the building.

No answer. I call out again, louder: "Joel! Joel!"

The place is windowless; there's no way I can peer out to see if he's gone back to the car. Suddenly I hear male voices coming from below and the crackle of field radios. It must be the Fish and Wildlife raiders, acting on their tip.

Joel would want to cover the raid, which will entail explanations to the raiders. He's well known, won a Pulitzer, knows the right law enforcement names. Though I have an old press pass, I'm no longer an employed journalist. Without him I'm afraid to show myself. So where is he? If he's around, he can't help but hear the men.

The elevator's starting up. I can't just stand here like an idiot. I glance at the fire stairs. Up or down? With the raiders on their way, I head instinctively for the top.

No sign of Joel on the fourth floor. I hear the elevator stop at three, and the raiders pile out. I finally find Joel on five, sitting on the top step, glasses off, head in his arms, looking dazed.

I rush to him. "You okay?" There's a faint yet cloyingly sweet aroma in the air.

He nods. "I got clobbered, coldcocked." He grins, amused by the archaic word. "You know, like in one of the old private-eye novels." He shakes his head, then winks.

He tells me that when I was busy taking pictures, he heard the elevator start to move. Figuring it could only be controlled by remote from the cellar or the top of the shaft, he decided to take a look. At the third-floor gate, when he saw the elevator was on five, he decided to take the fire stairs to the roof. By the time he reached five, smelled some kind of sweet scent, the elevator had started down again. He immediately went to the fifth-floor gate. From there he saw a man standing in the elevator. Actually, all he could see was the guy's shoulders and the top of his head. He yelled down, "Hey! You!" hoping the man would look up. The man did, but just at that moment someone smacked Joel on the side of the head.

"I went down," he tells me. "I remember crumpling slowly. I believe I actually saw stars. I think I was out for maybe a minute. When I came to, there was no one around. I've been sitting here since, trying to clear my brain." He sniffs. "Do you smell something or am I nuts?"

"Yeah, some kind of perfume."

"Reminds me of Chinatown," he says. "I don't know why."

I'm worried he may have a concussion. He says he's had concussions before and they felt much worse. I help him to stand. He wobbles at first, then regains his legs.

"I'm okay," he says. "Let's go down, see what's going on."

On the stairs he tells me that just before he was hit he caught a quick glimpse of the guy in the elevator.

"He looked short, but that could've been the foreshortening effect, since he was descending and I was looking at him from above. He had Asian features, but they looked phony—like they were frozen on his face, a frozen grin. I think he was wearing some kind of mask, the cheap plastic kind they sell in Chinatown. So . . . Chinatown mask, phony Chinese-waiter accent—fits together, doesn't it?"

"Meaning he's not really Asian?"

"Meaning maybe that's what he wants me to think."

"So he *is* Asian."

Joel shrugs. "Works either way. Anyway, I learned

something tonight—he's got a strong-arm guy watches his back."

Joel adjusts his granny glasses, employs his fingers to comb his goatee, then leads the way down. He recognizes the first person we encounter: Donald Buxton, chief enforcement officer in the San Francisco office of the Fish and Wildlife Service. While they trade information on their respective tips, I photograph the F&W animal control officers, assisted by personnel from the San Francisco Zoo, as they haul out crates and cages. The animals will be kept at the zoo pending disposition of the assets of Tan-Hing Enterprises.

Returning to Joel, I hear Buxton describe Tan-Hing as a shell company, based in Taiwan, specializing in the importation of rare tropical fish. In fact, F&W has long suspected the firm of dealing in black-market wildlife. Buxton received his tip just an hour ago via the F&W hotline. The anonymous informant used a fake-sounding Chinese accent.

Seven A.M.: As Joel and I depart Alameda Street, my eyes begin to smart. The sunlight this morning is shattering. It's going to be another brilliant San Francisco day. At my insistence we go immediately to St. Francis Memorial so Sasha can check on Joel's injury.

"Nasty bruise," Sasha says after examining Joel in the ER. "Until we're sure there's no concussion I don't want you to drive."

Joel, finally admitting to an awful headache, phones ice-goddess Kirstin, who taxis to the hospital to drive him home. When they drop me off on Russian Hill, Joel pats my hand.

"Exciting morning, right, kiddo?"

"Yeah . . . exciting," I agree. "What do you think's coming next?"

"Whatever." He peers at me. "Something bothering you?"

I think about that. There *is* something. "Ever hear of a sex-gun scene?" I ask.

"Sex-and-guns? Don't believe I have. Why? What're you onto?"

"Nothing, just curious."

He gives me his look that tells me he doesn't believe me.

"Sure . . . curious," he says.

I'm sitting in the Wongs' attic room, my first visit here in a week. It's Wednesday, eleven-thirty P.M. Though I don't expect to see any action tonight, I've come anyway, as if drawn by an invisible wire.

As expected, all is dark and quiet across the way. There's no moonlight, the sky's particularly black, and there's a heavy, thick, damp fog—rare here in the Mission—which tonight envelopes the entire city, clinging to every roof and cornice, creating droplets that catch in window screens and roll softly down panes of glass like tears.

The Wongs retired hours ago. As usual when I arrived we shared soft drinks and fruit, then together we climbed the stairs, they to their bedroom on the second floor, me to the attic. Though we communicate using only the most simplistic gestures, I've come to like them a lot: Grace with her warm friendly smile, Mr. Wong with that sweet faraway look in his eyes that makes me thinks he spends much of his time recollecting their silent early life in China.

Twelve-thirty A.M.: I awake suddenly from a dreamless sleep, immediately look across Cypress Alley. No action. The windows are dark. Then I hear it, the growling *varoom!varoom!* of the motorcyclist-enforcer. Impossible to tell where he is or how far away. I go to the window, open it a crack, listen to the growl as it fades.

I shrug. It's just the friendly neighborhood hit-and-run guy making his nightly rounds of intimidation. Then, suddenly, the growl comes at me again, louder this time, quickly growing into a roar. He's charging full speed down Cypress, just as he did the other night. A bearer of thunder, he passes beneath the window, squeals a turn at the end of the block, then storms back. This time he stops directly in front of the green door, backfiring his engine.

He knows I'm here. Someone in the neighborhood reported me. He's sitting in front taunting me: *Come out, girl—if you dare.*

My brain tells me to stay where I am. But I'm angry. The man now mocking me probably killed Maddy. Most likely his intentions toward me are equally murderous. So. . . do I just sit here quivering with fear? No, I don't think so. *No!*

I kneel on the floor beneath the window, call Kremezi on my cell phone.

"The motorcycle guy—he's here! Now! Popping his pipes! Listen!" I hold the phone up to the window. "Hear that? He's yours for the taking."

A long pause before Kremezi speaks. "Let me get this straight, Ms. Farrow. You're in the Mission inside somebody's house and the man you think killed your friend is on a motorcycle outside behaving in a threatening manner?"

"That's about it."

"So, if I leave now, what makes you think he'll stick around?"

"I'll keep him here, distract him."

"Jesus, don't do that! I'll be right over. Stay where you are."

"What if he leaves?"

"Then he leaves—which'll give us a chance to have a little heart-to-heart about civilians who get carried away with themselves, how risky that is and how it screws up the criminal justice system."

"Oh, I get it, Kremezi—there may be a killer over here but it's my behavior that troubles you."

"Still got that chip on your shoulder, I see."

I punch the power switch and cut him off.

I'm furious. The neighbor lookout turned me in to the drug dealers, the killer's downstairs and the cops don't care. For that matter maybe Kremezi's corrupt. Kind of hard to believe he investigated Maddy's hit-and-run and never heard about dealers on the block. But what riles me most is the schoolyard-bully arrogance of the enforcer making roaring noises down there like a bull snorting and pawing the ground before a charge. The whole neighborhood can hear him, and he doesn't care. He knows he owns the territory.

Well . . . I know a few things about schoolyard bullies, had to deal with them a lot when I was a kid. I was the girl who always blinked when she went outside, the one who wore dark glasses in class, the one who couldn't see colors. "Hey, Kay—your socks don't match!" "Kay wears dark glasses—she thinks she's a star!" I was different and got taunted for it. Not enough to cry about, but still, it hurt. Dad told me: "Hold your head high, darlin'. Don't let them get to you." And as for bullies: "Stand up to a bully, nine times out of ten he'll back down. Bullies are cowards underneath."

Is the enforcer-killer downstairs a coward? I've no doubt of it. Why does he wear that big black visor? For safety or because he's afraid of being seen? So . . . is there a way to see him, short of ripping the visor off his face? There is, and I've got just the tools to do it with.

Rapidly I unscrew Maddy's Pentax from her tripod, load it with a fresh roll of 120 film, then remove the strobe from my Contax and attach it to the Pentax. No automatic flash control on Maddy's camera; it will fire hot as I want. I set it for full, start toward the door, pause. The camera's great, but I'll feel better with a backup weapon. I glance around, don't see anything useful, until my eyes fall on Maddy's array of photochemicals. I pick up her STOP bottle filled with undiluted acetic, acid and stick it in my pocket.

On my way downstairs I hear a roar, the sound of the enforcer riding off in a cloud of soot. No matter, I'll wait in the alley for him to reappear or until Kremezi shows.

I pause outside the Wongs' open bedroom. Both appear to be asleep. Though I'm sorry they're deaf, I'm pleased they aren't bothered by the racket. It would not make me happy to bring disturbance into their lives.

Outside, as expected, the enforcer is gone, though, due to the thick night fog, the odor of his exhaust still hangs heavy in the air. It's chilly. I pull up my collar. The big 6×7 Pentax weighs a ton.

I can hear him now, perhaps two or three blocks away, roaring through the empty streets. The alleys too, I'm sure, the ones with the lovely botanical names which I explored with Sasha.

Yes, he's out there patrolling the neighborhood, intimidating the citizenry . . . which gives me a little time to scope out my environment. I find the niche where I hid from him last week. It's just the right size for me, an excellent place of concealment; a man or a larger woman couldn't squeeze in. I also note a beat-up VW camper parked in a carport across the alley. If chased out of my niche, I can dodge in there. If I slip into the space in front of the vehicle, he won't be able to reach me on his motorcycle. There's also a row of four garbage cans two doors down. I examine them; three are empty. I can roll the barrels into the alley as obstructions or fling their tops. Worst case, I can retreat back inside the Wongs'.

He's closer now. I can hear him on South Van Ness, ripping along the pavement. A screech of tires as he rounds the corner, then a roar as he zooms along Twenty-fifth. Another squeal as he turns into Capp. He's circling. In a few seconds he'll make the turn on Twenty-fourth. Then he'll come at me.

I step into my niche, hold Maddy's Pentax to my chest.

Varoom!varoom! He's backfiring at the end of Cypress, ready to make his charge.

Waiting for him, I'm pleased I'm no longer shaking, rather am tranquil and receptive as in aikido class. I drill my legs into the ground, then await the arrival of the demon.

Varoom!varoom! He's coming now, roaring toward me. I hear the throb of his engine, the explosions of his exhaust. With him too comes a wave of heat, as if he's pushing the fog before him. Noting that he and his machine are one, I will myself to merge with Maddy's camera.

When he emerges clearly from the fog he's but fifty feet away. It's then that I step out, face him, root myself, scorn his attack and blast him twice with my strobe. *Whap!whap!*

The brilliant light burns through his visor, stings his eyes. Mine too, for the reflection saturates my rods, temporarily shutting down my sight. No matter, I know just what to do. At the last moment, like a matador, I gracefully step aside, while he, unable to break the momentum of his charge, plows past.

Some achromats (I'm one) will retain an afterimage after a sudden burst of light. With my eyes shut I replay the moment his big black helmet exploded before my strobe. It was then that I caught a glimpse of the surprise on the lean, goateed face within. It's this image of his shock that I retain. Having stripped him of his mask, I feel my confidence soar.

He turns now, disoriented, reeling on his machine. Seems I blinded him as well. The moment he faces me I strobe him again, then run into the carport across the alley, on my way flinging a garbage can into his path.

He's raging. Making his machine growl loud, he charges after me into the carport, there tries to nudge me with his front wheel as I cower behind the fender of the camper. We're close now. For the first time I notice his clothing. Like some kind of self-dramatizing ninja, he's dressed totally in black. Though we're barely two feet apart, he can't reach me. Still, I can smell his sweat, the oil on his gloves, can hear him pant, feel the bursting fury behind his mask.

Whap! I strobe him for the fourth time. Immediately he rips his helmet off. We stare at one another. His eyes show the blank malice of a reptile, like one of those creatures I photographed at Tan-Hing. I give him back the cool stare of an aikido warrior, then raise the Pentax to take another shot.

Too late. There's a knife in his hand. He leans forward from his seat, grabs my camera, cuts the strap and rips it away. The pain's horrific, as though a hot wire just lashed my neck. While he heaves the Pentax at the garage wall, I pull out my bottle of STOP. As the camera shatters against the concrete, I twist off the cap, then fling the acid at his face.

Time slows. The moment is prolonged. I can actually see the liquid as it moves through the air, see the fear in his eyes as he realizes it's too late for him to duck. The acid moves toward him. He squeezes shut his eyes. Time speeds up. The liquid hits. He turns and screams.

I rush out of the carport, his shrieks and the roar of his machine splitting the air. Acetic acid is not like lye, it won't burn out his retinas, but it will sting badly and temporarily take away his sight. Figuring I've rendered him harmless, I'm surprised when he backs out on his machine, lines it up against me again, guns his engine preparing to charge at full speed.

I face him straight on. One of his eyes is shut, the other squints. He shows me the mean wily snarl of a killer. He holds up the knife, flourishes it at me and grins. I've no doubt now that he killed Maddy and intends to kill me too.

Strangely, I feel no fear of him, just curiosity as to which technique I should apply. I may as well be on the mat at Marina Aikido rather than standing here in a Mission district alley facing an armed opponent. He's the attacker, the *uke,* I'm the *nage.* The question for me now is how best to neutralize his intent. A strategy comes quickly to mind: control the center.

He's unstable on his machine, can barely see and, the worse for him, burning up with rage. He holds his knife in his fist and thus must steer one-handed.

I've practiced defending against a wooden *tanto* many times.

Don't be afraid of the steel. When you disarm him think of it as wood.

He charges. Again time seems to slow. The situation is clear. I go on automatic, start my sequence, find a rhythm that blends with his attack. A moment before he's upon me I turn aside, simultaneously grasping the wrist of his knife hand. While his motorcycle spins out of control, I continue to turn, twisting his wrist, pulling him off the machine, forcing him to the ground. The knife clatters to the pavement. The motorcycle smashes against the wall ahead. Completing my circle, I apply more pressure to his wrist. The motorcycle, still twisting, bursts into flames. I force his wrist back till I feel it snap, then go limp. Again he screams. The flames leap. I cut him across his neck with the side of my hand. Then, still turning, I step away from him, leaving him on the pavement as the pool of burning gasoline begins to spread. By the time I retreat to the opposite side of the alley, he's on fire, jerking spasmodically like a robot gone haywire.

I glance at my watch. The entire fight, from his first charge to his defeat, lasted less than forty seconds.

Kremezi arrives, then a fire truck and an ambulance. The enforcer is still alive, but burns cover much of his body. The medics cart him off. Kremezi drives me down to the Hall of Justice to make my statement.

From here, after relating the encounter in broad strokes, I phone Dad at home. Horrified by my story, he says he'll be right down. Kremezi leaves me alone for a while. When he returns he tells me the enforcer has been identified and, according to the doctors who've examined him, there's a bare twenty percent chance he'll pull through.

"Julio Sanchez. Did two terms at Pelican Bay. One very bad dude, Ms. Farrow. Hit-and-run's the least of what he's done. I've no doubt he'd have killed you if he could. Lucky for you he crashed."

I don't bother to protest that it wasn't luck, that I pulled Sanchez off his motorcycle, had him down and beat even before the fire. It's too complicated to explain how aikido works, and anyway, I doubt I can plausibly duplicate my moves. Better, I decide, to let the cops believe I was lucky, better to let the world believe it too. So long as drug dealers continue to operate on Capp, it'll be safer for me if they think their enforcer screwed up rather than suffered defeat at the hands of a woman.

"Darlin'!"

Dad bursts into the interview room, grasps me, hugs me hard.

And then, abruptly, everything changes; Kremezi turns deferential. No more talk of my interfering with police business. His supervisor, Inspector Girardi, appears, compliments Dad on having such a coolheaded daughter. In fact, I don't feel cool at all. My sangfroid, so firm back in the alley, deserts me. Sitting beside Dad I suddenly get the shakes. No stylized encounter on the mat, my struggle with

Sanchez was a dangerous, dirty street fight. Realizing how easily it could have gone the other way, I feel like a fool for having taken him on.

Dad continues to hold my hand through the interview. Inspector Girardi agrees with him there's no reason to release my name.

"I wouldn't hang around that neighborhood anymore if I were you, Ms. Farrow," Girardi warns. "There're vicious people there. If Sanchez dies, they may hold you responsible. Then they may seek revenge."

Dad escorts me home. I like the way he lavishes attention upon me, don't mind that he treats me as if I'm fragile . . . which he knows perfectly well I'm not. But instead of putting me to bed, as he used to do when I was a kid, he pours himself a huge belt of Scotch, then sits in my living room gazing out at the night-city.

"Grand old town, isn't it?" he says. "All those lights defining the hills. From up here you'd think it was paradise." He smiles. "Not like it really is, darlin'. Not like it really is."

After three days Sanchez is still on the critical list, the odds still high against his survival. I feel no pity for him. Though a good defense lawyer might get him off on the hit-and-run, I've no doubt he's the man who ran down Maddy.

Nights spent in my little spy nest at the Wongs are finished; I know I won't be able to return there again. Which leaves the matter of what Maddy was doing watching apartment 5. Though I understand I cannot go back now to the Wongs', I've no intention of letting the matter rest.

3
THE
CLUB

Kremezi calls. Julio Sanchez is dead. After hanging on at the Cal-Med burn unit for eight days, he succumbed.

"I interviewed him twice," Kremezi says. "He couldn't speak, so the way we did it I'd ask him a question, then he'd nod or shake his head."

"What did he say?" I feel weak in my stomach.

"Denied he had a fight with a woman. Said he was riding around the neighborhood, lost control, crashed against the wall, next thing found himself on fire. He also denied running down an old lady last month on Capp."

"And you believed him?"

"No, I didn't believe him. I'm just telling you what he said. The bottom line, Ms. Farrow, is he died a stand-up guy."

Suddenly I'm furious. "Excuse me! Because he didn't own up to killing Maddy, or because he refused to snitch on his pals?"

"Because he didn't say you pulled him off his machine."

"Oh, I see—better to die silent than admit he lost a fight with a woman."

"Don't get it, do you? No one'll be coming after you now. No one'll be out there looking for revenge. Thanks to his silence you're home free."

Kremezi, I decide, has pretty strange values for a cop.

"Of course I'm glad to be 'home free,' " I tell him, "but believe me, he killed Maddy, and he'd have tried to kill me again if he'd survived." I pause. "I expect now you'll be moving against the dealers."

"We'll be looking into that."

"Good. It's a forlorn neighborhood. I'd like to see it improved."

I talk tough with him, but the moment I hang up, I start feeling bad. I go to my bedroom, curl up on my bed and bawl.

It's not a lovely thing to be responsible for another's death. I know, of course, that I had no choice. It was Sanchez or me, and the fire was unforeseen. Still, according to the principles of aikido, one's goal should not be to hurt or retaliate, only to render one's attacker harmless. That was all I was trying to do.

Still I'm haunted. Early in the afternoon, I go into the darkroom to examine the pictures I took that night, rescued from Maddy's shattered Pentax. I never bothered to print up the shots, just glanced quickly at the negatives, then set them aside. Now I set to work making portraits of the man for whose death I am responsible.

Since I set the strobe on full in order to blind him, the film is greatly overexposed, but still there's sufficient image material to work with. Blinding him, of course, was my primary objective; taking his picture was a by-product. I didn't have to load the camera; I could have strobed him perfectly well on empty. But in the back of my mind was the notion that if I could also burn through his visor, I'd have a picture of Maddy's killer to turn over to the cops.

The portrait that emerges is not pretty. Sanchez's face is as slovenly as I remember. His jaws are pitted and there's a deep crooked gouge on his cheek that could be a souvenir of a knife fight. His mouth is mean, his goatee is scraggly, his eyebrows grow together in an unattractive way. But it's his eyes that grab me, the look in them of surprise in the first two shots, shock in the third, outrage in the fourth. It's like watching a man as his sense of invulnerability is shattered, then seeing hatred emerge out of the shards.

Joel calls to tell me he's no longer having headaches, that his mild concussion has healed. Now he's annoyed our Tan-Hing story didn't make much of an impression.

"Reptiles, snakes—people see them and go 'Yuck!' Believe me, if it'd been macaws and cockatoos, the readers would've wept crocodile tears."

He's also pissed at not hearing from his informant.

"Maybe he dumped me because the story didn't play big. Or because he thinks I'm burned over getting bopped on the head."

"He's not going to dump you, Joel. Who else has he got to use?"

I meet Dad for lunch at the Ton Long, a dim sum restaurant near his bakery. They know him here, greet him warmly. One of the tray waitresses even flirts with him in a combination of giggles and elementary Cantonese.

"Darlin', I'm losing it," he says, after she carries off her goodies to an adjacent table. "My Cantonese was never any good, but still I could jabber. It's been—what? Ten years since me and Rusty worked Chinatown? He, on the other hand, speaks better than ever."

He starts reminiscing about his days on the Chinatown bunco squad, trying to distract me, I know, from thinking about Sanchez. It doesn't work and it shouldn't, since the purpose of our lunch is to help me deal with my pain over taking a life.

"Okay," he says, finally meeting my eyes, "we know Sanchez was a slimeball killer, which makes dealing with what happened a little easier. But not that much easier, right?"

"That's right," I agree.

"But here's the thing, darlin'—you didn't do anything except pull him off his machine, and"—he winces—"break his wrist. The fire was an accident. Except not a total accident, because, way I hear it, most likely he brought it on himself."

I stare at him. "What d'you mean?"

"Something Rusty picked up down at the Hall. Seems Sanchez was carrying a firebomb, a Molotov cocktail–type deal. He was known for throwing firebombs at folks' houses. That's how he enforced silence in the neighborhood. What it looks like is when his motorcycle hit the wall, the bomb went off, then the fire spread back onto him. So what you got is a kind of poetic justice. The guy was hoisted on his own petard."

Dad beams.

"You know, down at the bakery I keep a big dictionary on my desk. Right before I walked over here I looked up that word 'petard.' Guess what? A petard was a kind of bomb that had a nasty habit of blowing up in its makers' faces. I also learned that it derives from the old French word for . . . I think the polite expression is 'breaking wind.' "

We're chuckling over this when three tray waitresses converge upon us. Soon the five of us are giggling together. I point to a plate of seaweed. Dad goes for shrimp toast. After the waitresses move away, we laugh some more.

"Feel a little better, darlin'?"

"A whole lot," I tell him. "Thanks, Dad. No more guilt."

Out on the sidewalk, as we're about to separate, he raises his finger.

"Almost forgot—I finally remembered where I saw that name before. You know, Ramsey Carson, one of the three

CFJ Realty Corp. guys who own that building. It had nothing to do with criminal activity. About a year ago there was a major gun auction at Butterfield and Butterfield. All sorts of historical stuff went for incredible prices. The big bidder, the collector who walked away with the best of the loot, was one Ramsey Carson, described in the *Chronicle* as a real estate investor. Gotta be the same guy, don't you think?"

THE GUN / *FIND THE GUN / WHERE'S THE GUN?*

Inside the magnificent new Main Library, due to the profusion of glittering surfaces and blinding natural light, I'm forced to wear my darkest wraps. I finally find a monitor in a relatively dark corner on the third floor. A quick periodicals file search combining the name RAMSEY CARSON and the word GUN yields thirty-six citations.

I read the articles on-screen. In the world of rare, historical and collectible guns, Mr. Carson, I discover, is a major player.

At the auction Dad mentioned, he paid $260,000 for the revolver alleged to have been carried by General George Custer at the Battle of Little Big Horn.

At another auction, held at Sotheby's in London four years earlier, he bought an Arab long rifle previously owned by the explorer and Orientalist Sir Richard Burton for a record-shattering £180,000.

But, I learn, Mr. Carson's acquisitions have not been confined to weapons associated with famous people. He's also a major collector of one-of-a-kind handmade British best guns, including the highest price ever paid for a pair of twentieth-century arms: $720,000 for matched Purdey sixteen-gauge over-and-under shotguns with special engravings by J. & B. Watson expressly executed for King Farouk of Egypt.

Thirty of the thirty-six citations are to articles about precedent-setting gun auction prices, four are to articles concerning real estate transactions by the CFJ Realty Corporation, and one is to a list, in which Carson is included, of donors to the San Francisco Opera Association. But it's the last citation, in a society column, that intrigues me the most, a throwaway reference by *Examiner* gossip columnist Schuyler Bigelow, known for his nasty pen, to Mr. Carson's role as founder of the Goddess Gun Club in Mendocino County.

When I click for full text, the library computer produces this:

> . . . *much talk in highly knowledgeable circles these last nights about bizarre goings-on at the veddy exclusive, veddy tony Goddess Gun Club near Mendocino.*
>
> *The G.G.C., as it's familiarly called by those in the know, was set up ten years ago by millionaire gun collector J. RAMSEY CARSON and his longtime friend and CFJ Realty Corp. partner, CHAPLIN D. FONTAINE for, and I quote from club by-laws as filed with the State Attorney's office, "recreation and good fellowship among shooters, hunters and firearms collectors, devoted to sport and the constitutionally guaranteed right to bear arms."*
>
> *All well and good, you may say, for who, except rabid members of the antigun crowd, would quarrel with such worthy objectives?*
>
> *But lately word has reached THIS DEPARTMENT that some G.G.C. activities may extend the meaning of "recreation" in ways unforeseen by certain distinguished charter members.*
>
> *There are rumors of contentious club meetings and furious resignations over what one source described as "activities unbecoming a true gentlemen's association."*
>
> *Be sure to watch THIS SPACE for further details as*

this delicious, pistol-whuppin' scandal continues to unfold . . .

Fascinated, I make another search combining SCHUYLER BIGELOW and G.G.C. Only one other item is produced, appearing in the Examiner three weeks after the first:

> *. . . several weeks back THIS DEPARTMENT promised further revelations about certain "scandalous" goings-on at the veddy exclusive, veddy tony Goddess Gun Club in Mendocino County.*
>
> *Contrary to our earlier report, it appears that all is actually quite well at the venerable G.G.C., differences between members having been resolved in what a source describes as "a traditional gentleman's manner."*
>
> *We're pleased that the troubles are now over in that hoity-toity gun lovers' paradise. Boys, of course, will always be boys, but boys with pistols can be . . . well, guntankerous . . . or so we hear!*

Interesting, I think, that in the first column Bigelow seems to salivate over the prospect of drawing blood, while a mere three weeks later, he appears eager to retract any implication that there's a scandal.

Deciding to look further, I define a search for all references to the Goddess Gun Club. I'm rewarded with thirteen citations, most references to the club's acquisition of additional acreage (I note three expansions over the past ten years); a small item about the filing of a lawsuit by a neighbor over excessive noise issuing from G.G.C. property; an even smaller item about the settlement of said lawsuit; an item about the accidental fatal shooting of a vagrant who illegally wandered onto G.G.C. land; another fatal accidental shooting of a poacher; and finally, a year-old article that makes me sit up straight in my chair: a third fatal accidental shooting involving club cofounder Chaplin Fontaine, which

took place between Schuyler Bigelow's two items about the
G.G.C.

I click on NEW SEARCH, then request articles on
CHAPLIN D. FONTAINE. In his obituary in the *Chronicle,* I learn that Mr. Fontaine was found dead on the gun
club firing range, victim of what the spokeswoman for the
Mendocino County Sheriff's Department described as "a
possible self-inflicted gunshot wound to the head."

Finding nothing further of interest concerning Ramsey
Carson, Chaplin Fontaine or the Goddess Gun Club under
its full name or acronym, I leave my computer station to
search out a Mendocino County telephone book.

I find it, along with all the directories for California, on
a disheveled shelf in the open stacks. At a reading table, I
look up the Goddess Gun Club. There's a telephone number but no address. I note the number, then turn to the
domestic subscribers section, where I look up Vincent Carroll, the man whose name appears beside the buzzer for
apartment 5 and to whose post office box address in Mendocino, Rusty informed me, PG&E bills for that apartment
are sent. Again a phone number, this one with an address. I
note both, then descend to the main lobby where, near the
ladies' room, I find a public phone.

Using my charge card, I dial Carroll's home number.
After five rings a woman answers. She sounds harassed, as
if maybe she's been out in the backyard hanging wash.

"Vincent Carroll please."

"Vince ain't here. Who's calling?"

"This is Mary in Mr. Carson's office. Any idea where I
can reach him, Mrs. Carroll?"

"Number one, I ain't Mrs. Carroll. There ain't no Mrs.
Carroll, not anymore. Number two, try him at the club,
which is what you should've done in the first place. He
oughta be there now . . . 'less, ha!ha! . . . he's out tomcat-
tin' round the county." She hangs up.

I dial the number for the Goddess Gun Club. A male
voice answers on the first ring.

"Vince Carroll please."

"Certainly. Who should I tell him's calling?"

"Mary in Mr. Carson's office."

"Right, Mary. He's out on the property. Give me a minute. I'll page him, then patch him through."

I hang up. No need to speak to Carroll. I found out what I wanted to know. The people who use apartment 5 on alternate Wednesdays are very much involved with guns . . . which lends credence to my belief, which I'd begun to doubt, that I observed a gun used as a sex toy the night I saw action through the window from Maddy's spy nest at the Wongs'.

Sasha, prince that he is, goes up to the Wongs' to collect Maddy's and my stuff, to explain, in sign, that I won't be coming back, and to leave two months' extra rent to cushion their loss.

When he returns, with Maddy's tripod, chemicals and sweater, he tells me that Grace Wong expressed sorrow. She'll miss me, she told him, just as she missed Maddy before.

As to the accident and fire in front of their door, she and Mr. Wong slept through the entire thing, only learning of it the following morning. Grace expressed to Sasha her hope that my departure had nothing to do with lack of hospitality. Sasha assured her it was simply because my work in the attic room was done.

I ask him if he's willing to drive me up to Mendocino on his next day off.

"Sure," he says, "on condition we eat a good meal, bed down in a cozy inn, then make love till dawn."

I phone Joel, ask if he knows the *Examiner* society columnist, Schuyler Bigelow.

"Baggy? Sure, I know him."

"People call him Baggy?"

"His friends do. That is . . . if he has any friends."

"Is he that malicious?"

"Venomous," Joel says. "Totally toxic."

He agrees to call Bigelow on my behalf. Ten minutes later he phones back.

"You're on, kiddo. Seven P.M., his place, for a drink. Be prepared to flatter him, but be subtle—he claims he can see through flatterers. I also suggest you wear your thickest suit of emotional armor, and if you want something from him be prepared to trade items in return."

"Sounds charming. Any other advice?"

"Yeah. If he tries to slap you down, smack him back in the puss. He claims to adore women—really he fears and loathes them. You'll never make him like you, kiddo, but if you handle him right you'll get his attention and respect."

The apartment building on Nob Hill, constructed early in the century in high Art Nouveau style, strikes me as appropriate for a society gossip—with its flamboyant facade of balconies and bays that billow out like the fronts of bombé commodes. My footsteps echo as I cross the marble-lined vestibule, then ascend the curving marble staircase.

Bigelow, no doubt for purposes of intimidation, keeps me waiting outside his door. I can hear him shuffling on the other side as he studies me through his peephole.

The moment he opens the door I understand why people call him Baggy. There're loose sacks of flaccid flesh beneath his eyes and bags of excess skin about his jowls. A decadent old man's face with wicked little eyes which gleam as they appraise me. I make my own eyes glow as I peer back.

"Ms. Kay Farrow, I presume," he says with a gravity affected, no doubt, for purposes of irony.

"And you, sir," I say, "must be the Gentleman Who Cannot Be Flattered."

He smiles slightly to show approval. He's wearing one of those at-home belted evening jackets with satin lapels you see on wealthy guys in old movies, and a pair of velvet slippers with the monogram *SB* elaborately applied to the tips. Having never seen a live human wearing such accessories, I'm amused.

He leads me through a living room fussily done up by a decorator.

"Nice room, but I rarely use it," he explains, as he beckons me into the adjoining study. "I'm far more comfortable in here—what I call 'my salon of bad taste.' "

He watches me closely as I take in his handiwork. Ah, the brilliance of such calculated vulgarity! Tiger-striped fabric on the couch and chairs. Leopard-spot fabric on the throw pillows. Execrable black velvet portraits of Marilyn and Elvis on the walls. And everywhere Barbie dolls, on every table, shelf and niche, Barbie here and Barbie there, not to mention her pals Skipper and Ken ... except, on close inspection, the goddesses' dresses are bloodied and ripped to mimic the clothing of murder and rape victims, or the little creatures are arranged as if engaged in bizarre sex acts. Joel was right about Bigelow—it's a woman-hater's collection.

I turn to him. "I see I'm in the room of a man who adores women."

"Well, aren't you the clever little lynx! Want a drink?"

I take a glass of wine, watch as he stirs himself a double vodka martini.

"Soft butch, aren't we?" he says, scanning my attire. "Black boots, black top, black everything—quite the brave young artiste. Glickman didn't tell me you were queer."

I shrug. "I'm not."

He snickers. "Oh, straight? Got a sweet, blond, milk-muscled boyfriend, do we, stashed away at home?"

I meet his eyes. "Have I offended you in some way?"

"*Offended* me? I'd *adore* it if you'd *offended* me," he responds. "Nothing I like better than a woman out of control. Unless, of course, its a divine feline creature licking my slippers like little Miss Courtney Barton here." He reaches down to scratch the ears of a fluffed-up Persian cat.

"I named her after my old second-grade teacher. How I hated that bitch! 'Bigelow! Stand in the corner!' 'Oh, yes, Miss Barton. But please ma'am, tell me why?' 'Teach you a lesson, young man.' Oh, the heat of her temper, the sting of her words! The lash marks, I'm afraid, still stripe my soul!"

"And so," I offer, "you named your loving cat after her to neutralize the pain."

He glances at me, startled.

I take a deep breath. I'm going to take Joel's advice, smack him hard.

"But it doesn't work, does it?" I continue. "The pain, I mean—it doesn't go away. Because in your heart you relish it. Recalling your humiliation in the second grade makes you feel alive. When you feel the old pain, the deadening, from years of putting people down, suddenly falls away. Your nerve endings tingle. You feel young again and vulnerable. Best of all, able once again to *feel!*"

He stares at me, astonished. I feel his rage rising. He's either going to throw me out for insolence or stop the stream of insults and start showing me respect. It can go either way—which is fine with me.

"I think I'd like to do up one of my Barbies like you, Kay Farrow—black outfit, camera, even the sneer. Then put her through some . . . hmm . . . shall we say . . . 'exemplary contortions'?"

"Why not just stick pins in her like a voodoo doll?" I ask. "Or is it the sexual degradation that turns you on?"

"Touché! Quite a piece of work, aren't you? Though I must say your little riff about my being dead inside is corny stuff. Still you get an A-minus. I like a girl who tries." He softens, offering a timid smile. "Please, from now on, call me Schuyler." He pauses, shyly. "May I have permission to call you Kay?"

Now that I've apparently passed his test, I decide to get to the point, telling him I've recently read some of his old columns in connection with a matter I've been researching. I tell him how disappointed I was when, after he promised further revelations about a scandal, he later appeared to backtrack, implying there was no scandal after all.

"Hmmm," he mutters, "doesn't sound like me. I try hard to deliver on what I promise. Still, people send me loads of items. Some unfortunately don't pan out."

I watch him closely. "The Goddess Gun Club scandal?" I ask. "Was that one that didn't pan?"

He freezes, actually seems to pale. "Oh, I see," he says, distraught, "you're here about *that?*" Suddenly he glowers. "Who *are* you?" he demands.

"Didn't Joel tell you? I'm a photographer."

He glares at my camera. "I can see *that!* Who sent you is what I mean."

"Nobody *sent* me. I've come on my own behalf." I pause. "You seem distressed, Schuyler. I'm sorry I've upset you."

He stands, starts to pace his little "salon of bad taste," stops to fasten his eyes upon one of the victim Barbies.

"I can't imagine why you bring that up," he says, "just as we were starting to get on. *Unless*—" He turns on me as if struck by a revelation. "*They* sent you, didn't they? Sent you here to bait me, even though I gave them my word I'd never mention them again. Well, young lady, here's a message to take back: *Schuyler Bigelow will not be baited.* Though gossip is my stock-in-trade, there'll be no more items about them. They and their godforsaken shooting club have been banished forever from my column."

I stare at him. He's serious. He actually takes me for a provocateur.

"For a guy who happily mutilates Barbies, Schuyler, you do get riled up. *No,* 'they' *didn't* send me. *No,* I *didn't* come here to bait you. *No,* I'm *not* an agent of the G.G.C. I'm working on a story, I reached a dead end, I thought maybe you could help. Perhaps you're scared." I pause, shake my head. "No, I don't think so. Mean and brittle as you are, you don't strike me as a guy who gets pushed around."

He's studying me closely now. All his awful affectations, previously displayed, are discarded as he weighs my claim of innocence.

"I believe you," he moans finally. "I'm so used to deceit I forget there are still honest people in this town."

He sits, grins, offers me a look of deep complicity. "All right, let's start over," he says pleasantly. "How may I help you this evening?"

"By telling me everything you know about Ramsey Carson and the G.G.C., for which I give you my word I'll never reveal you as a source and give you first crack at anything I find."

He's amused. "Your confidentiality promise is accepted. As for 'first crack,' of course, being a gossip, I love knowing everything that's going on. But as I told you, Ramsey, his pals and the G.G.C. have been banished from my column, so even if you come up with a good story, I won't run it."

"What can I give you then?"

"I'm afraid to tell you for fear you'll think me foolish."

"Come on, be brave, Schuyler! After all, a man who mutilates Barbies . . ."

"Yes, yes! All right." As he pauses I catch my first glimpse of his vulnerability. "Be my friend." He speaks the words simply, guilelessly. They are, I believe, the only sincere words he has spoken since I walked in.

"That's all you want of me?"

He nods. "But you see, my dear, I think it's actually quite a bit. Look around you." He gestures at the Barbies, smiles. "I'm wealthy, famous, feared, with a six-month backlog of nasty items in my files. And the truth is ... none of it means anything. Your friendship, on the other hand, would mean a lot. I don't know many young people." He smiles again. "So you see, Kay, my request is totally selfish. An old man's way of hanging on to youth. Anyhow, that's what I want. Grant it to me and we have a deal."

"Deal," I tell him. "Though I can't promise you much time."

"I won't ask for much, just an occasional drink, say once a month, a breath of fresh spring air in this old bachelor's dusty life."

Bargain sealed, he pours me another glass of wine, fixes himself another double martini, settles back.

"The first I heard of Carson was when he bought that pair of guns made for King Farouk. Never saw them myself, but I heard plenty of tales. For a while people who saw them could speak of nothing else. He'd bring them out at dinner parties, show them off to guests. Do you know about the guns, Kay?"

I shake my head.

"I gather they're spectacular, superbly made, absolutely gorgeous to people interested in firearms and such. But above and beyond the typical qualities of a matched pair of handmade English shotguns, it's the unusual engraving that makes this particular pair stand out. Erotic engraving, I'm told, totally pornographic, stupendously, deliciously obscene. Which is why Carson liked to bring them out after dinner, then pass them around the room. The men would guffaw, the women would giggle. 'Oh, Ramsey, what an awful dirty mind you have!' 'Oh, not *my* dirty little mind, dear. Just randy old King Farouk's.'"

I think back to the night at the Wongs' when I thought I saw the couple through the window playing with a gun.

"I've never heard of that kind of engraving on guns," I tell him.

"Neither had I. But since Farouk was famous for his obsessions with pornography and guns, I wasn't surprised to learn he combined them."

He smiles, the same thin begrudging smile that brings out the cross-hatching on his face.

"Look at my Barbies, displayed in flagrante delicto. Perhaps it's human nature to eroticize the objects one collects. I truly love my Barbies, enjoy stroking them ever so tenderly sometimes. Perhaps Carson strokes his guns as well. Wouldn't surprise me. In the end, they say, everything does come down to s-e-x."

I ask him about the G.G.C. He says he's heard it's extremely difficult to join, with laborious prescreening and interviewing by members culminating in a one-blackball-you're-out-type vote.

"It's a serious club, definitely not just a bunch of guys who get together to target-shoot and hunt. They've got this huge property up in Mendocino. Beautiful land. There's a compound on it including a luxurious lodge retreat where they eat, drink, make merry, puff on cigars, stroke their guns and do God knows what. They have a state-of-the-art firing range, stocked hunting grounds, everything their little-boy hearts desire. I hear there're celebrity members, a couple of movie stars, a big shot Hollywood director, a former governor of California, distinguished foreigners. It's men-only, of course, but I've heard they occasionally bring in party girls for fun and games. There are tales of 'rustic revels' — bacchanalian rites, orgies to celebrate the solstice, eclipses, Halloween. That's the thing about nasty boys, isn't it? Whenever they get the old urge to play nasty party games, you can count on them to come up with a good excuse."

He stops a moment, constricts his face; when he continues it's in a more serious tone.

"Then of course there's the matter of the 'accidents.' That's the real trouble up there. All those quote accidental shootings unquote—some reported, most, I hear, not. There are all these stories floating around. Tales of man-

hunts—catching poachers and vagrants, then setting them
loose to be stalked down and shot. Nothing anyone can put
his finger on. It's all really quite . . . strange."

"You're saying people have been shot dead and no one
knows about it?"

He shrugs. "So the rumormongers say."

"Schuyler, how can that be?"

He shrugs again. "I only have the stories unconfirmed.
As the saying goes, those who talk don't know and those
who know don't talk. Anything's possible if you're rich
enough. And from what I gather about the G.G.C., its
members are *veddy* rich."

I feel a hot flash of indignation, know the feeling well.
It's fueled many of my projects. It's what Maddy always
looked for in my work. "Your compassion comes out of
your anger, Kay," she'd say. "Don't fear it. Work with it.
Apply your outrage to what you see, use it to forge powerful images."

"What can you tell me about the scandal?" I ask.

"Ah, the scandal! That's where I stepped into it . . ."

He sits back to tell me the story.

It seems there were two factions within the club—a
small core group, the Inner Circle, formed around Carson,
that took part in the orgies and was responsible for the
mysterious shootings; and the majority of members, who
weren't involved, in fact knew nothing of these matters,
men who simply loved guns and had joined purely for
sport. Except that at a certain point, several of the outsiders
became aware of what the Inner Circle was doing. Which
led to the crisis reported in his column—angry meetings,
resignations, all that.

"Naturally," he says, "I can't tell you the name of my
source. Suffice it to say she was the wife of a member who,
discovering what was happening, became disturbed and
wanted to clean things up. Call these disturbed outsiders
the Reformers. They were led by a man named Chap
Fontaine, an erstwhile buddy of Carson's, one of his real

estate partners and, in contrast to the Inner Circle boys, a type rarely seen these sordid days. What we used to call, without an ounce of irony, 'a gentleman of the old school.' "

When Baggy wrote his first column about the scandal it looked as though there would be an exciting last-man-standing showdown between Carson and Fontaine. The common perception was that the Reformers would take over, throw the bad boys out, clean up the mess, set the club back on its old path straight and true and (this was the stinger) possibly provide information on the shootings to local law enforcement officials which might lead to the filing of criminal charges against Carson and his pals.

Baggy shrugs. "I appreciate what you said earlier, how I don't strike you as a guy who gets pushed around. I only wish that were true! Alas, though I'm brave enough when puncturing reputations and truly heroic when degrading Barbies, I confess I'm not a man who enjoys the prospect of receiving a bullet in the head. Which was, I was warned by an anonymous telephone caller, exactly what would happen if I ever again reported gossip about the G.G.C. I was instructed to write about the club one final time, retracting what I'd previously implied. Which I did, not just because of the telephone warning or the bullet that came shortly afterwards in the mail with my initials cut into the lead— let me show it to you!"

He steps over to the mantelpiece, brings down a small lacquer box, extracts a bullet, places it in my hand.

"Note the monogram. Not as pretty as the ones on my slippers. But it wasn't just the telephone threat or the arrival of this delightful item in the post that persuaded me. It was what happened to Chap Fontaine, his death by quote shooting accident unquote on the grounds of the G.G.C. Because, Kay, the way I heard it, there was no accident, no suicide either. What I was told, on good authority, was that Fontaine was shot dead by Ramsey Carson in a duel."

Baggy gazes at me.

"How does that strike you? True or not, when I heard it I felt I'd heard enough. Best, I decided, to do as I was told: retract the story . . . and ever afterwards shut up."

I stick around for another hour. Baggy, discovering I haven't eaten, disappears into his kitchen to rustle something up. While I wait I inspect several of the debased Barbies. Baggy's additions, I note, are intricate. He's not only carefully torn a raped Barbie's panties and bra, he's also fastidiously applied scratch marks to the poor dolly's plastic flesh. Looking at this mutilated specimen, I wonder if it's really going to be possible for me and Baggy to be friends.

He reappears with a delicious sandwich of cold chicken on crusty toast, accompanied by a greens and cherry tomato salad. As I eat he gulps down a third double martini, then starts to wallow in self-pity, spewing out *mea culpa*s and maudlin regrets over the way his life has turned, telling me that what I see when I look into his face is the wreckage of a man who once held great promise and then squandered it in pointless gossip.

It's half past eleven when I get up to leave. Too fatigued to walk home, I ask Baggy to call me a cab. He smooches me in the doorway of his flat, mutters, "If I weren't such an old nelly, Kay, you'd surely be the girl for me."

Waiting outside his confection of a building, I can't rid myself of the indignation I felt when he told me about the G.G.C. Orgies, mysterious unreported shootings, manhunts of vagrants, death-threat bullets sent by mail, a mortal duel—Maddy was, I now understand, onto something big, her own outrage so inflamed she was mobilized to take up her camera once again.

But how, I ask myself, did she find out about all this? What led her to find a place from which to spy on apartment 5? Particularly, I wonder, how did she know about the duel, which she mentioned in the little notebook she concealed in her folded sweater?

There was, it's clear, a lot more to the life of Maddy Yamada, photojournalist, than I ever knew.

Friday noon: Sasha and I depart San Francisco early to beat heavy exit traffic. By trading duty tours with another ER resident, he's managed to clear time for a three-day weekend.

We cross the Golden Gate Bridge in his freshly washed BMW. Though it's a brilliant day, hard on my vision, I'm able to protect my eyes with a pair of dark wraps. The effect's similar to placing a dark red filter on a camera when shooting with black-and-white film—heightening contrast and turning fields of blue, such as water and sky, to inky black.

When we reach the Marin side of the bridge I turn back, as always, to catch a final glimpse of San Francisco. Every time I cross the bridge, I feel the same frisson. There is the shining city, limned by wondrous Pacific light, clinging to its hills above the Bay. From the northern end of the bridge it appears a magical place—graceful city, fantasy city, white city of dreams and desires. Perhaps ephemeral city too, for there's always the chance at any moment the earth will shake and level it to rubble and dust.

We follow 101 through Sonoma County, past meadows edged by produce stands, vineyards lining the hills; then we follow the Russian River as far as Cloverdale, where we fork west on 128 toward the Anderson Valley.

As we cross this splendid land of vineyards and orchards, I tell Sasha about the curious lingo spoken here. Dubbed Boontling, it's little more than a special vocabulary of a thousand or so words developed in the last century by residents, many of them sheepherders and apple growers, as a way to communicate without being understood by strangers.

"A secret language?" Sasha asks, fascinated.

I nod. "That was the idea. People here were suspicious of outsiders. But with all the articles that've been written, there's not much secrecy left. Few people speak it anymore. It's become more of a tourism attraction than a private code."

Sasha loves my examples of Boontling, how a pay phone is called a "buckey Walter," sexual intercourse is "burlappin'," a cup of coffee a "horn of zeese."

Sasha smiles. "I bet I know how they came up with burlappin'."

"How do you think?"

"Someone saw a couple screwing on a roll of burlap."

I laugh. "Good guess, Sasha! You're probably right."

After passing through the towns of Boonville and Navarro, we follow a romantic winding road through an ancient sequoia redwood forest that takes us finally to the coast. From here it's just a few miles north to the Mendocino Headlands, alive with heather shimmering in afternoon light.

I've been here only once before, back in the eighties when I was an art student. That time too I came north with a boyfriend. It was autumn. Jeremy West and I hitchhiked up from San Francisco, bedrolls on our backs. We settled into a cheap room, then spent the weekend wandering the bluffs above the ocean, he with his sketch pad, me with my camera, both of us trying our best to capture the extraordinary beauty.

I still have the photographs I took that weekend, of the spume and spray of waves as they crashed against the cliffs, of seals sunbathing on rocks offshore, shots too that I took of Jeremy as he posed in a wonderful brooding windblown-hair-across-the-forehead Heathcliff manner.

He was an exceptionally handsome boy, talented and troubled. Though I didn't love him, I found him enormously attractive. That weekend in Mendocino was an idyllic time. On the bluffs we picnicked on local cheese and bread, smoked pot, then made ecstatic love in the clover. At night, wearing thick hooded sweatshirts to repel the chill, we wandered the bluffs again, cuddling one another, gazing at the moon and stars, while Jeremy swooningly cried out great chunks of poetry in French, rhapsodic verse by Arthur Rimbaud.

A few weeks later, back in San Francisco, we broke up. Jeremy quit school, then headed to New York to seek his fortune as a painter. Two years later I heard he was living impoverished on the streets of the East Village. A year after that I learned he'd OD'd on heroin.

As Sasha and I drive into Mendocino, memories of that earlier visit flood back. As we pass gray shingle houses and steep-roofed Victorians embellished with gables, I share my memories with Sasha, describe my feelings of sorrow and loss when I heard Jeremy had died.

"He painted tigers, Sasha. Huge magnificent striped tigers slinking through the forest or crouching in high grass. In those days no respectable Manhattan gallery would show such work. Gallery directors thought it trashy, fit at best for tourists. To be noticed back then, you had to paint like Schnabel or Basquiat. Jeremy was devastated. He had this huge talent but no sense of fashion. He told his friends he'd rather risk death taking drugs than paint to suit the marketplace."

Sasha listens well. He says he hopes coming back won't make me morose.

"Not at all," I assure him. "For three reasons. One, you let me talk about it, so it's out of my system. Two, I'm here on a mission. Third, I'm here with you."

Sasha beams as we turn into the drive that leads to our gleaming clapboard inn. We check in, unpack, bathe luxuriously in our private whirlpool-tub-for-two, make love on our king-size bed, then go out to explore the town.

We acquire a map, browse the boutiques, strike up conversations with sprightly shopkeepers. We obtain advice on restaurants and nature trails and where to rent a bike.

"The locals have an air about them, don't they?" Sasha says. "Like they should be envied for having figured out how to live here in paradise year-round."

In fact, I tell him, Mendocino's not quite as dreamy as it looks. In the back country, I tell him, just out of town, there're plenty of troubled people: paranoid marijuana farmers who grow and harvest pot on public land, ready to shoot anyone they think might be poaching their closely guarded crops; militias composed of equally paranoid survivalists, racists and religious fundamentalists, who, coming home from work, pull on fatigues, then practice maneuvers in the forest.

"It's an explosive California mix, people who hate the government, believe its agents will take away their guns, living side by side with zealous ecoterrorists who pound steel spikes into redwoods to tear apart loggers' chain saws. Winemakers, llama farmers, tax protesters, Second Amendment nuts, countercultural artists, as well as folks who just want to live 'off the grid' and school their children at home. They're all here coexisting precariously in paradise."

After a rest back at our inn and a good dinner, I persuade Sasha to join me as I change into working-class garb—jeans, boots and denim work shirt with white

T-shirt peekabooing through my open collar. Then I ask him to drive us six miles farther up the coast to Fort Bragg, a blue-collar town where I hope to obtain some information.

We choose the Paradise Saloon, a noisy redneck lounge on the main street, the kind of place working men and women might congregate Friday nights to drink, dance, blow off half a week's pay. There's a crummy neon sign outside, loud country music within. The entrance reeks of cheap beer. A couple of grizzled old guys with bloodshot eyes inspect us as we enter. Not hard to tell what they're thinking: *White girl, black boy—oh oh!*

Sasha, I'm pleased to note, is a good performer. He drops his accent and physician's manner, becoming a likable, new-immigrant escort to my petite, outdoorsy wildlife photography enthusiast. Objective: See if we can buy a few beers for local hunters in exchange for information on the G.G.C. Pretext: We're interested in discovering if there's some way I can get a photographic crack or two at one of Mendocino County's famous 150-pound tusked wild pigs.

We settle in low-key at the bar, waiting until the place gets used to us and we to it. After fifteen minutes I decide we've chosen well: the Paradise is friendly, its clientele a mix of locals and down-market tourists with lots of give and take between.

Confident our presence isn't an intrusion, I casually nudge Sasha in the side, our signal to start talking about my desire to do some animal-stalking photography. After a decent interval, Sasha turns to Joe the bartender (serious demeanor, drooping mustache, samurai-topknot hair) to ask where we might .get some good advice on local wildlife-watching opportunities.

Joe ponders, squints, peers about, finally gestures across the room. "See the guy over there—one with the bushy beard in the lumber shirt sitting with the blonde? Name's Hank. Little rough around the edges, but nice enough. Talk to him. Tell him I sent you over. He does a lot of hunting, so he can probably help. Or else steer you to someone else."

We thank Joe, finish our beers, order two more, then carry them across the room. Figuring Hank will feel less threatened by a female, I take the lead.

"Joe up at the bar said you could maybe give us some advice. Mind if we buy you a round?"

Hank, eyes blank, searches my face, scans Sasha's, then studies mine some more. Finally he grins.

"Sure, sit down," he says. "Pa always told me—'Son, never refuse a friendly offered drink.' " He sticks out his hand. "Hank Evans. This here's Gale Hoort."

We introduce ourselves; then Sasha summons the waitress. Hank and Gale both go for refills of the local ale.

I chitchat with Gale, trying to work up a quick bond. She's about my age, her nails are groomed to the nines and her blond hair shows dark roots. She tells me she works as a haircutter and hopes to open her own salon in another year. When she hears I'm a photographer and asks what kind, I tell her I do mostly catalogue work.

Meantime Hank and Sasha are talking baseball.

Hank turns to me. "Your buddy here sure knows the game."

"Did he mention he thinks a double play's a 'double cross'?"

Lots of laughter, another round of beers, more bonding leading to that warm, cozy, alcohol-haze feeling you sometimes get talking with strangers in a bar.

When there's a break in the conversation, Hank asks Sasha what he can do for us.

Sasha nods at me. Hank turns his head, then slowly, deliberately lowers his eyes to the level of my tits.

"My hobby's wildlife photography," I tell him, feeling as though he's stripping me to the waist. "We hear there's lots of wild game around. Thought maybe you could tell us where to look."

"Sure, there's plenty of good hunting if you know just where to go," he says. "What kinda game you interested in?"

"Wild pigs," I tell him.

A smile spreads slowly across his face. "Best eatin' pigs in California," he assures me, lightly touching his beard. "Some round here like to stick 'em. Some like to mow 'em down with a .44. Myself, I hunt 'em with a bow and arrow."

Sasha and I nod gravely.

"Course the dudes up at the Goddess, they go after 'em with a pack of hounds. Hounds'll run old mama pig up against a trunk, circle her, yap-yap-yap till the shooters come. Then one of 'em'll blast her with a custom-made fifty-thousand-buck nitro-express elephant gun. Likely as not the dude'll take out a dog or two with her. No matter. At the Goddess they got hounds to spare."

Jesus! I think. *He's talking about the club before I even mention it.* Subtly as I can, I ask Hank to tell me more about this "Goddess place."

He explains: "It's a highfalutin shootin' club. Two thousand acres of private huntin' preserve—lots of quail, wild turkey, black-tailed deer. Then there's bear, wild pig, bobcat if they're lucky . . . plus sometimes they stock the property with exotic game."

"What kind?" Sasha asks.

"Mostly African," Hank says. His eyes, crafty now, are finally off my chest. "Gazelle, zebra, even once, I heard, a rhino. Illegal, of course, but no one's going to mess with those boys. They got it made. Should see the private planes lined up weekends on the county airstrip. Anyhow, no way you'll get in there. They got security you won't believe. Trip wires, electronic surveillance, armed guards on platforms so they can see you coming. Poach around the Goddess, you risk your life. Gun or camera—doesn't matter. I only know a couple guys ever got in there, then out safe again. They had a helluva time too. Bagged plenty of top-grade meat."

Something about the way he imparts this last bit tells me Hank Evans was one of those lucky "couple guys." I study him as he confers with Sasha, outlining G.G.C. boundaries on our map to show us where we'd be well advised *not* to go.

"Course there *is* a way or two in . . ." he adds, "for those willing to take the risk."

He leers at Sasha, tempting him to ask. Sasha, I'm proud to see, continues to play his part, coolly responding that maybe Hank would care to go into that a little bit.

Hank smiles at Gale. "Hey, honey! We got us a *Mission Impossible* team here! Gale's been in the Goddess. Ain't you, honey?"

Gale tightens her lips and pouts.

"She didn't like it much," Hank says, giving us another cryptic smile.

Sasha, understanding that more alcohol is needed to further loosen tongues, beckons the waitress and orders another round.

While this is going on, Gale leans toward me, then cups her hand around my ear. "He's cute," she whispers, giggling, indicating Sasha. "I never been with a dark man. Is it true—what they say?"

Since I know she doesn't mean to be offensive, I giggle in return.

Two more rounds of ale and Hank's ready to confide. He leans forward, lowers his voice. The three of us lean forward too, so our heads are close.

"Tell you a secret," Hank says. I can smell the brew on his breath. "I not only been inside the Goddess, I'm one of the few outsiders killed game on the property. Not just once or twice. *Lotsa* times," he boasts. "Last visit, bagged me two doe with the bow and arrow. Beauties both of 'em." He closes down one eye to show canniness. "See, if you fire off a gun, they'll hear and come after you. I mean *hard.* They don't give a shit. They'd as soon shoot a poacher as plink a squirrel in there. There're stories around about them catching folks, setting them loose, then hunting them down. You know—'human game.' " Hank pauses for effect. "Maybe true, maybe not."

Sasha and I nod sagely.

Hank continues: "They got a huge perimeter, so what they do is bluff like when your poker hand ain't all that strong. Spread rumors the Goddess is impregnable, that they got all this high-tech shit in the trees—infrared detectors, remote TVs, like that—when the truth is the place's so big they can barely cover it."

I turn back to Gale. "Were you really in there?"

This time she admits it.

"They snuck me in," she says, "dressed me up like a boy when they needed waiters for this banquet affair. The catering company was short of guys, so one of my girl-friends at the salon made me up. Did a pretty fair job too. Got me in, anyway."

"Oh, she was cute," Hank says. "Should have seen her. Sideburns, mustache and the sweetest little-boy butt I ever saw!"

"Why waiters, not waitresses?" I ask.

Hank's happy to explain. "Stag function. Dancing girls, Asian strippers they brought in from the city. They even did this thing where a naked girl pops out of a cake. You know—like 'Ta-da!' " He thrusts up his arms to demonstrate the cake girl's exit.

"You saw all that?" I ask Gale.

She enlarges her eyes. "That wasn't the half of it."

"What was the other half?" Sasha asks.

"Oh, you don't wanna know," Hank says. "Got pretty down and dirty, didn't it, honey?"

Gale nods. "I didn't like it at all."

Since Gale strikes me as a girl who likes her sex as well as anyone, I wonder how down and dirty it could have gotten.

"Drunk rich kids' games," Hank explains, lowering his voice. "You know, gang bangs, shit like that."

I'm intrigued by the line Hank and Gale appear to draw between one-on-one screwing and group sex, which so greatly disgusts them. But I'm even more intrigued by my good fortune—steered by chance to perhaps the single most knowledgeable man in the county on the ins and outs of the G.G.C.

This is just too easy, I think, until I realize it's one thing to have stumbled upon Hank, another to get him to share his knowledge.

Gale, excusing herself to visit the ladies' room, is now table-hopping her way around the lounge. This gives me a chance to study Hank again as he and Sasha talk. He's a big meaty guy with a husky chest and broad back like my dad. His thick dark hair and bushy beard show streaks of gray, but more interesting, he has the dead-on gaze of a man who's been in combat. I figure him for mid-to-late forties, which would make him eligible for service in the Vietnam War.

"Sure, I did 'Nam, two tours," he tells me when I ask. "Spec six. Ranger battalion. Lurp mission leader. Now *that* was a lot of fun!" He guffaws. "Been huntin' since I was a kid, but got to love it over there. Course it was a different kinda game you hunted, know what I mean? Kinda like what they do up at the Goddess. Once you get a taste of that, hard to give it up . . . least so they say."

Sasha's appalled, but I nod to show Hank I understand. This is one angry dude, I decide, his anger free-floating, focused only when there's a target in his sights: rich hunters with expensive guns, politicians who betrayed the grunts, gun control enthusiasts, animal rights nuts, a doe innocently grazing in a grove of trees. Fair game is who-ever or whatever crowds his worldview.

When Gale returns she perches on his knee, circles one arm around his back and tugs playfully at the edges of his beard. I signal Sasha it's time to go. I'm nearly drunk, sleepy from the long day's drive, anxious to crawl into our huge downy bed back at the inn. I hand Hank one of my cards. He scrawls his number and address on a cocktail napkin in return.

"Next time you come up, gimme a call," he says. "Might take a look-see at some places we're not supposed to go." Big wink. "Best is middle of the week when they're not on high alert. Might get a crack at a wild pig if you're lucky. You shoot it, then I'll *really* shoot it, then Gale'll cook it, then we'll all eat it. All *right!*"

Next morning I get up early, take a quick shower, then walk into Mendocino in search of a bagel and ordinary cup of coffee. Returning to the inn, I find Sasha up. He's delighted I've brought him a double latte and croissant. While he munches and sips, he offers his views on our new friends Hank and Gale.

"Hank's an example of your American walking wounded," he says. "Know what he does for a living? Works for a septic pump-out service. When you and Gale were talking he told me his routine. He drives a truck up to the back of a house, pries up the septic tank cover, sticks in a big hose, turns on the pump that sucks all the crap up into the tank on his truck, hoses out the tank, reseals it, then drives off to some state-administered environmental disposal place where he dumps the pump-out . . . then on to the next call. Which means that basically he spends his days dealing with shit, which may explain why hunting's become his life."

I ask how he thinks Gale fits into this scheme.

"I think she adores him."

Sasha shaves and showers; then we go out to rent bikes. On the way he asks me what a Lurp mission leader is.

"LRRP, pronounced 'lurp,' for long-range reconnaissance patrols," I explain. "They'd chopper guys in, a few at a time, deep into enemy territory. There they'd make themselves invisible, live off the land, check out what was going on."

"Sounds dangerous."

"The word they used for it was 'hairy.' A lot of those guys never came back."

Just to see what happens, we bike up to the main gate of the G.G.C. like a couple of naive tourists.

The club access road isn't paved, forcing us to dismount whenever our tires get stuck in the sand. We confront a number of explicit signs along the way: "NO TRESPASSING," "PRIVATE ROAD," "MEMBERS ONLY" and, most unfriendly of all, "INTRUDERS BEWARE—ARMED RESPONSE AHEAD."

Approaching the steel-link gate, we hear the distant boom of shotguns, then spot a pair of guards. They're decked out in camouflage uniforms, holstered side arms, mirrored sunglasses and Foreign Legion–style black berets. One stands hands on hips by the gate in an intimidating legs-spread posture. The other stands legs-spread on a raised platform, observing us through a pair of heavy military binoculars mounted to a swivel.

Sasha asks how I see camouflage.

"I see their uniform fabric as mottled," I tell him. "I know what it is. In the forest it wouldn't fool me a bit."

The moment we cross an imaginary line a hundred feet from the gate, a siren starts to wail.

"We tripped it off," Sasha shouts above the shriek.

We stop. A good thing too, I decide, since I notice that the guard on the platform is now holding out a rifle with telescopic sight at port position before his chest.

The guard on the ground approaches, all hard face and surly mouth. On account of the mirrored shades I can't make out his eyes.

"Whaddaya want?" he snarls.

"Would it be okay if we walked in the forest?" Sasha asks.

"Members and guests only, jerk. Can't you read the signs?"

"Please, mister," I say. "All we're asking is to walk among the redwoods, listen to the birds, pick some berries maybe. We won't bother anything, we promise. *Please . . .*"

He laughs, turns to his buddy on the platform, shakes his head in disbelief. "Hear that, Paul?"

" 'Please, mister,' " the other one says, mocking my suppliant's tone. "That's the thing about this gig, Hal. You think you've seen it all, then a couple more loons show up."

The first guard laughs again, then jerks his thumb at Sasha. "Outa here! Both of you, before I set the dogs on you."

"Sorry to bother you," Sasha says, maintaining his dignity. "We'll be on our way."

"Don't come back neither," Paul on the platform shouts. "This is private huntin' and shootin' property. Wander around unauthorized you're likely to get shot."

We return to Sasha's car, hang our bikes on our rented bike rack, then head off on a roundabout route to another portion of the G.G.C. perimeter, where, Hank suggested last night, we probably won't be bothered.

It's here that G.G.C. property abuts a stretch of state land, a segment of the huge Jackson State Forest, encompassing groves of ancient redwood open to the public.

Mature giant sequoias are so tall and straight I feel humbled whenever I enter a grove of them. These towering trees, some fifteen hundred years old, which prosper so well in Northern California coastal fog, form a high crown canopy that filters out most direct light, creating a special dark world of soft shade beneath. Occasionally a slanting shaft of sunlight will break through the branches, illuminating the richly textured bark of the trees. But mostly the light at ground level is tempered and subdued, easy on my eyes.

We bike along trails, weave among the redwoods, following a swiftly rushing stream. Referring to marks Hank drew on our map, we depart the trail, hide our bikes in the brush, then proceed a hundred yards on foot to the G.G.C. fence just outside the trees, a simple affair of parallel strands of barbed wire strung a foot or so apart. It's just where Hank said it would be, well concealed from view. It's unlikely a hiker would stumble upon it unless, like us, he deliberately left the trail system to search it out.

The property line is demarcated by the fence and not much else. Areas on either side, once clear-cut, have long since grown over. Perhaps this portion of the G.G.C. perimeter isn't well tended because it's doubtful a poacher would try and cross here. However, in several places we find unrepaired rents in the lower strand, suggesting people have crawled through.

"How do they keep the animals in with such a crummy fence?" I ask.

"Hank says this is just their outer perimeter," Sasha says. "The stocked areas are fenced very well."

The notion that there might actually be African game within, zebras and gazelles, upsets me greatly. It's not just my awe of these gorgeous creatures, but contempt for the mentality that would import them to serve as prey. This is far worse, it seems to me, than the illegal animal imports of Tan-Hing, where the creatures at least were sold as pets. Here they're brought in as living targets intended to be slain to satisfy hunters' lust for trophies and the thrill of spilling blood.

We hike alongside the fence for a quarter of a mile, coming finally to a gate attached to its posts with heavy padlocked chains. On the other side there's a dirt track.

"Hank said there was a fire road," Sasha says.

"You know, if we wanted to we could climb over and walk straight in."

"And set off plenty of alarms. If they have sensors they'll be on the roads," he says. "They probably also run patrols."

"Anyway," I tell him, "if I wanted to go in, I wouldn't do it during daylight."

"It would be suicide no matter the time of day. Even with Hank I wouldn't try it. In fact, *especially* with Hank. If he was armed, even with just bow and arrow, he'd be fair game, and so would everyone with him."

Sasha's right, of course. Also, I have no valid reason to go in. So there're bad guys in there, they kill animals, shoot poachers, hunt down vagrants, engage in orgies, do gang bangs, fight duels—what else is new? There're plenty of bad guys in the world. Why single out these creeps?

And yet . . . I feel drawn here, convinced the G.G.C. is a locus of evil, convinced too that Maddy was somehow involved with it, and that her last photographic venture, so horrendously curtailed by Julio Sanchez, was an attempt to expose this evil to the world.

Sunday midmorning: I induce Sasha to drive me by Vince Carroll's phone directory address. Having established that Carroll is employed by the G.G.C., I feel an urge to photograph his face.

It's a nondescript ranch-style house in an uninteresting middle-class development named, according to the quaintly lettered sign, North Ridge Estates. Short stone pillars serve as sentries at the entrance. Carroll's place is just four houses in, distinguishable from surrounding homes only by the selection of specimen trees in front and the positioning of the garage vis-à-vis the front stoop and door.

As we pass, I spot a light Toyota pickup in the drive. Then, turning in my seat, I catch a glimpse of laundry flapping on a line in the backyard. Encouraged, since this was what I imagined when I spoke to the woman who answered Carroll's phone, I ask Sasha to hover for a while down the street in case someone emerges from the house.

He declines, saying that in a neighborhood like this you

can't drive in on a Sunday morning, park, then sit around in your car without arousing suspicion.

"A couple of strangers, you white, me brown—they'll think we're child-snatchers and call the cops. Look around, Kay. Tricycles on the lawns, basketball hoops above garage doors. This is a middle-class family community ... and we're the bogeymen. I say let's get outa here quick!"

He drives to the turnabout at the end of North Ridge Drive, where, in front of a faux colonial, I spot a FOR SALE sign on the grass. Just then a well-dressed woman pulls into the driveway, gets out, sets up an OPEN HOUSE easel sign by the curb, then unlocks the front door.

"Our lucky day," I tell Sasha. "We've come to look at real estate. We'll look at the house, then put the question to the realtor—how'll the neighborhood respond to an interracial couple? After that we can stroll around long as we like, and I can carry my camera too."

The realtor's name is Tami Lemmon. A perky blonde even shorter than me, recently divorced with two daughters, she tells us, she's had her license for just a year.

"Of course you'll be welcome here!" she says. "North Ridge is one of the friendliest developments in the area. Of course you should take a walk around! Then come back and give this place a real hard look." Tami squints. "It's a steal at one sixty-nine. I expect to sell it by the end of the day. Darn smart of you guys to get here first." She beams. "Early bird gets the worm!"

Approaching Carroll's house on foot, I spot a plump middle-aged woman with graying hair exiting the side door with a basket of wash.

I wave to her. "Howdy!"

"Howdy yourself," she bellows back. "Something I can do for you?"

I nod, approach. I recognize her voice. It's the woman I spoke with on the phone, the one who said if Vince wasn't at the club he was probably tomcatting around the county.

"We're thinking of buying the house up the street. The realtor suggested we walk around the neighborhood, see how we're received."

Her eyes flick over to Sasha, then back to me.

"How d'you expect to be received?" she asks.

"Well, that's the question, isn't it?"

"Is it?" She shakes her head. "Way I see it, folks generally get the reception they expect."

"You're saying—?"

"If you're lookin' for a friendly neighborhood, you won't find much better 'n North Ridge Estates. If you're lookin' for an unfriendly one, you'll probably find that here too."

"Well, thank you, Mrs. . . . ?"

"Call me Pris," she says, "short for Priscilla. You're . . . ?"

"Kay. This is Sasha. He's from India."

She smiles. "I didn't expect he was from Japan."

Sasha laughs. "Do you live here alone?"

She shakes her head. "I keep house for my kid brother. Kinda funny to find ourselves living together again after all these years, but now we're both divorced it makes sense." She rolls her eyes.

We stand together awkwardly; then she breaks the silence.

"Well, I got washing to hang, and you got the neighborhood to check. If you do decide to buy here, stop by again. I'll introduce you around. Meantime, good luck!"

What a nice intelligent lady, we agree, as we continue on our way. When we pass by again she's gone, probably back inside to fetch more wash. Sasha points out that even if brother Vince should pop out and show his face, it would be awkward for me to take his picture.

"You're right," I tell him, jotting down the tag number of his pickup. "We better get going before Tami Lemmon searches us out . . . since no other prospects have shown up."

Seven-forty A.M. Monday: We're parked in a pull-over area on Lake Hill Road, a good position to watch cars as they head out of North Ridge and turn toward town. We've been waiting here since seven, traffic's been sparse, but now the action's starting to pick up. With a telephoto on my Contax, I use the camera as a spotting scope to search for Carroll's pickup. Evidently the folks who live in North Ridge Estates are a punctual lot, eager to get to work on time; now there're so many pouring out of the development I'm having trouble keeping track.

"That's him!" Sasha says, starting his ignition.

"I can't see him."

"Yellow Toyota. Believe me, it's him."

"Thank God you see colors," I say, as Sasha pulls into traffic two cars behind the pickup. "The traffic light ahead—what color is it?"

"Just changing to red."

"Good! Stay on his right, then try and pull in beside him."

As Sasha executes the maneuver, I raise my camera to obtain a good clean profile view of Carroll just to the right of Sasha's head.

"Okay, my dear—turn to me now, but don't move a muscle. Gimme a big smile. I'm going to take your picture." *Whap!whap!* "Good! Now again!" *Whap!whap!* "Excellent! One more." And at that moment, Carroll, perhaps attracted by the improvised photo session in our car, turns and peers straight into my lens.

Whap! Gotcha!

"Okay," I tell Sasha, "I'm done. Let's go back to San Francisco."

Three days after my return, I meet Joel for lunch at the Macaroni House in North Beach, a triangular five-table place so compact that when new diners enter, those already seated must rise to let them through.

Joel's also in a restive mood, a fact he announces the moment he sits down.

"Now, kiddo," he intones, "is the spring of my discontent."

Having butchered half of one of my favorite couplets, he peers at me, awaiting my response.

"I don't know how to make it into 'glorious summer' for you," I tell him.

"Well, seeing you always lightens the load."

He's eager to tell me things are going well at home. Kirstin, he informs me, is building a nice business for herself reading runes. When her clients can't pay, as is often the case, she barters a reading for something of equivalent value.

"Such as?"

"One client gives her free lessons in macramé. Another, a potter, trades her ceramics. There's a professional dominatrix around the corner who's offered to trade sessions for readings. We haven't decided how to handle that yet."

I smile, ask how his investigation's going.

"There're lots of interesting stories out there, kiddo. No question there's a crisis brewing on the waterfront. But so far I lack the binding element. Who's stirring things up? Who's making it happen?"

"The guy with the Chinese mask?"

"Not a peep out of him since Tan-Hing."

"I still think you're being used, Joel."

"Of course I'm being used. What I gotta do now is use my user, turn the thing around."

After lunch we stroll the old Barbary Coast neighborhood, the network of narrow streets and cobblestoned alleys around Jackson Square. Here were situated the gambling dens, brothels and saloons that earned San Francisco its reputation as one of the most iniquitous port cities in the world. Where once men were shanghaied (drugged, then kidnapped to serve on ships literally bound for Shanghai), there are now elegant restaurants, fancy architects' and attorneys' offices, and pricey antiques stores offering treasures beyond compare.

At the corner of Gold and Balance, named for the assay offices that lined them during Gold Rush days, Joel turns to me and asks softly what I'm up to.

"I've known you a long time, Kay. Something's got you obsessed. I don't mean to pry, but maybe I can help." He shrugs. "Your call, of course."

Right then I decide to tell him everything, not only because he's helped me already and can surely help me some more, but also because I feel a need to confide. Though Sasha tries to be objective, as my occasional lover he cannot. Dad, of course, is hopelessly partial and overly concerned for my safety. Perhaps Joel, my most trusted friend, can provide the dispassionate advice I need. For he's right, I *have* become obsessed, and obsession, I know, can cloud my vision.

He listens as I recount the story, everything from the morning I learned of Maddy's death to my recent inquiries on the North Coast.

"It's taken me over," I tell him. "Maddy left me her cameras. When I got them I found that strip of film inside. I'm pretty sure that was an accident. Probably she just forgot. She certainly had no inkling she'd be killed. But still I can't help but feel it came to me by design, like a note placed in a bottle, then thrown into the sea . . . and everything that's happened since has flowed from that. Finding her spy nest. Witnessing the weird sex scene across the alley. My fight to the death with Julio Sanchez. Dad remembering the connection between Ramsey Carson and guns. It was my follow-up on that which led to the interview with Baggy Bigelow, which led in turn to the trip up north."

"Now that it's taken hold, you can't shake it, right?"

"I can't," I admit.

He smiles. "Getting a hunch, prying open a story, finding the more you look into it the deeper and more confusing it becomes—that sequence, kiddo, which you're now experiencing, is what my life's about."

"So what do I do now, Joel?"

"Basically you've got three choices. Let it go, put it aside, follow it wherever it leads. There's no greater compulsion than the last way, Kay. It's the storyteller's need, essential to human nature since the first storyteller told the first story to the first listeners seated around the first fire in front of the proverbial cave. 'What happened?' 'What happened after that?' they'd ask, for, being human, they craved to know. And for those of us who hear the calling, who are blessed or cursed with the need to tell the stories, there can be no choice—we must comprehend our story in order to tell it, and to comprehend it we must pursue it to its end."

*T*HE GUN / FIND THE GUN / *WHERE'S THE GUN?* I'm sitting in the Main Library at a study table surrounded by books, researching the history and legality of dueling in California.

I learn that the most famous duel in the state took place on September 13, 1859, between David S. Terry, then chief justice of the California Supreme Court, and U.S. senator from California David C. Broderick.

The issue was a personal insult supposedly delivered by Broderick in an antislavery speech. Terry, a saloon brawler, known for his skill with a bowie knife, challenged Broderick on "a point of honor." In fact, this was a pretext since Terry wanted California to become a slave state and saw the alleged insult as an opportunity to eliminate a political opponent.

The duelists, accompanied by seconds, doctors and witnesses, met in a secluded grove of Monterey pines near Lake Merced south of what we now call the Sunset. The weapons, chosen by Terry, were a pair of hair-trigger Lafoucheaux pistols.

Before the start of the duel, Broderick accidentally discharged his weapon. Terry then took careful aim and fired, hitting Broderick in the right breast between the second and third ribs. The ball ricocheted around inside Broderick's chest, ripping through various organs. Gravely wounded and in excruciating pain, Broderick held on for several days, then expired.

As a result of the scandal and the high status of the combatants, dueling was soon outlawed under Section 226 of the California Penal Code. In the twentieth century this antidueling statue has rarely been invoked. I can find only four cases since 1945 in which the charge was brought. In two, the opponents were recent immigrants settling matters in the traditional way. In the third the duel was fought to settle a business dispute; in the fourth, it was fought over a woman.

I learn that when the statute is applied, the prosecution must prove that the fatal fight occurred "by previous agreement or upon a previous quarrel." As a counter to the charge, the defendant may not claim self-defense. I also learn that a conviction for dueling carries a far lighter penalty than for first degree murder: a likely maximum sentence of nine years.

Tuesday morning: Finding an address in the San Francisco phone book for Mrs. Chaplin D. Fontaine, I walk over to the 2400 block of Vallejo in Pacific Heights to check out her building.

It's an elegant late 1920s high-rise with what must be magnificent views from the upper floors. A courtly uniformed black doorman with pencil-line mustache stands beneath an awning, guarding the gilded lobby behind.

He looks friendly so I nod to him and approach. His name's Sam, and, he kindly tells me, there're no current vacancies in the building, but, as there're quite a few aging tenants, apartments do occasionally come up.

"With a building nice as this," Sam says, "when they move out it's usually feet-first."

Just then one of the aforementioned elderly, a short natty gentleman wearing a checked suit, ascot and fedora, exits the lobby accompanied by a high-strung Jack Russell terrier on a leash. He gives Sam a hearty "Good morning," but before Sam can respond the little dog yanks the man around the corner, then starts to drag him down the hill.

I ask Sam about Mrs. Fontaine. He tells me she lives in the penthouse and that her late husband's firm owns the building.

"In this job you meet lots of different kinds of folks," Sam says. "We're not allowed to talk about our tenants, but I can tell you this—Mrs. Fontaine is a kind and classy lady. Everyone who works here likes her a lot."

Which could mean that Mrs. Fontaine is genuinely nice, or a good tipper, or that Sam would say the same no matter whom I asked about.

After more talk, about how rents are soaring in the neighborhood, I tell him I'd like to talk to Mrs. Fontaine but am shy about calling her.

"If you've got a good reason," Sam advises, "call her up and give it to her straight. She'll probably see you, but even if she blows you off she'll do it so nice you won't even know it's happening."

I wait till noon to give her a call. A housekeeper answers, "Fontaine residence," asks my name, then puts me on hold. A minute later Mrs. Fontaine picks up. There's a slight tremble in her voice as she asks how she may help.

I introduce myself as a photojournalist working on a story. I tell her I know that her late husband was a founder of the Goddess Gun Club, and ask if she'd be willing to talk to me about his involvement.

A pause. When she speaks again, her voice is filled with hauteur.

"*Who* did you say you were?"

I tell her more about myself, mentioning my books and photographs which have recently appeared in the *Bay Area News*. She says she saw my pictures of the landing of illegals in the Presidio but doesn't understand the connection to the G.G.C.

I tell her there is no connection, that it's a different story altogether and I'd prefer to explain my interest face-to-face.

Another pause. "You're an independent journalist?"

I assure her I'm independent, that at the moment I'm pursuing background information, and if she agrees to an interview I'll give my word that anything she tells me will be held in strictest confidence.

"That's nice," she says, "but since we haven't met, how do I know I can trust you?"

"Meet me, look into my eyes," I suggest. "Isn't that the best way? It's what I always do."

"All right," she answers finally. "I'll take you up on that. Come over for tea at five, I'll look into your eyes and then we'll see what we shall see."

She does have something to tell me, I think.

Sam's still on duty when I turn up. He gives me a wink.

"She's expecting you," he says, guiding me to the elevator. "I'll run you up."

On the way to the penthouse he tells me Mrs. Fontaine told him that if she decides her five o'clock visitor is unwelcome, he's to stand by to assist in putting me out.

"Oh, Sam! She thinks I wouldn't leave?"

"Just a security precaution," Sam says. "Some folks prey on the elderly, you know."

The elevator opens directly onto a lavishly decorated foyer. There's a tapestry on the wall depicting ladies and gentlemen in medieval dress, a richly patterned Oriental rug on the checkerboard marble floor, and two Louis XVI chairs that look like they belong in a period room at the de Young Museum.

Suddenly feeling underdressed, I glance back at Sam. He smiles encouragement.

"Ring the bell," he suggests.

There's only one apartment on the floor. I ring. A uniformed maid responds. She listens to my name, then politely asks me to wait. Feeling like a schoolgirl called up to the principal's office, I turn again toward Sam. He gives me another smile. I give him one back. Then I hear footsteps and turn to face my examiner. The woman who approaches is slim, wears a single-strand graduated pearl necklace and a well-cut designer suit, has precision-cut white hair parted at the side and a pale yet handsome face. She walks straight up to me with great assurance and peers intently into my eyes.

"Why, you're just a child," she says merrily. "A very nice one too, I imagine." She addresses Sam over my shoulder. "Thanks, Sam. That'll be all for now."

Agnes Fontaine and I sit side by side on a couch opposite a stone fireplace in her huge drop-dead living room furnished in a mix of Chinese and European antiques. Two large paintings, one by Helen Frankenthaler, the other by Willem de Kooning, hang on one of the walls. On the other are several pairs of French doors leading to an apartment-length terrace facing north. Through the glass I can see San Francisco Bay, the Golden Gate Bridge, Mount Tamalpais, San Pablo Bay and the lagoons and hills beyond.

While I peer about, she pours us each a cup of tea, then sits back as if to reappraise me. Her eyes aren't as sharp or laserlike as Maddy's, but they're plenty powerful enough. Though I don't see colors, I guess they're icy blue.

"I bought your books this afternoon," she says, gestur-

ing toward copies of *Transgressions* and *Exposures* on a
side table. "Impressive work for one so young. I hope you
don't mind my saying that, but at my age . . . well . . ." She
smiles slightly to herself.

She continues: "There was a time, long ago, when I too
wanted to be an artist. I went to art school back east, then
spent a year in Florence and another in Paris taking life-
drawing classes at the École des Beaux-Arts. I got so I
could draw pretty well"—she sniffs—"in an academic
sort of way. But I didn't have what it takes to be a real
artist. Luckily I knew it. So I came back to San Francisco,
married, had children, got involved in volunteer work,
most of it for arts institutions—all the conventional things
women of my generation did because there was really
nothing else for us, certainly not the possibility of careers."

She pauses. "Still, I always liked artists, liked having
them around. Chap and I often entertained them here." She
glances around the room. "Part of that was to give them a
place to come where they'd find a sympathetic ear. I've
bought a lot of contemporary art over the past thirty-five
years. If an artist was invited here, he could be pretty certain I'd buy an example of his work. I've got loads of art in
the apartment and more in three storage rooms downstairs.
Some of it's good, a lot of it isn't, but quality was never the
point. The purpose was to support people brave enough to
try to make something out of nothing. Which is what you
people do, isn't it? That's why I envy you. Not just
because you make art, but because you *dare* to make it. I
don't know where you get the courage."

Listening to her, I'm nonplussed. What is she trying to
tell me? That she envies me for daring to do what she could
not? I think it's not that simple. Perhaps she's saying she
wishes she could have been an artist because artists give to
the world, and, because she found another way to give, she
doesn't feel sorry for herself for lacking talent. But why, I
wonder, is she setting up this context for a conversation she
knows is going to be about her husband, guns and death? If

she wants to gain my attention, she's succeeded very well.

"I just want you to understand," she says, "why it was important for me to view your work before we spoke. I was prepared not to like what I saw in your eyes. But of course it's not what I might see *in* them that would tell me whether I could trust you. Many people fake sincerity. Rather it's what I could see *through* your eyes that would tell me who you were. In your books I saw what you saw. I saw the truth. It was then I decided I'd talk to you."

She waits for me to speak. I think a moment before I do. What she's said is extremely flattering. I decide to be direct.

"I'm searching," I tell her, "for answers to questions you'd probably rather not think about. If I ask about something too personal, please tell me and I'll go on to something else."

She smiles, refills our teacups, then repositions herself on the couch. "Ask me anything you like."

My first question is stunningly brazen.

"There's a rumor your husband was killed by Ramsey Carson in a duel. Is that true?"

She flinches slightly, then sets her features. Again, I'm impressed by how handsome she is, her superb bone structure and slightly sunken cheeks.

"I've heard the rumor. I don't know if it's true. I do know it *could* be."

"Please tell me more."

She sits back. "Chap and Ram were partners. Chap took Ram into his business when Ram was young, taught him to deal in real estate, helped make him rich. I'm not saying Ram didn't work for it. He did. He was a brilliant investor. Chap always said so. But without Chap, Ram would never have achieved so much. For years they were close. People said Chap treated Ram like a kid brother. Then, in the last year of my husband's life, there was a falling-out. We stopped seeing each other socially. The trouble wasn't over business, but over something that happened up at the club."

She visited the Goddess Gun Club only a few times, for the annual bring-along-the-wives picnic each spring. Shooting and hunting didn't interest her, but that didn't matter since the G.G.C. was set up as a sporting club solely for men.

The club was Ram's idea. Ram was the shooter. Chap liked to hunt once in a while, but it was Ram who adored shooting and guns. Some said he was obsessed, which was probably true considering the safaris he went on, the fortune he spent collecting firearms and the way he caressed them when he showed them off. There were, of course, his historical-association pieces, guns that had belonged to famous personages in the past. The coveting of these weapons she could understand. Then there were the erotic guns, guns embellished with erotic engravings and motifs, which Ram collected more avidly than anyone in the world. These she did not like at all.

"I found them pitiful," Agnes says. "But he loved to show them off, so what could one do except turn away and giggle and pretend they were too naughty to look at . . . which, I guess, was what he wanted. We'd humor him about them—me, Chap, their other partner, Orrin Jennett, his wife Laura, others in our circle. 'Oh, Ram—how *could* you!' That kind of thing. Truth is they bored me silly. Chap too. We just didn't get it. Phallus-shaped rear sights and triggers. Front sights made to look like a woman's . . . whatever they call it these days. And then the engravings, so elaborate—people doing all these things with one another. I want you to know I'm no kind of prude. The nude human figure has been a great subject for artists. When I studied art I often drew male and female nudes from living models. But what was depicted on some of Ram's erotic guns went beyond anything I've ever seen in art. It was pornography. There's no other word for it. Yet he so loved those guns, they were such a part of his life, there was nothing negative you could say without giving offense."

There was another aspect to Ram Carson, a hardness she felt in him. He could be courtly, as gallant as any man she knew. Aside from showing off his erotic guns, he was never vulgar in her presence. Yet she felt a kind of menace hidden beneath the veneer of good manners and dashing good looks. Like Hemingway, perhaps, if one can believe the tales of his bullying and brutality.

"We spoke earlier," she tells me, "about peering into people's eyes. Sometimes, when I looked into Ram's, I'd see this terrible dark thing. It was like looking at a tree with a leopard hidden in the branches. Even though you can't see the creature, you know he's there. It was that way with Ram, though no one ever mentioned it. Certainly not Chap, an excellent judge of character. I think Ram knew I saw something dark in him, for he was wary with me, cautious about what he said."

There was another thing, whispers about something sinister in Ram's past, nothing she paid attention to until after Chap's death when the rumor started that Ram had killed Chap in a duel. Then she remembered and tried to track the old whispers down. She didn't get anywhere. No one she asked would admit to having heard them. And since she couldn't remember herself, she had no choice but to let the matter drop.

"What kind of whispers?" I ask.

She looks past me at the Bay.

"That long ago, when Ram was young, he killed a man. Most particularly, killed him in a duel."

When she looks at me again, her face is contorted by a smile, a poor attempt to hide her pain.

"Preposterous, isn't it? Ram's now ... what? Sixty-four. Born a few years before World War Two. Assuming this duel took place at the earliest when he was, say, twenty-one years old, that would mean it was fought in 1956. A pistol duel fought during the Eisenhower years! Who would believe such a thing?"

But from the way she looks at me, I understand she *does*

believe it, and that she believes Ramsey Carson killed her husband the same way.

Distraught, she turns away. I sense her trying to maintain composure. Suddenly she rises, excuses herself, then rushes from the room. After she's gone, I walk over to the contemporary paintings to take a closer look.

The Frankenthaler doesn't do much for me. She's an important artist, just as Rothko is, but their work, like the work of Morris Louis and others of the abstract color-field school, is too color-dependent for my eyes. I'm attracted far more to painters who draw or work abstractly with line. The de Kooning reads well to me, a female figure rendered in edgy slashing calligraphic strokes.

When Agnes returns she's carrying a leather-bound photo album. "Come, let's sit," she says. "I have some pictures to show you."

This time, as we approach the couch, the sky has darkened sufficiently for me to take in the view.

"Glorious, isn't it?" Agnes says. "I try to sit here every afternoon at sunset. I like seeing the lights come on in the buildings, the night-city come alive. There's a lot of night in your photographs, Kay. You love the night, don't you?"

I tell her I do, explain about my vision, how I lack cone function and thus cannot see colors. Night, I tell her, is the time when I see best. She nods to show me she understands.

"This was Chap's," she says, opening the album, "where he kept pictures taken up at the club. I brought it out so you could see their faces—Chap's and Ram's of course, and the other men as well."

Most of the pictures are what I'd expect—group portraits of men dressed in hunting gear posing together with their guns. In some shots the poses are formal, the men lined up, as in team photographs, grinning at the lens, beside trophies of their hunt—boars' carcasses displayed head-up on the ground or killed deer suspended by their feet from the limbs of nearby trees. The hunters' faces bear grins of triumph: *How proud we are on account of what we've slain.* These are sportsmen's pictures taken to memorialize a shared experience, times spent tramping the woods tracking a quarry or waiting patiently in a blind.

The canny expressions of hunters who have outsmarted wild beasts—I've seen shots like these many times. Normally my eyes would glide easily across them. But these photographs are different. There are secrets here, secrets hidden in the faces. I study them as Agnes reels off the names.

"There's Chap with Ram beside him. There's Orrin Jennett, Frank Howard, Jack Stadpole and the director, Hoyt Hoge, up from Hollywood. Hank London, John Holmes, Rob and Gus Leavitt. Tuck Chubet, Carter Dixon, Dean Laneese, Chauncey Chase."

The names fly by me, male names, a roll call of Teds, Marks, Peters, Norms, an occasional Chris, a Caleb, even a Saul ... though most are classically WASP. Chap Fontaine and Ram Carson are in most every photograph, almost always together, their friendship evident in the way they nearly touch.

Fontaine has a smooth, contented winner's look. A temperate, round-faced, good-looking man with glossy combed-back silver hair, he never fails to grin, but his grin is never too exuberant. He's also a man so perfectly groomed that no matter the toils of the hunt, he never shows a smudge of dirt nor a single hair out of place.

Carson is also good-looking, but on another level—matinee-idol handsome with chiseled chin and nose, and a dark Byronic shock of windswept hair. Peering at his eyes in search of the darkness Agnes described, I catch only a glimpse of emptiness. Carson also shows the lascivious I'll-love-you-to-death grin of a swain, a rake, a beau, a gallant. It's the old Clark Gable lady-killer smile, the leonine kind that makes women go weak in the knees. I've been a sucker for it too—the dandy's smile, the smile of the heartbreaker, the guy who loves you so easy and so well. He'll love you, leave you, break your heart, but when he reappears, shows you that incredible smile, you forgive him and again throw yourself into his arms.

Ram Carson is simply incandescently handsome, and the camera loves him . . . which means he knows how to play to it. Also how to position himself. In nearly all the pictures he's in the center, the one about whom the others coalesce. Ram and Chap, Chap and Ram—there they are, always together, sportsmen and hunters, founders and leaders. They, the pictures tell me, *are* the G.G.C.

There are action shots in the album too, men dressed in hunting jackets with quilted patches at the shoulder, shooting sporting clays. Also combat side-arm shooting, under the guidance of a man I recognize as Vincent Carroll, in which club members in black T-shirts and camouflage fatigue pants take aim at human-form targets. These shots are scary, giving the lie to the aristocratic-sportsman look. This isn't conventional shooting club activity, it's pure militia stuff.

I ask Agnes about it. She agrees it doesn't fit with the rest of the pictures. She points out too that I won't find Chap among the side-arm shooters.

"That was Ram's project," she tells me. "He felt that as long as they had a place to shoot, they should offer combat training to members who were interested."

So, I ask her, what was the G.G.C., a rich man's sporting club or a gun nut's paradise?

"Both," she says. "But poor Chap didn't know it. He thought of it as a place where gentlemen who had achieved a certain level of success could mingle informally, bond in the male ritual of the hunt. He wasn't aware of all the evil things Ram was doing . . . not until the final year."

I mention Schuyler Bigelow's column about factions at the club.

"Yes, Baggy had that right," she says. "He's a nasty man, but his reporting's accurate enough."

So what, I ask, *was* Ram Carson doing that caused other G.G.C. members such distress?

She turns again to stare out through the French doors. Glancing out myself, I can hear nothing except her agitated breathing. When she turns to face me the light is so dim I can barely read her features.

"What Ram was doing, Ram and a few of his cronies, was to take the motifs engraved on the sides of his erotic guns and . . . bring them to life."

She shakes her head. "And worse. That's how Chap put it. He couldn't bring himself to say much more. He was so *aggrieved,* Kay, indignant that such things could be going on at his beloved club, and outraged that Ram was the one who'd instigated them."

When I ask her what kind of things, she shakes her head.

"There were probably crimes committed," she says. "Trespassers shot, things like that. And special hunting parties. 'Safaris' they called them, for which they'd hire drifters to play escaped convicts, then hunt them down. From the rumors Chap heard, not much mercy was shown."

She tells me how Chap felt betrayed by the man who was not only his partner, whom he'd nurtured and helped make rich, but also, he thought, his closest friend. It was, he told Agnes, like being stabbed in the back. And along with these feelings of outrage and betrayal, there grew in him an anger so deep it could only be assuaged by revenge.

He swore vengeance to her, night after night told her he'd get even with Ram, destroy him, bring him down. The first thing was to break off their business relationship—which didn't prove to be so easy. They were partners, along with Orrin Jennett, in a web of interlocking companies. Neither one held a controlling interest. There were all sorts of issues pertaining to the value of the properties and who had the right to buy the other out. Also, Jennett, protective of *his* investment, refused to take Chap's side,

which infuriated Chap, since he was the one who'd originally brought Orrin in. So there was also a feeling of being
double-betrayed, which only made things worse. Then
there was the matter of the club.

The G.G.C. was set up as a private association with three
classes of members—voted, charter and founding—with
nearly all the power in the hands of the latter. Since the three
founding members were Chap, Ram and Orrin, it came
down to the same insupportable situation as at CFJ Realty.

It was this intractability, she felt, that may have led to
the duel—if, in fact, a duel took place. If Ram indeed did
challenge him, Chap had been crazed enough to accept.

"Chap was an experienced woodsman," she tells me, "a
decent enough shot, but he knew he wasn't in the same
class as Ram. Ram was a tournament shooter. He had a
room filled with trophies. Chap had no business taking him
on in a fight."

Chap Fontaine, she assures me, was a civilized man,
ethical in business and personal affairs. He was intelligent,
rational, honorable . . . all the qualities one hopes to find in
a gentleman. But, like any man when his manliness is challenged, he was capable of behaving like a fool. Better to
die than be shamed, to fall on the field than be regarded as
a coward.

She sniffs. "Maybe it didn't happen that way. Maybe he
did shoot himself by mistake. But I'm certain of this—
Chap did not commit suicide. He was incapable of that and
far too angry to consider it."

That Sunday night she was sitting in this room, in the
very seat I now occupy, contemplating the sunset. It had
been a glorious display, she recalls, the kind we get every
so often in San Francisco—mackerel sky turned to the
color of blood as it caught the final rays of the failing sun.
She'd become lost in the magnificence of it, the vivid
phosphorescent glow that hung in the western sky even
after the sun sank into the Pacific. Then the phone rang, its

shrill sound cutting to her ears. She knew it was about Chap even before she picked it up.

She'd been getting intimations throughout the day, little whiffs that made her feel weak. Chap had gone to Mendocino Friday night in the private plane the club used to shuttle its senior members upstate. There'd been a determined look in his eyes when he kissed her goodbye. "I'll be back late Sunday," he'd told her. "By then everything will be resolved." He didn't say anything else, just nodded to her, then walked out the door. He didn't call her over the weekend. Yet when the phone rang that Sunday night, she knew it was someone else with news that would forever change her life.

It was Ram, his voice gravelly, filled with a kind of grievous gravitas.

"It's about Chap," he said. "There's been a shooting accident at the club. Doc Petersen's here, so he attended Chap right away." Ram paused. "I'm so sorry, Aggie. There was nothing Doc could do."

After Ram broke the news, the others came on the line with details of the sorrowful event. Petersen, their family doctor, a charter G.G.C. member, told her how it had happened. Then Vince Carroll, who was head of G.G.C. security, then Ram again, then Orrin . . . and she remembered none of it, just that Chap was dead, had somehow accidentally shot himself on the club range, that there'd been witnesses, people had gotten to him right away, but he'd never regained consciousness, had died painlessly . . . and they'd be flying his body back to San Francisco in the morning.

Perfect wife that she was, she wasted no time feeling sorry for herself. Instead she immediately called her children: Susan, who lived in L.A.; Junior, who practiced medicine in Palo Alto; Tom in Washington, where he practiced law. Next, Chap's attorney, Raid Harris, who was also Ram's attorney and lead attorney for CFJ Realty Corporation. Then . . . she was about to start calling Chap's close friends when she realized she'd already spoken to two of them, Ram and Orrin, and that the rest of their circle, at least the men, had been up at the club that weekend and thus already knew.

The same thing struck her later, the way they were all connected: through CFJ Realty and the G.G.C., sharing the same doctors, lawyers, bankers and friends, including a retired federal judge, two state senators, a justice of the state supreme court, a regent of the University of California and assorted fellow board members of the Fine Arts Museums and the San Francisco Opera Association. It was a closed circle. Even the owner of the mortuary that handled Chap's cremation and burial was part of it. Plus the wives, most of whom she'd known for years, worked with on committees, served with on boards, entertained one another in their respective homes, met for lunch at their downtown women's clubs.

The whole bunch of them turned out for the funeral, a lugubrious affair at Grace Cathedral. "Great turnout for Chap," people said afterwards. Ram Carson played lead eulogist, mouthing the usual platitudes: "Chap Fontaine . . . one of the last of a dying breed . . . a true gentleman whose word was his bond . . . We won't see his like again . . ."

After the burial, when Ram kissed her at the cemetery, his lips felt cold on her cheek. She asked him then about the "falling out." He dismissed it with a shake of his head.

"Sure, we had differences, Aggie. Business mostly. But nothing that could undermine a friendship of nearly thirty years. Without Chap there's going to be a big hole in my life. Let's not drift apart as people in these circumstances often do. I know that's what Chap would want."

Four days later she heard the first glimmers of the rumor that Chap and Ram had fought a duel.

She wondered to whom she could turn.

She went to see Raid Harris. When she started voicing

her concerns after condolences and small talk, he cut her short.

"Do you *want* to bring criminal charges against Ram, Aggie? Is *that* what you're asking me to do?"

His eyes were so stern, his tone so incredulous, she wilted, apologized, then listened passively as he recommended "an excellent and extremely discreet psychiatrist," who, as it turned out, was also a member of the G.G.C.

Raid Harris made another point: Ram and Orrin were proposing to buy out Chap's interest in CFJ Realty for "a most generous amount," more than it was worth. They wanted to bend over backwards, Raid said, to be fair to her and to Chap's kids.

"Under such circumstances it would be pretty ironic, Aggie, don't you think, if word were to get back to Ram you think he murdered Chap?"

The implication was clear: if word of such a horrible thought *did* get back, no telling whether the proposed buy-out would be nearly so "generous."

Not at all happy with Raid's reaction, she decided to hire an investigator, someone who would get to the bottom of the thing, come up with proof that Chap hadn't been accidentally killed or put the rumors of a duel to rest.

The obvious first choice was Lars Cosgrave, the most respected private detective in the city. His firm occupied a plush suite of offices on Montgomery Street, his receptionist had a British accent, he specialized in corporate investigations and worked with prominent attorneys on high-profile criminal cases.

Cosgrave listened politely as she sketched out her suspicions, but as soon as he heard the names of the players, he folded his arms.

"If you feel strongly about this, Mrs. Fontaine, *truly* believe a crime has been committed, I advise you to take your evidence directly to the Mendocino County DA."

When she protested she had no evidence, that that was why she'd come to him, he muttered "Indeed" to signal their meeting was over, then escorted her to the door.

Even after this rebuff, she was not ready to give up. She asked around, came up with the name of another private investigator—Susan Marzik of Marzik & Associates, a competitor of Cosgrave's, who, if not nearly so well connected, still had an excellent reputation.

Marzik turned out to be a soft-spoken fortyish woman with a serious demeanor. A San Francisco native, she'd spent twenty years as an L.A. cop, rising to the rank of captain, then moved back to the Bay Area to set up on her own.

Marzik told her that if it turned out Ram Carson killed Chap Fontaine in a duel, this was a very serious matter indeed. She proposed that she and an associate go up to Mendocino for a day, visit the scene, talk to the county coroner and the Sheriff's Department people and interview local witnesses. Marzik granted that such a brief overview would not be complete, but she was certain that if people were lying she'd pick up on it and thus be in a position to recommend an in-depth investigation. Agnes agreed, signed a retainer agreement, wrote out a check for thirty-five hundred dollars and went home feeling she'd done the proper thing.

Two weeks later she received Susan Marzik's report with "CONFIDENTIAL" embossed diagonally across the binder. The report, with tabbed sections and appendices, included detailed summaries of all the interviews along with photocopies of official county documents.

Five G.G.C. members—Carson, Jennett, Petersen, Jack Stadpole and Kirk Kistler—plus Carroll, the club security director, acting as range master that afternoon, had been present when the unfortunate accident took place. All six had made sworn statements as to what occurred. Marzik studied those statements carefully, then interviewed Carroll in depth.

Her summary:

Fontaine was practicing with a pair of 19th-century English percussion dueling pistols owned by the Club (photo attached). He loaded both pistols, placed one on his gun table, then went to the firing line to fire the other. After firing, he turned again toward the table, at which point the second pistol, perhaps jarred by vibrations caused by the firing of other weapons, discharged. The lead ball hit him between the eyes, killing him instantly.

All interviews, statements and coroner's photographs are consistent with the above account.

Because of a lack of powder burns, there is no possibility that the deceased shot himself or was shot by another at close range (under six feet).

Though we cannot discount the possibility that all witnesses lied in their sworn accounts, and there was, additionally, a cover-up by all the sworn law enforcement officers called to the scene, the likelihood of such an elaborate conspiracy is so remote as to be ruled out by common sense.

In addition, we have had an arms expert examine the pistols. His report (copy attached) verifies the delicate nature of the firing mechanisms and is consistent with the accidental discharge of the killing weapon as described in the witness accounts.

The only portion of the story which may be regarded as curious is the accuracy with which the accidentally discharged lead ball hit the deceased and thus caused death. Still, such things happen. Our research reveals that 25% of all accidental gunshot wounds are fatal.

Further, it is our opinion that rumors of a duel between Carson and Fontaine derive solely from the fact that the killing weapon was one of a set of antique dueling pistols donated by Carson to the Club, and otherwise have no basis in fact.

In short, we find the official account of the incident to be highly credible. Thus we cannot at this time recommend further expenditure of client's resources in pursuit of an alternative explanation of the matter.

Respectfully submitted,
Susan M. Marzik, Investigator

It's dark outside. A three-quarters moon, dominating the eastern sky, combined with the ambient light of the city is the only source of illumination in the room.

Agnes Fontaine shakes her head. "I didn't pursue it after that. I didn't see any way I could. And Raid Harris was right—the offer Ram and Orrin made for Chap's share of CFJ Realty *was* extremely generous. My son Tom represented me in the negotiations. I had no wish to see Raid again. Or any of the others. I've dropped them all . . . or perhaps they've dropped me. It doesn't matter. Those times are over for me. I'm no longer interested in putting up a social front."

She sets down her teacup. "I'm going to have a Scotch and soda. What about you?"

I ask for a glass of merlot. She smiles, says she's changed her mind, she'll have the same, leaves the room, returns followed by her maid carrying a tray. After the maid pours the wine and leaves, I turn to her.

"There's one thing I don't understand. When your husband discovered what Carson was doing at the club—the orgies, enactments of erotic motifs on his guns, shooting poachers, the safaris and all that—why didn't he go public or report the activities to the cops?"

"Probably because nothing could be proved," Agnes says. "No one ever said Ram or any of the rest of them were stupid. As for going public, that wasn't Chap's style. These men were his friends. He wanted to restore the dignity of the club, not bring it down in ruins. The way he went about it is the way he went about everything in life—working quietly, building consensus, then, when the time was right, making his move. He'd have wanted to keep it between Ram and himself, settle the matter privately between them."

Which, I point out to her, would have made an excellent rationale for a traditional gentleman's duel.

She sits in silence. I wonder what she's thinking.

"If there was a duel," I say gently, "someone must have talked. How else to explain the rumors?"

"Marzik said—"

"Because of the pistols—I know. And she doesn't think a conspiracy is credible with so many people involved. But isn't that what they always say: 'There just couldn't have been a cover-up. It's too farfetched'?"

She takes a sip of wine. "What are you thinking, Kay?"

"Assume for a moment there *was* a duel," I tell her. "If so, there were six witnesses. One was Carson, the other duelist. Then there's Jennett, your husband's partner, and Petersen, his doctor, and Carroll, a club employee. Suppose the other two were seconds? In which case all six would be involved. Since dueling's against the law, it wouldn't have been in anyone's interest to tell the truth.

"Then there's the gun mechanism. I don't know much about guns, but I do know that in the most famous duel ever fought in this state, the pistols also had hair triggers. On the other hand, a mortal shot between the eyes is consistent with the capabilities of an expert marksman ... which, you tell me, is what Carson is. As for a law enforcement cover-up, there was no reason for one. Again, I'm no expert, but I was brought up around cops. Think about it: The sheriff's people arrive, the witnesses, all reputable men, offer their statements, their story matches the observable facts. That a different story of a duel might also match doesn't mean there was a cover-up. All it means is that since the cops already had a credible explanation, they had no need to seek out an alternative.

"But I think the biggest hole in Marzik's report is her theory that there were rumors of a duel because old dueling pistols were involved. Isn't the more likely reason that a duel actually took place? Who, after all, at the end of the twentieth century would think to make up a tale about a duel? It's so improbable ... unless, of course, someone saw it. And I think if someone did, it would have been nearly impossible *not* to talk about it.

"Also, Marzik never mentions the rumors that years ago Carson fought a duel and shot his opponent dead. If those rumors are true, isn't that all the more reason to believe he may have done so again?"

Agnes is agitated. I feel her tension rising as I speak. After Marzik's report she gave up her quest for justice. Now, a year later, I turn up reigniting embers she thought were dead.

"I'm sorry," I tell her. "I'm stirring the pot. I know I have no right."

"But you *do*!" she says, voice firm. "And I'm grateful. You've suggested things I should have thought of myself." She pauses. "Chap wouldn't have rested till he had the truth."

She stands, goes to the wall, flicks a switch, illuminates the room.

"I see it so clearly now. They thought I was weak, that all they'd have to do is stare me down. Raid Harris, Lars Cosgrave, the bunch of them. They own this town. Marzik too ... or maybe she was just afraid."

Agnes is shaking. She starts to pace. It's as if all the rage she buried for a year is bursting forth.

"You say dueling's illegal?"

I explain the antidueling law and the possible penalties.

"If there's proof Carson shot your husband," I tell her, "he'd do better owning up to a duel than facing a murder charge."

"What about Chap? Takes two to fight a duel."

"He's already paid for his part in it, hasn't he?"

She nods. "Then there's the disgrace."

"Really, Agnes, I don't see any disgrace in what Chap did. Just the opposite. He faced off against a man who

betrayed his trust and who was by far the better marksman.
It's Carson who will be disgraced for shooting down his
benefactor, then behaving like a hypocrite at his funeral."

"You're right!" There's a snap to her voice now. "What
we need is proof! There ought to be a way to get it. Turn a
witness. Isn't that what they do?" She pauses in front of
the de Kooning. "You said that if there was a duel, all the
witnesses are implicated."

"Because they were parties to a crime, and later made
false statements to the cops."

Her eyes turn electric. I detect the glow of one who,
having believed she's lost a game, now sniffs the possibility of reversal.

"Ram's the one to get. Orrin too. He's no weakling and
he let Chap down. Petersen? He's a drunk. Then there's
Stadpole and Kistler—who may have acted as seconds.
My guess is Kirk acted for Chap, Jack for Ram. I wouldn't
want to hurt Kirk, especially since Chap trusted him. Also
I know Kirk would never have taken part in any of those
. . . affairs Ram organized. But Jack would. He's just like
Ram, a rake! Which leaves that local man, Vince what's-
his-name. I don't know him at all."

I don't say anything, let her talk on. I find it thrilling to
watch her. An hour ago she was in despair. Now she's
thinking of how she can claim some justice.

"Between Petersen and Stadpole . . . Petersen would be
the weakling. The local man too. He has a lot to lose. Say
Petersen broke and then maybe this Vince fellow—that
would be two witnesses corroborating each other's stories.
If Kirk joined in, it would be three against three. Ram,
Orrin and Jack would be finished then, wouldn't they?"

She clamps her jaws as if savoring their defeat.

"What I need is an honest investigator—preferably
from out of town. Maybe from down in L.A. where they're
not impressed by San Francisco money. A good tough
lawyer too, to file a wrongful death suit. Someone not
afraid of Raid Harris. A street-fighter type from Oakland

who didn't go to fancy schools, or someone Ram cheated, or whose wife Ram screwed. There should be plenty of those."

Suddenly she stops, covers her mouth with her hand.

"What am I saying?" She slumps beside me on the couch. "This isn't me talking. It's . . . someone else." She stares at me. "I feel . . . I'm going *mad*."

Trying to comfort her, I suggest she take time to think things through.

"It's a big step to go against people who were your friends."

She shakes her head. "*They were never my friends. They were Chap's . . . and he was wrong about them, every single one.*" She looks at me. "Tell me, Kay, what's your interest in this?"

I tell her about Maddy, her spy nest opposite the G.G.C. apartment, then the way she was killed and my suspicions that the G.G.C. may have been behind it.

"She was a photojournalist. It was her last story. I'd like to finish it for her if I can." I shake my head. "My boyfriend and I went up to Mendocino last weekend to scope things out. From what we saw, it's not only very difficult but extremely dangerous to try and enter G.G.C. grounds."

Agnes peers at me. Our dialogue seems to have run out of steam. I glance at my watch. It's nearly nine P.M.

"I'm sorry, I've kept you so long," she says. "You've been patient with me and now I'm embarrassed." She peers at me again. "Even though we've just met, I feel as though I know you. Perhaps it's your photographs. I saw power and truth in them. I trust artists, always have. Please excuse me a moment. There's something I want to give you before you leave."

When she reappears she's holding an accordion file.

"This is Chap's G.G.C. stuff," she tells me, "keys, property maps, building plans, everything he had pertaining to the club. Maybe, if you decide to go there, some of this will be of use. Keep it as long as you like. Neither of my sons wants it. They have no interest in the club, even though, as sons of a founder, they're members for life."

I thank her. She escorts me to the foyer, embraces me when the elevator arrives. As the doors start to close between us, I catch a glimpse of tears forming in her eyes.

Another doorman takes me down. Sam, he tells me, went off duty at six. Out on Vallejo Street it's chilly with fog oozing up from the Bay.

I turn east, walk down into the canyon of Van Ness, then up again to my own fog-shrouded neighborhood, Russian Hill. Standing at the peak, looking down Hyde Street toward misty Alcatraz Island, I feel a deep twinge of sorrow. After spending hours with Baggy Bigelow and Agnes Fontaine, I'm starting to see my beautiful city as a place where hypocrisy and duplicity reign.

Safaris! What kind of men are these that they are so ruthless in their pleasures?

It's then that I decide I shall return to the G.G.C., try and penetrate its grounds. I need photographs, evidence, the proof that Maddy wasn't able to obtain. "A suicide mission," Sasha called it when I floated the idea . . . but, as Joel says, those of us who hear the calling must pursue our stories to their ends.

Two-twenty A.M.: Joel and I are driving downtown through deserted night streets. At intersections I catch glimpses of Chinese characters on neon signs. As we descend Powell, the fog, thick on the hills, begins to break. At Sutter, we pass a foursome of tourists stumbling into the lobby of the Sir Francis Drake. We turn right on Post, glide by the elegant shops that front Union Square, then turn into the entrance to the Union Square garage. Joel pulls a ticket from the machine, the jackknife opens, we enter and descend into the huge underground space.

Slowly we pass lines of parked cars, methodically cruise each row, winding our way back and forth, searching for a dark gray Mercedes with the vanity plate JADE-5. No sign of life down here, no sound except the hum of our engine. The light is harsh, fluorescent, the shadows deep. The air smells of iron and oil. It's as if we've entered a space devoid of anything except gleaming metal machines arranged on a vast concrete floor broken occasionally by steel columns. Dead space.

There are, Joel tells me, eleven hundred slots in the garage. Unable to find the car, we descend to the second level, then the third, finally the fourth. Here at the bottom more empty spaces, more lifelessness, more dust on the hoods. And the vehicles, it seems to me, are uglier than the ones above—shapes less sleek, alignment less rigorous.

"Stop," I tell Joel.

He brakes the car.

"What's up, kiddo?"

"I've got a feeling, that's all."

We both stare around.

"Over there." I point to a dim corner, which, if I'm not mistaken, lies beneath the southeast intersection of Stockton and Geary.

"Think that's it?"

"I think so."

"You've got a hawk's eyes, kiddo."

"Yeah, at night I do."

Joel applies a little gas, very slowly approaches the corner, brakes again sixty feet away. He must sense the aura too, for there's something issuing from the dark vehicle in that corner—aloneness, morbidity, danger, the car sitting there like a snake poised to strike. We both feel it. And since neither of us is anxious to get out and discover why, we sit silent side by side staring at it, wondering what to do. Impossible to read the license plate, but the make is right, and, Joel assures me, the color.

"Your informant—what was his mood?" I ask.

"He wasn't jovial, if that's what you mean. No mention of me getting a nice treat this time." Joel turns to me. "Why d'you ask?"

"This place. The stillness. Down here you can't even hear the rumble from the street. Also, something in the air."

Joel sniffs, shrugs. "I don't know. Something ... maybe. You think—?"

I shrug. "Guess we better take a look."

He reaches to the back seat, picks a flashlight off the floor; then we get out of the car, both of us at the same time, and saunter cautiously toward the Mercedes. At thirty feet, Joel stoops, squints, shines his light on the plate.

"JADE-5," he says, smiling grimly. "Don't suppose it's booby-trapped, do you?"

"Do you?"

"Fuck it!"

He starts toward the car. I grab his arm. It doesn't take much strength to hold him back. "Let's circle around first. Maybe we'll see something."

We circle. His flashlight reveals nothing; the glass in the car windows is the kind that darkens under direct light.

"Useless," he hisses, flicking off his flashlight. Just then I catch a glimpse of a form inside.

"Do that again."

"What, kiddo?"

"Turn it on and off. Yes, just like that. Couple more times. Okay, that's enough. There's a guy in there."

"There is!"

"He's real still. He may be dead, Joel."

"Shit!"

I raise my camera. "I'm going to strobe him. Take a look."

Whap!whap!whap! As expected, my strobe defeats the glass, burns straight through to reveal a man on the passenger side slumped over the center console.

"I'll call the cops," Joel says.

He punches in 911 as I continue to shoot, circling the car. For years I've dealt with fear like this, hiding behind my camera, concentrating on photographing a gruesome scene so as not to yield to my terror. I pretend I'm a forensic photographer working every angle on the corpse. This way I don't have to ask who he is or what he did or how he died, just get the pictures, document the event, use my lens to distance myself from the horror. But then, after I've shot out the roll, I feel faint, squat on the cement floor, try to reload, am suddenly overcome by nausea and heat.

Joel kneels beside me. "They'll be here soon. You okay?"

"If I could just have some water or something."

"I've got water in the car."

While he goes to fetch it, I spool in a fresh roll. Then, as he holds the bottle to my mouth, we hear the sirens.

Joel has an oversize white handkerchief in his hand. "When they open those car doors it's going to stink." He sprinkles water on the cloth, shapes it into a triangle, ties it behind my neck, pulls it up over my nose like a surgical mask.

"Okay, kiddo?"

I nod. "Flashlight, water bottle, fresh hankie—you got it all."

" 'Be prepared,' my old scoutmaster used to say."

There're ten cops with us now, eight in uniform plus a pair of detectives. The car door's open and an assistant medical examiner is checking out the corpse. A police photographer with a crappy camera has pushed me aside. He wears bedroom slippers, loose khaki pants, a soiled V-neck T-shirt. Since Joel's known most of these guys for years, they include him in their banter.

"Asian male, mid thirties, hair disheveled, two bullet holes back of the neck," the AME announces. "Powder burns, like they pressed the barrel against him. One of those little .22 jobbies they like to use. Blood spatter on the dash. Shooter probably in the back seat, grabbed him by the hair, yanked his head back, fired twice, then pushed him forward. I'd say ten, twelve hours since the kill."

They've already run the JADE-5 plate. The car's registered to a Mrs. May Wing Ho on Clay Street.

"Typical Chinatown mob hit," the lead detective tells Joel. His name's Kingston, he wears a flashy striped dress shirt, badge clipped to the breast pocket. "Way they do it they go out together, drink tea, tell jokes, everything ha-ha-ha. Then, soon as they get back into the car, the schnook"—Kingston gestures toward the corpse—"gets it fast. They drive to a garage, an alley, wherever, get out, walk away. Later when we check we find the car was stolen a few hours before. Or maybe it wasn't stolen. Maybe it was loaned. Doesn't matter. There's never any evidence, just a dead guy with a couple of holes in the back of his head. Sometimes it turns out he ran up heavy debt or tried to move in on an established gang. Half the time we can't even run a proper ID."

"Is that a real Rolex he's wearing?" Joel asks.

Kingston raises the victim's arm, expertly strips the watch off his wrist. "Hmmm. Sure looks like it." He reaches into the man's back trousers pocket, extracts a wallet. "Well, looky here." He shows us a wad of hundred-dollar bills. "So maybe this time it isn't an ordinary Chinatown hit . . ."

I tell Joel I feel like throwing up. He smiles, helps me back to his car. After I'm seated, he leans in through the window.

"I feel trapped down here . . . like we're in a tomb," I whisper.

"We are," he says.

"You got tipped on this. Doesn't that mean anything?"

"Kingston, unfortunately, isn't the brightest cop in town."

"You recognized the dead guy?"

Joel nods. "You're pretty sharp tonight. Yeah, he's a Wo Hop To waterfront big shot name of Kevin Lee. Which, considering what's been going on, makes sense."

"What kind of sense?"

"Human smuggling, animal smuggling, a big boat blown up off China Basin. Seems like someone's trying to bust up the Wo Hop To rackets. Whoever's tipping me is laying down a trail. If he can assassinate Kevin Lee, he's telling me, he can do anything he wants."

Joel tells Kingston what he knows, then drives me home. As we ascend toward the street I start feeling better. Out in open air I breathe deeply, delighted to be free.

"Soon, I think, our informant's gotta tell me what he wants," Joel says. "He's setting me up, wants me to be too scared to refuse."

"What could he possibly want, Joel?"

"I don't know. But next time he calls I'm going to have it out with him. I'm tired of this shit, kiddo." Joel's mouth is twisted, his eyes cold with anger. "I'm going to tell him time's come to cut the crap."

On Russian Hill, when I get out of the car, I'm reeling with paranoia. Joel shakes his head.

"Great evening, huh?"

"Yeah, great evening. Night, Joel."

I wait till he drives off, then enter my building. As I ascend in the elevator, I ask myself: Are we mad or is it just the world?

Tonight I dream of cruising endless lines of cars, passing opaque windows hiding dead people still in their seats, eyes frozen open, staring out, revealed only when I blast their windows with my strobe.

I'm lying on my back in a grove of sequoias in Jackson State Forest, have been hiding here since closing time, half sleeping, half resting on my bedroll a hundred feet off the trail so as not to be discovered by forest rangers on patrol.

My bike is stashed in brush nearby. The moon, just a crescent, casts dimly tonight, barely enough to break through the canopy. My eyes, open for half an hour, are totally adjusted to the darkness. Even with meager moonlight, my night vision is superb. I can make out a squirrel poised on a branch high above, the texture of bark on the tree trunks, an owl standing like a sentinel on a low branch of a baby sequoia sixty feet away.

I can also read. I complete a final review of Chap Fontaine's G.G.C. security map, refamiliarize myself with details I've been studying for a week, then check my watch. Two-thirty A.M. Time to start my trek.

It's a weekday night. G.G.C. security should be lax, with just a skeleton crew of guards. My objective: steal as close as I can to the main lodge, take photographs at first light of the site of the orgies and the duel, then get the hell out. Purpose: to later distribute said photographs to Carson and his group, showing them that their security's been breached and there's someone who knows what happened. This distribution, hopefully, will cause dissension, making some of Carson's friends rethink their loyalty. For, I've come to understand, if anything's to be proven, people who know are going to have to talk.

I roll the map into my sleeping bag, stash it with my bike, then cautiously make my way on foot out of the forest to the barbed-wire G.G.C. fence, the one Sasha and I found when we followed the crude map Hank Evans drew for us at the Paradise Saloon. I'm wearing a black turtleneck, black jeans, black baseball cap, black hiking boots. My expedition camera, one of Maddy's, is a battered old all-black Nikon-F loaded with high-speed film. I carry no ID, nothing except a compass, my watch and a canteen of water.

The fence is just where it's supposed to be. This time, with Fontaine's detailed G.G.C. security map etched into my memory, I know the precise route to follow. I walk

parallel to the fence a hundred paces until I find a segment where someone's cut out a lower strand. I kneel,
push my camera through, then lie on my back and slither
beneath.

Though just a couple of yards outside of the state forest,
I'm in a different world, on G.G.C. property, a trespasser.
Club guards have shot people for what I'm doing. G.G.C.
security policy is succinctly laid down in one of Chap
Fontaine's documents: "Assume all trespassers are poach-
ers and treat them accordingly."

The moon, I think, *shines upon me. I'll be protected by
the night.*

I follow the barbed wire for two hundred yards, until I
spot the padlocked gate Sasha and I saw before. Here I
crouch, listening for vehicles. I can hear nothing but the
squeaking of branches in the forest behind and the sounds
of birds and small nocturnal animals in the scrubwood
ahead. When I'm certain there's no one around, I set out at
a ninety-degree angle to the fence, hiking deep into G.G.C.
property. I'm looking for a hunter's path which, according
to Fontaine's map, runs parallel to the fire road that starts
at the padlocked gate.

When I find it, I halt and listen again, then follow it
north. It's a two-mile trek to the main clearing and club
lodge. Hiking slowly and very carefully, I expect to cover
the distance in an hour, then find a position from which to
take photographs. The trail is poorly kept, signifying it's
probably not patrolled. Several times I stumble on roots
across the path. Once I trip, lose balance, am forced to use
my hands to break my fall. Pushing aside branches, I try to
avoid them as they snap back. Still I'm lashed twice, once
across my left side, the second time across my shoulder,
neck and upper arm. The sting is terrific. It takes all my concentration to keep from crying out. I touch my neck, feel a
welt. Bringing my fingers to my lips, I taste blood. I stop,
open my canteen, sip water, then apply some to the cut.

I'm working my way down a slope toward a draw. As

the slope steepens, I step off the trail, make my way through brush toward the bottom of the gully, then work my way along it across a dry riverbed of stones. I've come down here to avoid the first danger point, a secondary fence that's electrified and crosses the trail. In the rainy season, I know, this gully embraces a rushing torrent. Now in summer it's bone-dry.

As I hike, I wince at the sound of my boots as I stride across the stones. Too loud. I pause again. I want to return to the trail, but not until I'm certain the security fence is far behind.

Suddenly, a noise not far from where I'm standing. A loud snort, then another, then the sound of hooves clumping through the brush. I freeze. A wild boar! I must have passed within a few feet of him. He saw me, broke when I stopped, perhaps afraid I'd turn upon him. I'm in hunting country now.

Three-forty A.M.: I've been hiking for over an hour. Still no sign of the main clearing. I've evaded two more security points located as marked on the map, but now seem to have lost my way.

I pause, peer around. There should be a gunning platform ahead. No sign of it . . . or anything else man-made. Yet according to my compass I'm on course.

There's an incline to my west where, according to the map, another trail leads straight into the main clearing. I decide to cross toward it through the brush, find it, then hike parallel to it. That way I should come upon the platform.

After a while I find myself on a rise, a small dry plain, sweetened by juniper trees and piñons. The land's quiet here. No sounds of animals, birds or leaves and branches rustling in the breeze. In fact the air has suddenly turned still, giving me an ominous feeling. I pause again, and just as I do, hear a harshly pitched rattle a few feet to my left.

I freeze, spot the source right away—a small rattlesnake, black and white rings on its tail, hexagrams on its back which I know are probably green. Mean and deadly, it's close enough to strike if it has a mind to, and being young, is probably capable of emptying all its venom at once. But I know it has no mind, just the attack instinct of a reptile. If I move too fast I may spook it. If I stay where I am it may strike. Seeing no stick around, I start to back off. With my eyes still on it, I stumble, nearly fall backwards. Just then I see it scurry away. Gone now, but I wonder what other nasty creatures await me ahead.

I'm back in woodland, can smell leaf mold, fungus, something wild and gamy too, perhaps the leavings of a bear or herd of deer. The gunning platform is straight ahead, about three hundred feet due west, visible against the night sky, black silhouette against dark gray field. There's a railing on top, and what looks like a set of military binoculars mounted on a swivel. I hope they're not the night-vision kind. There may be a guard up there, though I can't see him. Hard to imagine a man standing watch, still and alert at this hour.

I know I'm near the main clearing. I pause a moment to reorient myself, recall the route I chose on Fontaine's map. I want to gain the high ground overlooking the shooting range.

I'm feeling nervous, can hear my heart thumping in my chest. There are G.G.C. personnel within calling distance, dogs too, which worries me, though I know the kennel is upwind on the other side of the lodge. I should have brought pepper spray, I think.

I choose a vector that will cut no closer than a hundred feet to the platform, start along it, moving carefully, wary of snapping twigs. I advance a dozen yards, pause, then advance again. My vision is enhanced. I can see every leaf, weed and stick on the ground so clearly that I forget that a vision-normal wouldn't be able to see half as well.

Hearing nothing but the sounds of my body in motion, I work to keep my breathing steady. I'm anxious to reach a vantage point where I can lie down safely, then watch the club grounds for others.

I'm past the platform. The ridge I'm heading for is just seventy yards ahead. There's an open stretch before me. I speed up a little, anxious to cross it, find cover on the other side. I step out briskly, then start to jog. Suddenly the ground gives way. I'm suspended in midair. It's as if all motion has stopped. There's a moment of perfect clarity as I grasp what's happened, that I've stepped on some sort of false-floor animal trap, am about to fall into a pit.

I'm strangely calm as I contemplate the possibility of being impaled on sharpened stakes below. Then the moment dissolves, the clarity gives way to terror, I feel myself falling, then let out a shriek as the ground disappears.

I hit the bottom hard. I try to curl my body, roll with my fall as I do when thrown in aikido class, but the ground is no dojo mat, and my fall has been from too great a height. My shoulder smashes into the earth. I scream out an enormous "NO!" expecting to die. Then I lie still, on my side, hurting, the breath knocked out of me.

Hearing myself whimper, I turn, look up at the sky. The view is narrow. The pit I'm in is at least three times my height, and its sides are inclined to keep whatever falls into it from climbing out. I've fallen, I realize, more than fifteen feet straight down. The whole left side of my body aches; my ribs are bruised. I squirm a little to see if they're broken, then stop, the pain too great. Lying back, trying to regain my breath, I hear the sound of an approaching vehicle. A few seconds later two straight beams of artificial light cut across the top of the pit.

What we got down there, Buckoboy?"

"It's human. Least I think."

The beams of their flashlights find my face, saturating

my retinas, blinding me, forcing me to squeeze my eyes shut.

"Yep, human all right. Hey, Chipper! I think we caught us a girlie."

"Whoopee!"

They go silent. Even with my eyes tight shut, I can feel their scrutiny, the cool penetrating gaze one applies to a wild creature one has trapped who now lies vulnerable at one's feet. The gaze that those who possess power turn upon those who are powerless. That gaze of curiosity: What will the poor creature do, how will she react to her entrapment and pain?

"You all right, sweetheart?" the first one, the one named Chipper, inquires. His voice, reedy yet gentle, wafts to me at the bottom of the hole. "Broke a few bonies, did you?"

"Maybe," I whisper back.

"Well, least she can speak, Buckoboy."

"Yep, she can speak."

"Go back to the truck, cuz, get the rope ladder, we'll haul her out, see what we got. Something tasty we can roast up nice for breakfast, or maybe something gristly and mean that won't taste no good at all."

The one called Buckoboy hoots, then departs. Chipper removes the light from my eyes.

"Open them up, sweetie. Take a gander."

I carefully open my eyes, blink to clear them, stare up at him looming high above.

He looks to be in his forties. He's dressed in a black commando uniform, has a rough weathered face framed by a rough beard, and his smile's twisted, more like a leer than a grin. He holds a rifle crooked beneath his arm, which terrifies me. He speaks nicely, calls me "sweetie," but I detect menace in him and am afraid.

"I ain't no monster, honey peach. But you're in big trouble. This here's private property. So what brings a little girlie like you creepin' round these woods middle of the night?"

I gasp. "I'm a wildlife photographer."

"Oh, are you now?" His voice hardens. "Well, that *surely* explains it—how come you got in here, got past all our surveillance, got nearly to the clubhouse and no one detected nothin' till you fell in our creature pit. Must be you got supernatural powers, girlie." He pauses, waiting for his sarcasm to wither me. "What's your name?"

"Ellie," I lie.

"Ellie *what*?"

I think fast. "Ellie Bigelow."

"So, Ellie Bigelow, what're you doing here? Answer me! *Quick!*"

"Taking pictures." I reach beside me, hold up my camera. "I was going to wait till dawn, then try and get some shots of animals."

He laughs scornfully. "You know this is a private sporting club?" I nod. "You saw our no-trespass signs?" I nod again. "But still you came in."

He waits for my answer. "I'm sorry," I tell him.

"I just bet you are . . . *now!* 'Cause now you're in for it, Ellie girl."

"Please," I whimper.

"Please—*what*?"

"Let me go."

"Ha!" He leers. "Give me one good reason I should?"

I think of a reason. "I promise I'll leave and never come back."

Chipper hoots. "Oh, I *know* you won't come back." He hoots again. "Bet your sweet tush you won't! Not after we're done with you."

He backs out of my field of vision. I can hear him mumbling to Buckoboy, then the two of them whooping it up. I strain to hear what they're saying. Phrases waft down to me: "little cunt bitch," "teach her a lesson." They want me to overhear, want me to be terrified . . . and much as I'd like to stay cool, I'm scared out of my mind.

Buckoboy throws down a rope ladder, climbs down into the pit, pistol in his hand, tells me to relax, says he wants to check my injuries before he moves me out. Just the sight of his gun held so close sets me on edge. I stiffen as he runs his fingers along my rib cage, occasionally probing my flesh. I'd love to throw him down, could probably do it, but I know that, facing men with guns, submission's my only chance.

Actually his touch isn't too harsh, but he's an unattractive man with a crudely clipped beard like Chipper's, small piercing ratlike eyes and breath that stinks of stale cigarettes. I can smell his clothing, his sweaty uniform shirt. I tense at his touch but try not to recoil. Last thing I want is to antagonize him.

He nods at me, grins, then shouts up to his buddy. "Don't think there's nothin' broken on this one. No weapons on her neither."

Chipper responds. "Good, cuz. Bring her up."

"You climb all right?" he asks.

"I'll try."

"Take it easy, one step at a time. If you fall don't worry. Little thing like you, I'll catch you."

He offers me some water from his canteen. I sip. He urges me to take a good long drink. Grateful, I oblige. Then he takes away my camera and hoists me up.

"Climb," he orders.

I start up the rope ladder. Sore as I am, I think he's right, that I'm badly bruised but nothing's broken. Having gotten bruised plenty of times in aikido class, I recognize the pain, know there'll be big ugly blotches on my skin for days, maybe even weeks. But, I think, I've been incredibly lucky. Without serious injuries, I'll be able to move, fight them if I have to. Perhaps these guys aren't as mean as they look. Then, just as I reach the fourth rung of the rope ladder, Buckoboy swats me hard across my butt.

"Git movin', bitch! 'Less you want some help." He smacks me again. I hate him for humiliating me this way, feel like shoving my boot into his face. *Play it cool,* I tell myself. *He's got a gun. Find out what their game is before you take them on.* Obedient, I scamper up the ladder.

Soon as I reach the top, Chipper grabs hold of me, yanks me up by my arms, holds me out squirming in front of him, sets me down, grabs my hair, pulls on it harshly, then throws me on the ground. This time I have the presence of mind to roll.

"Well, looky that!" he exclaims. "Little acrobat, ain't she?" He steps over to me, lays his booted foot on my chest, presses down. "Obey orders, you won't get hurt," he warns sternly, shaking his rifle barrel in my face. "Disobey, try to 'scape, try any fuckin' thing, you *will* get hurt, understand?"

Panicked by the gun he's wagging in my face, I nod.

"Little bitty thing, ain't you?" He turns back to the pit, calls down to Buckoboy. "Get your ass up here, cuz. Help me tie her up." He laughs. "Then we'll take her in for some 'terrogation."

"Oh, that'll be fun!" Buckoboy calls back.

My inclination is strong: *I must not allow them to tie me up.* While Chipper holds his gun on me and Buckoboy approaches with strands of rope, I start backing off. Suddenly Chipper dives at me, tackles me, brings me down, pounces on me and, while I struggle and squirm, quickly and expertly binds my ankles, then my wrists behind my back. When I holler at them, call them names, Chipper kicks me in my sore bruised side. I let out a scream, then submit as Buckoboy turns me on my belly and hog-ties me.

"Goddamn, she's a fightin' cat!" Buckoboy says. "Scratch your eyes out, you let her."

They lift me, then toss me into the back of their pickup as if I'm a sack of cement. Squirming to find a comfortable position, I listen as they talk about me, extra loud to ensure

I overhear, calling me alternately "the dumb twat," "the little cunt," "the stupid poachin' bitch," making references to how they're going to slap me around, make me "beg for it," make me suck their dicks.

"She looks like she's sucked quite a few, don't she, Chipper?"

"You betcha! And I bet she's taken it up the ass plenty a times. She got that look."

Their hoots are too loud, their threats too transparent, but I'm scared anyway, feeling an undercurrent that belies their bantering style. They not only want to intimidate me, they're also sending me a message: I'm their prisoner; they can do anything to me they want.

"She could go to the cops, squeal on us, couldn't she, Chipper?"

"She won't. She knows we'll come kill her if she does. Plus we'll make sure she signs the standard release form 'fore we let her go. *If* we let her go. We could just throw her back in the pit, then plow maybe two tons of earth on top of her. She won't be goin' nowhere then, will she, cuz?"

I want to think it's a game, that they're only trying to frighten me, make sure I won't trespass on club grounds again. But their coarseness tells me they couldn't care less about protecting G.G.C. property, that they're more interested in having fun at my expense. They don't seem at all like the disciplined guards Sasha and I met when we came to the main gate. Those two, mean as they were, at least presented themselves professionally. These two act like rednecks about to slip out of control.

That's what's so scary . . . and that I'm hurt and sore and tied up so uncomfortably in the back of their ratty pickup . . . and that they have guns, that my head's starting to swell up, that I'm hit suddenly with a wave of fatigue, that at a time when I should be most on guard and alert, I'm feeling dizzy, sleepy, on the brink of losing consciousness.

"We could turn her into a deer, cuz. You know, glue a

pair of horns to her scalp, give her two minutes' head start, then track her through the woods."

Images flood in of the G.G.C. safaris, tales of hired vagrants stalked through the forest like game.

But I can't sustain my dread. I feel too weak, too drowsy. I try to fight off the drowsiness, focus on my predicament, but the more I do, the more I feel myself slipping away. Then, feeling their smirks as they stare down at me, I realize with a sudden final terrifying gasp of clarity that I've been drugged.

It was the water Buckoboy gave me, *his* water from *his* canteen. Something was in it. I feel sleepy and numb. I hear them laughing, open my eyes for a moment to catch the manic leering pleasure in their eyes ... then give myself over to whatever it was they put into me ... close my eyes, feel my brain turn to mush, listen to my moans as if they're coming from a great distance, then feel a great black cloak slowly covering me up.

Every once in a while I become aware of my surroundings, then fade out again. Intermittently I realize I'm in a high-ceilinged room, spread-eagled on a pool table. A brilliant light, painful to my eyes, blasts down on me from above. I'm nearly naked, bare to the waist, wearing nothing but panties below. I can feel the heat of the pool table lamp on my skin. The side where my ribs were bruised hurts so much the pain brings me around. I struggle to open my eyes, see the men who stand above me, whose presence I feel, whose voices I hear—though I can't decipher what they say. The light hurts too much, I can see nothing but whiteness. Snow-blinded, I shut down, lapse back into slumber.

I'm going to be *raped. I know it!* They're going to use me, then, fearful I'll bring charges, throw me back into the pit and cover me up with earth. I'm terrified. I start to wail, then feel a hand come down hard on my mouth.

"Shush up, bitch!"

I feel something cold and metallic pressed against my neck. I don't want to yield to them. I want to fight them. I struggle to lift myself . . . but cannot. I'm paralyzed.

I'm still on the pool table . . . and the room is filled with guns. Hundreds of guns everywhere, terrible, terrifying guns in racks that line the walls—rifles, pistols, revolvers, guns mounted with scopes, gleaming metal barrels, glistening wooden stocks, the smell of gun oil, gun grease, the aroma so thick I can barely breathe.

The gun in front of me, the one they taunt me with, is covered with human forms. Men and women, cut into the metal, writhe together in ecstatic bliss. Their faces are frozen but their burnished bodies contort while their metallic flesh comes alive with gun-oil sweat. Even when the metal flashes and blinds me, I'm enveloped in the aroma of their sex.

I feel the gun as it caresses me, feel the metal on my skin, the oil as it transfers to my flesh. I arch myself up against it, writhe to touch it when it's pulled away.

"Oh, she likes it, don't she, Buckoboy?"

"Real juicy, ain't she? Maybe she likes it too much."

"No such thing as too much, cuz."

When the metal touches me again, I moan and lie back, then seek refuge in sleep. Just before I fall off I hear a bee buzzing in my ear.

The man lies on his back. The woman lies on her back beside him, hand on his cock, drawing it into her. On the other side, two couples cavort, a woman penetrated by two men, one beneath her, the other above her, while a second woman, sitting beside the three, plays upon the organs of the males with her fingertips.

A revelation: it's *they* who writhe and arch, not me. How could I have gotten so confused? My thinking's fuzzy, my brain is fudge, my eyes see clearly one moment, are blinded the next. I hear the smooth sound of the action of a gun as the breech is opened, then snapped shut, hear the click of the trigger as it's dry-fired. They're torturing me with this gun, touching me with it, then pulling it away, rotating it before me so the light catches the engravings and burns them into my brain. And through it all I hear the buzzing of a bee.

Though I hate them for this, I allow my mouth to go slack. I want them to think I like what they're doing to me. Then my will goes lax again, I close my eyes and turn off my thoughts. A bee is hiding in the corner. I hide within my soul.

Nothing more frightening to me than a gun. Is this the gun Mom used to shoot herself? How would they get it? It couldn't be the same. But the terror remains. What is it I fear most? A gun. And now they're pressing one against my flesh.

They're talking about me. The blinding light is no longer on me. I struggle to open my eyes, see their faces.

There're four of them now, the two with beards—my captors, Chipper and Buckoboy—a third man standing in the shadows and another, clean-shaven, whom I've seen somewhere before.

I stay quiet so they won't notice me. Though they're talking about me, they're looking at one another. The clean-shaven man is bawling my captors out, telling them they're stupid, telling them they shouldn't have abused me.

"We didn't hurt her none, just tried to scare the bitch," Buckoboy whines.

"What're these marks on her then?" the new man demands.

"That's from when she fell into the creature pit," Chipper says.

"Why's she undressed?"

Suddenly I realize I'm fully naked.

"Well, we just thought, you know—"

"Put something on her, for Christ's sake!"

"Oh, yeah. Well, see, her clothes got kind of ripped and all."

"Then find her some new clothes, you moron."

"You oughtn'ta talk to me like that, Vince."

"I'll talk to you any fuckin' way I want."

I can feel the anger between them, am relieved it isn't directed at me. The clean-shaven man, Vince, is my guardian, come to rescue me from my captors. This time, when I return to sleep, I'm no longer so afraid.

I'm in a vehicle again, not the pickup but a regular car, lying across the backseat. I squint. The light's dazzling. Must be morning. I catch a glimpse of two men in the front. We're moving fast. I concentrate on the driver, squint again, then open my eyes for just an instant, long enough to catch a flash-look at Vince Carroll, the man I photographed behind Sasha at the traffic light that day that seems so long ago.

Maybe, I think, this is the same car. No, that was a pickup too. Why did I hear a bee? Was it buzzing or whispering? The car lurches. I feel soreness in my side. The sunlight's so powerful I shut my eyes.

Are they taking me somewhere to set me loose, then track me as if I'm wild game? Shoot me? Dress me? Roast and eat me?

Bury yourself in a dream and maybe the pain and fear will fade.

The car stops. The back door is opened. They lift me out carefully so my body doesn't touch the doorway.

In open air, I feel the heat of the sun. Now, I realize, I'm clothed. No sound of traffic. We must be far off the road. They carry me for a time. I can feel the coolness as we enter shade. Then they set me gently down on resin-scented earth. Even so, I moan when my sore side touches the ground.

"She'll be fine here," the second man says. I haven't heard his voice before. "She'll wake up, orient herself, follow the path, find the road, stick out her thumb, hitch a ride."

"Leave the camera beside her."

"You're sure, Vince?"

"I took the film out. She finds her camera she can't say she was robbed."

I feel them staring down at me.

"She's really out."

"Like a light."

"She'll be okay?"

"Should be."

"She didn't sign a release."

"Doesn't matter. She'll be confused, not sure where she was, what happened. She'll never be sure, really. It'll all be very vague."

"They didn't really hurt her, did they?"

"They were about to. They would've I hadn't showed up."

"They're goofballs, both of 'em."

"Imitating their bosses. Wish I could fire 'em. Can't. Mr. Carson likes 'em, plus they know too much."

"Well, good riddance to her."

"Yeah, we sure don't wanna see her round again."

They stare down at me awhile longer. I breathe evenly

as if sound asleep. One of them touches me gently with the toe of his boot. I react slightly without breaking the rhythm of my breathing. They study me some more; then I hear them walk away. I wait a long time, till all sound of them is gone, then I fall back into real sleep.

It's hot. The sun's drilling my eyes. I feel around for my shades, remember I left them with my bike. I sit up, squint, shield my eyes with my hands, gaze about.

I'm lying on pine needles in a glade surrounded by pines. Maddy's old Nikon is beside me and also my canteen. I'm enormously thirsty. I pick it up, unscrew the cap, take a gulp of water, then, remembering how I was drugged, spit it out. I can't drink now even from my own canteen in case they spiked it too. I pour some of the water on my hands, sniff it, then rub it on my face. I feel woozy, but don't want to sleep anymore. I check my wrist, find my watch. Four o'clock. I realize with horror it must be four in the afternoon.

I'm even more horrified to discover that the clothes I'm wearing aren't my own. The boots are mine, but the jeans and T-shirt are not. Pulling them off, I'm grateful that at least my underwear's familiar. I inspect the pants and shirt. Men's clothes, freshly washed, sized far too large. I check the pockets. Nothing. I put them back on, then struggle to stand.

I've got to get out of here. I'm desperate for water, afraid of dehydration. I'm also hungry, but that can wait. A measure of hunger, I know, can make me feel powerful. Thirst will only make me desperate.

I take a step forward, feel dizzy, go to a tree, lean against it for support. I don't want to sit, am afraid if I do I won't find the strength to rise again. I must have water. Do I dare drink from my canteen? If I drug myself again, I'll collapse, then . . . maybe . . . die. No! I must find my way out of here, find people, help . . . and water. Water most of all.

I shut my eyes, hold my right hand over them, slightly

scissor open my fingers and peer between. If I squint, then crack my eyes open for a fraction of a second, I can see enough to create an afterimage which I can use to guide me as I walk. Take a few steps, blink again, capture another image, take a few steps more. A tedious process, but with luck, I should be able to blink my way out of here.

There's a path. Must be the way they brought me in. Follow it and I should find a road. There'll be no shade outside the woods. In open sunlight it'll be nearly impossible for me to see. Should I wait here for dusk and risk further dehydration? Can't! Got to get out of here while I've still got strength. Got to find water, then help.

Farther down the path I gain the impression I'm in some kind of park. No redwoods, so it's not Jackson State Forest, but I know there're numerous public wooded areas in Mendocino County. If this is public land, there should be picnic tables, trash barrels, pay telephones. I don't see anything like that. I think that if I do find a phone, penniless though I am I can still call 911.

I'm outside the woods, standing beside a dirt road, hoping someone will come along and pick me up. But who would stop for me? I'm hideously dressed and must look a wreck. My lips feel cracked and I smell of sweat. Anyhow, there's no traffic, so I cross to the shady side. Right or left? The light's more oblique now. If I walk with the sun behind me, I'll be able to see a little better. I turn left.

After walking a mile, I catch a glimpse of a structure off the road. I find a dirt track and follow it in. The track leads me to a cabin. No sign of habitation. The door's bolted, windows shuttered. Probably someone's weekend camp.

I look around the back. The windows here are shuttered too. I find an outhouse and a canister of propane, which tells me there may be provisions inside. I look around some more, discover a woodpile, a rusty axe hidden within. I take the axe to one of the back windows, smash it against the shutter several times. Six hard strokes and I splinter the wood. Unfortunately the window behind is locked. No choice but to break the glass. I smash it with the axe, undo the clasp, open the window and peer in. The room is dark, welcoming darkness. I crawl through, search around, find a propane stove, two Coleman lanterns and, in a cupboard, ten full sealed plastic gallon bottles of springwater.

I grab one, rip off the plastic top, hold it to my lips, drink. It tastes wonderful. I take another gulp, savor it, swallow it slowly. Then I sit down on a stool and do some serious drinking. After guzzling a quart of water, I take a few deep breaths, then shake my head to clear out the sludge.

There should be food here. I search the cabinets, find assorted packages of pasta, cans of beans, sardines and tomatoes. I fill a pot with water, light a burner, set the pot to boil on the stove. Next I find a can opener, open the tomatoes, put them in a saucepan, heat them up. I find a bathtub, beside it a barrel of what I assume is old rainwater. I strip off my clothes, stand in the tub, ladle water over my body, soap up and rinse. By the time I've washed, toweled off, found some men's clothes that fit me better than what I've been wearing, my pasta water is boiling. I cook up some spaghetti, cover it with heated canned tomatoes and devour my first meal in more than twenty-four hours.

Now that I'm clean, thirst and hunger assuaged, with the numbness caused by the drug quickly wearing off, I pace the cabin trying to reconstruct events.

I'm certain I wasn't raped, though I know I was threatened with rape, and that's illegal. I also know I was held captive and drugged against my will, and that's illegal too. I know further that I was caught trespassing on private land and because of that my hands aren't clean. Above all else, I know that the treatment I received at the hands of G.G.C. employees was odious beyond anything I've ever experienced.

Seething, I pick up the axe, am about to smash it into the cabin floor. I stop myself. I've done enough damage here. If I hadn't found this place, I'd still be wandering around. Thank God for this cabin, the water and food. Now . . . if I can only figure out where I am.

In one of the drawers I find a sheet of directions instructing weekend guests how to find the cabin. Studying the document, I realize I'm less than a mile from a paved road. I wash out my canteen, refill it with bottled spring-water, straighten up the cabin, scribble a note apologizing for breaking in, borrowing clothes and using provisions. I promise to pay for all the damage, sign the note, give my phone number and address, then close up the smashed shutters as best I can and walk back out the drive.

It's twilight. My vision's good. I'm striding fairly well. I feel much better, though there's still some cloudiness in my head. As for my anger, I try to put it aside.

I find the road, flag down the first vehicle that comes along. To my amazement, it stops. I run forward. It's a battered Ford Taurus with a young couple inside.

"Where you goin'?" asks the woman. She's got freckles and a friendly smile.

"Nearest public phone."

"We're headed for Fort Bragg."

"Fort Bragg'll be great!"

She exchanges a glance with her husband. He shrugs.

"Well . . . get in," she says.

I love you, people! "Thanks!"

Her name's Clarice. She chatters nonstop. I let her words wash over me while I think about what I'm going to do. Two things seem most important: report what happened to the cops, then retrieve my bike, bedroll, wallet and G.G.C. map from where I stashed them in Jackson State Forest.

Except I begin to wonder whether going to the cops is

such a good idea. I was a trespasser in possession of a G.G.C. security map. My intrusion into club property was obviously planned. How can I explain what I was doing there and why? Also, from what I've read, the G.G.C. is tight with local enforcement. Poachers have been shot, at least three have been killed; an unknown number of vagrants have been hunted down by G.G.C. shooting parties; a club officer and founder was possibly murdered in a duel on the firing range . . . yet, for all this, no club member or staff person has ever been arrested.

Still, impossible for me to accept what I endured. I simply can't let it go, thankful I wasn't raped or killed. The stuff Buckoboy and Chipper did to me, the attitude that made their abuse possible—that had to come from the top. A so-called gentlemen's shooting club that holds solstice orgies and sponsors guns-and-sex parties in the Capp Street apartment, that shoots poachers dead and partakes in manhunts is an environment where the worst kind of staff abuse is possible.

I sit up straight! Clarice is still gabbing but I don't hear a word. I'm thinking about what I saw that night from the Wongs' attic: the standing man, dressed in black, shoving the pistol into the mouth of the woman naked and on her knees. Then what Baggy Bigelow and Agnes Fontaine told me about Ramsey Carson's collection of guns engraved with erotic scenes. And then about the gun I saw when I was spread-eagled and drugged on the pool table in the club lodge, the gun they pressed against me, the gun I feared they would use to probe me . . . on which I saw naked men and women having sex.

Yes, what was done to me *did* come from the top. And what *might* have been done to me—that too! Vince Carroll told his buddy I'd wake up confused, wouldn't remember anything. Which must be why he thought it was okay to dump me in the woods without even a sealed bottle of water by my side. All that, I think, will have to be avenged.

". . . well, here we are, good old Fort Bragg," Clarice says. "Where should we drop you?"

"Paradise Saloon'll be fine."

A minute later they stop in front. I get out, thank them, wait till they pull away, then turn and enter the bar.

Bartender Joe, he of the drooping mustache and samurai topknot hair, doesn't recognize me at first. When I remind him, he smiles warmly.

"Yeah . . . sure . . . you and the Indian guy—I remember now. I set you two up with Hank and Gale."

For which, I tell him, I'm most grateful. I lean forward.

"I'm in trouble, Joe. Lost my wallet, got roughed up. Now I don't even have a quarter to make a call."

"No problem!" He slaps a ten-dollar bill down on the bar.

I thank him, but tell him a quarter's all I need, just something to put in the phone so I can get hold of an operator and place a call to Sasha collect . . . after which his quarter'll be returned.

He lays four quarters on top of the ten. "Pay phone's back by the toilets." He points the way.

Sasha picks up on the first ring. I tell him everything that happened. His groans of sympathy nearly break my heart.

"You should go straight to a hospital," he advises. "How can you be certain you weren't raped?"

"A woman knows."

He mulls that over, acknowledges that a woman probably does.

"They must have dissolved roofies in that water."

"Roofies?"

"Rohypnol, also called flunitrazepam. Someone doped with it wanders into our ER about once a week. It's like Valium, but ten times stronger. Knocks you out, clouds your brain. Know what they call it? 'The date-rape drug of choice.' "

I wince.

He tells me Rohypnol washes out of the system quickly, after which there's no evidence it was ever imbibed.

"If you want to bring charges, you should be tested right away. And even though you took a bath I still think you should get swabbed."

He goes quiet when I tell him I'm not going to a hospital and to please stop telling me I should. Also that I have no intention of bringing charges and why.

I ask him to give me Hank Evans's number so I can call and ask if he and Gale can put me up for the night. He finds Hank's number, reads it off to me.

"I love you, Kay. I worry about you," he says. "If anything happened to you—" I hear him choke up.

"I did something stupid," I tell him. "But now I'm safe. I'll deal with those G.G.C. bastards my own way."

I put down the phone, sob a little, catch my breath, then dial Hank's number. Gale picks up.

"We were talking about you just the other night," she says. When she tells Hank I'm on the line, he picks up the extension. After hearing my story, he says he'll be by in five minutes. I should wait for him out front.

When I try to return the ten dollars to Joe, he holds up both hands.

"No way!"

"You don't even know me, Joe."

"I like you just the same."

"What if I'm conning you?"

He laughs. "All the better. You need ten bucks that bad I'm glad to be the one gets conned."

Hank pulls up in a dark pickup just as I step out of the bar. He jumps out of the cab, wraps me in a big bear hug, the kind Dad always gives me, then hustles me into the truck, slams the door, peels off.

"Asshole bastards!" he says, apropos of the G.G.C. guys. "If I knew where to find 'em, I'd haul 'em out now and shoot 'em." He looks at me. "Why didn't you call me,

Kay? I'd have gone in with you. Armed too. With me along they'd never have gotten the drop on you." He pauses, gives me another glance. "It wasn't wild game you were looking to photograph, was it?"

"No," I tell him, "it was something else."

I like him enormously for not asking me what, not trying to coax out my secret. He just smiles slightly to himself, then praises me for getting as far as I did.

"You must be some kind of tracker."

"Not really. I had a security map. I memorized it. But the pit wasn't on it."

"Goddess security map—hot damn!"

He pulls up in front of a small wood shingle house on a street of other small wood houses set close together. There's a neat little front yard surrounded by a dog fence. Hank opens the gate, beckons me through. I hear a dog bark inside.

"Sure'd like to see that map sometime if you'd be willing to show me, Kay."

I turn to him at the front door. "You got it, Hank. It's yours."

Gale hugs me while their dog, a cocker spaniel, dry-humps my leg. Gale calls off the pooch, then stands back.

"You don't look too bad 'cept for the clothes. I'll fix you up with some of my stuff, at least get you into a pair of decent-fittin' jeans."

She's warmed up some lasagna for me, left over from their dinner. She beckons me into the kitchen, sits me down at the kitchen table, serves me. She and Hank sip beers while I eat.

Soon I'm blabbing away to them the way Clarice babbled to me in the car, telling them what I was really up to. After I've eaten we adjourn to their living room, outfitted with beautiful handmade furniture fabricated by Hank, a padlocked gun rack filled with shotguns and hunting rifles, and a second case containing finely wrought hunting bows.

"I know that Vince Carroll," Gale says. "He and my

brother played high school football together. Carroll used to be a deputy sheriff. Pretty nice guy. So now he's working for the Goddess . . ." She shrugs. "Go figure."

We talk some more. When Gale excuses herself to make up my bed, Hank offers to show me his den. He leads the way down to the cellar, through his woodwork shop, then to a padlocked door. He unlocks it, beckons me into a windowless room.

Here one wall is lined with books on the Vietnam War, the other with his collection of war souvenirs—photos of his fellow Lurp mission buddies, a captured Viet Cong flag, assorted VC arms and a half-dozen assault weapons including, he tells me, an M-79 grenade launcher.

"Some of this stuff's illegal," he says. "So, see, I don't take just anyone down here." He pauses. "You told me some of your secrets, so it's only right I show you some of mine."

"There's more?" I ask.

Hank grins. "Grenades, ammo, explosive matériel. After Ranger training they sent me to demolition school. That was the best part of it over there—blowing stuff up."

In the morning we drive to Jackson State Forest, hike in, find my bike and bedroll just where I left them. I ride the bike out, wait for Hank in the parking lot. He loads it into the back of his truck, then we drive back into Fort Bragg. I insist we stop at a print shop on the way to make him a copy of the G.G.C. map. We spread the map open, copy it in sections, then tape them together. Back in the truck, Hank studies it with the intensity of a pro.

"Yeah," he says, "uh-huh . . . um, interesting. They got themselves a sweet setup all right . . . but nothin' that can't be penetrated. Tell the truth, in military terms their security sucks. Like these sentry positions. I see about six different ways past. Army officer did it this way he'd get court-martialed after the attack. But course they're not expecting a real assault." He laughs. "They just wanna keep poachers out, and anyone who's heard rumors about their goings-on and gets too curious for his own good. But one guy equipped right, he could do damage in there. Create some real havoc, Kay. Wipe the whole damn Goddess off the map he had a mind to."

We return my rental bike; then he takes me to the bus stop, waits with me until my bus arrives.

"Got three pump-outs to do today," he tells me, "at a hundred per. Get paid per job, not the hour. Nasty work, but the compensation's good."

When the bus comes, he hugs me tight.

"Let me know, Kay, when you decide what you're gonna do," he whispers. "It'll be my pleasure to help you out. Two of us could have a helluva time in there. Get you some good payback while we're at it."

4

THE

BEE

My first couple of days back, I'm filled with rage, so irritable and angry I'm impossible to be with . . . and know it too.

"We're going to get you through this," Sasha says. "We'll do it together. Talk about it, open yourself up, don't be afraid to cry."

Waking up at his place, suddenly, in the middle of the night, I take him at his word, grasp hold of him, sob against his chest.

"I hate being a crybaby," I tell him in the morning.

"Don't think about it. Let yourself grieve."

And so I do, grieve for my loss of control, for allowing myself to be humiliated and abused.

"You didn't 'allow' it," Sasha says. "They drugged you, forced you."

"I hate them for their power, hate myself for giving in to it. I shouldn't have accepted their water, should have fought them from the start. I hate myself for being afraid of their guns."

I know that what I'm feeling is crazy, that my game

plan, if caught, was always to play fearful, submissive, dumb. But I still can't forgive myself for being
captured, even though I know if I'd fought them, banged
up as I was, I'd have probably gotten shot.

I turn up for aikido class midafternoon and again in
the evening.

Rita notices. "Training tough," she comments. "Committing to going for your *shodan*."

I neither nod nor shake my head, just show her an enig-
matic smile.

"Good, Kay!" she says. "Keep your own counsel."
Then she smiles to herself. I know what she's thinking:
Two can play the enigma game.

Sore as I am, I start slamming my practice partners
hard. They don't like it, and when their turn comes to be
the *nage,* those who are skilled treat me the same way.
Which is exactly what I want—to hurt, have my face
smashed into the mat. Throw and be thrown, slam and be
slammed—harsh training purges me, the pain releases me
from the anger I hate carrying around.

This evening, when I'm particularly rough on Phil, a
third kyu blue belt, a golden-boy type with the shag-cut
locks of a Greek god, Rita intervenes.

"You're getting to be one mean aikido bitch," she tells
me. "So let's see how bad you really are."

She orders me to come at her. I attack with all my might.
She throws me down so hard the breath's knocked out of
me, and the bruises, from the banging I took in the forest,
are reinflamed. Out of pride and to show her how little effect
her slam has on me, I spring up and go at her violently again.
Again she slams me down, again, again . . . and again. Soon
others in the class stop training to watch us, aware something serious is going on. A battle of wills between student
and sensei. There can be only one ending to that.

Rita goes about her task methodically, half-amused

expression on her face. *Okay,* her body language says, *you want to train with emotion, I'll show you real aikido power.*

She throws me, then tiger-walks around my fallen form. After the sixth very hard throw, I'm no longer able to spring up. When I do regain my feet, I'm angry, dizzy, hurting, panting hard. But the angrier and hotter I get, the cooler she becomes. Her wrist-holds turn painful. Even when I signal submission, she applies extra pain before granting release.

Now the entire class has stopped practice, spellbound by our show. No way I, a mere first kyu brown belt, can successfully attack a fifth-degree black belt. But still I try, reveling in the futility of my effort, eagerly plunging toward my inevitable defeat.

Suddenly, understanding me better than I understand myself, Rita changes tactics. She starts putting me down gently, after which she softly pats the top of my head. I can't bear such kindness. It's her tenderness that finally breaks me. When I start to weep, she pulls me up, embraces me.

"It's all right," she whispers. "You're through it now. It's over."

She releases me, calls the class into position, assigns a new exercise, then sends me to the side of the mat to do *ki*-flow exercises to regain stability.

After training she calls me into her office.

"Sit down, girlfriend. Tell me what's going on. Where's all this anger coming from?"

I tell her the essence of what happened up in Mendocino. I don't go into detail, just tell her I was caught someplace I wasn't supposed to be, was drugged, stripped and taunted.

"Soon as they figured out I was squeamish about guns, they ran one all over my body. They wanted to terrorize me." I look down. "I just wish—"

"What, Kay?"

"I don't know. Maybe, if I can get over that fear, I can start to deal with my anger."

She gives me an intense look. "How 'bout learning to shoot?"

The thought never entered my head. But the moment she verbalizes it, I feel it's something I must do. It's as if she knows instinctively what I need.

"I have a friend who specializes in teaching women how to use a gun. We served together in the Marines, taught together in Quantico. She's a master of weaponcraft and a terrific instructor. Now, like me, she's got her own school."

Rita writes out her friend's name, telephone number, an address in Nevada County, then hands me the slip of paper.

"Dakota Kass—is the name for real?"

"Oh, Dakota's definitely for real. Think it over. If you really want to get over your fear of guns, her classes are good as it gets."

I call Dad at his bakery, ask if he's free for dinner.

"Sure, darlin'. Want to do Chinese?"

We agree to meet tomorrow night at the Tan Yuet on upper California near where he lives.

In the darkroom, I print up enlargements of the shots I took of Vince Carroll at the traffic light the day Sasha and I tracked him in his car. After the prints are washed, I squeegee them, then study them as they dry.

Carroll has a pleasant, clean-shaven, all-American face—clear eyes, even features, the face of a respectable thirty-something member of the community. He could be a shop-keeper, small-businessman, even a deputy sheriff or security director at a private club. No hint of menace or of the tomcat-ting aspect his sister referred to when I phoned. Still, I can see why women might find him attractive. There's an inten-sity in his gaze, a willfulness in the set of his mouth. I also note the way his biceps bulge in his sleeves, and the tufts of light chest hair that show in the open V-neck of his shirt.

My savior or my nemesis? He rescued me from Chipper and Buckoboy, but thought nothing of dumping me, however gently, in the woods. He's in awe of Ramsey Carson, does his bidding, won't fire Chipper and Buckoboy because Carson likes them. The Capp Street apartment is listed in his name, and he was on the G.G.C. firing range when Chap Fontaine was killed.

I study his face, seeking some glimmer of pity, some little corner of contrition. I want to find a suggestion of the shared humanity I see in Dad and the faces of the many cops I've known, but all I can find are blank good looks.

So, who is he, I wonder—friend or enemy? Enemy, I decide, but one I may just be able to use.

I finish drying the prints, choose the most engaging one, turn it over, pick up a black grease pencil, write a note on the back in big block letters:

> *HI VINCE! NICE OF YOU TO GIVE ME BACK MY CAMERA. REAL CONSIDERATE ACT. IN RETURN HERE'S A <u>SHOT</u> I TOOK OF YOU THE OTHER DAY. I'LL BE IN TOUCH. YOUR SECRET ADMIRER.*

I reread my message, decide the tone's just right— brazen, sarcastic, slightly threatening too. Best of all, it sends a message: "I know who you are and where you live, which is more than you know about me. You're vulnerable, pal, so watch your back."

I scribble his name and North Ridge Drive address on the front of an eight-by-ten envelope, slip the photo inside, seal it, then drop the packet in the mailbox across the street.

I struggle to remember my ordeal in the gun room— what was said, done, what I saw and heard. My recollections are fragmentary, little bits and pieces as I slipped in and out of consciousness: metallic men and women writhing in erotic embrace; my tormentors' laughter; the smell of gun oil; the chill of the gun barrel as it grazed my flesh; flashes of steel blinding my eyes; a bee buzzing in my ear.

Sasha tells me that Rohypnol distorts perceptions, suppressing, exaggerating, creating a surreal nightmare world. As in a German expressionist film, he says, or a painting by Magritte. But still I feel there's something I saw, felt or learned in that room that imparted an important message, a secret hidden in my unconscious which I must drag out.

THE GUN/FIND THE GUN/WHERE'S THE GUN?

Maddy's words are now mine too. Find the gun, trace the gun, discover the meaning of the gun . . . then, maybe, my confusion will resolve.

I know that Ramsey Carson collects rare erotic guns, and that I, bound to the pool table, was taunted with exactly that kind of weapon. And that because I was in a drugged state, the characters engraved into the metal came alive, moved, screwed, even beckoned me into their orgy, and the glade in which their revelries took place became real as well. I smelled sweet air, heard whispering grass, saw butterflies flit, birds alight, was dive-bombed by a bee. Gun oil became sweat, gun grease became secretions, cocks swelled, labia opened and, throughout my ordeal, the bee hummed a message into my ear.

Follow me, it droned. *Follow me and I shall lead you to the honey.*

I phone Dakota Kass. Her voice-mail message is no-nonsense. I leave my name and number. An hour later she calls back.

"Rita told me about you," she says, "that you're uptight

around guns. I've had other students with that problem, cured most of them of it pretty well."

"Can you teach me how to shoot?"

"That's what I do, Kay. That and how to handle your-self in self-defense combat situations. Give me your address and I'll send you our brochure."

I ask when her next class cycle begins.

"There's still room in an intensive four-day course weekend after next. We can supply you with a gun and holster if you don't have one. Let me know. Classes fill up pretty quick."

Tan Yuet's one of those Hong Kong–style fish restaurants that look like nothing when viewed from the street. The usual Formica tables, overfilled aquaria, noise and chaos . . . until you sample the food. Then you can't imagine eating anyplace else. Salt-and-pepper-fried shrimp, smoked black cod, steamed flounder with black mushrooms and ginger—Dad loves it all.

After we give our order, the owner comes over to say hello. Dad introduces him, a handsome guy with sharp fea-tures and precision-cut black hair. His name's Jimmy Sing; he used to be a San Francisco cop. His sister, Soo-Lin, is married to Dad's former partner, Rusty Quinn.

Mr. Sing winks at me. "All very incestuous," he says. "Your dad and I both left S.F.P.D., both found new careers in food and couldn't be happier for the change."

When he moves away, I ask Dad what caused Jimmy to leave the Department.

"Caught with his hand in the cookie jar." Dad laughs. "Jimmy turned out to be a lot better restaurateur than he was a cop."

Dad's skeptical when I broach the shooting course, but once he hears my reason, he gives his blessing.

"I could teach you to shoot, darlin', but I think your

phobia's best dealt with by someone else." He looks at me. "Why now—if you don't mind my asking?"

I decide not to recount my experience in Mendocino, afraid he'll rush up there and confront Chipper and Buckóboy in a rage. He's always been protective of me, feeling my hurts, identifying with my vision problems, helping me learn to cope. The day Mom killed herself he waited for me outside the Art Institute in the rain, stood out on the sidewalk on Chestnut Street until class broke. Then, when I appeared, he took me in his arms, held me as he told me the sorrowful news.

"Time to get over it," I tell him, "time to face my demons."

Dad nods approval. "You're gutsy, darlin'. Always were." He looks at me closely, lowers his voice. "You seem to have gotten over the Sanchez thing pretty well."

"Thanks to you!"

At the end of the meal I ask if he remembers how he got me Vince Carroll's name.

"Sure, Rusty dug that up."

"Well, turns out Carroll's not in the dope business like you and Rusty thought. He's ex–law enforcement, used to be a deputy sheriff. Do you think Rusty could find out a little more about him?"

"Shouldn't be a problem, darlin'. I'll call him tonight. Rusty loves to snoop around."

The Personal Security Ranch brochure arrives, containing a number of photos of Dakota Kass, a petite woman, about my size and build—blond, intense, a bundle of coiled energy, decked out in cowgirl clothes: buckskin jacket, western boots, wide-brimmed hat. She looks good in combat stance holding out her gun. The cost of her four-day extended-weekend course is six hundred dollars, ammunition extra, lunches included. There's a special double-occupancy rate for students at a nearby motel, or, for those willing to rough it, free bunk space in an outbuilding at the school plus a moderate surcharge for meals.

I call her, tell her I want to sign up for the course and that the bunkhouse accommodation will be fine. When I mention I'm nervous, she assures me I'll get over it quick.

"You were probably nervous the first time you walked into Rita's dojo," she says. "But once you stepped onto the mat, you were too busy for stress. It'll be the same thing up here."

The bad dreams continue, the partially recollected nightmare of my ordeal. Though determined to crack the code of the gun, find the key to my lost memory, I find myself stymied, the secret still elusive, hovering just beyond my reach.

Sasha, intent on helping me work it out, suggests I try and draw what I saw.

"I'm a photographer," I remind him, "not a draftsman."

"Surely you took drawing class at art school?"

"Yeah . . . but it's been years."

"Were you good?"

"Not bad."

"Well then, why not try it?"

I shrug. Maybe he's right. Since writing often clarifies my thinking, perhaps drawing will do the same. Then I laugh. "I know why you want me to draw the gun. You want to see what those erotic engravings are about. As if you need any ideas along those lines, Sasha!"

This morning I put on my heavy shades, then walk down to the Art Institute. At the supply store, I buy a sketchbook and a good set of charcoal drawing crayons.

Returning to my apartment, I set to work trying to re-create the scenes on the gun.

My first efforts are pathetic. I draw the people as stick figures. Then, when I try to refine them, the women come out looking like pinup girls and the guys like cartoon hunks. I rip out the sheets and tear them in half. The figures weren't like that at all, they were beautifully, indeed superbly, engraved.

By midafternoon I'm satisfied I've got at least one scene down fairly well: a woman sandwiched between two men, their six legs emerging at divergent angles from the sprawl, while a second nude woman sits beside them tickling their genitals, the focus of the composition.

Having gotten the figures right, I do my best to re-create the setting—trees, grass, a sylvan glade.

Working on these elements, I suddenly remember the setting wasn't woodsy, rather was a clearing in a jungle, with numerous animals—monkey, fox, leopard, gazelle and variety of birds—curiously watching the humans cavort.

Recalling the detailed manner in which the animals were engraved, I try sketching them on separate sheets. There was, I remember, something special about them, a strong particularity and an intensity about their collective gaze.

Again, my first efforts are poor, the animals coming off like creatures in a comic strip. But as I work I realize that though they were better drawn, they were rendered a little like cartoons. It was their faces, I remember, that were individualized . . . in the manner of cartoon animals. Then I get it! They had human features incorporated into their animal faces. Though they were unmistakably animals, their countenances were portraits, so well drawn there could be no question that they were based on real people. So—four faceless humans having sex in a clearing, observed by a virtual zoo of human-faced animal-voyeurs hidden in the foliage.

Whose faces? I wonder. G.G.C. members? Ramsey Carson's "inner circle"? Whoever, they were expertly transposed by the engraver. Then I wonder: *Was this the gun that Maddy was looking for?*

Tonight I drop in on Sasha, show him my drawings. He's entranced.

"You draw beautifully, Kay."

I nod. "I forgot how much I used to like it. I could never paint. The colors always defeated me. But drawing was something I could do as well as anyone. So I worked hard at it. Then, in art school, I got interested in sculpture— which is also monochromatic. I wanted to be a sculptor till I discovered black-and-white photography. Until last night, I doubt I've drawn anything since sophomore year."

He holds up the jungle scene. "Quite a picture!"

"Yes, and the engraving's even better. Whoever did it was a real artist. I think this scene's the main panel on one side of the gun. There's another jungle scene on the other side, plus smaller scenes on top of the lever, the bottom plate and the trigger guard. There's also scrollwork, phalluses and vulvae, beautifully stylized, repeated over and over as a motif. The engraving's highly erotic, but I wouldn't call it pornographic. It's not vulgar. In fact, it's extremely refined. The best sort of erotic art really, except there's something creepy about it when you see it on a gun."

Sasha nods. "The eroticism of violence." He takes my hand, brings it tenderly to his lips. "Even touching you with it, they were committing a kind of rape."

"Yes," I murmur sadly. "That's what it was. Which is why I hate them more than I can say."

We go out to dinner in North Beach. Finding a free table at Rose Pistola, we order a half-bottle of sauvignon blanc, a split bowl of pasta rags with pesto and a plate of deep-fried anchovies.

We talk while we wait for our food.

"You're sure it was a real bee?" Sasha asks.

"Of course! Why not? Bees fly in through windows, then get trapped. I remember—this one dive-bombed my head."

"Could it have been a fly?" he asks.

"No way!"

The bee bothers me. Its buzz was so loud it's hard to believe it wasn't real. True, in my delirium that night I thought I could hear the sounds of the jungle, the chirping of the watcher-animals, the heavy breathing and moans of the lovers in the glade. But on some instinctive level I believe the bee must be the key. It was too prominent, too pervasive, buzzed too loud, I remember it too well.

Sasha, understanding my frustration, suggests I try and free-associate.

"You mean like this: Bee, bees, hive, honey, sting, queen, drone . . . sex?"

He raises an eyebrow. "Is that where the bee leads you?"

"The context was erotic."

"Give it another try."

"Hmmm. Bee, hive, honey, honeycomb, honeydew, honeysuckle, honeymoon . . . sex."

He laughs. "You're hilarious."

Later that night, after gently making love to me, Sasha, who's been quietly thoughtful since dinner, turns to me in the dark.

"I wonder if you're a synesthete."

"Jesus!" I turn to him. "What's that?"

"I already know you are—the way you 'hear' colors, associate them with musical instruments."

"The crimson sound of flutes, the gold of clarinets."

He nods, pats my hand. "Don't worry—synesthesia isn't a disease. It's not even a psychological condition. Just a phenomenon certain people experience, a crossover of the senses. Some synesthetes 'hear' colors. Others 'taste' sounds. Or they associate a particular shape with a particular word. A synesthete might say, 'This chicken tastes too round.' "

"That's kinda poetic."

"Often it is. Drugs such as LSD and Ecstasy can cause synesthesia. Rohypnol too. It's known to distort, exaggerate, transform sounds into visions, visions into tastes and smells. So I'm thinking—why not the reverse?"

"You're saying I made up the sound of the bee?"

"Not at all. I think you converted it from something you saw. I think you saw a bee somewhere on that gun, and the image got transferred in your mind into the sound of a bee buzzing in your ear."

I'm excited hearing this, but still confused. "Why just the bee?" I ask. "Why not all the other creatures on the gun?"

Sasha smiles, the smile of a wise psychiatrist. "What was so special about that bee? That's what you have to discover. My suggestion is stop puzzling over the sound. Instead draw the bee, draw it over and over until the image tells you why you converted it."

Dad calls. Rusty ran a background check on Vince Carroll. Dad gives me the results.

"You were right, darlin', Carroll was a deputy sheriff, pretty good one too, it turns out. He was doing fine, on the promotion fast track, then it all went sour. Happens to the best of 'em. This was a police brutality case with Carroll the key witness. Seems one night his partner got drunk, arrested a suspect and beat him . . . which, maybe, wouldn't have been so bad except the arrestee was innocent. Carroll tried to stop him, the partner turned on Carroll, knocked him out. At the trial, Carroll told the truth, his buddy went to prison, three years state time, which made Carroll a snitch. He stuck around, but no one would work with him. Eventually he was forced to quit. Then, like a typical out-of-work cop, he got depressed, got divorced, began to drink. He'd about hit bottom when he lucked into a good job, security director for a gunning club. The money was good too, lots more than a deputy makes. But they say something changed in him. He started out this straight-arrow type, incorruptible, pure blue flame of justice, but after the trial he turned bitter, told his friends it wasn't worth being a good cop, no one appreciated it, no one cared about anything except greasing his own wheel. He also went around saying everyone in county law enforcement was on the take from the marijuana growers, talk that didn't make him very popular. That's about it, darlin'. People Rusty talked to say Carroll's not a guy to mess with. I'd stay away from him I were you. I know his kind. Got a lot of rage bottled up. You open the bottle, the rage flies out, then anything can happen."

If you don't drive a car, it's a long trip to Nevada City. I take a Greyhound to Sacramento, change for Reno, get off at Auburn, pick up the local Gold Country line that takes me into the historic center of town. From here, as instructed, I call Personal Security Ranch from a pay phone. Twenty minutes later a guy in a cowboy hat pulls up in a dusty pickup. He gestures for me to jump in.

His name's Mike, he's about my age. As we drive I'm able to get a few things out of him, namely that he's "Miss Dakota's" number-one ranch hand and Mr. Fix-it, doing most everything around her place from gunsmithing to heavy labor. Also, that he's got an M.A. in comparative lit from Yale.

"Dakota's the finest tactical handgun instructor I ever met," he tells me. "Great shot too. No one, man or woman, can outgun her. Not even me, and I tell you, I'm pretty damn good. I got nothing but respect for the lady. You come to her green, you leave combat-trained. She works your butt off, but when you leave you know your stuff."

Sounds good to me.

We wind our way through the hills, past deserted mines, then descend into a valley on a dirt road. It's rugged country, the road's powder, we raise a trail of dust. The Sierras loom above us, majestic peaks, snowcapped in winter and, Mike tells me, so colorful in autumn people come from all over the West to view the foliage.

He turns to me. "You're color-blind, aren't you, Kay?" I nod.

"Dakota told me. Shouldn't affect your training though. You get your sight-picture right, you got it made." He makes a pistol out of his hand, fires off three mock shots. "Do the ol' Mozambique!" And then, before I can ask him what he means, he announces: "Well, here we are."

We drive in through a cow gate. Personal Security Ranch, it turns out, occupies what was once a kids' summer camp. Many of the wooden structures, bleached and baked dry by the sun, are partially decomposed, but the main building, a ranch house, has been nicely restored.

Dakota Kass opens the door. At first I don't recognize her. Though she's wearing a holster and gun, she appears smaller and more feminine than in the photos in her brochure. Perhaps it's her hair. Now it hangs free, swings as she moves, while in the photos it was tied back. Also, in the photos she wore shooting glasses and ear protectors, and stood in aggressive combat postures.

She greets me with a smile. "Come meet the others," she says.

We enter a main room decorated with ceramics, saddles, horse blankets, a rack of rifles and a large painting of a historical Native American encampment. Five women stand about awkwardly, sipping Cokes and beers. I'm rapidly introduced to Cheryl, Diane, Caroline, Lydia and Liz. Four more will be joining our class, Dakota tells me, making a total of ten.

While Dakota confers with Mike, I mingle with the women, all of whom wear holstered side arms. They turn out to be an interesting group. Cheryl, I learn, is a web site designer, Diane a rancher, Caroline a "mom," Lydia a high school soccer coach and Liz an attorney. Each comes from a different part of the state. When they hear I'm from San Francisco, a certain amount of merriment erupts.

"We think of San Francisco as gun control territory," Liz explains.

"Also Sodom and Gomorrah," says Cheryl, adding that she's from San Jose.

Dakota rejoins us. "Couple months back, we had a woman from Berkeley. That *really* caused a stir!"

Laughter, then more conversation. I learn that Diane, Lydia, a woman named Sharon and I will be sharing the bunkhouse, while the others will be staying at a motel ten miles away.

Mike is assigned to fix me up with a weapon. After showing me to the bunkhouse so I can stow my gear, he leads me to a small outbuilding just off the range, unlocks the door, then, inside, works the combination on a closet-size safe.

In it, neatly stowed on racks, is an array of small arms, pistols and revolvers of different sizes and calibers.

"Dakota thinks you'll be happy with a 9mm automatic," Mike says, picking out several pistols, extracting their magazines, showing me they're clear, then lining them up on a table.

I stare at the guns.

"Before I hand one to you, here're the three basic gun handling rules: Act as if every gun is always loaded. Keep the muzzle pointed away from people. Never place your finger on the trigger. When I hand you a gun the slide'll be open. Even though I've checked to make sure it's clear, you do the same, okay?"

I nod.

He picks up a pistol. "This is a Glock, a gun a lot of people like. It's ergonomic and very well built." He offers it to me. "Go ahead, take it."

I reach forward tentatively, then pull back.

"Hey, don't pussy out on me, Kay."

I turn on him. *"Excuse me?"*

"Just goading you." He laughs. "Dakota's orders, a method we use when a lady acts squeamish. Please don't take it personal."

His eyes are so sad and his smile so sweet I accept his explanation. Five minutes later I'm handling pistols the way I handle cameras in a photo store, picking them up, testing them for heft, looking for one with the right "feel." I like the Glock, the Beretta, the Sig-Sauer too. But when I pick up the Heckler & Koch, I know I'm handling something special.

"H&K—yeah, she's a beauty." Mike leads me outside, shows me how to hold it in an isosceles stance.

"Still feels good?"

"I like it, Mike."

"Then she's yours for the duration. Come back in, I'll show you how to clean her and take her apart. Since you already got safety shade wraps, I'll fix you up with ear protectors, holster and belt, then we'll head back to the house for chow."

I lie awake for an hour huddled in my sleeping bag atop my bunk, listening to the even breathing of the other women and the wind howling in the hills. I'm thinking about shooting and guns. There was something very aggressive in the isosceles stance, so different from the self-effacing posture I assume in aikido while awaiting attack. In a funny way it reminded me of the alert focused stance I take when working with my camera. Perhaps, I think, firing bullets won't be all that different from shooting film.

Again I dream of the erotic gun, enter into the world engraved upon its steel, smell the bodies of the lovers, feel the eyes of the animals, their curiosity, the intensity of their gaze. Again the bee flies around me, dive-bombing and buzzing, whispering in my ear. But the buzzing is so harsh I cannot hear the whispered words.

We meet on the range promptly at seven A.M., ten women decked out in matching baseball caps and T-shirts bearing the Personal Security Ranch logo. Even at this hour the sunlight's fierce, forcing me to wear my strongest, darkest wraps. Dakota, hair in a ponytail, T-shirt blinding white, paces before us addressing us in staccato military style.

"This," she soberly informs us, "is a cold range." The gracious hostess of the night before is now a drill sergeant barking out her rules. "That means if you're not about to shoot, you stay holstered and empty. Since we'll be working with deadly weapons, the first half hour this morning will be devoted to safety. The first rule here is very simple: Even though this range is cold, we act like every gun is always loaded."

We learn how to load and unload, then how to "show clear." We learn other commands: "Rack the slide." "Cock and lock." We learn not to look at the target but at the "sight-picture." We learn how to stand, grip the gun and control the trigger.

Shortly after eight I fire my first round. Dakota stands behind me, supervising, encouraging, explaining how I must squeeze the trigger slowly, so that when the gun fires I surprise myself.

The jolt is strong, but I hold steady, and at her command, fire again. By the time I empty my magazine of eight, I'm exhilarated by the sound, the smell and, most of all, the fact that I've not only broken through my phobia, but also shot a target at which she shows little scorn.

Some of the women are experienced shooters. Three of us have never fired a gun before. But even the experienced members are attentive to what Dakota tells us next.

"What we're doing has nothing to do with competition shooting. Those of you who've done that view it correctly as a sport. This is not a competitive-shooting class. You get no points here for marksmanship. Defensive shooting is combat, stopping an assailant with lethal force. It's about tactics and speed, mind-set and focus, most of all about wanting to survive. Remember this: Your gun is not an article of sporting equipment. It's a weapon. Don't think of it any other way."

She tells us we must learn to be instinctive shooters, that when we leave we must be able to draw from our holsters, then accurately fire three shots at ten yards, two to the chest target, one to the head target, all in a second and a half—an exercise she calls "the Mozambique."

We learn that since defense tactics are counterintuitive, we must practice, practice, practice until the tactics become second nature.

We learn about ammunition: that military ammo, called "hardball" or full metal jacket, is cheap and great for practice, but that it's no substitute for hollow point, which is more deadly and has far greater stopping power.

"People always ask: 'Do I shoot to injure or shoot to kill?' The answer," Dakota says, "is neither one. You shoot to stop—which may mean killing. You don't think about that. Your object is to stop your attacker at any cost."

Refreshing words in view of my confrontation with Julio Sanchez.

We practice clearing jams when a shell fails to eject (a "stovepipe") or fails to feed. We learn that all guns jam, and that knowing how to clear a jam can make the difference between survival and death. Mike places dummy rounds in our magazines to provoke deliberate jams, which we must then clear speedily or hear Dakota's ominous refrain: "Sorry, you lose, girl—you're dead."

After three hot hours on the range, we take a fifteen-minute break, then regroup in a wooden building furnished with a blackboard and semicircle of chairs. Here we take two hours of classroom instruction. I nurse the sore web of my hand, while Dakota lectures us on California law concerning use of deadly force; gunfight tactics; speedy decision making in crisis situations; how to behave with police after a gunfight and how to deal with post-gunfight trauma.

After lunch, it's back to the range for three more hours of hands-on practice, then two more hours of classroom instruction, then a cleanup break, then dinner for those of us bunking at the school.

After dinner Dakota beckons me aside for a private evaluation.

"You could be good," she tells me. "You've got excellent hand-eye coordination, your shooting's more accurate than most and you're cool under pressure. No question your aikido training and photographic work have developed your psychomotor skills. I've only two negative comments. You're still a little scared, still flinch more than you should. I'm pretty sure I can get you over that. Your other problem is indecision. You pause too long before you shoot. In a gunfight, those hesitations will get you killed."

"But aren't I right to be certain of my target?"

"Of course! But you've got to learn to trust your instincts. To do that you need to trust me more. I know four days isn't a lot of time to build confidence, but I'd like you to give me the benefit of the doubt." She peers into my eyes. "You don't like to give up control, do you, Kay?"

"No," I admit, "I don't."

"Neither do I. But there're times when we've got to. If you want to become a good defensive shooter, stop second-guessing yourself and your instructors. Combat's different than taking a photograph. There, if you miss the shot, you miss the shot. It's not life-and-death. Combat *is* life-and-death. If you miss, your opponent gets a chance to kill you. So you can't afford to miss. You've got to be certain every time."

In my bunk, I try to work it out. Taking a picture of a person is a way of "shooting" him, but the stakes, as Dakota points out, aren't nearly as high. A camera is a tool and so is a gun. One records images, the other kills. The difference lies in the irretrievability of the act. Take a lousy picture and you get a lousy picture. Take a lousy shot, and maybe you get shot yourself.

But it goes deeper. Taking a photograph is an act of capture, while firing a weapon is an act of destruction. If I'm not fast enough on the range, maybe it's because I'm trying too hard to make the perfect shot, compose the sight-picture too well, turn the target into some kind of work of art. I've got to stop worrying about how the target's going to look. Accuracy, not marksmanship. Fire, stop the aggressor, save myself.

On the second day, classroom work takes a different form. Dakota describes actual gunfights, diagrams the positions of the shooters, shows us videotaped interviews with the survivors, analyzes what happened, then asks us to extract the lessons.

The lessons are clear: Speed, confidence, focus prevail. Indecision, fear, reluctance to fight all lead to loss.

On the range I become more aggressive. And my photophobia, as in the dojo, bothers me less than expected considering the intensity of the light. In the various confrontation exercises—close-up shooting, pivots and turns, fast draws, quick reloading, shooting while moving, firing at moving targets, shooting from prone position, shooting while rolling, shooting from improvised cover— I try not to think, just react as if my life depended on it.

Dakota rides me, Mike is compassionate. They employ a whole spectrum of techniques—shouting orders, coddling, mocking my failures, sympathizing with my difficulties, forcing me to anger, whipsawing me with their "good cop/bad cop" routine. I'm not the only one to get such treatment. Each woman has her deficiencies. Our instructors smartly focus on our weaknesses, then present us with exercises to correct them.

"Don't be afraid of stress," Dakota exhorts. "Stress can be your friend. Let it feed your energy."

When there's a break I go up to her. "Rita's always telling us pain can be our friend."

Dakota smiles. "Stress, pain—they're pretty much the same, I think."

At dusk we practice low-light shooting, then, after dinner, go back out for a two-hour session of night shooting. As expected I'm superior at both, by far the best in the group. But Dakota refuses to compliment me.

"Yeah, you're accurate, Kay," she tells me, "but frankly, your tactics suck. Also I'm clocking your Mozambiques at one point seven, one point eight. Gotta get it down, way down. Speed it up or you're not going to pass the course."

Suddenly I'm in a sweat. To go through all this, lay out so much money, spend four days with my eyes constantly bombarded by light, my ears assailed by noise, then fail— the prospect's unimaginable.

Now, focusing my anger on Dakota, I stop blaming myself for being wimpy and slow.

She wants me to go in and blast, fine, I'll blast her stupid targets to shreds! She wants me to do a 1.5 second Mozambique, I'll give her a fuckin' 1.4!

Combat shooting's not like aikido. There're no spiritual depths, least not that I can see. For all the talk about thinking of your gun as an extension of your arm, I find it totally unlike weapons training at the dojo. Here the aim is not to disarm or neutralize your opponent's energy, it's to put a hole in his head. Stopping means killing. Render harmless means render dead. It's the finality that makes it so difficult. When I think about it, I'm not able to do it.

Nine P.M.: No moon. One by one Dakota has us crawl through the dust, pistol in hand, while she activates a moving target mounted on a wire. I fire twice, roll, fire a third shot at the target head.

"Got him," Mike yells. "You killed him, Kay. You get to live!"

Suddenly, caught up in his fervor, I roar out my delight.
"*That's* what I want to hear," Dakota shouts. "When
you're visceral, you're engaged."

Day three: I'm on a roll. Maybe getting too cocky for
my own good. I'm so used to thinking before I shoot, com-
posing the frame, asking myself what I want from the shot,
that now, released from all that, my shooting starts getting
wild.

Dakota notices, pulls me off the firing line, assigns
Mike to run me through special drills. He takes me to
another range on the other side of the ranch, talks me
down, then walks me through the basics once again.

"Yeah, of course it's fun," he tells me, "but it shouldn't
become a game. Combat's serious. We don't shoot with
paint balls here. Stay steady, cool, alert. Now let's see you
do some Mozambiques."

Dakota lectures us on split-second decisions, differenti-
ating, for instance, between a child holding out an ice cream
cone and a short person threatening us with a revolver. She
reviews situations where cops made terrible mistakes, mistook a crowbar for a rifle, a cap pistol for a real pistol, a colleague reaching for a badge or a criminal reaching for a gun.

We learn about different carrying techniques especially
suitable for women, the pros and cons of manufactured-
for-women guns (Dakota scoffs at them, telling us small
guns are harder to shoot and have a more vicious recoil),
how to keep a gun when there're kids in the house, how to
defend one's home, special problems facing women when
they shoot.

On the range we practice combat against two and then
multiple assailants, emptying our pistols and speed-
reloading, advanced tactics such as knowing when and
how to retreat, close-up shooting (fifty percent of all law
enforcement shootings take place within nine feet), accurate medium-distance shooting (fifty feet), sweeping a

building, working a corner, shooting from vehicles, weapon retention, disarming an armed assailant, quick-draw strokes, step-back techniques, one-handed shooting, weak-hand shooting, alternate shooting stances and, for me the most crucial drill of all, spot target assessment in crisis situations.

Tomorrow afternoon, after morning drills, we'll be tested on our skills, culminating with individual sessions inside Dakota's "Fun House," a two-story window-less building tricked up with little rooms, creepy dark corners, staircases both ordinary and spiral, pop-out targets that emerge from closets, mannequin opponents who unex-pectedly materialize.

Invited by the motel women to join them for dinner at a roadhouse just outside Nevada City, Diane, Lydia, Sharon and I listen raptly as they speak with awe of the difficulties and vicissitudes of the Fun House—rumors that it's unbeatable, that no one gets through it alive, that it's devised to humble even the most adept student, that course graduates refer to it as "Dakota's revenge."

We go around the table, each telling what brought her to the ranch.

Lydia, it turns out, was raped last year at gunpoint. Liz, a divorce attorney, tells us she's being stalked by the hus-band of a client who blames her for ruining his life. Cheryl, the web site designer from San Jose, lives in fear of her ex, a cop who beat her, and on the day she told him she was leaving, grabbed her and held a loaded pistol to her head.

When it's my turn, I tell them that two weeks ago I was caught trespassing on private property, and since the guys who caught me had guns, I was afraid to use my martial arts skills to fight them off.

"Seeing how terrified I was, they thought they'd have themselves some sport, so they tied me to a pool table, then probed me with a gun barrel. Now I dream about it. Every night I dream about it. I came here to get over the nightmare, and to learn how to handle myself if I'm ever in that situation again."

We break up early. Tomorrow, after all, is a big day. Everyone wishes everyone else good luck. Then it's: "Night. See you on the range."

I'm inside the Fun House, having just stepped through the door, Dakota right behind me, so close I can feel her breath on my neck.

It's hot in here, maybe a hundred degrees. The air's close. My T-shirt's sticking to my back. I smell gunpowder and shoe leather, gun oil and sweat.

I inch toward an archway.

"Step in," Dakota says, "then sweep the room."

I step in and sweep the way we were taught, staying away from the walls, holding out my gun, moving it in arcs. No one here, so I move on.

The next room's small, with a closet near the corner, door slightly ajar. Someone's hiding in there—I know it!

I move out of range of the closet, make sure there's no one else in the room, then approach from the side. Suddenly I reach out with my foot and kick the door open all the way. At the same moment I yell: "Throw it out, dickhead!"

Alas, no one's there.

"You just gave away your position," Dakota says.

The next room's a narrow hall with two sets of stairs, one leading to the second floor, the other to the cellar.

I decide to ignore the cellar. No way can I safely descend. Anyhow, we were taught not to pursue an intruder, rather retreat to a safe room, take cover and defend.

I move toward the stairs leading up. Just then the cellar door slams. As I turn toward the sound, I catch a glimpse of a figure at the top of the stairs. I turn back, fire up at him three times, a classic Mozambique. Then I turn back toward the cellar door, just in time to catch sight of another figure. I'm about to blast him when I realize he's a kid.

"Go back to the cellar," I yell.

"Good, Kay!" Dakota whispers. "You didn't shoot little Johnny. But you still got to deal with the bad guys upstairs."

No way, I realize, am I going to be able to mount those stairs without stepping into someone's line of fire.

"No!" I whisper back. "I'm going back to the cellar where I can protect little Johnny best by covering the door."

Dakota doesn't say anything, just moves behind me as I skittishly inch my way back down into the hall. Just then I hear a door fling open. I flatten myself against the wall, Dakota right beside me.

"He's coming down. What're you going to do?" she whispers.

I don't answer, instead count silently to three, then step out fast and rake the stairs with fire: *Bam!bam! Bam!bam!bam!* Then nothing, just the echo of my shots and the smell of gun smoke hanging in the air. I step back, continue toward the cellar door. Just as I reach it, it flies open. Since little Johnny's hiding in there, I hold my fire. A big mistake. A man-size mannequin pops up, gun in hand.

"You're dead, Kay," Dakota informs me deadpan. "When you turned your back on the door, he slipped in. Also, you made a big mistake. You've only got one round left. After you blasted the stairs you should have changed magazines. Even if you'd fired at the big guy, he'd have had the advantage."

I holster my pistol. "Okay, so I'm dead—what happens now?"

Dakota grins. "Basically it was an impossible exercise—so you pass."

We all pass. If we didn't, Dakota says, she'd feel as though she failed. We hug one another. Four days of stress. We're bonded now, sisters-in-arms. We exchange addresses, promise to stay in touch. Cheryl offers me a lift to San Jose. From there it's but an hour by bus to home.

Tuesday morning: I enter a store called Gun City near the Hall of Justice. At the counter, a kindly middle-aged woman asks how she may help.

"I'm looking to buy an H and K P7M8."

"Certainly . . ."

She pulls a carton off the shelf behind, opens it, lays the pistol before me on a black velvet pad, the kind you'd find on the counter at a jewelry store.

I pick the weapon up, rack the slide, eject the magazine, inspect it, slam it back, cock the gun, dry-fire.

"Just what I want. I'll take it."

I hand her my credit card, sign the necessary papers. She hands me a booklet: "The Gun-Owner's Guide to Staying Legal in California." After the obligatory ten-day waiting period, I can return to pick my weapon up. The entire transaction takes no more than five minutes.

At eight tonight I load my pockets with quarters, walk down to Polk Street, find a public phone in a bar, dial Vince Carroll's home number in Fort Bragg.

Vince picks up on the second ring.

"Know who I am?" I ask.

"Sorry, ma'am, I don't."

"You never heard me speak, did you?"

Silence. "Who is this?"

"Your secret admirer," I tell him cheerily.

Another silence, this one longer. "What do you want?"

"You said I wouldn't remember anything. Let me tell you, I remember plenty."

"Look, I can't talk now. How can I get in touch?"

"You gotta be kidding!"

"I'll meet you anyplace you want. You name it, I'll be there. I'll come alone."

"Sorry, Vince, you haven't earned enough trust for that."

"What do I have to do to earn it?"

"Chipper and Buckoboy—give me their full names and home addresses."

"Sorry—no can do."

"Yes *can* do. You don't like them, you'd like to get rid of them. I can take care of that." Silence. "Also I want the gun."

"What gun?"

"You know the one I mean."

"We've got hundreds of guns . . ."

"The special gun. The one with the special engraving."

"You're nuts!"

"Am I? Must've been my overnight at the club made me this way. I know things about you, Vince. About your law enforcement career. How you testified against your buddy. That took guts. But there was no guts in what was done to me. That was a coward's game. You know it too."

"Like I said, I'll meet you."

"I'll think about it. Meantime, you think about showing me good faith. I want those names and addresses. Next time I call, be prepared to give them to me. Understand?"

"Hey, don't hang—"

But I do hang up, then slump down to the floor, hands trembling, clothing drenched in sweat.

I'm sitting in my living room sipping coffee, staring out at the city sparkling in the night. On my lap sits the sketchbook in which I've been trying determinedly yet fruitlessly to draw the bee.

No use. I can't seem to get it right. No matter how many times I draw it (and I'm getting expert now at drawing bees), it doesn't ring a bell with me, doesn't fit with the scenes on the gun.

I wonder about myself. I think Dakota's gun course has helped restore my confidence, badly shaken after my encounter in the gun room. But still I feel I'm carrying a burden, one I want very much to lay down. Ever since my fight with Julio Sanchez something's happened to my fun-loving self. I know the last thing I want is to become a woman harboring a grievance, one who's been hurt and can't get over it.

Knowing I must see through my plan to let my grievance go, I return to sketching. I think of Maddy's good counsel whenever I was working on a project and became stuck:

Keep struggling with it, Kay. Struggle on it till you work it through. It'll be the times when you don't feel like going on, yet force yourself, that you'll make the breakthroughs.

Butterfield & Butterfield is on San Bruno Avenue in the warehouse district. I arrive at nine A.M., an hour early to ensure I get a decent seat. Dad told me about this auction, called it "the gun sale of the year."

I set my leather jacket down on a chair, then check out the exhibition in the main gallery. Hundreds of historical arms—dueling pistols, salon pistols, flintlocks, single-shot derringers, Civil War muskets, percussion carbines, nineteenth-century Colts, Springfields, Winchesters and double-action revolvers—are laid out on display tables and in locked glass-door cabinets. There's also a huge array of twentieth-century small arms—Mausers, Rugers, contemporary Colt and Smith & Wesson pistols and revolvers—plus bullet molds, powder flasks, bowie knives, dirks, sabers, cutlasses, assorted edged weapons and a huge Colt Gatling gun mounted on a gun carriage.

But the excitement in the gallery is focused on fifteen or

so handmade shotguns manufactured by the famous British gunmaker firms Purdey, Holland & Holland, Boss, and Westley Richards. I join a small group of connoisseurs covetously gazing at these exquisitely made hunting and field arms whose allure, I understand, is based not only on their beauty, craftsmanship and superb condition, but also on their noble provenances.

Two sporting guns in particular attract attention, a twelve-gauge Boss made for Edward VIII when he was Prince of Wales, and an over-and-under made by Westley Richards on commission for T. E. Lawrence—Lawrence of Arabia. It is this gun that I am hoping will attract Ramsey Carson to the auction, for I have come today not to drool over weapons but to observe the bidding and the bidders.

Nine fifty-five A.M.: I return to the auction room to reclaim my seat. The setup is formal, an elevated lectern in front for the auctioneer, TV monitors above so everyone can see slides of the items as they come up for sale, a couple of hundred chairs lined up in even rows to the back of the room, two long tables on either side, ten telephones lined up on each, attended by auction house employees poised to take bid orders from collectors around the world.

I check out the crowd. Ninety percent are men, some in suits, others in windbreakers, still others in polo shirts, western shirts with string ties, even one paramilitary type dolled up in fatigues. Noting the way these prospective buyers banter back and forth awaiting the start, I strike up a conversation with my neighbor, an elegant gray-haired gentleman with intent eyes and an ironic smile, decked out in dark blazer and striped bow tie.

Explaining I'm new to the game, I ask if he wouldn't mind helping me identify the important players. Saying he'd be delighted, he hands me his card ("Cutler 'Cut' Beresford, Rare Gun Appraisal," with a Nob Hill address), then points out several major dealers, adding that close observation of their bidding from the start will reveal much about the current state of the rare gun market and prospects for today's sale.

I look for Carson, don't find him, think about changing my seat to obtain a better viewing angle on the crowd. But most of the seats are already taken. Figuring I'll spot him if he comes in, I settle back to watch the show.

The first several lots, nineteenth-century Colt percussion revolvers, are rare and pricey, so at once there's tension in the room. The bearded, shaved-headed auctioneer quickly takes control, working with a few aggressive bidders with whom, Cut Beresford tells me, he's worked out signals in advance. I can't see the face of the most active bidder, seated in the first row, but notice that he keeps his head down except when he raises, at which point he tilts it up just the slightest bit. He buys the first two lots at prices considerably above the estimates.

Things move swiftly. Bidding rarely lasts longer than a minute. The tenth lot is hotly contested between the nodding gentleman in the first row, a stern-faced man in a striped shirt seated in the rear and a telephone bidder who eventually captures the prize, a pair of engraved Colt dragoon revolvers, for $310,000, causing a murmur to ripple across the room.

After the flurry over the rare Colts, things settle down. New bidders, competing for medium-priced items, show more passion than those going for the big stuff. These men, identified by Cut Beresford as collectors bidding for themselves, grin or grimace depending on the outcome of the contests.

An hour passes. The fine shotguns are about to reach the block. Scanning the room, I notice the arrival of several new players sporting a different kind of clothing and demeanor. Decked out in silk ascots and tweeds, they carry themselves with the erect confidence of old-school British gentlemen. No gaudy grins and loud guffaws from these types, rather the sophisticated smiles and charm of gun-collector aristocrats.

An engraved twenty-gauge Parker is the first fine shot-gun to come up. Once again tension rises and bidding becomes intense. A man in a plaid golfing cap vigorously wiggles his pen. Three telephone bidders are also in the game, plus one of the dealers who had been fairly quiet during the bidding on the Colts. Golfing Cap gets the Parker, then, perhaps puffed up by his success, again starts wiggling his pen to gain a matched pair of Purdeys. He wins the Purdeys, competes for a Holland & Holland, but is defeated by a bidder on the phone. He tries for another Holland & Holland, fails again. Dejected, he sits out the next two rounds.

Concentrating on the travails of Golfing Cap, I barely notice the man who slips into the seat three to my left. But after Golfing Cap's second defeat, I give the newcomer a glance, then nearly double-take. It's Carson, I'm certain of it, dressed in a white shirt, sober tie and dark pin-striped business suit, scanning the room, taking in the vibes.

Our eyes meet, he smiles slightly, then, when I match his gaze, narrows his eyes with curiosity. A moment later he scans past. I study him but not too long; I don't want him aware of my interest. He looks just as he did in Chap Fontaine's G.G.C. photographs—leonine and intensely masculine, with a weathered face and appealing Clark Gable squint, his hair perhaps slightly more silvered than before, but still very much the swain/gallant. The animal magnetism is apparent too, for, I note, I'm not the only one aware of him. Cut Beresford whispers his name in my ear. Then: "Watch him on the big sporting guns."

When I check out Carson again, he's done with his sur-vey. Now he sits back, leg casually crossed over his knee, arm resting carelessly on the back of the neighboring chair. The Edward VIII Boss is up. Bidding starts high at $100,000. As it escalates, I twice notice the auctioneer focus on Carson, his stare met each time by a barely per-ceptible shake of Carson's head. $200,000. $250,000.

$270,000. $275,000. The gun is finally won by a telephone bidder at $280,000.

Another matched set of engraved Purdeys goes for $110,000. Then comes the Lawrence of Arabia gun. Again, the opening is $100,000.

This time, as the bidding rapidly escalates past $200,000, I detect complicity between Carson and the auctioneer, Carson neither nodding nor shaking his head, simply staring, coolly meeting the auctioneer's eye, as if calculating the best time to enter the fray.

Bidding on the Lawrence gun reaches $285,000.

"Going once," the auctioneer declares.

Suddenly there's activity at the telephone table. A phone relay man, hitherto silent, calls out $300,000.

Dead silence in the room. Then the man who's just been outbid calls out $305,000.

$325,000 from the phone.

$330,000 from the rear.

$350,000 from the phone.

A brief silence as the room reacts.

The auctioneer looks to Carson. This time Carson evidently gives some kind of signal, for the pleased auctioneer announces "Three-sixty from the center."

$375,000 from the phone.

$385,000 from the center.

$400,000 from the phone.

Cut Beresford leans toward me, whispers: "Probably a rich Saudi at the other end. Or D'Arcy Chambers in Dublin. He's a big collector and Lawrence of Arabia buff."

"Four-ten from the center."

"Four-fifty from the phone."

"Four-sixty from the center."

"Four seventy-five from the phone."

The auctioneer stares straight at Carson. There's a force field between them. I lean forward to better watch Carson's face. His stare is frozen. The auctioneer calls out first warning. Carson winks his right eye twice.

The auctioneer calls: "Four ninety-five from the center."

This time silence from the phone.

First warning. Second warning. "Sold!" Amidst ardent applause, the Lawrence gun is hammered down at $495,000.

Two lots later, Carson slips out of his seat. I turn to watch as he strides up the aisle, nodding to acquaintances, shaking congratulators' hands, then takes a standing position in the back, arms folded, master of the room.

"Look at him, he's happy now," Cut Beresford whispers, "but give him a couple weeks. He'll be on the prowl again. Collector's syndrome. I see it every day. The more they get, the more they want."

I thank Cut for his tutelage. During an interval, I slip up the aisle myself. At first I'm disappointed. Carson's no longer standing in the rear. Then I spot him in the lobby with two other men, equally well dressed, the three of them spouting hearty good humor, carrying on the way men do at stag functions and sporting events.

I go to the lobby counter, pretend to peruse auction catalogues while listening in.

"Had to be Chambers," Carson says. "Been chasing my ass for years."

"You sure own his ass today, Ram."

"He's probably throwing up right now," the second man says.

"I *like* that image." Carson tongues his lip. "Old D'Arce on his knees in front of the toilet vomiting out his bile. Best part is he's knows it's me who beat him."

The three guffaw. "Ha!ha!ha!" They slap one another on the back.

"Way to go, Ram!"

"Ram-the-Man! Go get 'em, pal!"

"I always do," Carson says, smug grin plastered on his face.

Big smiles all around, more guffaws, more "Ha!ha!ha!"s. Another round of slaps on the back, followed by slap-palm handshakes. Then the two other men move toward the door, while Carson, still aglow from his triumph, resumes his arms-folded Master of the Universe stance at the rear of the auction room.

I'm home alone tonight. After dinner I carry my coffee to the living room window, stare out at the city so still behind the glass. The towers of the financial district, aglow with lights, appear as stark abstract forms against black cumulus clouds, their edges etched by the three-quarters moon. I know there are passions roiling out there, but from here the city seems serene. As I sip I wistfully consider how greatly I would like to find that same serenity within myself.

Again I try to sketch the bee. With each attempt the quality of my drawing improves, but I can't seem to get it right. Like the animals in the foliage, it should have a face, which, for some inexplicable reason, I cannot manage to draw. I flip back through my sketchbook, look again at my drawings of the animal-voyeurs. The monkey has a face, as do the leopard and the pelican. So—why not the bee?

I pull out Chap Fontaine's album of G.G.C. photographs, find the men I spotted with Carson this morning in the auction house lobby. Both were younger than Carson, and for all the chumminess between them, behaved more like acolytes than equals. In the photos, dressed in T-shirts and shorts, they show the lean builds, carved features and aggressive stances of males thrilled to participate in a hunt.

I study their faces, take in their most prominent features, then try and sketch them, exaggerating in the manner of a cartoonist. Then I try superimposing these sketches on sketches of several of the animals. The face of the first man, the hearty one, fits well on the fox. The face of the

second, the one who conjured the image of the defeated
D'Arcy Chambers throwing up, goes nicely on the body of
the crocodile. And Ramsey Carson's face well suits the
leopard, who, in my sketch of the engraving, is the alpha
animal.

I search the album for a face that will fit the bee, but
find nothing that works or even sparks a memory. Perhaps,
I think, the bee did not stand among the other animals, but
lurked elsewhere within the scene.

I phone Cut Beresford. Courtly as ever, he invites me
to his Jones Street flat at four this afternoon to answer all
my questions concerning rare guns and gun engraving.

I take an early aikido class, my first since my return
from Nevada City. Afterwards Rita asks me how it went
with Dakota. I tell her it went well, that I'm no longer gun-
shy and have even purchased an automatic.

She nods, but I detect a measure of disapproval. "Lethal
force—don't know, girlfriend. I prefer what we do here,
applying just enough force to do the job."

"I prefer it too," I tell her. "I've also decided about the
shodan. I want to go for it."

She brightens. "Great! If you work hard you'll be ready
by the end of the summer. Then you can take your exam on
retreat."

The prospect of being tested for my black belt in front
of several hundred devoted aikidoists from all over the
state is frightening and exhilarating at the same time. The
judges at retreat exams are big shot Japanese instructors.
At some retreats as many as thirty people are tested.

Rita, sensing my anxiety, reaches for my hand.

"You can do it, Kay. Work with me every day and I
guarantee you'll be ready. You need this now. I really
believe you do."

Cut Beresford lives but three blocks from Baggy Bigelow, but his apartment could not be more different. While Baggy dwells in a hothouse salon of twisted Barbies and calculated "bad taste," Cut receives me in an underfurnished white living room—so blindingly white I must ask him to draw the drapes so I can see.

Even then I must wear a pair of dark red wraps to make out my surroundings—one wall composed of floor-to-ceiling shelves of books on the history of guns, another covered with framed engravings of gun mechanisms. As for actual guns, there's not one in sight, which surprises me until Cut explains that he himself is not a collector, rather a scholar of firearms specializing in authentication and appraisal.

He's even more nattily dressed than at the auction, in a light linen suit and floppy bow tie. He raises his eyebrows when I broach my interest in erotic guns.

"Kind of an esoteric subject," he comments.

"You mean—for a woman?"

He smiles. "Actually not. One of the most important collectors of erotic arms is Baroness von Heinholz. I visited her castle outside Munich a couple of years back. She has incredible stuff, most of it engraved sixteenth- and seventeenth-century German wheel-locks and eighteenth-century French flintlocks."

I'm surprised. "They made erotic guns back then?"

Cut nods. "It's an old tradition, though you don't hear much about it. Pieces rarely come on the market. There's only been one article written about them, a chapter in a book by an expatriate Englishman, privately printed back in the 1940s."

When I explain I only just discovered such firearms exist and am eager to learn more, he goes to the bookcase and retrieves the book, promising to send me a photocopy of the applicable chapter.

Back in his chair he eyes me wisely. "Yesterday you were sitting next to the number-one erotic gun collector in the world. But you knew that, didn't you?"

I admit I did.

"Is there some reason you don't want to talk to Carson about all this?"

I nod. "He's hot on the chase. I figured you, an expert, could give me a cooler view."

Cut smiles. "You're right about Ram. He's a pretty formidable character, obsessive, prideful, acquisitive. He probably wouldn't like it if you tried to pick his brains." He eyes me. "So you want a cool overview?"

"I'd love it, Cut—if you have the time."

He nods, starts to talk, his presentation intelligent and concise. The decoration of objects, he reminds me, is a natural human impulse. Since prehistoric times, men have marked stone, carved wood, drawn pictures on the walls of caves. Erotic decoration also goes back to early times, men and women having always been fascinated by sex. Thus we have numerous ancient Greek vases painted with erotic scenes, as well as erotic mosaics and frescoes. Hunting and war weapons, being mystical objects, were always decorated, and of course hunting and war, by tradition, were purely masculine pursuits. So, Cut asks, is it at all surprising that we find erotic decoration on edged weapons and, with the invention of gunpowder, firearms as well?

"Since you put it that way, not surprising," I agree. "But what astonishes me is that it's still going on. Erotic art and pornography I can understand. Beautiful, finely crafted weapons—I understand that too. But why combine them, especially now when there's so much sexual openness? What I'm asking is—what's the connection between guns and sex?"

"Ah!" Cut grins. "You've got it wrong. It's not about *guns* and sex, it's about aggression and sex, which go perfectly together, always have. Why? You'd probably do better asking a psychologist. I have my own theory, namely that hunting and war are actually erotic activities which stimulate us, make our eyes glisten, cause us to breathe hard and salivate. I think we're hard-wired for blood sports. If we didn't like killing so much, we wouldn't do it, in which case we'd be an entirely different species— soft, kind creatures no doubt, but probably quite boring. Not artists, builders, hunters, warriors. More like sheep grazing peacefully in meadows."

"You think eroticized violence is at the root of civilization?"

"A philosophical question, but since you ask, yes, I do. And if you look at things from that perspective, erotic guns aren't nearly as odd as they seem. Just listen to the way soldiers talk. Look at the phallic shape of guns. It's a natural connection, and the fact that such guns are still produced is in the great tradition of decorated arms. Gun engraving, remember, is a genuine art form, of which erotic engraving is a natural subset." He looks at me. "But you know, Kay, interesting as all this is, I don't think it's what you've come to hear. I have a feeling there's something specific you're looking for. If you tell me, maybe I can help."

He looks at me in such a sympathetic way I'm tempted to tell him everything. But, I remind myself, I barely know this man. Better, I decide, not to reveal too much.

"There's a particular erotic gun I'm interested in."

"Contemporary?"

"I think so."

"I know the work of all the top engravers. There're not many, perhaps fifty in the world. It's a dying craft. If you can describe the engraving, I might recognize the style. It would be better, of course, to see the actual work."

I bring out my sketchbook, show him my drawing of the two couples in the glade. Watching him as he studies it, I detect no shock or amusement at the subject matter, rather the demeanor of a connoisseur closely inspecting a work of art.

"If the engraving's half as good as this, it's very good indeed."

"It's a lot better," I tell him. "I made the drawing from memory."

"Interesting . . . Work this fine and detailed is what we call *bulino*. But the scrollwork, this entwined sexual organ motif along the edges, looks like classical engraving of the British school."

"What's *bulino*?"

"A method akin to banknote-style engraving, developed in Italy, named for a special engraver's tool. The classic engraver works two-handed, setting a fine chisel, called a scriber, then gently tapping it with a small hammer to gouge the steel. A *bulino* artist works with just one hand, carefully controlling his tool, cutting the steel with great precision fine line by fine line. With *bulino* you get a kind of photographic realism with attenuated shadings as delicate as in a halftone, pictures that seem literally to come alive when light strikes the metal. It's demanding virtuoso work, so finely wrought that if you were to ink the gun you could actually pull off a print."

He squints at my drawing. "Not many people work at this level. I wonder . . ." He shakes his head. "I've never seen this gun. I'm sure of it. But it reminds me of work I've seen in Ram Carson's collection." He looks up at me. "Is that why you don't want to talk to him?"

"That's another reason," I admit.

"Ram has a pair of erotic guns originally made for King Farouk. Jock Watson and his daughter decorated them. He was a genius engraver. In his heyday no one could touch him. But I think if Jock engraved this gun, I'd have heard about it. He died thirty years ago. All his work's been catalogued. And Jock didn't work in *bulino*."

Cut starts flipping through my sketchbook.

"Nice close-ups," he says of my animal portraits. "This gun must have incredible detail."

He flips another page.

"Hmmm! What's this?"

He holds up one of my failed sketches of the bee.

"Something I think I saw on the gun," I tell him.

He sits back, smiles. "Well, that's it. The signature."

"Signature?"

Cut nods. "Jock's daughter, Bee. This was the way she signed her work."

"*Bee* Watson?"

" 'My little honeybee'—that's what Jock always called her. He doted on the girl. Taught her everything he knew. Wanted her to become the best gun engraver in the world. And for a while there she absolutely was the best. Then she gave it up. At least I thought she did. But now that you show me this—"

Cut talks on, but I stop listening. I feel a delicious shiver, the same kind I've felt when making a major breakthrough in my work.

Bee Watson.

Suddenly it comes together. David Yamada spoke of Maddy's mysterious visits to her old friend "Bea" who lived in the Mission. This Bee, whom I mistook for Bea-short-for-Beatrice, has to be the same person.

And then I smile, for with this revelation comes the recognition that the bee in my nightmares was indeed trying to whisper me a message.

I phone David Yamada at Kalei-doscopics. The video-game-freak receptionist answers.

"How's the iguana?" I ask.

"Joe? Right now he's under my desk munching a head of celery."

When David comes on, I remind him about the letters from Bee he found in Maddy's papers.

"Right. Two letters from way back when."

"Can I see them?"

"Gee, I don't know, Kay. I mean, I guess ... if you really think ..."

"You don't sound very enthusiastic."

"May I ask what this is about?"

"I'd rather not say just now."

"Gee, that doesn't seem fair, considering the circumstances."

"What circumstances, David?"

"Oh, you know ..."

"I'm afraid I don't."

When he starts to stammer, I let him twist. One thing I

learned from our previous encounter: David Yamada reveals as little as he can.

"Considering she was my stepmom, I think I'm entitled."

"All right. I've developed some information about a woman named Bee—B-e-e, not B-e-a. I want to find out if it's the same person."

"How would a couple of old letters help with that?"

I'm getting fed up with him. "When can I see them, David?"

"I'll try to stop by tonight."

" 'Try' or come?"

"I'll come at seven."

"Good! I'll be waiting for you downstairs."

After we hang up, I ask myself why he's acting this way. Then something occurs to me. I call the San Francisco Museum of Modern Art, ask to speak to Sam Levine, associate curator of photographs. When Sam comes on he tells me how sorry he was we didn't get a chance to talk at Maddy's funeral, which gives me just the opening I need to ask about Maddy's archive.

"David Yamada tells me he turned it over to you guys."

"Yeah, all her negatives, tons of prints, plus twenty or so boxes of papers."

"Anyone been through them?"

"We've looked through most. A treasure trove. We've already had inquiries from a couple of would-be biographers. Trouble is once they hear stuff's embargoed, they cool off."

" 'Embargoed'? What does that mean?"

"Sorry, Kay, I thought you knew. David Yamada's condition, part of the deed of gift. There're two sealed boxes, not to be opened till the year 2030. Even we can't look at them."

"What's in them, Sam?"

"I've no idea. But the only gap in the material concerns Maddy's life before 1957, the year she took up photography."

Hey, a miracle! Found a parking space on Russian Hill!"

The affectionate peck David applies to my cheek seems a bid to reestablish himself as the older-brother-I-never-had.

He looks forlorn when I tell him we're not going up to my apartment, rather to a coffeehouse down the street.

"What's up?" he asks as we walk down Hyde. A cable car sails by, giddy tourists hanging off the sides.

"What's in those embargoed boxes over at the museum?"

"Just stuff Maddy didn't want people to see. At least not till all concerned have passed away."

"It was her decision?"

David nods.

I look at him. He lowers his eyes. I'm pretty sure he's lying.

At the corner of Union we pass Swensen's Ice Cream. An aroma of vanilla issues from the door.

"You told me you kept some stuff back."

"Yeah, just some papers concerning my dad, their love letters, stuff like that."

"So how come you kept the letters from Bee?"

"Hey! Here we go again—you the interrogator, me on the hot seat."

"Make you uncomfortable?"

"Seems weird, that's all."

"You brought the letters?"

He nods, pats the breast pocket of his jacket. "Since there's nothing in them, certainly nothing to do with Maddy's work, I didn't see any reason to send them over to the museum."

We're standing just outside the cafe door.

"What do you think's in the sealed boxes?"

David shrugs, then looks away.

Not true, David. You know.

We enter, order espressos. While we wait, David places the Bee letters on the table.

I nod but make no move to pick them up. Instead I peer at him, knowing my gaze makes him uneasy. One of Maddy's best lessons concerned dealing with a difficult subject. "Don't pounce," she'd say, "don't provoke, simply gaze until the person discloses himself or the scene jells and comes together."

Finally he speaks. "I think they contain stuff she didn't want people to know about."

"I can't imagine she was ashamed of anything."

"I didn't say she was ashamed, Kay. But she wanted to protect people who're still alive."

"Until 2030? Except for you, me and her students, she didn't know anyone likely to live that long."

David shrugs again. "Beats me."

I give him a glance to show I don't think it beats him at all. Then I pick up the letters.

David's right, they're innocuous, written in the kind of informal chatty tone one might expect from an old friend. I wonder why Maddy kept them along with her love letters from Harry Yamada.

Finding nothing in the texts, I study the extraordinary handwriting, a beautiful loopy flowing cursive script, the writing of a calligrapher or artist/engraver, a conclusion validated by the beautifully engraved crosshatched letters *BEE* in the upper left corner of the paper. Then I check the signatures. In both cases, beneath the *B* there's a tiny drawing of a bee.

David, I notice, is watching me closely.

I put the letters down. "You're right, not much here."

"What're you looking for?" he asks.

"Some hint as to who this woman is."

"Did you find it?"

I nod, point to the bees. "I've seen this signature before."

He's attentive now, leaning forward, staring into my eyes. "Where?"

Noting a light screen of perspiration on his forehead, I lower my voice. "On a gun," I tell him softly.

The moment he hears the word, he slumps back.

"What's wrong, David?"

He shakes his head.

An idea comes to me. "You're covering up something about Maddy that has to do with guns."

He stares at me, stands, tosses down some money, then rushes out the door, leaving Bee's letters behind.

She was my teacher, my mentor, my coach, my friend, also my surrogate mother. There was something incredibly lustrous about her—the luster of wisdom, the same luster that drew one to her eyes. She was the most honest person I ever knew and her art was clear, radiant, uncompromising. Yet now I know there is a secret in her past, hidden in those sealed boxes embargoed at the museum—the same thing that caused her, despite illness and old age, to set up the little spy nest on Cypress Alley.

THE GUN / FIND THE GUN / WHERE'S THE GUN?

Maddy's quest has now become my own. And there's only one way, I think, to get to the bottom of it.

BEE / FIND BEE / WHERE'S BEE?

First thing in the morning I phone Dad. Having just finished baking hours, he's happy to talk. I tell him I need another favor from Rusty, copies of Maddy Yamada's phone bills the last three months of her life.

"Don't know, darlin'. That's a heavy request. Rusty could get in trouble someone found out."

"Will you ask him, Dad?"

"Better if you ask him. He's always asking after you.

Why don't you call him, butter him up? You know, wax him a bit. I think he'll do anything you want you ask him nice enough. He could never resist sweet talk from a pretty lady."

I love Dad's mixed metaphors: "sweet talk, butter up, wax." I call Rusty, set up a meeting with him after work.

He lives in a small one-story house out in the avenues off Santiago, the vast flat Sunset district south of Golden Gate Park between Mount Sutro and the Pacific. It's a neatly kept little masonry house on a neatly kept block, built, like its neighbors, in typical California bungalow style.

Arriving at twilight, I notice an Asian man washing his car next door, a trio of Asian girls skipping rope on the sidewalk. The neighborhood, once a favorite of cops, has become heavily Asian the last few years. Houses here that used to be cheap have lately become very expensive.

Rusty opens the door, beams, hugs me tight, then stands back to take me in. His petite wife, Soo-Lin, stands giggling just behind.

Soon we're seated side by side on a couch in the living room done up in busy faux pan-Asian decor—lacquered Korean chest, ceramic Cambodian elephants, reproduction Ming-style chairs arranged beneath framed ornate Japanese kimonos on the wall. Soo-Lin serves us tea, then sweetly withdraws, fulfilling what must be Rusty's fantasy of a submissive Asian wife.

"Jack keeps me up to date on all your doings, Kay. Lately seems like the only times he calls are to get you information."

I thank him for the background information on Vince Carroll. I give him Maddy's phone number, ask him for final-months records of her calls.

Rusty nods. "No problem. Always glad to help you out." He folds the slip of paper bearing Maddy's number, takes a sip of tea, then glances at me and smiles.

"Up to your neck in it, aren't you, dear? The waterfront thing your pal Glickman's been writing about."

"Don't know if I'm quite up to my neck in it, Rusty. Up to my kneecaps maybe."

He laughs, much too heartily, I think, as if I've made a truly witty remark. Then, too suddenly, he turns dead serious.

"Bad business, Kay. Tong wars. People get hurt in those kinda deals. Innocents most of 'em. Journalists too, when they stick their heads into it. Stick your head in too far someone might chop it off."

I gulp. "Do you know something, Rusty?"

"Just what I read . . . and hear around."

"What d'you hear?"

"No one's got anything against *you,* Kay. Everyone likes you fine. It's Glickman they don't like. The way he pries. There're people around who'd like to see him get it good."

Jesus! "What're you telling me, Rusty?"

"I know Chinatown . . . even better than your dad. There's stuff going on in the cellars there he's got no idea about. Get out of it, Kay. Get out now while you can. Glickman needs a shutterbug, there're plenty of others he can use."

"Joel's my friend."

"Then do him a favor, tell him to lay off. Take a vacation. Hawaii maybe, or better still, South America."

I stare at him. "That sounds like a threat, Rusty. Is this why you asked to see me?"

He grins. "Did I ask, Kay? Way I remember, it was you called me."

"Dad's suggestion."

Rusty shrugs, takes another sip of tea, then beams at me the way he did at the door.

"Not a threat, Kay. Just a warning from someone doesn't want to see you hurt. You know how a cop feels about his partner. It's the same thing with your partner's kids.

You care for them like they're your own." He glances at his watch, stands. "Time to call you a cab. Don't worry— I'll get right on those phone bills for you. So great to see you, Kay. Real glad we had this chance to talk."

In the cab I start to shake. *What was Rusty telling me?* Surely more than just a general warning about "tong wars."

I look out the window. We're on the Great Highway heading north. Fog's closing in, the kind of heavy damp San Francisco sea fog that can make your teeth chatter even in midsummer. As we swing around Sutro Heights Park, I have the driver pull over, then get out, walk a few paces into the park, pull out my cell phone and call Joel.

He picks up immediately. "Where are you?" I ask.

"Just cruising around. How 'bout you?"

When I tell him where I am, he offers to come pick me up. "Walk down to Cliff House," he says. "I'll meet you in front."

I agree, start back toward the street, then stop. A large statue, partially hidden in a grove of pines, seems to emerge out of the fog like an apparition. I walk over to it, look up, examine the carving on the pedestal: *DIANA*.

Of course! It's the famous statue of Diana, Goddess of the Hunt, patroness of the G.G.C.—a slim beautifully sculpted female figure holding a bow and arrow, standing beside a slain stag. At the solstices and equinoxes, pagans and goddess worshippers assemble here to leave garlands around her neck and nosegays at her feet, while on these same occasions, up in Mendocino County, Carson and his friends misappropriate the marvelous creature's legend.

The fog surrounds me as I stand on the promenade behind the Cliff House restaurant, looking out at the water.

I can see nothing, can only smell the ocean, its salty mol-luscous essence. The night is windless. I can hear bells in the buoys, foghorns from ships plying the coast and the barks of sea lions cavorting on Seal Rock.

I like this spot, so popular with tourists, preferring to visit it at night when there's barely anyone around. Dad, knowing how much I liked to go out when the sky turned dark, used to bring me here at dusk. Then my photopho-bia would recede and my keen night vision would engage. Many evenings we'd stand by this very balustrade gazing at the water rimmed by moonlight or, as tonight, bound by fog.

At other times, daylight times, I remember him taking me into the Camera Obscura situated on the terrace below, where, inside the strange dark chamber, constructed after a design of Leonardo da Vinci, I would gaze at the projected image of the ocean without being snow-blinded by the brilliant light outside. Seeing the Camera Obscura now, basically a camera-shaped shack with a turret poking up out of its roof, I decide it's the perfect place for my meet-ing with Vince Carroll.

Joel pulls up in his VW. He looks vulnerable tonight, not the prize-winning investigative reporter I know and admire, rather a worried, narrow-shouldered, bespectacled, bearded guy wandering the city in a shabby car.

I beckon him to get out, stand with me at the balustrade. Never a man to stand when there's an available seat, he reluctantly agrees.

"Can't see anything," he complains, taking up a posi-tion by my side.

"Well, Joel, isn't that the story of our lives?"

"Depressing," he mutters. "I'm shivering. Can we please get back in my car?"

"Sure. Just wanted you to feel the lostness here."

We take El Camino del Mar through Lincoln Park, swing in silence by the Palace of the Legion of Honor, where the fog breaks the symmetry of the facade. Then we drive through Sea Cliff, past mansions hanging like aeries above the fogbound coast.

"Some nights I drive around for hours," Joel tells me. "Through residential areas, never downtown. I like the look of houses when it's dark, the windows lit up inside. It gives me a feeling. You know . . . melancholy." He shrugs. "Sorry. I can't explain it."

I've never known him to talk like this. Normally he's so focused it doesn't occur to me he has moods.

"You called me for a reason," he says.

I tell him about Rusty Quinn, how he and Dad were partners on the Chinatown bunco squad, how they stayed close even after Dad quit S.F.P.D., how Rusty became Dad's and, later, my source for information normally accessible only to cops. Then how Dad suggested I go see Rusty, and how this evening, I did.

Joel listens as I tell him what Rusty had to say, but says nothing, just drives on into the Presidio, then down to the spot where we waited together that night so many weeks ago for what turned out to be the most daring act of human smuggling ever perpetrated in San Francisco Bay.

He cuts the engine. "You think your dad set it up so Rusty could warn you?"

"That occurred to me, but I doubt it."

"Rusty wanted you to know he knows what's behind the tips. Have you thought through the implications of that?"

I nod.

"Funny thing, kiddo—I thought of it myself a couple times, but it seemed so damn implausible that it was a cop thing. Just didn't figure."

"And now?"

"What Rusty said sure makes it seem possible. I wish he'd told you more."

"He won't, Joel. All he wants is for me to get out of it.

That's his obligation to Dad. What he doesn't know is that warning me off is probably the best way of keeping me in."

Joel smiles. A foghorn moans. The Golden Gate Bridge is invisible, totally wrapped in fog. Only the slightest glow breaks through from the highway. In the windless night, we can hear the swish and clatter of cars crossing above.

"If the tips were from a good cop doing his job," Joel says, "he'd have made those busts himself. He wouldn't have called in the Coast Guard, Immigration, Fish and Wildlife. But if he's a bad cop looking to break a gang so he can move in on its action, what better way than to tip off those guys, then sit back while the whole thing self-destructs?"

"So why you, Joel?"

"To send the message. Also, like Rusty told you, maybe the tipster doesn't like me. He could be someone I once wrote about, crucified in an article, called to account. I've done four series on corrupt cops, made more enemies than I care to count. It makes a sinister kind of sense, I think—use me, then pull out the rug."

"Or ambush you."

"Yeah." Joel nods. "That too."

"Rusty has this from his contacts in Chinatown. That's what he meant when he spoke of stuff going on in the cellars. I think he was referring to Chinatown cops. Can you do something with that?"

"I sure as hell can try."

He starts up the car, drives on through the Presidio, along the Marina, then up to my building at the crest of Russian Hill.

"If this is about cops, it could get dangerous," he says. "If you want to bug out, I'll understand."

"You kidding? I want the pictures. I want to be there for the finale."

He grins. "Sounds like you, kiddo. Don't worry, we'll be careful now we've got an advantage. We don't yet know what's going on, but we're starting to get a rough idea I think."

At midnight I call Vince Carroll. Sister Pris answers, annoyed at being woken up.

"Helluva time to call," she mutters.

"Sorry. It's club business."

"Yeah, I know, the usual crisis. Gimme a minute while I kick little bro awake."

A couple minutes later Vince comes on the line, his voice groggy from sleep.

"It's your secret admirer," I tell him cheerfully. "Ready to give me those names?"

"Oh, shit!" He drops the receiver. I wait while he picks it up. "Still there?" he growls.

"Answer the question, Vince."

"You'll get them when we meet."

"And the gun?"

"Fuckin' impossible. You should know better than to ask."

"Okay, we'll put that aside for now. We'll start with Buckoboy and Chipper."

I give him his marching orders. Tomorrow he's to dress in a dark business suit, then drive into the city alone and unarmed with just the beeper I know he carries as director of security for the G.G.C.. He'll be watched, I warn him, along the way. He's to park close as he can get to Cliff House, then, no later than three P.M., descend to the beach. He's to stand there awaiting my beeper message, which will be a string of sevens. When he gets it he's to go to the nearest pay phone on the Cliff House terrace and wait for it to ring. If I decide he's been a good boy, I'll call and tell him what to do next. If I decide he's jerking me around, I'll pursue another course of action.

"That's it?" he asks when I've finished.

"Too complicated for you, Vince?"

"I can handle it."

"Give me your beeper number."

He gives it to me. "You're one tough lady, aren't you?" he asks.

"Not really," I tell him. "A secret admirer—that's all I am."

Two-thirty P.M.: Having paid a buck for admittance, I'm standing inside the Point Lobos Camera Obscura. Built in the 1940s, it's one of the more quirky San Francisco sights, a holdover from a now defunct amusement park called Playland at the Beach. The owners bill it as "the biggest camera in the world." In fact, that's about what it is, a walk-in twenty-five-foot-square light-tight box with a tiny aperture in its turret. The turret rotates slowly, scanning the immediate area. Light enters through the aperture, strikes a mirror, which projects the image down through several lenses onto a six-foot-diameter horizontal parabolic plate. The effect is marvelous, a sharply focused live picture of activity outside. It's like watching a movie with the action taking place in real time.

I feel safe standing here. New Age–type music plays softly, enhancing the mysterious effect of the incoming light. As usual the place is empty. If people come in, it won't matter; they rarely stay too long. The darkness nurtures me, and since the room is nearly black, my night vision is engaged. Moreover, since the aperture-turret turns, I have a perfect continually changing view of the beach and surrounding area, including the terraces above, enabling me to observe my surroundings through 360 degrees without being seen.

At 2:50 I spot Vince Carroll walking down to the beach dressed in black. I observe him awhile, enjoy the spectacle of him standing sweltering among sunbathers and volleyball players in his dark suit. Every once in a while he checks his watch, betraying his impatience.

Each revolution of the turret takes approximately three minutes, causing me to lose sight of him from time to time. But the turning enables me to make sure no obvious confederates are lingering nearby. Though I don't think Vince brought backup, I take this part of my surveillance very seriously. Yes, there're plenty of people around and I feel safe inside the camera, but I don't want trouble when I leave.

At 3:05, with Vince in full view, I dial his beeper, punch in a string of sevens, then hang up. I watch as he rips the beeper off his belt, studies it, then strides toward the terrace, all the while tracked by the rotating turret of the Camera, which, perhaps on account of its shabby exterior, he seems not even to notice.

His body language on the terrace tells me he's upset. A young woman in a sports bra is using the pay phone. He's wondering if I'll wait or give up. I don't think it occurs to him I can see everything going on.

The young woman completes her call, departs. Immediately Vince moves to the phone. I let him wait awhile, then dial. He snatches up the receiver on the first ring.

"Hot out there?" I ask him.

He looks around. "Where are you?" he demands.

"Not so fast, Vince. First you're going to give me the names."

"That wasn't the deal."

"It *is* the deal," I tell him sternly. "Names and addresses, then we meet."

He gives me the names: Chipper's is Dale M. Drew; Buckoboy's is Morton F. Lawry. Both reside at the same address, 121 Kemppe Street in Fort Bragg.

"So it's the Dale and Mort show?"

"Uh-huh."

"Lovers?"

"Cousins."

"Okay, I'm going to relay this to a friend, then I'll call you back and tell you what to do."

I immediately call Joel's number, leave the names and address on his voice-mail. If something happens to me, at least he'll have the information.

As the turret swings again from beach to terrace, I check to see how Vince is doing. He looks worried now, probably thinks I've abandoned him. I dial the pay phone. Again he snatches it up.

"Come down to the Camera Obscura on the lower level," I tell him. "Give a dollar to the man in the booth and enter. You'll be contacted." I hang up, then watch as he looks around, finds the shack, nods and strides toward it.

I lose sight of him while the turret once again scans the beach. A few seconds later I hear him outside purchasing his ticket. I position myself on the far side of the parabolic plate, then wait for him to enter.

My eyes, of course, are well adjusted to the darkness while he's been out in blinding sunlight. He'll see the moving image on the plate, will likely be mesmerized by it, but to him I'll be just a form in the dark, my features lost in shadow.

"Move to your right," I instruct as he enters. "Stay on the other side of the plate." As he edges to his right, I edge to mine, positioning myself near the exit.

"This is wild!" He gestures at the moving image on the plate. "I'd no idea. You could watch me the entire time."

"Never mind that. We've got business. I didn't like the way you left me in the woods. No water—"

"I left you a filled canteen."

"I couldn't drink from it. It could've been drugged."

He shakes his head. "Sorry. I didn't think of that."

"You were also wrong about my not remembering anything. I remember plenty."

"What are you going to do to those guys? Turn them in? Won't do you any good. Nothing'll happen to them. But they'll know who you are, then you'll *really* have something to worry about."

"I'll take care of them my own way."

"Good. You'll be doing me a favor."

"I want the gun, Vince."

"I told you, that's impossible. What do you want it for anyway?"

"To destroy it."

"You're dreaming!"

"Why? Chipper and Buckoboy got hold of it. They were going to rape me with it. I'm sure they would have if you hadn't come along. I owe you for that. That's why I'm talking to you now."

"Sorry. You'll never get it. It's the club ritual gun."

"I've heard about those rituals."

"Then you know why you can't have it."

Though I've no clear idea what he's talking about, I nod as if I do.

"I know what happened to Chap Fontaine," I tell him. "You lied to the cops. That's obstruction of justice."

He stares at me, trying to read my face.

"I think you're better than the rest of them," I continue. "I think you'd be happy to see the whole house of cards collapse. And it's going to. When Carson killed Fontaine he went too far. There were witnesses. Witnesses can be turned. Better to be one who turns than one who's turned upon."

"You're crazy!"

"I know about Capp Street. I've got pictures taken through the windows. I know about the hunting parties, the 'safaris.' How many people have been killed?"

He casts down his eyes, doesn't answer.

"It's not me who's crazy, Vince. It's the guys you work for. You know it too."

He's badly shaken, no longer fascinated by the moving

picture on the plate; rather he's struck by the implications of what I've said.

A man and a boy enter the Camera. They stare at the moving image on the plate, the man explains how the apparatus works, then, after a minute, they depart.

"Who are you?" Vince demands.

"Who are *you?*" I ask. "Good cop or bad?"

He starts to sputter something, then his voice peters out.

"A snotty shooting club for rich guys is one thing," I tell him. "A secret orgy and manhunt club where they ream people with a gun is something else. The club's going down, Carson and his friends with it. Help me get that gun and I'll try and keep you out of it. Stay loyal to Carson and take your chances."

"I can't help you," he whispers. "Don't you understand? If anything happens to that gun they'll know I'm involved." He pauses. When he speaks again it's in a tone so low I can barely hear him. "They'd kill me for that."

Difficult to argue with a man who tells you he'll be killed. Clearly he's more afraid of Carson than of me. With good reason, since he's seen what Carson's capable of. But I'm not interested in his reasons. I want the G.G.C. destroyed.

I tell him to remain inside the Camera another five minutes; then I put on my heavy shades and slip out the exit door. A minute later, I'm on the terrace of Cliff House beside the same phone where he got my call. I wave toward the Camera turret, then enter the restaurant, cross through the dining room and bar, exit by the front door and grab a cab.

I tell the driver to take me to Japantown, then watch through the back window as we drive away. No cars follow. As we speed down Geary, I say I've changed my mind, ask to be dropped at the corner of Arguello. Here, to make absolutely certain I'm not being followed, I take a slow walk around the block. Satisfied I'm in the clear, I stride over to City Stone Ground, Dad's bakery on

Clement. I can smell the aroma of the bread even before I reach the door. I peer through the window, spot Dad in his baker's whites, talking to one of his Russian refugee staff. He must sense me looking in, for he turns and waves.

"Hey, darlin'!"

Reading his lips, I imagine I can hear his voice even through the thick plate glass.

Tonight I phone Hank Evans in Fort Bragg. Gale answers.

"Hey, how you doin', Kay?"

"Great! I got the names of the guys worked me over at the G.G.C."

"Whoa! Let me call Hank."

When Hank comes on I give him the names, the Kemppe Street address and the information that Chipper and Buckoboy are cousins.

"I'll take care of them," Hank assures me.

"Please, nothing violent, Hank. Scare them, make them crawl, but don't seriously hurt them, okay?"

"Don't worry yourself about it. Job's as good as done."

"They're gun guys so be careful."

He laughs. "I'm the ultimate gun guy. Anything else you want besides an apology?"

I ponder that for a moment. "No," I tell him, "I think an apology will do just fine."

Tonight I ask myself: What am I getting into? How far am I prepared to go?

Maybe, I think, it's time to pull back, put aside my anger. To understand should be sufficient, to exact vengeance is perhaps too much. But it's hard to feel any pity for Chipper and Buckoboy, parodying the arcane pleasures of their bosses. They were gross, they violated me. I want them violated back.

Rusty faxes me printouts of Maddy's last three phone bills, listing not only her toll calls (which were few) but also all her incoming and outgoing local calls. Finding my own number several times, I try to recall our conversations. The calls were brief. We were probably firming up appointments. Still, the memories make me sad.

I start with numbers Maddy called that bear Mission district prefixes. I find several, assemble a list. Jim Lovell, the self-taught street photographer Maddy took on as a student, lives in the Mission, so I eliminate his number, then start calling the rest.

One turns out to be an antiquarian bookseller on Valencia, the second a bookstore at the corner of Mission and Twenty-fourth, the place where, several times, David Yamada dropped Maddy off. There's a call to a photo lab on Guerrero, and four calls to what turns out to be a doctor's office on Seventeenth Street.

Next I check my list against the printout of incoming calls with Mission prefixes. Very quickly I discover seven calls to Maddy's number from the same doctor's office.

I call the number again, this time ask to speak to the medical records clerk. After considerable clicking, a woman with a Creole accent picks up. I tell her I'm trying to gather the records of a woman recently deceased. I give her Maddy's name. Several minutes pass, then she comes back on.

"We never had that patient here," she says. Before I can respond, she disconnects.

Curious, I think. Why would Maddy call and receive calls from the office of a Mission district doctor?

Joel phones. He tells me he's been going through all his old articles and notes on police corruption, pulling out names, assembling a list. Over the last three days he's been on the phone checking up on every cop he ever wrote about—which ones are still with S.F.P.D., which ones are dead, retired or in jail. He's also cross-checked for Chinatown and waterfront connections. So far he's come up with what he calls "one very interesting possibility."

"Can't tell you more now," he says. "Just wanted you to know I'm not sitting on my butt."

Thursday, five P.M.: I'm at the foot of the exterior stairs of a decrepit wooden Victorian on Seventeenth Street between Shotwell and Folsom. A battered moving van is parked in front. Sweaty men are carrying out furniture—chairs, desks, a giant TV. A couch and several disassembled beds are piled by the rear of the truck, waiting to be stowed.

I squeeze by the movers, enter the foyer. A woman in a soiled nurse's uniform, looking harassed, intermittently issues orders in Spanish to the movers while speaking in heavily accented French into a cordless phone.

When I appear she stares through me. Finally noticing me, she motions me toward a large room to her right.

I enter what looks to be a reception area where two women, standing just feet apart, are shrieking at one another in Creole. They pay no attention to me. One, dressed as a nurse, is weeping copiously. The other, in high heels and stylish suit, appears to be making demands. While I wait two movers with Ecuadorian Indian features and squat physiques lift a heavy filing cabinet and carry it out.

"Excuse me."

The women turn to me together.

"Who are you?" snaps High Heels. I'm about to explain when she cuts me off. "Who let you in? Can't you see we're busy here?"

"Must have been Marie-Claire," the nurse says.

The other nods. "If you're from City Health you're too late. Dr. Desaulniers has left and he won't be coming back. Last night he flew to Haiti."

"Leaving us to pick up the pieces," adds the nurse, breaking down in sobs.

Having stepped into what's clearly a difficult scene, my first instinct is to withdraw. But not, I decide, until I find out about the calls.

"Look, I'm not from City Health and I'm not looking for Dr. Desaulniers. I'm trying to find a woman named Bee."

"*Bee!*" High Heels turns to the nurse and laughs. "Hear that? She's looking for Bee!"

"Of all the days," sighs the nurse, working to recover.

"Bee hasn't been here in months," High Heels tells me. "Not since Madame Desaulniers died."

"What did she do here?"

"Hear that?" High Heels cries. "What did she *do?* Want to tell her, Claude? Or should I?"

Claude resumes sobbing. The two Ecuadorian movers reenter, pick up a rolled rug, while a third removes a framed portrait of Jean-Bertrand Aristide from the wall. The three, exiting together, nearly collide at the door.

"She did absolutely nothing, that's what she did," High Heels says. "Her visits here were worthless."

"Where can I find her?"

High Heels throws up her arms. "I have no idea where she is. I don't want to know where she is. I don't care where she is."

"Ask Marie-Claire," Claude suggests. "She may know."

I step back into the foyer. Movers are hauling a large oak bureau down the stairs. Marie-Claire, now off the phone, warns them to be careful.

"Excuse me, can you tell me how I can find Bee?"

Marie-Claire stares at me, confused. "Bee? The therapist? She hasn't been here in months."

I nod. "Do you know where she lives?"

Marie-Claire shakes her head. Then, just as her phone rings, something seems to register. "She's got a place out in Bolinas. Try there," she says, waving me away. Then, into the phone: "Yes, that's right, all appointments have been canceled. Dr. Desaulniers has gone back to Haiti. He's been appointed Deputy Minister of Health."

Saturday morning: Sasha's day off and he's delighted at the chance to depart the city. We drive past pedestrians and joggers thronging the walkways on the Golden Gate Bridge, are entranced by the clusters of sailboats in the Bay lining up to race. As we're coming off the bridge, I spot a close pack of bicyclists climbing the trails of the Marin Headlands. Local weathermen have predicted a ravishing, breezy, fog-free summer weekend.

We wind our way along the coast on precarious Route 1, laughing at our vertigo on the switchbacks. Arriving at Stinson Beach dizzy and nauseous, we resolve to take the longer northern route on our return.

A funny place, Bolinas. There's no sign telling you where to turn off. As often as highway authorities put one up, a posse of xenophobic residents tears it down. But it's not hard to find the town if you have a map, and then when you get there, you wonder what the grand to-do is all about. Like who would want to come to this bedraggled village where burned-out druggies and scrofulous dogs roam the streets, food stores look like they should be closed down by the health department, and aging gray-haired hippie-movement refugees sporting faded tie-dyed T-shirts stagger about in a meditative daze?

We receive disapproving glances when we park on the main street. Evidently Sasha's shiny BMW is not an approved vehicle here. Our first stop is a real estate office where I ask the lone attendant, a freckled girl with multiple piercings in her eyebrows, if she knows a woman named Bee.

She shrugs. "Sounds familiar. What's her last name?"

When I tell her it's Watson, she repeats the name, then chews it. "Sorry," she says. Then, with a smile: "Did you check the phone book?"

A few doors down we come to a natural foods store where varieties of nuts and grains are displayed in open sacks.

I ask the long-haired boy at the counter if he knows a Bolinas resident named Bee Watson. Never heard of her, he says. I'm about to leave when he calls me back.

"There's an old woman called Bee. Don't think she's got a last name."

Excited, I ask where I can find her. He stares at me, confused. Then he steps out from behind his counter, leads me down an aisle to the honey section, scans the shelf, extracts a jar, hands it to me, then returns to his post.

I examine the jar. The label, beautifully hand-lettered, reads: "Bee's All-Natural Honey." At the bottom is the bee signature that appeared on the Bee Watson letters and the gun.

Exhilarated, I carry the jar back to the counter, purchase it, ask the boy where Bee the beekeeper lives.

He shrugs. "Maybe up on Overlook," he says. "Anyhow, you can try."

We drive up to Overlook, find an irregular row of small odd-looking craftsman houses, some with strangely angled roofs, others with turrets, still others shaped like silos.

"I wish you could see the hues," Sasha says. "Some are done up in rainbow colors."

A boy about eight years old is practicing with a pogo stick beside the road. We stop. I ask him if he knows where we can find a woman who keeps bees. He stares at us, terrified, then rushes toward the house behind, a geodesic dome.

"Mommy! Mommy!" he cries.

A huge obese woman with prematurely gray hair waddles onto the porch. She eyes us suspiciously while admonishing the boy. "Goddamnit, Wave—I told you not to talk to strangers."

"They want to know where the bee lady lives," Wave says.

He steps behind her, hides, starts playing peekaboo with us from behind her hulk. She waddles closer.

"We're looking for Bee Watson," I tell her.

"Who's looking? Sherlock Holmes?"

Sasha's laughter makes her grin. Wave grins too, then crouches down between her legs.

I hold up my jar of honey. "We're looking for the woman who makes this."

"That'll be Bee. Never knew her last name." She gives us directions. We're to take a dirt road right, then make a left at the fork. "You'll know it when you get there," she tells us. "Buzz-buzz-buzz."

"Buzz-buzz-buzz," echoes Wave.

We follow her directions. Soon enough, we come upon a sign bearing the bee signature followed by an arrow. As we approach, the road becomes deeply rutted. We pass a rusted-out pickup, then spot an old Volvo parked beside a tarpapered shack, with a trailer set up on cinder blocks behind. Though I don't hear any buzzing, I smell sweetness in the air, then make out a short plump woman on the other side of a field of wildflowers. She's wearing a beekeeper's helmet with fine mesh veil and appears to be puttering amidst a set of hives.

Evidently she hears us, for she turns and waves. A few minutes later, she walks over. When she lifts her veil I see a lovely sweet-natured English face crowned by silver bangs. I recognize her at once as the unknown mourner who wept so copiously at Maddy's funeral.

She seems to recognize me as well, for she nods at me and smiles.

"I know who you are. You're Kay," she says. "Dear Maddy used to talk about you all the time." Her smile is warm, her accent British.

"Lovely day, isn't it? A good day to sit down and talk. There's a nice spot of shade behind the house. Would you and your young man like to join me for some tea and honey?" She grins. "Best honey in the world. You have my word on it!"

Bee is small, with fine hands, a woman of exuberant gestures. She's also bouncy. As she speaks, she sometimes stands up out of her seat.

"Oh, she was a gunslinger!" Bee says. " 'Deadeye,' they called her. 'Sharpshooter!' 'Miss Sure-Shot!' All the words like that. And her eyes! Well, you remember her eyes, Kay. To see them once was never to forget them. Blazing eyes! Eyes that'd melt you down like wax. She could shoot wicks off burning candles, suit marks off playing cards tossed in the air. She did that wonderful old Annie Oakley trick too, shooting backward using a mirror. She'd shoot the cigarette out of your mouth. Once, when a fella challenged her, said he could shoot the pants off her, she literally shot the pants off him, actually shot off his waist button and his trousers fell to his ankles. He hobbled away and fell in the mud—*kaboom!* They called it 'trick shooting,' but it wasn't. It was honest shooting. As honest as the girl. And never in my life did I meet anyone more honest than Mandy Vail."

We're sitting in a little patio set up between her trailer and the tarpaper shack, shaded by branches of a big Monterey pine arching overhead. The sand floor's been raked. There's a freshly painted round metal table and three white metal cushioned chairs. Three slightly chipped Chinese teacups, three fancy old silver spoons and a pot of fresh unpasteurized honey in the middle, honey so good, buttery, pungent with wild herbs, that the only descriptive phrase that comes to mind is "nectar of the gods."

I feel like I've just been hurled down by a stupendous aikido throw. It's like I'm on the mat now, all the breath knocked out of me, and I need a good jolt of something to bring me back. So I dig my spoon deep into the pot of honey, bring it to my mouth and suck the marvelous substance off. There! That's better! I'm revived, though still amazed. And yet it all makes sense, is so utterly logical I don't know why I didn't think of it before.

Maddy Yamada, she of the intense gaze, the laser-sharp eyes, the perfect eye-hand coordination, she who could perfectly nail a moving subject with her Leica at two hundred feet, one of the greatest war and action photojournalists of her generation—why couldn't she also have been an expert markswoman in her youth? It's all of a piece, gunslinging and photography. I learned that from Dakota. But still, to think that my Maddy, who hated violence and detested guns, had once been Mandy Vail, Wild West show sharpshooter—the concept boggles.

"She was a great cowgirl. Great horsewoman. Her entrances were terrific. She'd come in like a gust of wind."

Bee Watson glows as she speaks of it. Sasha, sensing my excitement, takes my hand.

"She'd gallop into the ring," Bee tells us, "white-brim cowgirl hat hanging from her neck, fringe flying behind her buckskin jacket, Winchester pump rifle slung over her back, twirling her pearl-handled six-guns, one in each hand, and, even while she held the reins of her steed, firing at floating helium balloons. Such carriage! Presence! She was irresistible. Everyone loved her. And oh yes—it was love that put an end to it too, that turned it all to bitter ash."

I start asking questions. I struggle to obtain the facts: How did Maddy learn to shoot? How to explain her prowess with guns? How did she land in a Wild West show? How did Bee come to know her? What was she like before the transition to photography? I want to hear the saga of her early life, and Bee is eager to recount it. I have the feeling this is a story she's been waiting to tell. Now that someone finally wants to hear it, it bubbles out of her like champagne.

Maddy Yamada was born Amanda Vail in Medicine Bow, Wyoming, in 1931, only child of Jim and Dilly Vail, hunting guide and hunting-camp cook. It was her dad who taught her how to shoot.

Jim Vail, regarded as one of the best professional tracker-hunters in the state, made good money accompanying rich, powerful men out to bag elk, cougar and bear—oil men, industrialists, generals and politicians, even, one time, a former President of the United States. The Vails ran a class operation, supplying burros, tents, camping gear, trophy carriers, everything a serious hunter might need. And the food rustled up by Dilly, wild game prepared over open fires, was considered some of the best hunting-camp food in the West.

Amanda—or Mandy, as they called her—inherited, they said, the deadeye aim of her Wind River Shoshone grandfather on her mother's side, a famous hunter in his time. Even from her infancy people would comment on her eyes, how bright they were, how they burned like little fires in her face. She was an active, highly intelligent, tomboy-type girl, with a feisty nature, a winsome smile and almost frightening powers of concentration.

By the time she was five she was plinking rabbits. At twelve she was winning shooting competitions. At fourteen she was junior state champion. Wild West shows, long in decline, had pretty much died out during the Great Depression. But after World War II there was a revival. Mandy was sixteen when she saw her first show. She was bowled over by it.

In 1948, just seventeen, she moved on her own to Laramie to study mathematics at the University of Wyoming. She loved math, excelled at it, took pleasure in its logic, certainty, proofs. While attending college, she decided to take up "fancy shooting." Asking around, she found a coach, an old-time showman shooter named Tom Sewitt, who had actually known Annie Oakley when he'd worked as a stable boy in Buffalo Bill Cody's Wild West before World War I.

From Tom, Mandy learned some of the immortal Annie's favorite moves: behind-the-back shooting, mirror-shooting, shooting backward using only the blade of a bowie knife as her mirror. Under his coaching she learned to fire six shots with her revolver in one second, to fire at six clay targets all thrown into the air at once, breaking each before it reached the ground. She could split aspirin tablets, puncture brass bus tokens, shoot chunks out of golf balls in flight, cut a rope while Tom spun it as a lariat, reduce clay targets to powder, explode lemons thrown in the air, "pulp" tomatoes, "scramble" eggs, reduce apples to applesauce. She could also create cartoon pictures with bullet holes by firing at a backlit screen. She'd fire six dead accurate bullets in a row. *Boom-boom-boom-boom-boom-BOOM!* Above all, she learned the great trick of trick shooting: there is no "trick" to it, just practice, practice, practice.

The first year with Tom she shot thirty thousand rounds. The second year forty thousand. In 1950, at the age of nineteen, without a word to her parents, she took the train to Denver to audition as a fancy shooter for the Great Western Circus. The proprietors watched in awe as the bold girl with the flaming red hair performed. After her exhibition, they hired her on the spot.

In the circus they announced her, just before her entrance, as "Mandy Vail, Deadeye Shooter."

The crowds nourished her. She reveled in their wonder and applause, loved the greasepaint, the costumes, the drumrolls, the smell of the sawdust, the way the spotlight followed her around the ring. Hunting in the woods was fun, higher mathematics presented a challenge, but performing in public was best of all—it made her feel alive.

Bee Watson, five years older, was traveling with the Great Western Circus too, not as a performer but as company armorer, in charge of maintenance and safekeeping of the edged weapons and small arms used in the show. A rebel herself, she had fled her father's engraving shop in London the year before to seek adventure in the American West. She came over on a contract to engrave Colt revolvers, soon tired of it, then hooked up with the circus.

Though she loved engraving, she hated the thought of spending her life breathing the bad air of an engraver's shop. The circus was fun, gave her a chance to travel and engage with life. Shortly after Mandy joined, she and Bee became fast friends, going out dancing, flirting with men, sharing hotel rooms and confidences.

"I don't think Maddy—I'll call her that from now on, but remember, she called herself Mandy back then—I don't think she had much romantic interest in boys before we met," Bee says. "They were more like brothers to her, hunting pals, shooting-competition rivals she could easily defeat. But being always on the road, moving from town to town as we did—that put the pressure on. The circus was a sexual hothouse. Everyone was sleeping with everybody else."

Bee had come to America in search of adventure; now she found it in men's arms. She'd take a circus-crew member as a lover for a month, then throw him over for someone else. Or else meet a man at one of the dance halls she and Maddy frequented, spend a week of bliss with him, then wave goodbye when the circus train pulled out of town.

With Bee's guidance and encouragement, Maddy too joined the fun, flirting, kissing, indulging in petting, all the while retaining her virtue. She was seeking true love, and that, at least around the circus, was in short supply.

And, too, she scared men off. Bee thought it was her eyes.

"They seemed to consume you, gobble you up. A lot of men couldn't take it. There she was, young, beautiful, immensely talented and admired, and yet there was this forbidding thing about her too. Yes, her eyes, and perhaps also her purity, by which I don't mean virginity. More like the purity of her intent. There was no nonsense about her. No claptrap. Not only did she shoot straight, she was a straight shooter in every sense. Charlatans, fakes, frauds and poseurs, silver-tongued pretty boys with well-practiced seduction patter—the circus was full of them—were wary of her because they knew she could see straight through them. Better to stick with their own kind, or court a playful girl like me who was just out for fun."

But there were others who felt challenged by Maddy's discrimination, who vowed they'd be the first to bed her. One in particular, a stagehand and roustabout named Ram Carson, was determined to woo her with his charm.

"Wait!" I lean forward, head reeling. "You're talking about Ramsey Carson, the real estate tycoon in San Francisco, the one who collects erotic guns?"

Bee nods. "I see you've done your homework, Kay. Yes, that's the one."

"So that's the connection!"

"You know the story?"

"No," I tell her. "I don't know anything. Just that Maddy was spying on an apartment owned by Carson in the Mission, where Carson and his gun club pals did, you know . . . whatever."

Bee laughs. " 'Whatever'—I like that. Because, God knows, they were certainly doing *something* up there. But I'm getting ahead of myself. Unless you want the story backward."

No, I tell her, I want it straight, the way Maddy would have told it, in sequence, as it happened.

Bee nods. " 'Tell all the Truth but tell it slant.' Emily

Dickinson wrote that. Of all your Yank poets, she's my favorite. I'll try to tell it to you straight, Kay, but since I know only my own version and the events took place long ago, please forgive me if it comes out a little crooked sometimes."

Carson was an immensely handsome young man, several years younger than Maddy. He was muscular and headstrong, with a poetic veneer that hid the coarseness beneath. At first Maddy was taken with him. Perhaps, she confided to Bee, Ram, so much like a character out of a Jack London novel, was worth her time. Bee, who'd had a fling with him herself, did not encourage her friend.

Very soon Maddy became disillusioned. Ram was a marvelous dancer, a terrific kisser, had drop-dead good looks. But there was a mean streak in him which Maddy soon perceived: the way he bullied the horses, became belligerent when he drank, picked fights with smaller, weaker men while playing up to those above him. There came a point where she refused to go out with him, refused even to dance with him or speak with him in private.

This, unfortunately, did not dampen Ram's ardor. Perhaps because no girl had ever rejected him, he refused to take his dismissal seriously. On the contrary, like many egotistical men, he took it as a ploy. She must be trying to excite him, he told his friends, make herself more desirable by playing hard to get. Impossible she could resist him if he set his mind to her seduction. He decided then to change tactics, court her the old-fashioned way, sending notes, flowers and intermediaries to plead on his behalf.

He even attempted to recruit Bee for this purpose: "We had a good few weeks together, you and I," he told her, "but Mandy's the girl for me. Help me win her, Bee. Please."

When Bee laughed he was taken aback.

"She doesn't like you, Ram. Accept it and leave her alone."

But he wouldn't. And when Maddy finally did meet someone she liked, he became coldly furious.

The other boy was named Tommy Dunphy. He was the same age as Maddy, also a performer, a recent recruit to the Great Western Circus, hired to play several heroic roles—Wyatt Earp in the O.K. Corral sketch, and Colonel George Custer in the big spectacle piece, "Custer's Last Stand."

Tommy was an actor, not a shooter, though he fired off blank cartridges in his scenes. Ram, who was a shooter, hated him from the start, first because, being an actor, Tommy was far higher in the circus pecking order, and more important, because Maddy was attracted to him.

At first their relationship struck Bee as brother-sister stuff. Tommy was pretty rather than handsome, had beautiful almond-shaped eyes, sensual lips, shag-cut golden hair that curled over his ears. He wasn't a good dancer or a particularly good kisser; in no sense was he a ladies' man. But there was a boyish sincerity about him that appealed to Maddy, a naïveté equal to her own. Even more attractive was his natural sweetness. Tommy was friendly, modest, self-effacing, generous and, perhaps most in his favor in Maddy's eyes, totally without guile.

They became secret lovers. Those first weeks even Bee didn't know. They'd meet after evening performances, go off together on long walks about the fairgrounds, then disappear to quiet corners of the encampment or to empty compartments in the circus railway cars. Bee began to notice changes in Maddy, a new quietude, the way she glowed and sometimes sighed aloud. It was only when she saw them practice shooting together that she understood what was going on.

It was a classic triangle: the beautiful girl, the pretty blond boy she'd chosen as her lover and the dark handsome boy who wanted her, was spurned and now smoldered in silent fury.

Everyone in the troupe knew how Ram felt. He continued to tell his friends, with an insistence that belied conviction, that the reason Mandy Vail flirted with Dunphy was to make him jealous. He would win her, he promised; they would see. Why else did she evade his glances unless she was afraid she'd yield to him if she did not?

Yes, everybody knew ... except Maddy and Tommy, too wrapped up in one another to notice. Bee doubted that Tommy, as a featured player, was even aware of Ram's existence. As for Maddy, in her bliss she even forgot he was around.

One day Ram left a lengthy love letter for her, the silly, preposterous letter of a lovesick boy. It was filled with weakly expressed affection coupled with pompous pronouncements. It was all about him, not her, *his* distress, *his* needs, without any regard for feelings she might harbor or had ever professed. He accused her of playing him for a fool, taking up with another to make him jealous. But, he wrote, he was ready to forgive her now that the time had come to end the charade and admit to how she truly felt. "I'm the only man for you," he wrote. "We were meant for each other. There can be no other in your life." It was an obsessed, grandiose, lunatic letter, a little scary too.

Maddy was upset by it. Showing it to Bee Watson, she confessed she had barely noticed Ram lingering about the last few weeks, and had never encouraged him during the brief time they'd dated.

"He's so egotistical. What am I going to do? I can't just ignore this, Bee. Or can I?"

Bee agreed Maddy couldn't ignore the letter, that she had to send a message, something that would make Ram understand his cause was hopeless and he must henceforth leave her alone.

"I don't want to ridicule him," Maddy said, "but everything about him fills me with scorn."

Bee agreed. Ridicule was not the way. But a terse response was necessary. Ram had to be shaken out of his delusion.

There was a famous story about Annie Oakley, probably apocryphal but a good vignette nonetheless. Idolizing

Annie, Bee and Maddy both knew of it. And in these circumstances, it seemed to carry a relevant lesson.

Sometime in 1887, during the stupendously successful season of Buffalo Bill's Wild West at Earl's Court in London, Annie received a written offer of marriage from a self-described French count. Enclosed was a photograph of the gentleman, along with writing to the effect that he'd surely commit suicide if she refused.

Annie, it's said, shot out the eyes in the suitor's portrait with her revolver, scrawled "Respectfully Declined" across the bottom and mailed the picture back.

What Maddy said she liked about Annie's response was the combination of contempt and personal esteem. The bullet holes represented a highly emphatic "NO!" while the word "respectfully" showed a lady's regard for a gentleman's feelings however absurd.

Thus, in emulation of her idol, Mandy Vail tacked Ram Carson's handwritten letter to a corral post, marked off thirty paces, turned on her heel and emptied her Winchester into it, creating a large X of bullet holes across the paper. She then retrieved the punctured document, carefully refolded it, scribbled a brief note to the effect that as much as she was honored by Ram's sentiments she was in love with another, and asked him as a gentleman to kindly leave her alone.

In retrospect, Bee felt, the rebuff was too harsh, but then both Maddy and Ram were young and the whole affair smacked of boy-girl melodrama. Another mistake, Bee admitted, was Maddy's assumption that Ram Carson was a gentleman.

Her response to Ram's love letter was deeply wounding, especially as word of it spread around the troupe. Ram had acquired enemies. When they heard how Maddy had X'ed his letter with bullets, they reminded him of his boasts and taunted him for his failure to win her heart.

He couldn't take his hurt and anger out on Maddy, or

even on Bee, whom he believed to be the Svengali behind Maddy's atrocious act. They, after all, were merely girls; a man could only fight a man. He thought about beating up Tommy. No doubt he could do it; he was far stronger and good with his fists. But, he reasoned, administering a beating, however pleasureful, would only win sympathy for Tommy, drive him further into Maddy's arms and ensure that he, Ram, would be fired from Great Western.

There was another means to redeem his honor, he decided, a way far more meaningful and poignant. Maddy, being an expert shooter, respected good shooting performances by others. Moreover, she'd been teaching Tommy how to shoot. If Ram could lure Tommy into a shooting match and win, he could prove he was the better man in the very field in which Maddy excelled. Victory in such a contest might not win her back, but it would be sweet, would defeat Maddy and his rival and thus partially settle the score.

Impossible, of course, to understand how the final plan evolved within Ram's brain. But, Bee believed, there must have come a point when, brooding over his humiliation, seeking a suitable revenge, he realized a conventional shooting contest wouldn't do. Such competitions were usually good-humored affairs in which defeat was lightly taken and hands were shaken at the end. Ram required something darker and more serious.

"I think what occurred to Ram," Bee says, "as he nursed his wounds in his roustabout's bunk, was something like this: Sure, to beat Dunphy in a shooting match would be fun, but not nearly painful enough. This guy and Mandy have got to be made to hurt. So what about a real man-to-man gunfight, a duel? Call him out, face each other with pistols, fire at will, may the best man win."

As Bee says this I start to tremble. Heat rises to my head as the hidden symmetry starts coming clear. To calm myself I take another slug of Bee's honey. Then I remember Agnes Fontaine speaking of rumors of a deadly duel in Ram Carson's past. Could this have been the one, with Maddy the inciter?

It was all madness, of course. Bee imagined the paranoia swirling inside Ram, the brooding over and nurturing of the injustice inflicted upon him, the crazed sparkle in his eye as he devised his scheme, the satisfaction as he contemplated his vindication.

The troupe was performing in California at the time, working the Central Valley along the railway line north to south: Redding, Chico, Yuba City, Sacramento, Stockton, Modesto, Merced, Fresno, Bakersfield.

It was just outside Stockton that the duel took place. Maddy had left the circus several days before on a two-week visit home to Wyoming. Her mother had fallen ill, her father had called on her to help and Maddy, a loving and obedient daughter, arranged a special leave with management, then fled to her ailing mother's side.

Ram must have calculated this was the time to strike. With Maddy around, there was a chance she'd intervene and stop the fight. Or worse, if Ram knocked Tommy off, she'd step in and face off with him herself, in which case Ram would certainly be killed.

He also must have calculated the insult extremely carefully, for it was essential that Tommy Dunphy be riled up enough to fight. From what Bee heard, the offense was brutally delivered in front of others just after a morning rehearsal of the O.K. Corral sketch in which Tommy starred.

It was a hot, humid summer day. The rehearsal had just finished. Tommy and the other actors, dirty and sweaty from their work, pulled themselves off the ground, flicked the dust off their clothes, then started toward the dressing area to change out of costume and shower.

It was at this point that Ram interjected himself.

"Hey, Dunphy," he yelled. "You draw a gun like a girl." People turned. Tommy stood frozen, then looked around to see who'd spoken. When his eyes met Ram's, he broke into a smile. "Very funny," he said.

"No," Ram replied, "isn't funny. It's true."

Ram approached, then stopped, spread his legs in a gun-slinger stance and continued with his taunts.

"I think you're a girlie-boy, Dunphy. You act mighty girlish the way you draw. Way you play patty-cakes with Mandy Vail too. She's your boyfriend, right? That how it goes?"

Tommy kept smiling. He couldn't believe what he was hearing. *Who is this guy? One of the roustabouts. What's his problem anyway?*

Tommy wasn't one to seek confrontations. Off stage he was gentle and shy. Still, aspersions upon his masculinity and gross disparagement of Maddy could not be borne. People were watching him. He was a featured player; he played heroic roles. He knew the man facing him was trying deliberately to provoke him, but he couldn't let such insults pass.

"Who the hell are you?" he demanded.

"I'm Ram Carson. You're Girlie-boy Dunphy, right?"

There was a sneer on Ram's face, the sneer of a playground bully. Tommy understood that this was serious.

"You need a lesson in manners, Carson."

"You the one to give it to me, girlie?"

"You look kind of girlie there yourself."

"Guess we should settle this then. You don't box, so a fistfight wouldn't be fair. But you draw and shoot, least you pretend to. So let's see who shoots like a girl. Let's settle this with guns."

Again Tommy looked about. He'd just received a challenge issued in the manner of a western movie, the town bully calling out the hero on Main Street, townspeople assembled to see which man backed down.

"Whatsamatta? Afraid to shoot without little Mandy around to help? You're a chicken-livered coward, ain't you? Cluck-cluck-cluck!" Ram delivered the jeer in a barnyard falsetto.

Mocked beyond endurance, Tommy rushed at Ram, who sidestepped, causing Tommy to plunge headlong into the dirt. Ram leaned down, gave Tommy his hand, helped him up, brushed him off.

"You've been challenged, Dunphy. If you're not too chicken to take it up, send a friend to speak to mine." Ram indicated his best buddy in the crowd. Then he laughed, and strode back to his job.

Word spread quickly around the circus. Bee, appalled at the prospect of a gunfight, immediately sought Tommy out.

"He didn't seem like the boy I knew," Bee tells us. "It was as if his personality had totally changed. Suddenly here was this cocky kid, all juiced up, full of himself, raring to fight.

" 'Carson made a big mistake calling me out,' he told me. 'In the show I draw a gun and fire at people every day. And under Mandy's coaching, my shooting's gotten pretty slick.'

" 'But this is real, Tommy,' I reminded him. 'Not a show. You're an actor, Ram's a fighter. He's jealous of you 'cause Mandy likes you. That's what this is about.' "

Tommy told Bee he knew all that, had been so informed that afternoon. Which was all the more reason to go through with the duel—not just to defend his own honor, but Mandy's too. Anyhow, it was too late to call it off. The seconds had met. Everything had been arranged.

"Frankly," he told her, "I think Carson'll chicken out. He knows I can shoot, but he thinks I'm a coward. When he finds out I'm not, he'll apologize, you'll see. And if he doesn't—well, I'll just shoot him down."

There was no reasoning with him. As far as Bee was concerned, both guys were behaving like little boys. Ram had played cleverly on Tommy's pride, and now, it seemed, Tommy had psyched himself into thinking he could take Ram on.

There was a part of her that found the situation ludicrous, believed the duel couldn't and wouldn't take place—that someone would have sense enough to stop it or that the boys themselves would call it off.

Later, she would hate herself for not taking the affair more seriously, for being so maddened by Tommy's posing that she didn't go to circus management and, failing their intervention, to local cops. Later she learned she wasn't the only member of the troupe who felt this way. No one really believed there'd be a duel. It was 1955, Eisenhower was President, this was the United States of America. A real gunfight just seemed . . . impossible.

They met at dawn when everyone in the troupe was still asleep, four young men, the two duelists accompanied by their seconds, in a clearing in a eucalyptus grove not far from where the circus was encamped. Tommy, she understood, dressed to be seen, wore one of his costumes from the show, an elaborate gunslinger's outfit with handmade shirt, tooled holster, boots and spurs. Ram, on the other hand, dressed to kill, wore a tattered old T-shirt, faded jeans, a wrangler's jacket and a battered holster casually belted about his waist.

The seconds had agreed on rules. The weapons would be .32 caliber, the same as Maddy used in her act. The combatants would stand facing one another separated by sixty feet, each one's gun loaded with a single round. At the count of three, each could draw and fire at will. Failing a hit, both guns would be reloaded, then the duel would proceed with the distance closed to fifty feet, and failing again, to forty. Between rounds either combatant could call the fight off. An apology for his remarks by Carson or a concession by Dunphy that Carson's remarks were true would also constitute a stop.

"I imagine them standing there in the morning summer fog," Bee tells us, "Tommy sweating, his heart pounding wildly in his chest with the realization that this time the fight would be real. Meantime Ram stands cool, heart rate normal, eyeing Tommy with the poise of a hunter awaiting his chance to kill. Neither boy willing to back down, each seeking satisfaction for his injury, the two bound together by shared feelings for the absent Maddy, who, were she present, would have instantly shot the guns from both their hands.

"I imagine the early-morning chattering of birds perched on the limbs of surrounding trees. Tommy's tension as the seconds step back to make the count. The sense of inevitability that pervades him, the mood of doom. His belief that fate has drawn him to this encounter, and that fate alone will determine the outcome. Above all, the aura of unreality, that this isn't, can't be happening, that in a moment some person or force will intervene. And Ram, all the while measuring his opponent, feeling his weakness, knowing he holds his life in his hands and can take it at his whim.

"The voice of Ram's second as he solemnly makes the count: 'One. Two. Three.' Each boy draws his gun, then waits for the other to fire. That would be each one's way of showing he's not a coward, that he can face up to a bullet without a flinch. Suddenly the sun breaks through the canopy. A beam of light, shimmering with fine dust, falls upon Tommy's face. It's like the sudden heat of the spotlight picking him out during the show. Unnerved, Tommy's hand begins to shake. Ram grins, taunting him with his smirk. Infuriated, Tommy fires wildly, missing Ram by fifteen feet. Birds, startled by the explosion, break from the trees. Then the clearing goes still.

"Ram again smiles to himself, lowers his gun a little, then raises it slowly. Tommy, understanding that this is real, wanting to run yet fighting his instinct to flee, stands stiff and rigid as a post. Ram's grin widens. Raising his gun further, holding it steady, he slowly squeezes his trigger. The roar. The bullet hurtling through space. Tommy, knowing he'll be struck, perhaps bending forward a fraction to facilitate the collision. The bullet smashing him square between his eyes. Tommy collapsing slowly to the ground."

Bee sits back, shakes her head. She's been telling the story with such intensity she's out of breath.

"So awful," she says, "so sad. Everyone who knew Tommy was heartbroken. This talented young man suddenly cut down . . ." She sighs. "The tragedy changed all our lives."

Maddy, receiving news from Bee by telegram, never returned to Great Western. Instead she stayed with her mother until her death several months later, then disappeared, never again to perform in fancy shooting exhibitions, and as far as anyone knew, never again to fire a gun.

Ram Carson was arrested, charged with manslaughter. Later, through the intervention of a smart public defender, he was recharged with dueling under the California anti-dueling statute, pleaded guilty, received a five-year sentence, was sent to San Quentin, served three years and was released.

Bee left the circus too, to return to England and her father's shop.

"I wanted to make something of myself," she tells us. "I was determined to become the finest gun engraver in the world. Later some said I was." She shrugs. "I'm not sure. But I was good. Several times my father told me I'd surpassed him, and he was among the very best."

Watson & Watson, Gun Engravers. They won prizes, received royal patronage, had a list of clients willing to wait five years for commissioned work. Bee took a year off, traveling to Italy to learn *bulino* technique from the masters of Val Trompia. When she returned she and her father, Jock, collaborated on a number of special pieces for King Farouk of Egypt in which erotic motifs engraved by Bee in *bulino* style were surrounded by Jock's exquisite traditional English-style scrollwork.

"Are those the guns now owned by Carson?" I ask.

Bee nods. "When I heard he bought them, I was mortified. I hadn't heard about the sale. But even if I had, I couldn't have afforded to buy them back."

She empties her teacup on the ground, refills it. "I became a specialist in erotic arms engraving. After people saw what we'd done for Farouk, we received requests from collectors around the world. There aren't many serious ones. Maybe a dozen, fourteen at most. Von Heinholz in Munich, of course. She and Carson are the most aggressive. Jansen in Denmark. Eric Templesman down in L.A. An Argentine billionaire named Masconi. The one they call 'the Turk,' who lives on quai d'Anjou in Paris and whom no one in the business has ever met. I engraved guns for most of them, though not for Carson. At least not knowingly. I'll get to that in a moment. That's when I started signing the pieces with my little drawing of a bee, to keep the erotic work separate from our mainstream product. We were, after all, a respectable firm with clients who'd have been appalled if they knew what we were doing on the side."

In 1965, crossing the Atlantic on British Airways after a brief vacation in the States, Bee opened a plastic-covered airline copy of *Life* magazine to find a series of astounding photographs taken in Vietnam attributed to a photographer named Maddy Yamada.

The pictures were austere and moody, printed in stark black and white, a series of portraits of Vietnamese men and women, young and old, whose lives had been deeply affected by the war. What was most powerful about these pictures was their depth, the sense Bee had that she could feel the emotions of the subjects. And there was amazing tension too in the contrast between the sharply etched portraits and the soft-focus scenes taking place just behind: raging fires, churning helicopters, heavily armed soldiers marching past.

It was, Bee thought, the disconnect between foreground and background that gave these pictures their extraordinary power. Curious about the photographer, she leafed through the magazine to a page where there were snapshots and biographical sketches of contributors.

She didn't immediately recognize Mandy Vail. Ten years had passed since she'd last seen her, the picture was small, not much bigger than passport size, the woman in it wore a flak vest, had short-cropped hair and three cameras strung about her neck. But there was something familiar in the face. It was the eyes, of course, Mandy Vail's eyes, blazing eyes that seemed like they could light up the world. Bee turned to the brief bio sketch, from it learned that Maddy Yamada was a freelance photojournalist who lived in San Francisco. No mention of Wyoming, a past as a fancy shooter, nothing but those bare-bones facts.

Bee turned again to the photographs, wanting to be sure they were as strong as she had thought. Then she looked again at the little snapshot of the photographer. This time she was certain. It *was* her Mandy. No one else she'd ever met had eyes like that.

When Bee returned to London she wrote Maddy a note, expressing admiration for the work, recounting her own activities since she'd left Great Western, ending with an expression of hope they might meet again, then mailed it off to Maddy care of *Life*.

It was nearly a year before she received a reply. Bee's letter finally caught up with Maddy in Tokyo, where she'd gone after spending a year in 'Nam. She was delighted to hear from her old friend. There'd been big changes in her life since their circus days. After Tommy's death she'd lost her heart for shooting and guns, given them up, moved to California, finished college, become interested in photojournalism. Meantime, she'd married one of her teachers, a Nisei university professor of engineering named Harry Yamada, a marvelous man, twenty years her senior, supportive of her new and dangerous career.

She'd love to see Bee again, Maddy wrote. She had fond memories of their days together on the road. Sad that those wonderful times had ended so tragically. But, she went on, she believed in renewal and redemption, even in the case of Carson. She hadn't seen him, of course, but heard he also lived in San Francisco where he'd embarked on a career in commercial real estate. She had no intention of seeing him, yet she harbored no ill will. Of all the friends from the old days, her old pal Bee was the only one she truly missed.

Years passed. Bee and Maddy continued to correspond. Meetings were planned, in Paris, London and New York, but failed to take place on account of family obligations or work. The exchange of chatty letters began to ebb, replaced by brief notes scribbled on the inside flaps of Christmas cards.

More years passed. Maddy became world-famous. Bee subscribed to *Life* in order to follow her work. In the late sixties and early seventies Maddy's photographs appeared twelve times on the magazine's cover.

Meantime Bee's reputation grew. In 1970, her father passed away, leaving her as sole artist/engraver at the Watson & Watson firm. She took in apprentices, attempted to train them, but the pay was low, young people were impatient for advancement, and the handmade British "best gun," always a luxury item, was becoming prohibitively expensive.

By 1975 Bee had restricted her work to special-order one-offs for wealthy collectors. She no longer undertook commissions for standard hunting scenes, would only engrave scenes which had never previously been applied to arms.

Among her seventies and eighties favorites:

A pair of matching Granger sidelocks collectively called "The Justine," commissioned by the Turk, consisting of eight erotic scenes from Marquis de Sade's novel of the same title, embellished with gold and platinum inlays.

A Purdey called "The Oscar," commissioned by a famous British stage and screen actor, depicting key scenes from the life of Oscar Wilde.

"The Venus," a heavy-gauge Krieghoff over-under deeply incised with motifs from Leopold von Sacher-

Masoch's *Venus in Furs,* on commission from an Austrian collector.

An erotic gun called "The Goddess," ordered by an exclusive gun club in California, the scenes incised in *bulino* on a period virgin (unengraved and mint condition) Parker model Invincible, one of only three such guns known to exist.

I turn to Sasha. He holds his head in his hands. When I look again at Bee, she peers at me, eyes open in surprise.

"I've said something wrong, Kay?"

I shake my head.

"But something's upset you. I can tell."

"Why don't you show Bee your drawings," Sasha suggests.

I nod, pull my sketchbook from my camera bag, open it to my main drawing of the G.G.C. ritual gun, hand it to Bee.

She studies the series. "Yes, of course, this is 'The Goddess.' Not exactly, but fairly close." She looks at me, searchingly. "So you've seen it! This is why you've come."

"Not only seen it. It was nearly rammed into me," I tell her quietly.

"Oh, my God!" Bee drops her teacup; it hits the ground, rolls beneath the table. She shakes her head. "Bastards!" Tears pulse from her eyes. "Those awful little shits!"

"I was drugged," I tell her. "Luckily, before they went too far someone came along and stopped them."

"Hyenas!" Bee bites off the word. "I hate them! I told Maddy what they were doing. It made her furious. She vowed she'd stop them. Then—"

Bee blinks, shakes her head. She seems confused. Dazed myself, I ask for a time-out. The story has grown too entangled. In the space of an hour I've learned that years ago Ramsey Carson killed Maddy's first lover in a duel, and now Bee has learned that I, Maddy's student, was nearly raped by the gun she herself engraved for Carson's G.G.C.

Sasha helps me up; then together we follow Bee, who has offered to show us her hives.

We stop first at her shack, where she issues us beekeepers' helmets with veils, gloves and all-white jumpsuits, a necessary precaution, she tells us, since bees will often attack darkly dressed people, mistaking them for marauding bears.

On the walk to the hives she also tells us how, in 1988, she began to suffer from arthritis. Within months, the condition grew worse. Finding herself unable to complete commissions because of pain, she sold the London engraving shop and moved to California, where she'd long yearned to live.

Here, after trying various arthritis remedies, including conventional anti-inflammatories, she heard about apitherapy, the use of bee sting venom to relieve the pain of arthritis and other diseases.

At first she was skeptical. Then, because her name was Bee, she wondered if the coincidence could be karmic and therefore worth exploring.

"That probably sounds 'touchy-feely Bolinas' to you," she says, "but the truth is I was desperate. The pain was terrible. So I thought why *not* try it. I knew I wasn't allergic to bee venom. I'd received many stings in my girlhood and had never gone into anaphylactic shock. So I went several times to an apitherapist who placed bees on various of my acupuncture points. The stings didn't bother me much, and afterwards, to my surprise, my pain would practically disappear.

"No one's sure how it works," she tells us. "And there are plenty of old fogies who don't think it does. Lots of theories. One is that the venom boosts the immune system. Another that it promotes nerve transmissions. A third, the one I subscribe to, that it boosts the body's production of cortisone by as much as a thousand percent. All I know is it works for me."

She tells us how her experiences with apitherapy led to her training to become an apitherapist herself. Which in turn led quite naturally to her becoming a beekeeper, producing honey for herself and a limited production which she sells to local stores, along with bee pollen and beeswax.

Even from a distance we can hear the buzz. As we approach the hives, it grows louder and more ominous. I glance at Sasha, can see he's doubtful.

Bee says she believes bees can detect human fear, so if we feel uncomfortable, she warns, we probably oughtn't to come too close. She has four hives, she tells us, two inhabited by Carniolan bees, two by Italian. Both produce a wonderful mixed-flower honey from the nectars of coastal heather, lavender and bramble. She adds that she herself consumes a cup and a half of raw honey per day, to which she attributes her present good health and sense of well-being.

"Beekeeping is a Zen-like craft," she tells us. "You must move carefully, decisively. When you do it well, you feel an extraordinary connection with the earth. People have been keeping bees since ancient times. There are cave paintings of men gathering honey. The Greeks adored it, consumed it with milk and bread. The Romans cooked with it. Aristotle kept bees. Malta, in corrupted Greek, means 'honey island.' Then there're the bees themselves, fascinating creatures—the way they work, organize, the strange hypnotic dance the gatherers do to describe locations of nectar. My parents, for some reason, named me Bee. And back in the engraving shop my dad would call me his 'little honeybee' when I worked hard. I never thought much about it, just accepted it as an expression of his love. Now I wonder if he saw in me something of what I've since become. For as much as I loved engraving steel, I feel far happier and more in touch doing this."

She shows us the stack of trays in the hives, the bottom box, the hive body or brood chamber, presided over by the queen, the screen called the queen excluder that keeps the queen out of the supers where the bees make and store honey, and the uppermost shelf, which she calls "the attic," the only level from which she takes honey away. She tells us how, in cool weather, she sedates the hives with pine smoke, removes the upper shelf, brushes clinging bees off, then retrieves the precious thick golden fluid.

An hour later, we're back at the patio table beneath the big pine, sipping tea again and feeling more relaxed. The sun is lower now, my vision is better. I take the opportunity to closely inspect Bee Watson's face.

Already I'm enthralled by this extraordinary woman, fascinated too by her amazing life. Studying her, I see surprisingly smooth skin for a person of her age, deep laughter lines, warmth and wisdom in the eyes and a suggestion too, in the curve of the mouth, that she has felt pain and loss yet has never given in to bitterness.

She and Maddy finally got together, their first meeting since August 1955. Though nearly thirty-five years had passed, they at once felt easy with one another, reminiscing, exchanging news. And then instead of falling silent, as is often the case after exuberant initial exchanges between reunited friends, they soon found a warm, effortless camaraderie.

Maddy confided that, on account of slower reflexes and failing vision, she expected to give up active photography in a few years.

"I'm going to devote myself to my students. I wish I could do something completely different the way you have, Bee," she said. "But I made my big career switch years ago."

Bee asked Maddy if she'd ever regretted giving up shooting. Maddy responded she had not, that taking pictures was far more gratifying.

"More weighty too," she told Bee, "in that the 'shots' are permanent. I can contemplate them. They're not just marks on a target that gets torn up."

"Some of your old targets were works of art," Bee replied.

Maddy laughed. "At first I missed the show, the drama of it, the spectacle! But later I got to like hiding behind my camera." She paused. "Of course, it isn't like that. Took me years to realize it. Though my face never appears in my pictures, I think I'm more present in them than I ever was trick-shooting before a crowd. The crowd's huge now, hundreds of thousands, looking closely at images I make with my hands and eyes. Those images *are* me. They reflect my vision. When I study my old pictures I continue to learn things about my subjects, but I believe I learn a great deal more about myself."

From time to time Bee and Maddy would meet in the city for lunch, or phone one another just to chat. Twice Maddy came out to Bolinas for weekends. On these visits they slept in adjoining hammocks strung up outdoors. Maddy loved the country, told Bee sleeping out like this reminded her of her Wyoming girlhood. Both times Bee tried to lure Maddy into picking up one of the rifles she kept around the place. Maddy refused.

"I just can't do it," she confessed. "It's a phobia. The notion makes me sick. I tell my students to photograph what they fear. And I've been photographing men with guns for years. But photographing and handling are two different things." Maddy paused. "You see, I think if I picked up a gun now, I'd feel a great desire to fire it. And if I did that . . . no telling where it might lead."

They spoke very little of Carson, Maddy simply mentioning again that he'd succeeded in business, had become rich and was occasionally cited in society columns as one of the more eligible bachelors in town. She didn't think Ram knew she lived nearby, or ever connected the Mandy Vail he'd once thought he loved to Maddy Yamada, photojournalist.

All this time, Bee kept up her gun-collector connections. Occasionally she'd receive requests, through the old

Watson & Watson firm, for special-order erotic engraving.
She turned all such commissions down. She'd lost interest
in engraving, had embarked upon an entirely different sort
of life. Still, she wasn't one to burn her bridges. She loved
gun-world gossip and solicited it in her letters.

She'd been aware for a time that a new collector of
erotic guns had appeared on the scene and was aggressively
buying everything in sight. It was only with the sale of the
Farouk guns that she learned that this was Ramsey Carson.

At first she couldn't believe it. It seemed too great a
coincidence. She made inquiries, and little by little, information filtered back. It took a while before she beheld the
grand design. When she did she was appalled.

Carson, she learned, was founder and president of the
same California gun club that had commissioned the erotic
engraving on the Parker Invincible, "The Goddess." She
also heard that ugly rumors about the club, particularly its
ritual use of "The Goddess," were circulating in gun-
collector circles.

Through her network of friends Bee was able to track
these rumors back to an American film director, also a
major gun collector, who claimed to have attended several
Goddess Gun Club orgies. This gentleman had not been
discreet; the club, Bee learned, was now the talk of gun-
collecting Hollywood. Rumor had it that a top-ten male
movie star had applied for membership.

Bee, not wishing to upset Maddy, kept this news to herself. Still, as the artist who had engraved "The Goddess,"
she felt distress over these awful tales. The erotic guns
she'd worked on so lovingly over the years had been
engraved to satisfy the yearnings of connoisseurs. The
notion that one of these arms with its inherent mystical
power, which by her labor she'd turned into an object of art,
was being corrupted by misuse began to haunt her dreams.

She phoned Ramsey Carson's office to request a meeting. An hour later he called her back.

She was struck by his voice, so slick and smooth. She

could hear nothing in it of the aggressive roustabout from
Great Western days.

"Been a long time, Bee. I was sad when I heard you
sold the shop. For years I admired your work. I even hoped
to commission something from you one day."

"You *did* commission something."

A little chuckle. "Yes, 'The Goddess.' So . . . you
knew?"

"Not at the time. I do now."

"I also have the guns you and your dad engraved for
Farouk."

"I know that too."

"Then I have no secrets from you, Bee. I wouldn't have
used an intermediary except I was afraid you'd turn me
down. Because of what happened . . . though it's been
years. I've changed a lot. I'm sure you have too. At least I
know your engraving's improved." Another little laugh,
then the sincere tone favored by flatterers. "Your work's so
good, Bee. The best! No one touches you. Perhaps no one
ever will. When we acquired that Parker, you were the
only one we had in mind to engrave it. I was pretty sure
you wouldn't refuse me, but you understand, I couldn't
take the chance."

Oh, yes, she understood! If she'd known "The Goddess" was for Ram, she'd have turned him down cold.

"What brings you to town, Bee?"

"Just traveling," she said. Before she called she'd
decided she wouldn't mention she lived nearby. "And
since I'm here I'd like to see your collection."

They arranged to meet in two days. When Ram offered
to send a car for her, she told him she was staying with
friends in Marin.

"Bring them along, why don't you?"

"I think not, Ram. Not everyone's so taken with erotic
guns."

He laughed. "I create a scandal every time I bring mine
out. It's just like I dropped my pants. People want to look

away but can't. Which is why I do it, of course. To stir
folks up, get the juices flowing . . . so to speak."

His home, on a quiet block in Presidio Heights,
reminded Bee of townhouses she'd seen in Paris: gated
street entrance leading to cobbled courtyard, gray stone
building with mansard roof behind. Crossing the courtyard,
Bee noted a great surround of blooming jasmine suffusing
the entrance with a nearly overpowering bouquet.

She barely recognized the dashing, perfectly coiffed,
middle-aged man who opened the door. She searched his
face for the handsome eighteen-year-old she'd known
back in Great Western days. That boy habitually wore
T-shirts, jeans and cowboy boots. This man was decked
out in gleaming black shoes and a beautifully tailored dark
pin-striped suit.

Most striking, the strutting youth she remembered had
been transformed into a man who appeared to know
exactly who he was. No awkwardness about him; now
every gesture seemed assured, every modulation of expression carried weight. Ram Carson had turned himself into a
convincing San Francisco gentleman.

He escorted her through a large living room reminiscent
of great rooms in English country homes—grand fireplace, sofas covered in faded chintz, life-size ancestor portraits of aristocratic men holding guns, accompanied by
slavish dogs. Then up a sweeping staircase to the gun room
on the second floor.

The decor here reminded her of numerous gun rooms
she'd visited through the years: glowing Persian rug, dark
paneled walls, finely built cabinets with glass doors to
exhibit the precious arms. There was a refectory table in
the center upon which several guns were displayed, and
deep, richly upholstered opposing leather Chesterfields
where gentlemen could sit and handle these marvels of the
gunsmith's art.

He handed her a glass of hundred-year-old cognac, then started showing his collection. Bee was impressed. Though smaller than the von Heinholz hoard, it was, Bee thought, better selected, each example being a "best of class."

The Farouk guns were as she remembered. Holding them again, running her fingers over the engraving, Bee felt tears spring to her eyes. These were the first arms that she and her father had engraved together.

"Tell me about them, Bee," Ram asked. "What was Farouk interested in?"

She shrugged. "Guns and sex, in equal order. When he found out they could be combined, he went berserk combing the world for fine engravers."

"So there were other guns?"

"Many. But none so fine as these. He was a vulgar man as kings go. Roly-poly fellow, spoiled and rich, without a thought in his head. He ate too much. Couldn't get enough of macaroni and cheese, which he'd slurp down with gallons of orangeade. He collected everything—art, sex toys, ancient sculptures, obscene cuckoo clocks. If Farouk coveted something, he bought it, or stole it if he could. He'd go into the houses of rich Cairenes, take what he wanted, and no one dared say a word. He collected women too, as if they were baubles. After a night of sex, he'd hand out jewelry which he'd tell them was from the royal treasury but which would turn out to be made of paste. He even made a pass at me—"

Ram laughed.

"Why not? I was pretty then."

"Yes, Bee . . . I remember."

"He had bad breath and stupid patter. I made it clear I couldn't stand him . . . which excited him no end. My father knew that once you delivered goods to him you'd never see a cent, so he insisted on full percent in advance and got it. We decided to engrave the guns as magnificently as we could, in the vain hope we might improve His Majesty's atrocious taste."

Ram's eyes sparkled as she spoke. He couldn't get enough of her gossip. Soon the center table was covered with erotic guns, Bee spellbinding him with anecdotes about this gun and that, the infatuations of one collector, the foibles of another.

A large amount of cognac was imbibed. There finally came a point when Bee felt the time was right to broach her concerns about "The Goddess."

"I've heard stories about how you use it," she told him. "It would be good to know the truth."

Ram smiled at her. "Private club business," he said, making a zipping motion across his mouth. Then, narrowing his eyes: "But remembering how you were in the old days, Bee, I doubt you'd disapprove."

"And those faces you had me put on the animals—they're the faces of club members?"

"Of course. Did you recognize me as the leopard?"

Since she hadn't at the time, she shook her head. "Bunch of voyeurs, aren't you?" she asked gaily.

"Some of us like to watch, others to partake. Think of it this way, Bee—a bunch of horny guys getting our rocks off after a hard day trekking through the woods."

Horny guys getting our rocks off! This was the first real vulgarity to escape his lips that night, the first phrase he'd used that didn't jibe with the image of the polished gentleman. The expression infuriated her, but she concealed her anger. She had to probe further, confirm the rumors about "The Goddess" or assure herself that they were false.

"Orgies can be enjoyable," she said, smiling. "So long as everyone's in on the game."

"True . . . though sometimes a little resistance adds to the fun."

"I can imagine 'The Goddess' racked nicely on the wall presiding over your revelries."

"Sometimes we bring it down," he said. "Lots of ways to use a gun."

"The Parker Invincible's a great gun, Ram. I bet you've fired it."

He smiled. "Used it in many different ways. 'The Goddess' "—he modulated to a thick German accent—"can be a vikid little inztrument."

He tittered then, and she felt sick, since he'd as much as owned up to the rumors.

"I want it back, Ram."

He stared at her, waiting for the punch line.

"I mean it. I'll pay you for it, of course."

He stood, wobbled a bit, then regained his balance. Though he'd been drinking steadily since she arrived, he seemed a man well used to alcohol. She knew the type. The more they drank, the cooler, smoother, slicker they became.

He stared at her again, smirk growing on his face. "You think because you engraved some figures you have some claim to ownership?"

"I made 'The Goddess.' "

"Wrong!" He shook his head, angry. *"We* made 'The Goddess.' You were just our decorator."

"I think I'd better go, Ram."

"As you like. But before you do, there're a couple other items I want you to see."

He turned, unlocked another cabinet, pulled open the glass doors with a flourish.

"Remember this?" he asked, holding out a battered old Winchester pump.

She stared at it, confused, since it was not of a piece with the rest of his collection.

"You don't recognize it?"

"Should I?" she asked.

He smiled again. "Turn it over."

Reluctantly she took hold of the gun. On the obverse side she found a pedestrian engraving of a girl firing a rifle from a horse, an engraving she'd made more than forty years before for Maddy. This, she recognized, was the gun Maddy had used to shoot the X in Ram's note.

"Where'd you get this?"

"Mandy left it behind. A friend kept it for me till I got out of prison."

He returned the Winchester to its rack, pulled out another gun, a battered small-gauge revolver.

"Recognize this one, Bee?"

She stared at it, knew immediately what it was. The thought made her want to vomit. She turned away.

"Yep, my old trusty, the one I used to kill Dunphy. Humble though it is, it's precious to me. I like to use it when I party too. This gun"—he kissed the barrel—"has seen lots of passion."

Raising her eyes from the revolver, she stared into his face, saw how now the Janus mask had cracked, the slick front slipping off even as she gazed, oozing off like melting wax. In its place she saw a countenance filled with malice, eyes dancing with gloat. Ram, she realized, had neither mellowed nor matured. The strutting bully had become a monster.

She didn't wait for him to call a cab, instead ran from the gun room down the stairs, then out into the night. In the courtyard she could still hear his laughter echoing from within the house.

She had a job those winter days that brought her into the city, an advanced cancer patient, Marguerite Desaulniers, who was suffering incredible pain. The woman's husband, a homeopathic Haitian physician named Paul Desaulniers, had tried everything: hypnosis, acupuncture, even Demerol, to no avail. Reluctant to give her morphine for fear she would thereby recognize she was terminal, he turned to a colleague, who recommended Bee as an expert, highly empathetic apitherapist.

Bee took the bus into the city three times a week, box of bees in hand, to administer sting venom to Madame Desaulniers. There quickly grew a bond between them.

Bee would place the bees, induce them to sting, then stay with Marguerite until her pain subsided.

They talked a lot during these sessions. Bee was naturally effusive and believed conversation was a good way to distract a patient. Marguerite, it turned out, loved to talk about sex, so the two spent hours sharing confidences. From these exchanges Bee learned about the prowess and proclivities of Paul Desaulniers. She also found she could make Marguerite giggle by describing the erotic guns she'd engraved.

One afternoon, after one of these exchanges, Bee told Marguerite the story of Ram Carson and revealed her concerns about the misuse of "The Goddess."

At their next session, Marguerite told Bee that when she passed on Bee's tale to her husband, he'd grown thoughtful, then recounted a story about a patient, a Chinatown prostitute who called herself Georgette, who turned up one night badly injured at the Desaulniers clinic, telling a strange story of being hired to entertain a group of white men who then sodomized her with the barrel of a loaded gun.

At the end of the apitherapy session, Bee, as usual, went downstairs to brief Dr. Desaulniers on his wife's condition. After giving her report, she asked him about Georgette. Dr. Desaulniers filled in a few details.

Georgette was a petite Chinese girl whose presenting symptoms were serious rectal and vaginal tears.

"She told me she was an illegal immigrant," Desaulniers told Bee, "working to pay off her debt to the Chinatown gang that had smuggled her in. That night she was sent by her pimp to take part in some sort of hunting-gun consecration ritual. Though she received nothing for this service, her pimp, she believed, was paid very well. She told me that other girls in her predicament had suffered the same fate, receiving injuries that ended their pleasure-girl careers, forcing them to labor in sweatshops to work off their indentureships."

Bee was extremely agitated that night when she left

Desaulniers's office. The tale of a gun-sex ritual was too great a coincidence. Was it possible, she asked herself, that there were two groups of men, members of the Goddess Gun Club and the group who'd hired Georgette, who indulged in this strange mode of play?

On her way to her bus stop, Bee decided not to go straight home to Bolinas. Instead she stopped at a pay phone, called Maddy, told her she had something important to confide, then took a city bus to Maddy's apartment.

Maddy listened, incredulous, as Bee described the stories she'd heard about Carson, and then her meeting with him two months before.

Even before she finished, Maddy expressed great distress over the fact that Bee had kept the encounter secret.

"He has my old gun! My God, Bee! Why on earth didn't you tell me?"

Then, when Bee told her about the other gun, the pistol with which Ram had killed Tommy, Maddy exploded in anger.

"You're right, he *is* a monster! To think I spent all these years trying to forgive the bastard. Now this!" Maddy's eyes glowed with fury and pain.

It's twilight now. A breeze wafts to us from off Bolinas Lagoon. Bee, I can tell, is nearing the end of her tale.

"You remember how she was last winter, Kay, how difficult it was for her to get around. Still, she was determined to do something about Ram. 'We can't leave it like this,' she said. Right away, that very night, she made up her mind. There was unfinished business. An old wound had been opened. The time had come to close it for good. 'I want that gun,' she said. And I knew she didn't mean the Winchester or 'The Goddess,' but the revolver Ram had used to kill Tommy."

Maddy had a plan. She had no intention of going after

Ram with a gun. She had finished with firearms years before. She had another weapon now, her camera. They must find this Georgette, she said, interview her, discover everything she knew. Then they'd have a starting point. If they could get incriminating pictures, document what Carson and his pals were doing, they'd have the leverage they needed to get all three guns back, and maybe put the Goddess Gun Club out of business.

"This was the old Maddy speaking," Bee tells us, "the girl I'd known in Great Western days. And though one part of me found her plan farfetched, another was just as angry and just as determined to quash the evil Ram Carson was still inflicting upon the world.

"We went to Chinatown together on several nights. We must have looked pretty peculiar—two elderly women, one with a camera and blazing eyes, the other, me, more timid but taking courage from Maddy's grit, prowling the alleys off Grant and Stockton, trying to engage with prostitutes, persuade them to help us find Georgette.

"We never did find her. But we found others who told similar tales—about a group of cruel men who kept what the girls called a 'fuckhouse' in an apartment in the Mission. Tales of nice-looking, well-dressed, well-spoken Anglo men who liked to play kinky party games which ended in a penetration ritual with loaded guns. These parties were terrifying, they told us, especially if you were afraid of guns. To make an example of them, the pimps would send girls who needed disciplining for withholding money or failing to meet their nightly quotas. And since several girls had come back badly injured, just the threat of being sent was enough to drive some to try and return to China.

"One girl described what she called 'the play' in great detail. Even I, who over the course of my career had engraved a good fifty erotic guns, was shocked. Maybe it's because I have a special feeling for guns, an appreciation and respect for their beauty and power. Of course firearms are deadly. But they can also be works of art. Decorating them with erotic motifs—well, perhaps that's just a step away from using them as instruments of erotic cruelty. But however short the step, for me it was enormous. I'm no prude, Kay, but still . . ." Bee shakes her head. "I just didn't get it."

It's dark now, and getting cold. Sasha and I help Bee carry the tea paraphernalia into her trailer. I rinse the pot and cups in her kitchenette; then the three of us sit together on the semicircular couch in the rear of her tiny trailer living room.

"There isn't that much more to tell," Bee informs us.

She's calmer now, her gestures less emphatic. The nervous bounciness of the afternoon is gone.

"Maddy was finally able to persuade one of the girls to show us the location of the 'fuckhouse.' Sorry to use such a vulgar word, but that's what they all called it. She showed us the building, pointed out the apartment windows. We found a name on the building register, but it didn't mean anything to us. Anyway, following up on a name wasn't what Maddy had in mind.

"She was looking for a vantage point from which she could stake out the apartment and take pictures. There was this odd-looking wood structure in the alley that ran behind. We went back there and she studied the situation, decided there was a window on the third floor that would give her a decent view.

"She was really incredible. I don't know where she got the energy. It was as if she were on a mission. She told me that this was life-or-death for her, that she couldn't rest till it was resolved. And that if she couldn't take the kind of photographs she needed, she'd try something else, such as confronting Ram Carson on the street. 'I'll photograph the hell out of him, hose him, strobe him till he's blind,' she said. She meant it too. She had fantastic energy. Though it was clear to me she was very ill, she never once complained.

"I offered her apitherapy. She turned me down. She

wasn't in pain, she told me, just fatigued. But you'd never know it the way she moved. Over and over she repeated the same thing, almost like a mantra: 'What he's doing, Bee—it can't be allowed to go on.' "

THE GUN/FIND THE GUN/WHERE'S THE GUN?

Maddy's words, boldly written and underlined in her notebook, now finally make sense. But I don't think it was her own old Winchester she wanted, or "The Goddess," or even, particularly, the murder gun. The "gun," I believe, was just the pretext. What she wanted was to shut down the G.G.C., forever stop their cruel exploitation, their terrible terrifying games of sexual power.

"She rented the attic room, then spent nights there waiting."

Sasha looks at me. I know what he's thinking: that in a sense it's turning into *my* story now.

"I spent many nights there with her. We'd stand watches, one of us sleeping, the other looking out. It was weeks before we saw anything. Finally one night we did."

Bee shakes her head. "We saw little corners of things, flashes. They were suggestive, but didn't tell us much. Whatever we were seeing certainly wasn't any kind of evidence. Maddy was frustrated. I'd never seen her in such a state. 'Bee, I've lost it,' she told me. 'I don't know how to photograph this stuff. I can't see a damn thing.'

"One night when I started to clean the window, she stopped me. 'They'll see us,' she said. 'One inkling they're being watched and the game's up. They'll pull the blinds, then we'll never catch them.'

"She brought in another camera, a big one. But even then she had problems. 'The view angle's too narrow,' she said. 'The focal plane's too critical.' She told me this wasn't the kind of photography she was used to. It required a highly technical approach, and she'd never been much of a technician. 'I'm just an old gal with a good eye,' she said. Still, she was determined to make it work. She vowed to stay at her post till she got explicit pictures. 'Sooner or later I'm going to nail the bastard,' she'd tell me. 'Then we'll have the leverage we need.' "

This doesn't sound like the Maddy I knew at the end of her life, the patient, probing teacher who guided and counseled me. More like the young aggressive Maddy, the girl who took a camera off to war and, against all odds, brought back the goods.

"I think sooner or later she would have nailed him too," Bee says. "She had me convinced. She was going to stick it to Ram Carson if it was the last thing she did." Bee shrugs. "Then, one night . . . well, you know what happened—"

Bee starts to sob. I put my arm around her. I'm amazed it's taken this long for her to break. For it seems to me that the story she's been telling is really the story of her own life. Or, perhaps, the entwined lives of three people who came together by chance when they were young.

"It amazes me how the three of you ended up living so close to one another," I tell her. "You meet up years ago when you're kids, then, in old age, meet again, still trying to work out your passions."

Bee nods. "We *didn't* work them out, Kay. It was over when Maddy was killed. As far as I know, Ram never found out she lived in San Francisco. He certainly never knew she was stalking him. I've thought about telling him. Maybe if he understood, he'd feel some remorse. But I doubt it. I think he's grown so hard and heartless nothing can reach him anymore. And frankly, I've no desire to see him again."

She wipes her eyes, blinks to clear them.

"I told you about our fling, how we were lovers for several weeks before Maddy joined Great Western. I don't like telling you this, but it's part of the story too. You see, I was crazy about Ram back then, thought he was the cat's whiskers. He was the handsomest lover I ever had. Yes, he was selfish, but he knew how to make a girl feel good. I was jealous when he started going out with Maddy. Of course I kept all this to myself. Her friendship was too important to me. I didn't want to lose it." Bee pauses. "I fibbed when I told you how he came to me for help and I told him his cause was hopeless. I'm afraid the truth's not quite so pretty."

I squeeze her shoulder. "It's okay, Bee. You don't have to tell us if you don't want to."

She shakes her head. "No, I must. What happened was I played the part of confidante, pretending I'd help him out. I told him she was just flirting with Tommy to make him jealous, and that if he wanted to win her he should write her a letter expressing his love, that if he did that she'd be moved."

Bee exhales. "I knew Maddy and Tommy were in love. But I wanted to hurt Ram and I knew a stupid letter would be his undoing. So you see, Ram had it right. I *was* the Svengali. It was *me* who encouraged Maddy to follow Annie Oakley's lead, nail his letter to the corral post and shoot it to shreds. It was *me* who put everything in motion, started the chain that led to all the tragedy. Today, telling the tale, I realized I must take responsibility." She hangs her head. "In some awful way, you see, I believe that in the end everything that happened has been my fault."

Sasha and I drive back to the city in darkness, along the lonely deserted roads of West Marin. After Bolinas, we turn toward Olema, epicenter of the 1906 earthquake that devastated San Francisco and started the great fire that burned the city down. From there we follow a road named for Sir Francis Drake, who in the sixteenth century visited this coast, but failed to discover San Francisco Bay. This road takes us back to civilization. An hour later we reach the Golden Gate Bridge.

"It wasn't Bee's fault," I tell Sasha. "But believing it is, she carries around a huge load of guilt."

Truth is I don't think anyone's guilty. But I do think

Carson is totally evil. What seems especially awful is that
he *could* have changed—served his prison sentence, come
out a better person, then worked hard, made something of
himself, found redemption, all the things he pretends he's
done. But it didn't work out that way. Instead he got
worse. The orgies with the guns. The safaris at the club.
Shooting down his friend and benefactor in a duel.

It's as if he feels he's above the customs and laws gov-
erning the rest of us, that no rules apply to his pursuit of
pleasure no matter how cruel or spiteful it may be. He
needs those pleasures. Without them he feels empty. Yet
his pursuit has made him totally hollow. Such evil, I
believe, must be destroyed.

Driving up Lombard toward Russian Hill, Sasha turns
to me.

"Now that you know what Maddy was up to, what are
you going to do?" he asks.

I look at him. I don't respond, but I think he knows the
answer.

5

THE

GUN

Returning to San Francisco, I find a message from Hank Evans. I immediately call him back.

"Quite a night," Hank tells me casually. "Paid a little unexpected visit on the cousins."

I tense.

"I'm sending you a tape of what they said. Their apology and all. You'll hear a little kickin' and screamin' at the start. Never mind. Just filter it out or fast-forward to the end." Hank pauses. "I believe now they're truly sorry they messed with you, Kay. Ha! Sorry they ever met you."

I put down the phone. *Jesus! What did he do to them?* Of course, the truth is I don't want to know. I decide that when the tape comes, I'll run it down to the end, listen to the apology, then throw the damn thing away along with my awful memories of the gun room.

I'm attending aikido class every day now, working hard, practicing all the requirements for my black belt exam.

Today, to get me ready, Rita puts me through a truly frightening drill. She blindfolds me, then sets attackers against me in pairs. At first I perform poorly, stumbling and losing my sense of direction. After each encounter, Rita places her hands on my shoulders, calms me, sets me facing the *kamiza,* then leaves me to deal with the next pair.

After four clumsy bouts, I start to find the flow. By the time the seventh pair come at me, I'm feeling really good.

"I like training blindfolded," I tell her at the end. "I want to practice like this every day."

She shakes her head. "Once a week's enough." She wants me to concentrate on defending against wooden sword attacks, on switching techniques when called on to do so and, most important, on freestyle defense against four attackers at once.

Handling multiple attacks will be the culmination of the exam, the last thing the examiners will see me do. There's no way I can fake it, and there'll be plenty of eager attackers. At other people's exams, I've jostled for the chance to take part in these cluster assaults. It's great sport, an opportunity to go at someone while helping him prove his mettle. Whenever I attack I feel relaxed, knowing I'm going to be thrown. This time the pressure will be on me to properly apply the throws.

Midnight: Joel and I have been driving for nearly an hour to reach this place at the southern tip of San Francisco Bay. Now, a little north of Milpitas, we approach a network of salt ponds, part of the vast San Francisco Bay National Wildlife Refuge.

We're on a street lined with sleek low-rise office buildings, overflow from Silicon Valley on the other side of Dumbarton Bridge. There's not a car or person in sight, and the only illumination, besides a few security lights, is moonlight reflected off of dark glass facades.

We pass slickly designed company signs: Netmatics,

SysCascade, DataTrans. Then we dead-end at an empty
overgrown field smelling of salt weed. It's as if we've
arrived abruptly at the edge of civilization—behind us,
soulless, glossy, futuristic buildings; ahead nothing but
marsh and emptiness.

Joel pulls over, cuts the ignition.

"Ever been down here?"

I shake my head. "I remember hearing about some sort
of island community, but I never knew where it was."

We get out of the car. Joel checks his watch: 12:10.
"We're nearly an hour early," he says.

"Do you care?"

He shakes his head. "Let's try and get in."

His source called him two hours ago, told him to come
here at one A.M., then hung up, leaving Joel no time to
"have it out with him."

"It's been so long since he called I decided to do what he
said. After all," Joel tells me, "the guy hasn't failed us yet."

He hands me a flashlight, locks his car; then we walk to
a gate in a wire security fence. It's not locked. We walk
through, shut it behind us, then start down a narrow path.

I can smell the salt strongly now. The moonlight illuminates an occasional power cable girder-tower. The salt
pond ahead is crossed by walkways constructed of wood
planks, elevated several feet above the wild grass.

"A salt company works these ponds," Joel tells me.
"They dike off the sloughs, cutting off the flow. The sun
evaporates what's left of the water, then they come in with
machines and harvest."

We walk about a mile before we reach a second gate,
this one padlocked, but with an easy way around for people on foot. We continue down the road, heavily rutted
now. Every so often Joel stumbles, then grabs my arm.

"Glad you can see in the dark, Kay. Tonight you're my
Seeing Eye pooch."

I peer around. In the distance Mission Peak and the
Valpey Ridge appear as dark forms against the night sky.

Lights twinkle in the Mission Hills. Far in the distance I can hear the sound of a receding train.

Joel points at the trestle ahead. "Only way in is to walk the tracks."

These are, he tells me, the old tracks of the South Pacific Coast Railroad, now used by Amtrak and CalTrain. Once on them I'm better able to see where we are. With moonlight shining, everything's as clear to me as it would be to a vision-normal at midday. I make out the remnants of ruined duck blinds in the salt marshes, and the outlines of our destination, the ghost town known as Drawbridge, once a refuge for gamblers and prostitutes at its northern end, respectable families who built vacation shacks at the southern. Drawbridge, Joel tells me, was a paradise for fishermen and duck hunters. They came out here to shoot ducks by the thousands, many later served up at San Francisco's finer restaurants.

"It's one of the weirder places on the Bay," Joel says, stumbling across the ties that hold the tracks.

We're on the trestle. There's water on either side. I smell the powerful aroma of wetlands—pickleweed, marsh grass, mollusks and slime.

Joel points out how Drawbridge is situated on an island. He says no one's lived there in years.

"You're not supposed to come out here without a guide. The refuge runs a few small tours in summer. Of course people are fascinated, so kids sneak in, druggies too looking for a place to party. There's been a lot of arson over the years. Many of the old shacks are burned out."

I look where he points at ruined buildings standing like empty husks—pilings collapsing, roofs broken by years of weather, walls bashed in by intruders.

"You can still find faded lettering on the structures. Over there's the Sprung Hotel, where the roulette wheel was supposedly etched with the names of the good-time girls upstairs. The building beside it was a gun club."

My ears perk up at that.

He's still talking when I hear an approaching train. Turning, I see it, bearing down on us fast. It's a passenger train, and it's coming at sixty miles an hour. We jump off the tracks, then lie beside them and hug the earth lest the suction draw us in. As soon as the train passes, I hear what sounds like a series of small explosions. I stand, see flashes of light amidst the ruins of Drawbridge, then hear the roar of an outboard as a speedboat pulls out, then takes off heading north across the Bay.

"Something just happened down there," I tell Joel.

He gapes at the ghost town. We step back onto the tracks, then jog till we're off the trestle.

Decomposing structures are visible now on either side, decaying boardwalks too.

"Oh, Jesus!" Joel moans, stumbling toward the prone figure of a man lying facedown in a patch of weeds.

I move forward cautiously, camera in my hands. Joel speaks to the man, but he doesn't move. I notice dark stains on his clothes. I crouch down, touch him warily. He's still warm, but dead I think. Carefully I turn him over while Joel shines his flashlight on his face. He's Asian, young, late teens or early twenties, and he *is* dead, head and body torn up by bullets.

"This just happened. The guys who did it sped away."

"There's another one over here." Joel points at a body fifteen feet away. "There's another too."

I recoil, frightened now, understanding we're squatting at the center of a scene of slaughter.

It takes us but a few minutes to find six more dead youths. And for all we know, there're others. Joel's worried there may be survivors who'll take us for the killers. He hustles me down a boardwalk into a ruined shack that smells of dry rot and salt, pulls out his cell phone, dials 911, reports in a whisper where we are and what we've found, then suddenly drops his phone.

"What, Joel?"

He points across the room. Through a broken doorway I

spot a male figure propped against a wall, legs spread, arms at his sides, gazing straight at us, pistol lying in his lap.

"He's dead too," Joel says.

We both start to shake.

"Let's get out of here," Joel whispers. Outside the shack he checks his watch, looks at me, shivers. For the first time since I've known him, he looks truly scared.

"We got here early. We weren't supposed to see the shooting. He wanted us to trip over the bodies, freak out, whatever. But we saw more than we were supposed to. Least you did, Kay."

I nod. "I saw the boat."

"Recognize it if you saw it again?"

"Maybe. I caught a good look at the stern and some of the letters and numbers on the prow."

"Not good," Joel says. "When the cops get here keep it vague and don't tell them about any numbers. I have a pretty good idea a certain former cop I've been investigating is behind all this. So be real careful, understand?"

I set to work with my Contax documenting the scene, using my strobe to blitz the fallen bodies against the ruins of Drawbridge and the night. I strive to create raw, stark, flattened images of carnage through extreme contrasts of light and dark, to convey the brutality of the slaughter, the butchery of it, the way the old-time tabloid photographers did when they covered gangland slayings with Speed Graphic cameras and synchronized flash.

Laboring, I quickly work up a sweat. Meantime Joel sits on the ground, one arm wrapped about a knee, the other clutching his cell phone to his ear, dictating his story to his editor. Since the *Bay Area News* is a weekly, he'd normally have plenty of time to write, but tonight, by coincidence, the *News* goes to press. Realizing he has a chance to scoop the dailies, Joel is reporting the Drawbridge Ghost Town massacre as spot news.

I catch several of his phrases as I work: ". . . Asian street gang members . . . Wo Hop To triad . . . bloodbath . . . culminating event . . . battle for control of the San Francisco waterfront . . ."

Although we were a good hundred yards away when the shooting occurred, heard shots but saw nothing but flashes from guns and the escaping boat, Joel is so skilled he can re-create the scene, describing "twisted bodies of Asian youths," "cold salt marsh grasses flecked with blood," "what looked to be a devastating ambush in this remote ghost town at the bottom of San Francisco Bay."

Like me, I realize, he is plunging into work to distance himself from the surrounding horror. Maddy told me she did the same in Vietnam: "I set myself the task of creating powerful images. It was the only way to keep my sanity."

The cops come in like an invading force, Feds along with Coast Guard, harbor patrol, county and municipal law enforcement, arriving by chopper, squad car and boat. Within minutes, fifty or sixty uniforms converge.

We're herded aside, questioned, swiftly conducted out of the area, driven to the Hayward police station. Here we're separated, then questioned by a succession of investigators from different agencies. Again and again I'm asked to describe what I saw. Following Joel's advice, I give a vague description of the boat. When a detective asks me why I didn't photograph it, I explain: "It was middle of the night. I didn't want to get shot. I was a hundred yards away, too far to strobe, and I don't work with a telephoto lens."

"Then how come you saw it at all?"

"I have good night vision."

He shakes his head. "Yeah, sure . . ."

They release us at dawn, escort us back to Joel's car. It's been ticketed. Seems we parked in a no-night-parking zone.

"We're getting near the endgame," Joel tells me as we drive back toward Oakland.

I think: *I'm near my own endgame too.*

"What's the name of this game anyway?" I ask.

Joel shrugs. "Those kids were ambushed. They must have been lured there for some sort of illegal exchange. Money for drugs, guns, whatever. An exchange is always the most dangerous part of a deal between crooks. At first I thought this was a game about takeover and power, since the purpose of every tip seemed to be to place me as a witness when a criminal act was being sabotaged. Then things changed. We got the tip to go to the garage where we found the body. Tonight was the same thing on a bigger scale—go out to Drawbridge and find a bunch of Wo Hop To boys who got massacred."

Joel pauses. The sun's rising just behind us, casting long shadows, painting the hills ahead with morning light.

"I don't think it's just a takeover attempt," he says. "It's a war of extermination. Whoever's behind this doesn't just want to put those guys out of business. He wants them all stone-cold dead so he can take control and never look back."

That makes me shiver. "Back at Drawbridge you said you had a pretty good idea who's behind this."

Joel nods. "Give me the numbers you saw on that boat, kiddo. If I can track the boat back to him, we'll be ready to play the endgame our way."

Back home, exhausted, I find a small package in my mailbox. I open it in the elevator, inside find an audio-tape cassette with "INTERROGATION" written in block letters on the label.

Upstairs, I jam the tape into my tape deck, fast-forward

a quarter of the way in, then switch the machine to play. I hear thuds, obscenities, Hank Evans making fierce demands, disgusting little whines and howls from Chipper and Buckoboy, who, I imagine, tied up and helpless, are being methodically beaten and kicked.

I can't say that image pleases me much or that it totally disgusts me either. Rather I find it satisfying in a repulsive sort of way, since, basically, human scum is getting what it deserves.

No need, I decide, to listen to the cousins whimper their feeble apologies. Any remorse extracted this way will of necessity be insincere. Still, there's something slightly satisfying about having this proof that they were punished—something akin, I imagine, to the meager contentment of a rape victim considering the daily grind of her attacker in prison.

Tonight I phone Vince Carroll. As usual sister Pris answers, then fetches Vince. I hear them quarreling in the background.

"The kitchen's a goddamn mess. Your night to wash dishes."

"Know what, sis? You sound just like Mom."

I hear her laughter dwindle as Vince moves to pick up the phone.

"Hello," he says.

"It's your—"

"—secret admirer. I recognize your voice. Someone did a real job on Chipper and Buckoboy. You wouldn't have had anything to do with that . . . by any chance?"

"Don't know what you're talking about."

"Uh-huh." He laughs. "So what's on your mind, nameless one? If it's that goddamn gun again, forget it."

"I already have."

"Really! Well, now we're getting someplace."

"You were an honest cop, Vince. Testified against your partner. Took a lot of heat for that."

"So?"

"Time to be honest again. Tell the truth about how Chap Fontaine was killed."

"Look Ms. Whoever-you-are, honesty suits me fine. But I have no interest in getting killed."

"You won't get killed. All I want is that you come into town, meet with me, then the two of us go see Agnes Fontaine."

"Mr. Fontaine's widow? I remember her. Nice lady."

"She is, and now she deserves to know what happened to her husband. I think she's entitled to that. I believe you do too."

A long silence, which I have no intention of breaking. Vince is either decent or corrupt. If the latter, nothing I can say will affect him.

"Well . . ."

"Well what?"

"I'll think about it."

"Please do."

"You're not holding my feet to the fire on this?"

"I'm done threatening you, Vince. I only want you to talk to Mrs. Fontaine because you know it's the right thing to do. If you don't see it that way, I won't be happy, but— I mean this—I won't bother you again."

Another silence. I do mean it. I'm done coercing him. He saved me from rape, possibly saved my life. Now that my tormentors are taken care of, I have no further scores to settle. It's Maddy's scores that concern me now.

"I always liked Mrs. Fontaine," he says. I detect something wistful in his voice.

"She thinks well of you too," I tell him, though I have no knowledge whether this is true.

"I didn't think she noticed me. Being just a club employee and all."

"She noticed you. And she knows you're honest."

"Yeah. So tell me something, Ms. What's-your-name—"

"Name's Kay."

"Nice name. So tell me, Kay—how come you know so much? What were you doing the night you fell into Chipper's creature pit?"

I tell him I was looking to take some photographs, background shots in and around the range where Fontaine was killed, which I'd mail to all the witnesses, hoping to provoke at least one to break and talk.

"You're a cop," I tell him. "You know how it works. Takes just one witness to start the ball rolling. The little guys deal, plead and testify. The big guys get convicted and go to jail."

"Wouldn't've worked."

"Probably not."

"What's your connection to the Fontaines?"

"No connection. My interest in this is a very long story, too long and complicated to explain."

Another long pause. Again I wait him out. "I agree with you," he says finally. "I think Mrs. Fontaine *is* entitled to know the truth. As for my telling anyone else or testifying in court, don't count on it."

I assure him I won't and that there won't be any tape recorders or cops listening in when he and Agnes talk. He agrees to come into San Francisco tomorrow afternoon. I tell him I'll identify myself fully when we meet.

Hanging up, I'm sure he knows that once he speaks to Agnes there'll be no turning back. But like any man contemplating a serious act of betrayal, he has an easier time considering the consequences in increments.

Five P.M., Tuesday afternoon: Vince Carroll and I are standing in the marble foyer just outside Agnes Fontaine's penthouse door. Sam the doorman stands in the open elevator, waiting for us to be let in. I'm nervous. Having seen both sides of Agnes, the ultracivilized patroness of the arts and the angry widow, I'm wondering just how Vince will be received.

The moment she opens the door, I know things will go well. She smiles, embraces me, then greets Vince as a social equal. She ushers us into her art-filled living room, seats us facing the fireplace, pours us each a cup of tea. Then she focuses on Vince, recalling G.G.C. functions at which they've met, adding how grateful she is that he's come to see her and how well she understands the courage that must take.

"I think it's only right you know what happened," Vince tells her with touching awkwardness.

Agnes nods to acknowledge his generosity, then arranges herself to hear his story.

He mumbles something unintelligible, glances nervously at me. I think: *Oh, God, he's tongue-tied.* But then he finds his voice. Within minutes of our arrival he's describing the events of that Sunday afternoon a year ago as if they only just took place. The stiff way he holds one of Agnes's precious teacups in his brawny hand puts the seal on his sincerity. Hard to think this big burly guy pouring out his heart isn't telling the truth.

"Please understand, ma'am—I liked Mr. Fontaine very much. He was always straight with me, looked me in the eye, treated me with respect the way you have today. Not like some others, I can tell you." Vince shakes his head. "Far as they're concerned, I'm just a servant."

"Anyway, I knew Mr. Fontaine didn't like what was happening around the club. He wasn't the sort of gentleman who'd do those kinds of things. I think it's better I don't go into too much detail. Kay knows what I'm talking about and I guess maybe you do too. Point I'm making is Mr. Fontaine was a real sportsman, not like Mr. Carson and some of his friends. For them the club's a place to do a lot of stuff's got nothing to do with hunting and sport."

Agnes nods, eyes fastened upon Vince with intense interest. Whatever anger she may feel, she conceals it well.

"At ten that morning, Mr. Carson calls me into his

office. 'There's going to be a duel this afternoon on the range,' he says. *A duel?* I look at him. 'Excuse me, sir, what was that?' 'A duel between Mr. Fontaine and me to settle our differences. Club business. Nothing that need concern the staff. I want you to dismiss all employees after lunch.' I stare at him. He stares back, eyes cold as ice. 'You understand what I just said, Carroll? I don't want anyone around not party to the affair. This is an internal club matter. I'm informing you because you're security director, and if someone's hurt or whatever, you're going to be the one to call for medics. In that case we'll have a cover story worked out.' "

Vince shakes his head. "I tell you, ma'am, I saw a lot of strange things take place at that club. Things I've never told a soul. But I never heard anything like what Mr. Carson told me that morning. A duel with loaded guns to settle differences, to—I want to get this right—'set the direction for the club for the next hundred years.' I thought I knew what he was talking about too, whether G.G.C. was going to be a decent hunting and shooting club or a place for weird parties and the other stuff they were doing, the safaris as they called them."

Agnes nods to show she understands and that he needn't feel embarrassed or worry about giving her offense.

"I did like I was told. No choice if I wanted to keep my job. We had this discussion about what the 'cover story' would be, then I went to talk to the staff. I kept telling myself nothing was going to happen, that this was just another of Mr. Carson's peculiar games. He played a lot of games, the gentleman did—if you want to call him a gentleman. He and his cronies were into a lot of strange stuff. They're not just gun enthusiasts, you understand. They're in love with their guns. They worship the damn things. Guns to them are like gods. They keep an apartment in a seedy part of town where they party like you wouldn't believe. I never attended one of their gala nights, as they called them, but I've been in there afterwards to clean up the mess. Not a pretty sight. So, like I said, after lunch I dismissed the staff. Not many members around that day. Most had left early in the morning. The few who stayed behind were personal friends of Mr. Carson and Mr. Fontaine. So when it looked like things were shaping up to happen, I went to talk to Mr. Fontaine.

"I found him resting in his bedroom with the door closed. I knocked, said my name, and he invited me in. He was lying on his bed in just his undershirt and shorts. He waved to me. I approached, told him I understood there was going to be a duel with a pair of old pistols they kept in the gun room, and I wanted to make sure he was in agreement with that, because if he wasn't I'd take steps to put a stop to it and escort him safely off club property if that's what he wanted me to do.

"He thanked me, said he appreciated my concern, and that yes, there would be a duel, and I needn't worry too much about it, he could hold his own as a marksman against any member of the club. Anyway, he said, those old dueling pistols were wildly inaccurate, so probably nothing much would happen beyond a single exchange of shots. At worst, he said, somebody might get clipped in the arm, though he even doubted that. And if someone did get hurt, Doc Petersen would be there to bind the wound.

"He turned serious then, told me this was an important turning point for the club, that he and a number of members didn't like the way things were going, and rather than have a big fight about it and go to court, he and Mr. Carson had decided to shoot it out in a gentlemanly fashion with the understanding that if he lost he'd resign and those who felt the same way would go with him, but if he won, then Mr. Carson and his crowd would resign, and—I remember he winked at me when he said this—that would probably be a relief for staff as well.

"I thanked him for being straight with me and assured him I'd be there and make sure everything was conducted properly and on the up-and-up. And that if at any time he didn't feel right about the duel or decided he didn't want to go through with it, he should tell me and I'd take care of the matter. I also told him that if Mr. Carson won and he resigned, I'd resign my position too."

Vince disengages from Agnes, lowers his eyes, shakes his head.

"I should have listened to him more carefully than I did." Vince looks up at me. "How could there be winner and loser if there was going to be a single exchange of shots with no one hit? There couldn't. But I wanted to believe what Mr. Fontaine said." He looks at Agnes again. "Ma'am, I'm not saying he lied, but what he told me didn't add up. I'm sorry I only realized that when it was too late."

"He probably didn't want you to worry, Vince," Agnes says. "I'm sure that's why he fibbed. You're right. What he said didn't make sense. If there was going to be a winner and a loser, then someone had to get hit."

Vince, absolved, appears relieved, further confirming my belief in his account. Still he hesitates. Agnes quickly picks up on the reason.

"I know it's not pleasant for you to tell me the details, but it's important for me to know, for our children too—to know how their father died."

"He died honorably, ma'am. You can be sure of that. That's what everybody said, that Mr. Fontaine died honorably on the field." Vince scratches his chin. "Gotta tell you though, I don't put much stock in that kind of talk. I don't see anything honorable about two men firing antique pistols at each other. Seems more like murder to me, especially considering one of them was the better shot, that he'd practiced a lot with those particular old guns, and had the far colder heart—which is what it takes to stand up to a loaded gun aimed at your face.

"See, they weren't standing all that far apart when it started. Offhand I'd guess thirty feet. The other men, the seconds, Mr. Stadpole and Mr. Kistler, together they measured off the distance with a tape. It was extremely hot that afternoon, in the nineties. The glare was such you couldn't look anywhere near the sun, but the line Mr. Stadpole and Mr. Kistler laid out was drawn so there wouldn't be any direct light in anybody's eyes. Mr. Fontaine and Mr. Carson waited at opposite ends of the range. They weren't speaking. Nobody was. Dr. Petersen lay in a lounge chair with his medical bag and a bottle of Scotch. He'd been drinking since before lunch. I'd say he was near blind drunk when it came time for them to start.

"When everything was ready, the two who were going to fight took off their shirts. Then I remember feeling a whole lot better about the thing, figuring they were going to put on bulletproof vests, and that way if someone did get hit he'd probably get knocked down but wouldn't be killed. Then, when I realized they weren't going to put on anything, they were going to face each other half naked like that, I got scared.

"So there they are, two over-sixty guys facing each other, stripped to the waist. Then Mr. Stadpole and Mr. Kistler bring out the loaded guns, announce that one loaded one and the other loaded the other, then Mr. Kistler takes the gun he loaded over to Mr. Fontaine, and Mr. Stadpole takes the one he loaded to Mr. Carson.

"I remember how Mr. Carson sort of waved his around. He aimed it here and there, sighted along the top of it, then held it by his side and pulled it up fast like he was practicing to raise and fire it in the duel. But Mr. Fontaine, he didn't do any kind of rigmarole, just held his weapon in his right hand pointed down, watching Mr. Carson with this curious expression on his face. He was cool, Mr. Fontaine was. I don't think he'd had even one drink before he came out. But Mr. Carson was more than cool, he was so cold he damn near froze you with his eyes. Not that he looked at Mr. Fontaine once. All through it he acted like Mr. Fontaine was just a target he was aiming to hit, never mind he was flesh and blood.

"Time comes for them to take positions. Each stands

behind his line, looking at the other, gun held by his side. Mr. Stadpole and Mr. Kistler stand opposite each other too, so the four of them make this kind of diamond shape. Then Mr. Stadpole asks if each man is ready. Mr. Fontaine nods. Mr. Carson calls out, 'I am ready, sir.' Then Mr. Kistler says in this deep voice he has: 'Gentlemen, you may fire at will.'

"Mr. Carson, he seems amused, like he thinks the situation is funny. Mr. Fontaine, I can tell, doesn't like that one bit. He raises his pistol, aims it carefully at Mr. Carson, who then, I swear, laughs aloud. Suddenly Mr. Fontaine swivels ninety degrees and fires at a target across the range. And—this really got to me—even with that antique weapon he hits it near the bull's-eye.

"Mr. Carson looks over at the target. 'Nice shot, Chap,' he says. Then he raises his gun, aims it straight at Mr. Fontaine, smiles this wide Cheshire cat smile of his and fires. Just then a big hole appears between Mr. Fontaine's eyes.

"I couldn't believe it! Mr. Fontaine fires at a paper target, then Mr. Carson shoots him in the head! Mr. Carson's still smiling when Dr. Petersen runs over to Mr. Fontaine to check his heart. Dr. Petersen turns and announces Mr. Fontaine is dead. Mr. Carson nods, cold as can be, hands over his gun to Mr. Stadpole, then tells me to take care of business. While I go inside to call the sheriff's office and the medics, they move a few things around to fit the cover story they worked out earlier."

Listening to Vince's narrative, amazingly similar to Bee Watson's account of the duel Carson and Tommy Dunphy fought forty years before, I'm filled with a troubling sense of déjà vu. The same chill in Carson, the same smirk to intimidate his opponent, force him to fire first, and of course, the same failure of nerves in Chap as in Tommy, the refusal to fire directly at his adversary. Tommy fired his gun off wildly. Chap Fontaine turned his on a target to demonstrate by his accuracy that he could kill Carson if he wished. But, I understand now, a duel isn't about marksmanship, it's about, in Vince's words, coldness of heart.

"So Chap never fired at Ram?" Agnes asks, tears forming in her eyes.

"That's how it was, ma'am."

"Ram shot him down in cold blood?"

"No doubt in my mind."

"And no one said anything?" Now the tears start to stream down her cheeks.

Vince lowers his head. "I should have, ma'am. I know that now."

He describes the arrival of the sheriff's deputies and the story the seconds told about how Mr. Fontaine had been fooling around with a pair of old pistols when one went off by accident and caught him between the eyes. Then how they called Agnes to give her the news, and how, afterward, Carson, Stadpole and Petersen went to the club bar to celebrate, and how even after Carson had downed half a dozen vodkas, Vince could still see the ice in his eyes.

"What about now, Vince?" I ask.

He looks at me, not sure what I mean.

"Are you going to speak up about it now?"

He goes silent for a time, then looks up at Agnes and nods.

"I decided last night, I'm going to tell what happened. I'm hoping Mr. Kistler will back me up. He went into the bar when they were celebrating, had harsh words with the gentlemen about the way the duel had gone down. He resigned from the club, as did quite a few other folks, all Mr. Fontaine's friends. I think when word got around, everybody felt bad about it. Except Mr. Carson's group. They were happy as larks."

"It's going to take a lot of courage to speak up," Agnes says.

Vince nods. "I know. I thought about it all night. There's an assistant DA I know up in Mendocino name of Jules Lampone. He's young, smart, true-blue. I'll go to him, tell him my story, ask him to put me up before a grand jury. Kay told me about the antidueling statute and how

Carson killed a man in a duel once before. When the grand jury hears what I've got to say, it'll be pretty hard for them not to indict the creep."

There's a fine moment as we leave. Agnes, eyes still wet, takes both Vince's hands in hers and thanks him for telling her the truth. His eyes water up as he asks her forgiveness. She opens her arms to him, grips him tightly as they embrace.

Outside, in front of Agnes's building, Vince appears greatly relieved.

"You've been pretty rough on me, Kay, with all your 'secret admirer' crap. Never thought I'd tell you this . . . but I thank you for it now."

"Time's come for me to thank you too, Vince—for saving me from those redneck shits. But next time please leave me a sealed bottle of water, okay?"

He laughs.

I turn serious. "There's something else." He looks at me. "Do you know anything about the hit-and-run took place on Capp Street back in April?"

He lowers his eyes. "The lady?"

I nod.

"The motorcycle guy who patrols for the dealers up there, he told us some old biddy was snooping around. So Carson offered him a couple of hundred to get rid of her."

"Kill her?"

"Nothing like that. He just wanted her scared off. But the motorcycle guy was a nutcase. Carson should have known better than to use him. That's the chance you take when you deal with a psycho, that he'll think the only way to get rid of someone is to do her."

So it *was* Carson, not the dealers up the block, who was responsible for Maddy's death. And of course he had no idea the "old biddy" was his old love, Mandy Vail.

I am outraged!

Struggling to keep my voice steady, I thank Vince for his candor. "What'll you do now?" I ask him.

"Give notice," he says, "then start looking for a job. Or maybe go into business with my sister. Couple of ideas we've been kickin' around."

Wednesday, one A.M.: Vince Carroll and I are staked out across the street from 4106 Capp, in the exact place where Maddy stood the night she was killed. There's still a little residue on the concrete curb of flowers left in the days just after Julio Sanchez ran Maddy down.

It's been two weeks since Vince turned state's evidence in the matter of Chaplin Fontaine. Four days ago a Mendocino County grand jury, having taken testimony from Vince and Kirk Kistler, handed down a bill of indictment against Ramsey Carson, charging him not only with dueling but also first degree murder. Jack D. Stadpole, Orrin R. Jennett and Dr. Henry L. Petersen were named as coconspirators.

Vince has persuaded ADA Jules Lampone to make the arrests tonight, not up in Mendocino but down here in San Francisco, in a manner calculated to inflict maximum distress and humiliation upon the arrestees. The plan is for Lampone and his squad of deputies to raid apartment 5 in the midst of the group's fortnightly sex-and-guns orgy, handcuff the indicted men, then drag them down to the street, where I'll be waiting to hose them with my Contax and strobe.

I know exactly what I want from this evening's shoot: coruscating images that will totally disgrace these guys, thus vindicating Maddy's interrupted quest. I want to discredit them for my own reasons too, because of what I endured in the gun room of their hideous club. Far as I'm concerned, everything Chipper and Buckoboy did to me was but a parody of their masters' rituals.

While we wait for Lampone, I ask Vince how it went when he resigned.

"Club officers were pretty pissed," he tells me, "Carson especially. When I told him me and Pris were planning to take over a bed-and-breakfast in Fort Bragg, he said that sounded like wimpy work, and if I ever wanted another job in the security field I shouldn't expect a recommendation."

"Like you'd really want a recommendation from a convicted felon, right?"

Vince laughs. "G.G.C. security's in bad shape these nights, what with Chipper and Buckoboy quitting, and now me." Vince looks at me closely. "This would be a good time to break in, assuming someone wanted to. They keep some pretty nice guns in there, you know . . . including the one you're interested in."

I decide to let that pass, though it does spark off a couple of ideas.

"Any other creature pits not marked on the security map?"

He shakes his head. "Mrs. Fontaine gave you her husband's map, didn't she?" Again I don't respond. "Well, figures." He sniffs. "We couldn't reckon how you got in far as you did without inside help."

"Something else I've been meaning to ask you, Vince. These safaris you mentioned—how do they persuade the vagrants and drifters to play?"

"The players weren't vagrants and drifters, Kay. They were illegal aliens," he says, "Asians all of them. Carson knows this Chinatown racketeer who's like a contractor— he supplies whatever kinds of humans you need. Party girls like the ones upstairs. Men to run through the woods like game. And if someone gets hurt in the process, it doesn't matter. The people are expendable. If they get damaged it's built into the price."

"Jesus! Are these guys totally evil?"

"Yeah, I think so, pretty much," he says.

Just then a convoy of four law enforcement vehicles pulls up, two S.F.P.D. prisoner-transport wagons, a squad car full of Mendocino County deputies and a lead car holding Lampone along with a female San Francisco ADA acting as local liaison.

This is my first look at the straight and righteous Jules Lampone, who doesn't look at all as I expected. I had in mind a big Italian type with mustache and football player build. Lampone, it turns out, is balding, narrow-shouldered, scrawnily built, with a slender, clean-shaven face, slightly crooked smile and rasping high-pitched voice.

"Happy to meet you," he says, lightly shaking my hand. "Heard a lot about you from Vince."

I thank him for exclusive access to tonight's "perp walk."

He smiles. "Yeah, I love a good old-fashioned dog and pony show. Favorite part of the job. Something biblical about it, checking out the suspect's demeanor, searching for remorse or lack thereof." He winks. "Always helps the prosecution when they pull their jackets over their heads . . . like Adam and Eve covering up . . . sort of."

I like the guy. He's got the killer instinct it's going to take to put Carson away. I wish him good luck as he, his deputies and counterpart enter the building across the street.

It feels strange standing here tonight, just where Maddy stood four months ago, waiting, as I imagine she did, for the orgiasts to troop out. She wanted to photograph their faces, with the intention, I believe, of tracking them down later and confronting them. I can't help but think how much she'd love to be standing here with me waiting to photograph those same men at the depth of their disgrace.

It's been years since I've covered a real perp walk, not since I worked as a staff photographer for the *News*. It's a ritual of the news business: the shackled suspect(s) marched out for full display to the press, still photographers scrambling for position, reporters yelling queries ("Did you do it, Jack?"), each perp sending his particular message by the way he handles the ordeal:

Head held high, expression proud ("I got nothing to be ashamed of").

Big smile, rapid-fire repartee with favorite reporters ("These monkeys'll never put me away! See you all in court").

Head ducked or hands held in front of face to conceal features ("I can't see you, therefore you can't see me").

Suspect in tears ("I'm contrite as I stand before you broken upon the wheel of my shame").

It's barbaric, also quite wonderful, I think, integral to the criminal justice system, the public's right to see the accused, read his or her face, essential to our sense of urban theater. I've looked at old engravings of French aristocrats driven in carriages to the guillotine, observed the blankness in their faces as they pass through the mob howling for their blood. I saw that same lostness when I was part of the pack, the look that says: *This isn't, can't be happening to me.* Back then I developed my own techniques for covering a perp walk, techniques I'm eager to employ tonight. Tonight's different too from those Hall of Justice stakeouts. Tonight I've got the perp walk to myself, and it's personal. I want to nail a certain son of a bitch.

Waiting below, I hear no screams of denial issuing from the windows of the second floor, nor do I see silhouettes of club members resisting arrest. As I well know, the bedroom of apartment 5 fronts on Cypress Alley. The Wongs, I'm certain, have long since gone to sleep. But I have a sense that many neighbors are watching now, aware that something important is happening in the neighborhood. I hope they're watching, I hope everyone is. I would like everyone to see the coming parade of shackled fools.

Movement in the building lobby. I make out figures heading for the door. I glance at Vince. He's nervous; I understand why. I think it's brave of him to show himself tonight to those he has betrayed. Of course he was never one of them, was merely their servant, and a servant offering evidence against his masters is in the great tradition of bearing witness.

I race across the street. With my lens set on autofocus,

I'm prepared to hold my camera wherever necessary to nail Carson hard.

Lampone appears first, grin of triumph on his face. *Whap!whap!* Got *him* good! Let's see who's next.

Four handcuffed G.G.C. flunkies, deputies' arms looped in theirs, try to do a classic cover-up. *Whap!whap!* My strobe burns through to expose their shame.

Next come four Chinese girls, makeup messed and hair askew, complaining shrilly that they didn't do anything, don't know anything, they're just waitresses catering a private party.

When they spot me they start to beam. *Whap!whap! whap!* I fire away at them. *Right, that's it! Make pretty for the picture!*

Carson's next. I'm all worked up for him. The momentum's built, the adrenaline's pumping. *Whap!whap! Whap!whap!* I blast him in quick bursts, the way Maddy taught me trained assassins do. He peers at me through the blinding light, trying to make me out.

"Hi, Mr. Carson!" I yell at him. *Whap!whap!*

"Who's the bitch?" he mutters to his deputy escort.

"Over here, Mr. Carson, sir!" I coax. "Come on, sir! Say cheese!"

He turns away in disgust, but still he won't bow his head. I hold my camera low, walk alongside of him shooting up to catch his face from beneath. *Whap!whap!* He tries to ignore me. That's fine. *Whap!* I want to catch his entire repertoire of expressions. Already I imagine a full page in the *News,* a dozen mug shots splashed across in even rows, all of the same man, Mr. Big Shot.

"Get away from me," he growls.

Whap! "Great!" I tell him. "Keep it up! Come on now—let's see more emotion!"

"Who brought in this cockroach?" he demands of his escort.

"Special arrangement by the DA's office," the deputy replies deadpan.

Carson looks at me curiously. *Whap!whap!*

"Oooh, *niiice,*" I tell him.

"I've seen you before. It was at the auction. You were sitting in my row."

"You got it!" *Whap!whap!*

"Who are you?" he demands.

I move in close, so close I can smell him, feel the warmth of his breath upon my face. He glares at me. I glare back. Then I hose him mercilessly: *Whap!whap!whap!whap!whap!*

He squints, then cowers before my assault.

"My eyes!" he cries. *"You're hurting my eyes!"*
Whap!whap!whap!whap!

"Just one more," I tell him. "Come on now—show me the cold dueling stare, the one that unnerved Tommy Dunphy and Chap Fontaine."

"Who are you?" he demands again.

Whap!

"That one's for Mandy Vail!"

At that his features contort. If only for a moment he appears to wince, then hardness again fills his face. No chance, I know, to break a man cold as this, but it's nice to think I may have opened him up a crack.

"And these are for me!" I tell him. *Whap!whap!whap! whap! whap!*

Thirty-six exposures shot. The roll's finished. I drop my Contax, let it hang loose about my neck.

"I want to come see you when you get bail," I tell him. I stick my business card into the breast pocket of his shirt, then turn my back and walk away.

Russian Hill, two A.M.: I become aware of her as I'm pulling my key ring from my pocket . . . a furtive movement behind, then an elongated shadow on Hyde cast by the streetlamp at the corner. If it weren't so late, I wouldn't hear her. The cable that carries the Hyde Street cable cars shuts down around one in the morning, eliminating the low-grade whirring beneath the street that blots out most subtle sounds above.

I turn, spot her coming toward me. I wonder: Has she been waiting for me in the shadows of the bushes that line the perimeter of Sterling Park? I go on guard, wondering who she is and what she wants. Then, as she moves closer, I see she's no taller than me. A moment later, I recognize her.

Actually it's double recognition. I identify her first as one of the four Chinese girls escorted by the cops out of the Capp Street apartment. But as she comes closer I realize tonight was not the first time that I've seen her. There's something unmistakably familiar about her face. It's her eyes, I think, much larger than normal in a face so small. Then my second act of the recognition: she's the girl I discovered hiding in the Presidio months ago, the night Joel and I covered the landing of illegals near Fort Point.

Her hair's long now, her expression no longer fearful, her body language no longer furtive. She looks older, less naive. And now she speaks some English too.

"I dream of you many nights," she tells me in a throaty singsong whisper. "I want to find you to say thanks you. I do not know where to find."

She's smiling at me, holding out something in her hand. It takes me a moment to figure out what it is—my black sweatshirt, the one I gave her off my back so she could escape without being spotted by the I.N.S.

"You made it, I'm so glad," I tell her.

She grins, holds my sweatshirt to her heart. "Thanks to you," she says. "When tonight I see you it is my dream." She embraces me. "You save my life."

She kisses my sweatshirt, presses it forward to return it, then starts bawling in my arms. I hold her close. This meeting, so unexpected after such a stressful night, moves me so much I begin to bawl myself.

"My American name—Lucky," she says in her lilting singsong, grinning through her tears.

I invite her upstairs. In the elevator I ask how she found me.

"Chinese man," she replies.

It seems that after the arrests, the four girls were interviewed in a paddy wagon by a Chinese-American cop. Deciding there was no reason to hold them, he released them at the Hall of Justice. But Lucky refused to leave. She begged the cop for the name of the white woman who was taking pictures at the scene of the arrests. She told him that I had aided her and now she needed to find me to thank me properly. Fortunately the cop was softhearted. He got the information from the DA's office, including my address.

I offer her coffee. She asks instead for tea, accompanies me to the kitchen, insists on preparing it herself. Watching her, I can't help but feel pride for my role in her escape. That night, touched by her plight, I did what I could. Now, to my surprise, I learn that my small act of kindness may have helped her survive.

Or did it?

As we sip tea in my living room, Lucky describes her life since the night she landed. She recounts her saga in broken English, how she found her way out of the Presidio, changed the twenty-dollar bill I gave her at a Chinese laundry in the Richmond, then, asking directions, learned how to take a bus to Chinatown. Once there, she found the address the illegals on her boat had been told to memorize in case of separation. Of her group of 130 souls, only fourteen made it into the city.

Within a day she was put to work as a dishwasher in a busy Chinatown restaurant. She soon graduated to trainee waitress, then to full waitress, probably, I decide, on account of her appearance, her large, heartbreakingly beautiful almond eyes.

Over the last few months she's moved from restaurant to restaurant, employer to employer, her contract changing hands each time, sometimes as often as once a week. But these promotions have had no effect upon her lifestyle. She continues to reside in a bare room with nine other girls, all illegals, sleeping on the floor.

Still she's managed to learn some English and the customs of her new country. Her hope, the hope harbored by all the girls she lives with, is to attract a Chinese man with American citizenship wealthy enough to buy out her contract, wed her, then pay whatever it costs to regularize her situation.

Though I nod to show her I understand her words, I can't help but wonder if she's telling me the truth. If she's only a waitress, what was she doing tonight at the G.G.C. party apartment?

Perhaps she anticipates my question, for suddenly she goes silent. Then, after a pause, it pours out of her, a mixture of English, Chinese, sobs and wails.

I can't make much out of what she's telling me beyond her feelings of desperation and shame.

"I no street girl!" she repeats emphatically. "No comfort girl. No!"

Then amidst the flurry of moans and whimpers I hear the name "Jimmy" repeated several times—Jimmy this, Jimmy that, a bad man, she makes clear, a man who frightens her, a man she doesn't like.

I'm trying to calm her, to get her to explain herself more clearly, when she utters the words "Tan Yuet"—and then I sit up straight.

"Tan Yuet restaurant?" I ask.

"Yes! Same same!" She leans forward, nodding excitedly. "Tan Yuet!"

I sit back. Is this Jimmy she's been talking about, who, I've gathered, is the man who sent her to the G.G.C. party tonight—is he, I ask her, the same restaurateur with sharp features and precision-cut black hair introduced to me by Dad as ex-cop Jimmy Sing?

"Same same!" Lucky seems as amazed as I that I know the man she's talking about.

"Jimmy sent you tonight?"

"Yes! See, Jimmy *bad*. I *no like*. I try leave job. He say, 'No! Now for punish you go fuckhouse!' He make me go. I cry, but he no care. He *make* me."

Jesus!

But even as I try to comfort her, assure her I'll try and find a way to help her out of the exploitive cycle in which she's been enmeshed, the implications of her story ricochet within my brain. And then, suddenly, like a handful of loose iron filings abruptly patterned by the presence of a magnet, all my disparate notions lock into a scheme so clear and overarching that even as I'm frightened by the revelation, I'm exhilarated by it too.

Night. Joel and I are standing at the base of a ladder of iron rungs built into the concrete wall of a warehouse. We're in the commercial waterfront area of Sausalito, just across the Golden Gate from the city—a district of boatyards, dry docks, ship's chandlers and storage buildings, all near the huge structure that houses the San Francisco Bay Model.

There's no one around. The area's dead quiet, and now the night fog's coming in, heavy summer fog filling the air like thick black smoke. It chills me to the bone.

I secure my camera to my belt and start up the ladder, shivering as I climb. "This is it, kiddo," Joel mutters. "We're at the endgame now."

The ladder we're climbing was built into the wall as a convenience for workmen servicing the roof. The only problem, seems to me, is that if we run into trouble, this ladder's going to be our only way down.

Actually, it feels good to scale the side of a building like I'm Spider-Woman. Cold as the fog is, I'm glad it's around me blanketing me from view.

When I reach the top, I step over the building parapet, then vault down lightly onto the gravel-on-asphalt roof. I jounce on the roof a couple of times, checking it for safety, then go back to the edge to see how Joel's doing.

He's not happy. His eyes are bugged out, reminding me of the Jimmy Stewart character in *Vertigo*. If he's scared of heights, I think, the descent will be even tougher for him than the climb.

He's breathing hard when he reaches the top, grasps the parapet, then heaves himself up. He shakes his head, mumbles, "I'm really out of shape." He sits down on the asphalt to regain his breath.

Ever since I told him Lucky's story, he's been hot on the trail of Jimmy Sing. An ex-cop who deals in illegal immigrants—that in itself would make Jimmy suspicious. But the fact that he's also Rusty's brother-in-law, and Rusty tried to warn me off our story, put us both on high alert.

Joel has discovered that years ago Jimmy worked in a police intelligence unit whose mission was to penetrate Chinatown gangs. He ended up part of a crew of corrupt cops all caught and sent to prison. Jimmy served five years. Now it looks like he's up to the same old stuff.

Lucky, meantime, has been installed in a spare bedroom in Joel's house, where she's live-in nanny to little Roland. She has sanctuary, Roland Glickman has a loving caregiver and ice-goddess Kirstin now has more time for her runes—a perfect arrangement all around.

I leave Joel to check out the skylight, a low hut shaped like a huge coffin, with a pitched roof composed of safety glass with wire hexagons embedded within. The inner surfaces of the panes have been painted black, giving the glass a dull matte finish. But there're patches which have escaped the brush, large enough to allow me to peek through.

I bring my face close, stare down. A few seconds later I feel Joel come beside me and do the same.

There're lights on below, the kind of strong directional spots you'd expect to find in a photographer's studio, illuminating the area directly beneath. I estimate the distance to the floor at thirty feet. I can easily make out a half-dozen men moving about. They wear dark tracksuits with white racing stripes down the legs, the same kind worn by Lucky and the other illegals the night they landed at our feet. I hear conversation, a mix of English and Chinese, which reaches us clearly or fades off depending on the position of the speaker. I also hear the sound of pry bars splitting wood as the men break open several of the dozen or so wooden crates spread out on the warehouse floor.

It's a perfect setup for photography, well lit, with the wattage so strong the players are unlikely to look up lest the harsh light hurt their eyes. I snap an 80mm lens onto my Contax, which is loaded with high-speed film, press it to my spy hole and peer in through the finder.

Yes, they're splitting open crates, then removing wrapped objects from straw packing. I start taking pictures, then feel Joel's hand on my arm. I turn to him. He points. Using my viewfinder, I follow his lead, noting two men, dressed differently than the others in slacks and Hawaiian-style hang-loose shirts, moving about like supervisors.

I focus in on them. One, clearly Chinese, wears a shoulder holster containing a huge pistol, probably a .45. When he turns I recognize him.

"No question—it's Jimmy," I whisper. "How did you know he'd be here?"

"Checked to see if he had a boat. He has four, all berthed here in Sausalito. One has numbers that matched the numbers on the boat you saw at Drawbridge. Next I checked around the waterfront, found out he rented this warehouse. I called you tonight after I followed him here." Joel grins. "They call it, you know—investigative reporting." He pauses. "What about the other guy? Recognize him?"

Heart pounding, hoping against hope, I look carefully at the other man through the viewfinder. Immediately I'm relieved. There's something strange about his face, as if his features are frozen or he's wearing some sort of mask.

I nudge Joel, whisper: "Is he the one you saw in the elevator the night you got conked?"

"Could be," Joel whispers back.

I peer at the man again. Due to the foreshortening effect caused by having to look down, I can't be sure, but there is something familiar about his build.

"Hey!" Joel nudges me again. "They're unwrapping down there."

I move my camera a little to the left. The two supervisors have joined the workers surrounding a man unwrapping an object extracted from the crate. As I watch I'm suddenly aware how close my position is to Maddy's in the Wongs' attic: unseen observer poised with camera behind panes of dirty glass watching a strange situation unfold.

As the object is unwrapped, the men cluster closer, momentarily blocking my view. Then, amidst cheers, the man in the center holds the object up for all to see. It's a weapon with a thick, mean-looking barrel.

Guns again!

I hear Joel take in his breath. "Shit! That's a grenade launcher! Keep taking pictures, Kay—long as you can. I'm calling in the Feds."

He retires to a corner of the roof. A few seconds later I hear his voice as he whispers into his cell phone. Meantime more weapons are unwrapped. I recognize an AK-47 from one of Dakota's slide lectures at the ranch.

I'm scared shitless. Smuggling guns is serious business. Meantime we're trapped here on the roof. I go over to Joel, still speaking into his phone.

"Let's get out of here right now!"

I secure my camera, climb over the parapet. I have my

feet on the top rung of the ladder when Joel grasps my
hand.

"You don't want to stay for the fireworks?"

I shake my head. "Not up here."

"Then you better scurry down quick, kiddo. Feds're
already on their way."

"Come down with me," I plead.

He releases my hand. "Sorry, can't climb down fast
enough." The look in his eyes tells me he means it.

I catch the sound of sirens in the distance. I nod to Joel
and start down. Ten feet from the ground, I hear the sirens
again, closer and louder. I leap the last few feet, make a
quick dash for the next building, turn the corner, quickly
reload my camera, then crouch down, ready to cover the
bust.

Suddenly it's dead quiet again. There's also an aroma of
burning eucalyptus in the fog, probably wafting from one
of the controlled burn-offs taking place on Angel Island.

What happened to the sirens?

Maybe, I think, the Feds are sneaking up. It's then I
realize I'm in a dangerous situation. When the Feds arrive
I can get caught in a crossfire, or worse, mistaken for a
member of the gunrunning gang.

Just then I hear sharp sputtering like firecrackers coming from inside the warehouse. Seconds later I catch sight
of Joel on the edge of the roof wildly waving his arms.
When he sees me he cups his hands around his mouth.

"Hide!" he yells down to me. "It's some sort of double
cross. Fuckers're shooting it out."

Then, before I can react, the warehouse door bursts
open and the two men wearing Hawaiian shirts rush out.
The bigger one with the frozen features disappears into the
night. Jimmy Sing, gun drawn, pivots, then fires back
through the warehouse door.

Jimmy empties his weapon, changes magazines, but
before he can raise his pistol again, he takes a burst of fire
and falls. He rolls out of sight of the doorway, lies still. I

wait for someone else to rush out, but after the echo of the shooting fades, the night turns so silent I can hear only my own short hard gasps.

Again I look up at Joel. He's gesticulating. Not understanding, I shrug. Again he cups his hands about his mouth. "Other guy—he went toward the Bay Model building," he yells.

Just then another burst of automatic fire from the warehouse, followed by the sound of shattering, then a huge crash inside.

Joel ducks. When he reappears he's frantic. "They heard me. They shot out the skylight. *Shit!*"

I make a decision. An instant is all it takes. Joel's stuck on the roof, bad guys with guns know he's there, there's a loaded pistol lying thirty feet away from where I'm crouched and the summoned law enforcers have yet to show up.

I move on instinct, the way Dakota taught us at the ranch, run to Jimmy, check to be sure he's dead, grab his gun, race back to my position, where I assume an isosceles stance, gun extended and gripped in both hands, covering the warehouse door, ready to perform "Mozambiques."

If anyone comes out that door, I'm going to fire at him, not to kill or injure but to stop him from going after my friend standing helpless on the roof. This is what I trained for in Dakota's Fun House . . . though I never thought I'd put her training to use.

I'm relieved when two vans pull up and government SWAT team members pile out. I immediately lower Jimmy's pistol, then fade into the shadows to watch.

The men, dressed in black with the letters A.T.F. stenciled on their backs, get a quick shouted briefing from Joel. Four of them scurry up to join him on the roof, while the rest assume positions around the warehouse door.

Now that Joel's safe, there's nothing for me to do here except pick up my camera again and document the arrests. But I have business far more pressing. I make my way along the edge of the adjoining warehouse, circle it, then run into the shadows of the huge Bay Model building where, according to Joel, the second man in the Hawaiian shirt may have fled.

The Bay Model, operated by the U.S. Army Corps of Engineers, is an enormous working model, hundreds of feet across, of San Francisco Bay and the Sacramento–San Joaquin river delta. Dad used to bring me here when I was a kid; I always liked it because the lighting was dim. The huge structure that houses it was built during World War II for construction of Liberty ships. The Bay Model was created in the 1950s to study the effects of dams, floods and dredging on the ecology of the Bay.

The vaultlike main doors are tightly shut. Since this is U.S. Army property, it's hard to imagine anyone trying to break in. But then, walking along the north side of the structure, I notice something glittering on the ground.

I stoop, pick the object up. It's a face mask with Chinese features, the cheap plastic kind sold in novelty shops, vulgarly called a "Chinaman mask."

Detecting an aroma, I bring the mask to my nostrils. A familiar scent of cologne, cloyingly sweet, comes off the plastic. I've smelled it before, faintly in the warehouse the night we went into Tan-Hing Enterprises, the same night Joel got conked after thinking he saw a man descending in the elevator wearing a Chinese mask. I also smelled it more recently and a lot more strongly on Rusty when he hugged me at Dad's bakery and again the night I went to see him at his house.

Rusty. I've suspected as much ever since Lucky's revelation. I just haven't wanted to believe it. Now, finding confirmation, I feel bad, for I know that when Dad finds out it's going to break his heart.

Near where I'm standing there's a service door flush to the side of the building. I go to it, turn the handle and pull. To my surprise it opens. Running my fingers along the inside edge, I discover the clasp's been taped.

I slip inside, shut the door quietly and, still holding Jimmy's pistol in both hands, make my way cautiously down a short corridor, then through the center slit of a plastic humidity barrier. There's a pair of swinging doors on the other side. The moment I ease through them, I'm hit by a blast of warm dank air.

I stand amazed by the sight ahead. The Bay Model is spread before me, a vast arrangement of sculpted concrete slabs covering two acres of interior space. A few low-wattage lamps cast dim light, endowing the model with a surrealistic glow. I make out roads, bridges, marshes, mudflats, cities, towns and parks. Most exquisitely, I can also survey the three connected bays, South, Central and San Pablo, as well as the Golden Gate and a small hunk of the Pacific on its other side. The model is molded to show the contours of the Bay bottom, also islands, protruding rocks and shoals. There's water flowing through it. I hear the clicking and beeping of computer-controlled meters and monitors, as if some kind of experiment is under way.

I'm standing, I realize, approximately on the edge of the San Pablo Straits in San Rafael. I stand very still, scanning and listening. If, as I suspect, Rusty's here, there are hundreds of places for him to hide.

Then I spot him on the model overlook rotunda, the first stop for visitors entering through the main door. He stands in clear sight, still as a statue, facing me beside an exhibit. He must have seen me the moment I came in.

"Hi there, Kay!"

His words resound in the huge space, bounding off the columns and girders that support the ceiling. There's gravity in his tone, great sorrow too. I wish I were closer so I could read his face.

"Jimmy's dead," I call back, my words echoing. "A.T.F. guys've got the warehouse surrounded. It's over, Rusty. Time to turn yourself in."

"That what you think, Kay?"

"What else can you do?"

He doesn't answer, instead moves down to the Corps of Engineers exhibit, then over to Oakland Harbor, stopping when we're but sixty feet apart.

"I see you got a gun. Know how to use it?"

I nod.

"I got one too," he says, raising his hand, showing me a police revolver. I can make out his face better now. I've never seen so much intensity in it. The man across the water isn't the jovial Rusty Quinn I remember from my girlhood. Tonight he looks like a man caught in a trap, desperately seeking escape.

"You want to shoot it out, Rusty—that's what you're saying?"

He laughs, lowers his gun, sticks it in his belt. "No, uh-uh, I don't want to shoot it out. Least of all with you, dear."

I lower my pistol. "Shall we disarm then, throw our weapons into the water?"

"Good idea."

"You first, okay?"

He chuckles. "Spoken like a true cop's daughter," he says merrily. "You're still Jack's darlin'—yeah!"

"There's no way out, Rusty."

"I think there is," he says. "This is a big place. Lots of ways outa here."

"Better go then. I won't try and stop you."

"Sure do appreciate that, Kay."

He steps over the barrier, into the foot-deep water, then starts clomping toward me, at each step shedding water from his shoes. When he reaches Alcatraz, he steps upon it, balancing himself precariously on the island model.

"Best you go now, Kay. Turn around and leave."

I shake my head. There's something dangerous in his face. I decide to try and stall him. "Let me take your picture first, Rusty. Okay?"

He smiles. "Always the little shutterbug. Sure, take a shot. Make it good too. 'Rusty in the Bay.' Or better,

'Rusty at Bay.' Ha! I kinda like that one, don't you?"

Dakota taught us never to give up a weapon, but tonight, following my instinct, I take a chance. I stoop, then deliberately place Jimmy's big .45 down on the concrete to show Rusty I'm not his enemy, to mollify and hopefully defuse the craziness I feel coming off him in waves.

When I rise, I'm holding my Contax in my hands.

"How do you want me, Kay? Jolly Old Rusty? Or"—he makes a mock-comic twisted face holding up the corners of his eyebrows—"Rusty, Scourge of Chinatown?"

To my amazement he starts preening for me. I can't tell if he's trying to humor me, or is on the verge of committing a violent act.

"I like Jolly Old Rusty," I tell him. "In fact, I love that guy."

"You got it, Kay!"

He turns ninety degrees, then strikes a bizarre pose, head held high at a weird exaggerated angle, left hand above his eyes as if gazing far ahead the way North American explorer-scouts are depicted in nineteenth-century panoramic paintings of the West. I follow his sight line. He's looking west toward the Pacific, where a vast expanse of ocean would be modeled if the Bay Model were miles wide.

I frame him in close-up through the 80mm. There's so much madness in his face, suffering and paranoia, it hurts me just to look. There's something else too, a vague, gentle lostness in his eyes, a quality Maddy used to call "dream-murder."

"Hey, hurry up!" he shouts. "It's tough standing still. Go for it, girl! Shoot, for Christ's sake!"

I activate my strobe, start to fire.

Whap!whap!whap!

"Got the goods now, do you, Kay?"

"Yeah, I got 'em, Rusty," I respond, lowering my camera.

Then, before I can do anything, so fast I haven't even

time to try, he pulls his revolver from his belt with his right hand and sticks it in his mouth. Still holding his left hand over his eyes as if to protect them from the ravenous, raging rays of a blinding, all-consuming imaginary sun, he pulls the trigger.

The explosion bursts across the huge building like a crack of thunder. Then, as if an earthquake has struck, a miniature tsunami sweeps across the model of the Bay.

Four A.M.: Back on Russian Hill, I smell a faint trace of sandalwood in the air when I come through my apartment door. It's Sasha. He's let himself in. I find him asleep in my bed. I gaze down at him, so happy to see him. What flash of intuition has brought him here knowing that tonight of all nights I really need him?

I strip off my clothes, take a long hot shower, then nestle against him in the sandalwood-scented sheets. He moves a little, feels for me, cups my breasts with his hands. *Yes, please hold me, Sasha.* I want nothing more now than to fall asleep in his strong dark arms.

Eleven A.M.: I'm standing in front of Dad's bakery, having traveled to the Richmond by bus. Baking time has long passed though the wonderful aroma of bread production is still in the air. Most of this morning's loaves have been delivered to client restaurants, while the remainder are on sale at the front of the store to walk-in customers.

Dad, I learn from his manager, is at the Russian coffeehouse up the street taking his midmorning break. I saunter up there, catch sight of him through the window sitting at a table wearing glasses and reading today's *Examiner.*

I watch him awhile, note the absentminded way he drinks his coffee, bringing it slowly to his lips, taking a sip, then another, replacing the cup on the table, then turning the page.

I have no desire to go in there now and wreck his tranquillity, but there're things he must be told. I don't believe I pushed Rusty to kill himself. I can't imagine him submitting to arrest and disgrace. I'm pretty sure he would have ended his life if only for the sake of Soo-Lin. That's the trouble—I'm just pretty sure, not sure a hundred percent.

"Dad."

He looks up, shows me a big grin, removes his glasses.

"Hey, darlin', sit down. This is great! What brings you out?"

Suddenly he looks concerned. He knows I've not come bearing happy news.

"What's the matter? You look tragic."

I sit beside him, take his hand in mine, blurt it out: "Rusty's dead. Shot himself last night. Worse, I saw him do it. I'm sorry, Dad—he was in deep, deep shit. He must have felt it was his only way."

We walk back to the bakery, get into his car, drive out to Lincoln Boulevard, then down to the parking area near Baker Beach. It's foggy; there's hardly anyone around, just a dozen or so hard-core nudists lying faceup on their towels hopeful the sea fog will lift.

"God, I hate guns!" he says.

We're walking on the sand just above tide line. There's seaweed and driftwood strewn by the waves.

"I'm sick of them too," I tell him. "Lately they seem to have taken over my life. I bought one after I took that shooting course. Cost me a bundle. Never fired it. Now I don't want it anymore."

He's less surprised than I'd have thought about Rusty going bad, says it was always in him, the temptation, and that it's a fine line that separates criminals from cops.

"We play the same game, you see, except on opposite

teams. The law's on our side, that's the difference. As for right and wrong, who's to say?"

I know he doesn't believe that, but understand why he must say it. It's hard enough for him to have lost his closest friend. To despise Rusty for turning corrupt isn't possible for him yet. Perhaps it never will be.

He puts his arm around my shoulder, holds me against his side.

"I'm just so sorry you had to see him do it, darlin'. Just so damn sorry, that's all."

We drive over to Rusty's house in the Sunset. While Dad goes in to visit with Soo-Lin, I wait in the car. There're masses of Chinese people coming and going. Soo-Lin lost both a husband and a brother last night.

Dad isn't gone long. When he comes back out, I notice a bitter sadness in his face.

"She couldn't look me in the eye," he says. "She knew what he was doing. She knew all along. For all I know, she pressured him into it."

He pauses, then smacks his fist into his palm. "But pressure—that's no kind of goddamn excuse."

Though Ramsey Carson posted bail within eight hours of his arrest, it's two weeks before he calls.

"I want to talk to you about Amanda Vail," he says, smooth, deferential. "I was wondering — may I take you to lunch?"

"I don't do lunch," I tell him, working to keep my voice steady. "But I'd be happy to come see you at your house. I've heard a lot about your gun collection, Mr. Carson. I'd like to see it too, if that's all right."

"Sure! We'll kill two birds. Here, tonight, eight P.M. We have a lot to talk about, I think."

I turn up at eight in my usual tough-girl photographer garb—black boots, jeans, T-shirt, black leather jacket, Contax camera around my neck. Though I don't plan on taking any pictures tonight, I wear my camera as an emblem.

The house is as Bee Watson described, even more luxurious, I think. The blooming jasmine in the courtyard emits a perfume suggesting sweet and careless wealth.

Carson is dressed like a British sportsman in town for the day—tweed jacket, tattersall shirt, gleaming shoes, dark flannel slacks. He greets me with a smile perfectly composed, not at all like the distraught character I saw two weeks ago doing a perp walk in manacles.

He shows no sign of worry on account of his forthcoming trial. Perhaps he thinks the charge of murder will be dropped, and that a plea to having fought a duel will only add to his mystique.

He escorts me up to the gun room, offers me a drink, smiles when I ask for a glass of water. He shrugs, pours one for me, then a large cognac for himself. He swirls it in a snifter, then, donning a pair of white cotton gloves, proceeds to show me the Farouk guns I've heard so much about.

Though they're extremely well wrought, I'm not really very interested.

"Actually there're a couple of other guns I'd rather see," I tell him.

"Oh?" He raises an eyebrow. "You must be quite the connoisseur."

"Show me Mandy's Winchester and the revolver you used to kill Tommy Dunphy."

He stiffens. "You're well informed, Ms. Farrow. I don't usually show those guns to strangers."

"You want to know about Mandy, don't you? That's why you invited me. So let's cut the crap."

He gazes at me, amused. "Bitchy little broad, aren't you?"

I grin.

He grins back. "All right. It's not like they have any real value, you understand."

He opens a cabinet beneath one of the gun racks, pulls out the weapons, lays them on the refectory table beside the Farouks. They appear pretty scruffy in such exalted company, beat-up stocks and dull metal barrels beside a matched pair of gleaming masterworks of the gunsmith's art. But the way Carson handles them tells me that for him they carry a lot of meaning. I'm going to have to play my cards cleverly, I think, if I'm to walk off with them tonight.

As I move to touch them, he winces slightly. Perhaps he thinks I too should put on gloves. I ignore him, pick up Maddy's Winchester, fondle it, am surprised at how small and light it is. I feel a strange sensation too—the same slightly squeamish feeling I get when working with her cameras.

"Here's my proposition. I'll tell you the full life story of Mandy Vail, whom I knew extremely well. In return I want these guns."

He scoffs. "Not much of a deal, Ms. Farrow."

I study him, the astute real estate investor. He negotiates deals every day, while I barely do one a year.

"Suppose," I ask him, "I throw in the shots I took of the goings-on in apartment five."

He turns grim. "You're bluffing."

"Think so? Ever notice the attic window in the little house across Cypress Alley? It's got a view right into the bedroom. I staked you out. So did Mandy . . . before you paid a street enforcer two hundred bucks to scare her off." I stare at him. "You didn't know the 'old biddy' was Amanda Vail, did you? Or that she was known the last forty years as Maddy Yamada, one of the most respected photojournalists in the world?"

"That can't be," he says, sinking into one of the chesterfields, pomp deflated, self-assurance draining from his eyes. "Not her. Couldn't have been. I don't believe it."

"It was her all right. And you had her killed."

Though he continues to shake his head, he knows I'm telling him the truth. "Tell me what you know?" he says finally. And, when I shrug, he whimpers: "Please."

"The guns?"

He waves his arm. "Take them. Take the goddamn things. They're just worthless junk anyway."

It's after midnight when I finally leave, having told him Maddy's story and answered numerous questions about her life and work. Now I carry the weapons out in a splendid English leather gun case probably worth twenty times the value of what's inside.

I'm exhausted. Bee was right about Carson being emotionally dead. There's barely, I think, the tiniest pith of human feeling in him. Recounting Maddy's story, I felt as though I were talking to an empty suit. Though stricken at first by the news that it was his beloved Mandy he'd ordered chased away, he could only relate the episode to himself.

"Way back when we were young I was crazy about her," he told me. Then he shook his head. "Hard to feel much of anything for her now, except . . ." He winced. "She made a damn nuisance of herself."

I stared at him, incredulous. "A nuisance! You call her *a nuisance?*"

He shrugged. "Hiding in a little room behind a camera—that wasn't the shooter I fell in love with when we were young."

Well, I think, as I wait now for my taxi outside his gate, impossible to feel anything for him. He's a killer, a monster. Even his madness fails to move me.

Maddy, I think, would know just how to photograph him—mercilessly, straight-on, full-frame, beneath a relentless noonday sun, letting the harsh light strip him to the very core of what he's become, exposing his ice-cold killer's eyes so that they meet the viewer's gaze.

Six days later: Hank Evans and I, faces painted dark and dressed in black fatigues, lie beside one another on a rise behind a large felled oak not two hundred feet from the main compound of the G.G.C.

It's exactly 12:15 A.M., the sky is studded with stars; behind us hangs a delicate crescent moon. The air tonight is sweet, redolent of resin and bay leaves. The ground's so dry I hear the crackling of tiny twigs whenever I make the slightest move.

Though I told Dad I was sick of guns, I'm not finished with them yet, there being a few loose ends to tie up before I expel them forever from my life.

Hank, preparing to leave me here while he ventures into the very heart of G.G.C. property, is on a high.

"Gonna be a piece a cake, Kay," he whispers. "Fun too. That's the best part. You're going to see how much fun it is."

His plan, to probe right to the clubhouse, do his business then safely retreat, has been meticulously prepared. He's come in here twice this week to haul supplies, reconnoiter and check his route. Meantime I phoned Vince Carroll, told him to go away for a few days, preferably someplace where he'll be seen by lots of witnesses. As a result he and Pris have gone off to Tahoe for a week to attend a workshop/seminar: "How to Operate a Profitable Bed-and-Breakfast Inn."

An hour ago Gale Hoort drove us to our starting point, a spot on a fire road that intersects with the southern perimeter of G.G.C. grounds. From there we made the trek to our present location in less than forty minutes. We walked single file, I following in Hank's footsteps at thirty feet, the two of us communicating by hand signals. No snakes this time, no animals breaking through the brush, no tripping over logs, or branches springing back to lash my face. I've had the pleasure tonight of prowling the forest with an expert woodsman, one moreover who's been an army ranger and Lurp mission leader in Vietnam.

Hank checks his watch. "It's time," he whispers. "If I go now, I'll have forty minutes in the clear."

He's referring to the G.G.C. security check-in procedure, disclosed to us by Vince. The club, he informed us,

has four guards on duty on weekday nights, hired through
a contract security service. The men are new to the area
and perfunctorily trained. Three are stationed on tree-high
guard platforms, one of them at the main gate, the other
two on either side of the club compound. The fourth man
sits in the club security office monitoring motion detectors,
security devices and the guards' field radios. Each guard
must check in hourly with the office on a regular rotation,
starting at five minutes past the hour. Thus our window of
opportunity will last from now to 1:05 A.M., more than
enough time, Hank believes, to accomplish the mission
and withdraw.

After he rises to a crouch, I help him slip into his backpack. Inside are fifteen half-pound blocks of C-4 plastic
explosive wrapped in waxed paper, fuse igniters, gas tank
charges with timers, heavy-duty padlocks, remote detonators and two hundred feet of detonation cord. The electronic unit to set off the detonators stays here with me.

In addition we both carry a field radio, water canteen
and flare gun hooked to our belts. I also carry my cell
phone to call Gale when we're ready for pickup, while
Hank wears a holstered army-issue Colt .45 and a ban-
dolier containing a half-dozen extra magazines.

I've been worried about that Colt, afraid he'll use it.
The only condition I've set for tonight is that no guard or
guard dog be harmed. Hank's given me assurances. He's
going to create diversions to pull off the guards and will
neutralize the dogs by placing his own locks on the kennel
gates. But, he's also warned me, if anyone shoots at us, he
won't hesitate to return fire.

"Not to kill them, Kay, but to force them to take cover."

Though I'm not crazy about the idea, I can think of no
alternative, for I've decided that under no circumstances
will I submit to capture here a second time.

Hank, giving me a farewell pat on the back, crawls out
from behind the oak trunk, then starts to move, belly to the
ground, toward his next position fifty feet away. We both

have our field radios turned on with the understanding that we'll use them only in event of an emergency.

As I watch him crawl away, I ask myself what I'm doing here, whether I've become so addicted to danger and excitement I've lost my common sense. Aikido used to be enough for me. On the mat I found all the excitement I required. But since my fight with Julio Sanchez, I've been appalled by my apparent craving for more. Even the sickening experience of being abused by Chipper and Buckoboy failed to slacken the hunger. Finding Kevin Lee's body inside the car, tripping over Wo Hop To bodies down in Drawbridge, staring into Rusty's eyes at the very moment he blew out the back of his head—all that violence hasn't daunted me, seems rather to have increased my appetite. Tonight I hope to purge myself of the need.

Hank's out of sight now, but I know pretty well where he is, moving stealthily along the lengthy wall of boards and sand that constitutes the rear of the G.G.C. firing range. Back there he's out of sight of the guard on the near tower, assuming said guard is even awake and doing his job.

Two minutes later Hank reappears. Though I see very well in darkness, I pick up his pair of Russian army-surplus night-vision binoculars in order to follow him as he moves among the service buildings, then toward the kennels to place his locks. This is his first task, which could turn dangerous if the dogs become excited and start to bark.

Give him five minutes to reach the kennels, one to place the locks, five more to reach the vehicles in the service parking lot, five to set his gas tank charges on the cars and propane tank, then sneak away.

As I wait for him to reappear at the side of the lodge, I think about the different motivations that have brought us here to rain ruin upon the G.G.C.

For Hank the desire springs from a long-seething rage against rich dilettantes who have created a fiefdom by fencing off fine hunting lands previously open to all. He hates them for importing game, hunting with expensive firearms, despises their power, snobbery, hypocrisy, exclusivity, rough and illegal treatment of poachers and apparent immunity from the laws and social norms that prescribe his life and those of his friends. It's a blue-collar rage he feels, anger against privilege fueled by tales of the revelries and orgies that take place at the club. In the end, I think, it's the same strain of fury that possessed Russian peasants as they observed their aristocratic masters living decadent lives of pleasure at their expense.

My anger is sharper, more personal, for I was bound to the pool table, then threatened with the ritual gun. The men who abused me have been well punished, but for me that's not nearly enough. I want the whole enterprise destroyed, most particularly the site of my degradation. "If you're going to blow the place up," I told Hank, "don't forget to do the gun room for me."

I catch sight of him now at the corner of the lodge. He rises, waves his arm to signal that so far things are going well. The diversion explosives are set, the detonation cord is strung. In exactly one minute he'll ignite the fuses. Then when, hopefully, the guards are drawn away from their towers, he'll break into the main lodge to inflict some truly serious damage.

I check my watch, then huddle down. It's so quiet now, so still, I relish my knowledge of what's about to happen. As a surge of power washes over me, I think that, indeed, the old adage is true: knowledge *is* power . . . and tonight the power belongs to me.

A flash of light. Then a huge report. The *Boom!* crashes across the compound, rages against my ears. I duck, quickly slip on a pair of heavy shades to protect my eyes. When I look up again, it's in time to see the first fireball rise like some kind of weird gaseous specter from behind the lodge, quickly followed by a series of explosions on the far side of the compound.

The fireballs come quickly—two, three, four, five! Within seconds the smell of burning gas wafts to my nostrils. The light of the fire sets the nearest tower in silhouette. I observe the guard standing at the railing, then scampering down the ladder to the ground. I pick up the night-vision binocs to watch him as he races toward the front yard of the lodge, meets up with another man, probably the guard stationed in the security office, then the two of them as they run toward the back to see what's happening in the parking lot.

Since I certainly don't want them to get hurt, I send them a wish-message: *Don't go too close! It's not your club! Run away! Let the G.G.C. be damned!*

A huge blast lights up the sky. Must be the propane tank, I think. *What a diversion! Jesus! I hope Hank didn't plant any more explosives back there.*

We figured it would take the fire department at least fifteen minutes to reach the club, a good two hours after that to get the fire in the rear under control, by which time we would be long gone.

I think of Hank now inside the lodge building, setting his charges, molding them to doors, light fixtures, the grand piano in the lounge, beneath the mahogany bar. Then sticking in the detonators, turning the detonator switches on, moving always toward the gun room, pool table in the center and all the fabulous guns gleaming brilliantly in their cherrywood racks.

Mold some C-4 to the gun vault too while you're at it, Hank. Blow all their precious firearms sky-high. Blow up the videotapes of the orgies, the club records, logs, accounts and membership rolls. Take out the antiques, paintings, lugubrious hunting trophies mounted on the walls. Don't forget the leather couches in the lounge, the big oak club officers' table in the dining room, the range in the kitchen where the succulent prime steaks are grilled. Take it all out! Every trace. Leave nothing behind but smoke and ash.

Hank's running toward me now. He doesn't even bother to hunch low or crawl, just runs openly across the main yard, crosses the firing range where Chap Fontaine was killed, then leaps his way to cover in the trees. Half a minute later he flings himself down beside me.

"Best time I've had in years," he says, panting. He turns to me. "Great diversion, huh?" There're beads of sweat on his face, exultation in his eyes.

He reaches for the device that will set the detonators off.

"How do you want it, Kay?" he asks. "One at a time or all at once?"

"I think all at once will be just fine," I tell him.

"Yeah!" He smiles. "Well then—here she blows!"

He pulls all the switches together, then clamps his hands to his ears. I do the same. There's a brief pause, barely long enough for me to sigh, then an explosion so loud and violent it dwarfs the diversion explosions many times over. The entire main lodge of the club seems to rise up into the air, hang there a moment, then collapse. Secondary explosions erupt. Flames leap. Acrid smoke clouds the air. Plumes of dust rise, shimmering pillars. I grin. We are destroyers wreaking vengeance, flinging down lightning bolts upon our enemies.

"We're outa here," Hank says, gathering up his stuff. "Oh, by the way, I got something for you." He reaches beside him, hands me a gun, the one gun in the world I'd know anywhere—"The Goddess."

"It's the one you wanted, right?"

"Oh, Hank! I can't believe it. You're fabulous!" I plant a kiss on his cheek.

"Couldn't resist taking a souvenir," he says. "Listen, I want to double-time it out if that's all right."

"Sure."

"Halfway to the road, we'll give Gale a call."

At that he starts to move, I following again at thirty feet, the two of us jogging stealthily through the forest. Holding "The Goddess" before me, I feel like Diana herself, Goddess of the Hunt, loping jubilantly, triumphantly through the moonlit woods.

News of vastly destructive nocturnal explosions at the G.G.C. is the lead story on tonight's late news. I watch from bed as Sheila Troy, Channel 6's glamorous on-scene reporter, offers an analysis before the smoldering wreckage of the club.

"Sheriff's office sources attribute the explosions to disgruntled hunters in the local community," she reports. "These men, according to these same sources, have long resented the Goddess Gun Club for its strict policy toward poachers, some of whom have actually been shot by G.G.C. guards. It's no wonder, these sources tell me, that resentment has built to the point where an attack has taken place. In addition there are mercenary groups in Mendocino County who may have had reason to want the exclusive shooting club burned down. Estimated damage due to the blaze, including buildings and artifacts—six point four million dollars. One law enforcement source, close to the sheriff, tells me that the sabotage was so well executed he estimates a commando squad of at least a dozen men worked with military precision to bring it off."

Four guns to dispose of now . . . and I know just where each one must go.

I take my new H&K straight to Gun City, tell the woman behind the counter I've changed my mind and would like to sell the pistol back.

She picks it up, examines it. "Never been fired," she notes. "I can't give you full price. How's eighty percent? Or you can leave it here on consignment. I'm fairly certain I can sell it for you, but of course not for what you paid."

I happily accept a twenty percent loss, figuring it's a fair price for ridding myself of trouble. I'm glad I'm over my gun phobia now, glad too I've discovered that guns aren't me.

Tonight I phone Bee Watson, tell her I've got something for her. We arrange to meet tomorrow in Bolinas. Sasha has agreed to drive me out at noon.

Next I call David Yamada. At first he's shy with me, stumbling over his words. Then he apologizes for his behavior the last time we met, rushing out of the coffee shop without saying goodbye.

"That's okay, David," I tell him. "I understand. Since then I've learned all about Maddy's past, her career as a fancy shooter in the circus."

Silence. "I should have known you'd find out. Maddy always said you were relentless."

"I found Bee Watson. She lives out in Bolinas. She told me everything. I even have the old Winchester Maddy used to use."

He gasps.

"This is important, David. Please tell me the truth. Was it really her idea to embargo her early papers? Or did you decide that on your own?"

"I did what I thought best," he tells me. "She didn't want people to know."

"When she was alive—sure, I understand. But now that she's gone it doesn't make sense. I believe her past informed the deep humanity of her work. Her whole life, the fancy shooter as well as the socially concerned photojournalist, is present in every photograph she took."

"I guess."

"Anyhow, you should know I'm going to present the rifle to the museum, also an interview tape I'm going to make with Bee. I feel very strongly that Maddy's full story must be known. Meantime I hope I can persuade you to revise the terms of your gift."

Silence again. "I'll think about it, Kay."

"Thank you. I know you'll do what's right."

He chuckles. "You don't leave a person much room to maneuver."

"Probably my worst failing," I admit.

The moment Bee sees "The Goddess," her eyes widen. She hugs me, then lightly runs her hands over the gun, caressing the engravings with her fingertips.

"It's for you," I tell her. "You made it. Now it's yours again."

Soon her desire gives way to squeamishness. "I don't know, Kay. It's stolen property, isn't it?"

I assure her that as far as anyone knows, every single gun in the G.G.C. gun room was blown up or consumed by fire.

"I understand," she says, "but you see, it's a Parker Invincible, a great gun, the rarest and finest Parker ever made. I'll have to return it to them. I'll ship it to them anonymously." She smiles. "But not the engraving. I'll take off all the steel first."

Sasha drives us out to Point Reyes, then into the National Seashore. We park at the head of Tomales Point Trail, then hike through coyote brush, following the curves of the moors into the Tule Elk Reserve. Perhaps because it's a weekday afternoon and the fog's closing in, we pass only two other hikers coming the opposite way. En route we stop to observe herds of elk. An occasional rabbit leaps across our path. At six P.M., when we reach the grassy slopes of Tomales Bluff, there's no one else around.

The view from here is wondrous: open ocean to the west, the mouth of long narrow Tomales Bay to the east. Waves crash against the rocks below, churning spume, showering land's end with spray. Fishing boats bob on the swells. The fog makes the place seem otherworldly, uniquely strange.

It's from here that we've decided to cast away the revolver Ram Carson used to kill Tommy Dunphy in their duel. Sasha offers to hurl the murder gun into the water. He throws well. The little gun flies high, clears the rocks, falls into the mouth of the bay, which, Bee tells us, is prowled continuously by great white sharks, devouring fish and anything else living or dead that crosses their murderous paths.

I phone Baggy Bigelow. He turns frosty as soon as he hears my voice.

"You welshed on our deal, Kay. We were to become friends, see each other once a month. Now two months go by and you call out of the blue. I'm deeply hurt. Hurt to the quick."

I think he likes feeling hurt, that he nurtures himself licking his wounds. As for me, whom he fancied as his "new young friend"—how delicious it must be for him to savor the pain I've inflicted by my neglect.

"Look, Baggy, I've been busy as hell bringing down Carson and the G.G.C. Who do you think found a witness to the duel with Fontaine? Who do you suppose blew up the club lodge?"

"My God, girl!" In an instant his frostiness melts to syrup. "You've got an item for me?"

"I've got a whole column."

"Please, dear, bring your sweet tush straight over here. I and all my Barbies are panting, breathless for your company."

OH, HOW SWEET IT IS!
by
Schuyler Bigelow

THIS DEPARTMENT has learned more about the weird and bizarre goings-on at the veddy exclusive, veddy tony, all-male Goddess Gun Club in Mendocino County, lately blown up by persons unknown.

A highly knowledgeable source, exclusive to THIS COLUMN, reveals that among numerous valuable firearms lost in the catastrophe was a particular weapon which club insiders called "The Goddess."

Sounds perfectly innocent, right? Maybe so . . . until
you learn that this weapon, an antique Parker shotgun,
was embellished with engravings of pornographic
scenes watched in turn by a group of animal-voyeurs
bearing the caricature faces of leading members of the
club.

Lately making the rounds at Pacific Heights dinner
parties—you know the kind, those veddy exclusive
little gatherings of eight or ten—has been a game
of "zoo," i.e., match-the-critter-to-the-member.

Here, for your delectation, DEAR READERS, is a
short list of animals and G.G.C. members whom knowledgeable folk are trying to match up. See what you can
do with them.

CRITTERS: Monkey; Fox; Leopard; Wolf; Pelican;
Gazelle; Ostrich; Crocodile.

MEMBERS: Jack Stadpole; Orrin Jennett; Raid
Harris; Ramsey Carson; Henry Petersen; Tuck Chubet; Carter Dixon; Chauncey Chase.

And there's more! Scuttlebutt has it that "The Goddess" was used in a veddy unseemly manner during
certain arcane "rituals" conducted on club premises,
rituals that mirrored the activities engraved upon the
gun itself. Oh, dear boys! If only those burned-down
G.G.C. walls could talk!

On a more serious note: A year and a half ago THIS
DEPARTMENT made mention of contentious G.G.C.
meetings regarding certain "recreational" goings-on
at the club, and, a few weeks later, that differences
between members had been resolved in "a traditional
gentleman's manner."

Now all the world knows that a gun duel was fought
between cofounders Ramsey Carson and his real estate
business partner, the much loved and greatly missed
Chaplin Fontaine. Fontaine was killed in the duel,
about which witnesses lied to local police. Later, Carson eulogized Fontaine at a hypocritical memorial ser-

*vice in Grace Cathedral. As reported in THIS NEWS-
PAPER, indictments of several of San Francisco's
leading citizens have since been handed down.*

*It can now be revealed that this was not the first gun
duel fought by Mr. Ramsey Carson. Nor was it the first
duel in which he killed an opponent. Future columns
will supply further details on this gentleman's rather
amazing histoire.*

*Query: Is the aforementioned histoire relevant? The
case prosecutor seems to think so. Carson's indictment
for murder, as opposed to merely dueling, is based on a
legal theory that an experienced duelist facing off
against an inexperienced opponent is akin to a professional prizefighter taking on an ordinary Joe in a bar,
i.e., assault with a deadly weapon. And for such a person, who has killed before, to engage in a duel is
indicative of "intent to kill."*

*Let it now be recounted that after THIS DEPART-
MENT first wrote about the club, an attempt was made
to intimidate your FAVORITE COLUMNIST by an
anonymous caller who threatened him with "a bullet in
the brain" should he continue to file items about the
G.G.C. A couple of days later a bullet engraved with
his initials was received in the mail.*

*Now far be it for THIS DEPARTMENT to impugn
the reputation of any particular person by accusing him
(or her) of issuing this obnoxious ultimatum. Still, it's
important that you, DEAR READERS, understand that
THIS DEPARTMENT will never be intimidated by
threats, no matter how vicious and no matter how
exalted or well connected the source.*

*Over the coming weeks we shall offer further revela-
tions about G.G.C. goings-on, including some, shall we
say, veddy strange parties held in an apartment in the
Mission, an apartment situated in a building owned by
(surprise!) CFJ Realty Corporation, a company bear-*

ing the initials of its original owners, Carson, Fontaine and Jennett.
    STAY TUNED!

The end of summer: My life is coming together. All the endgames have been played out, all the mysteries resolved. I still miss Maddy, her nurturing friendship and sometimes sharp critiques, most of all her powerful eyes, which could see intentions in my work I barely knew were there. But I keep reminding myself that I must become my own coach and best critic now.

The painful memory of my ordeal in the gun room has greatly diminished. The humiliation has been well paid back. It's time to put all that behind me. Sasha says that to allow oneself to feel humiliated is to grant to one's tormentors an unseemly power.

And so I concentrate on the future, which now is to achieve my *shodan* in aikido. I train hard every day, working with Rita, practicing techniques, looking forward nervously to the exam.

Tonight, coming straight from evening practice, I drop in on Sasha without calling him first. He's delighted; his liquid eyes light up. He gazes at me, insists we make love at once—never mind a shower first.

"But Sasha—I'm so sweaty."

"Never mind." He licks his lips. "I like you that way."

He picks me up, carries me to his couch, gently lays me down. Then he undresses me, makes passionate love to me, bathing my body with his tongue.

Later, as we're hugging one another, he tells me he adores the fact that I see him in black and white. It's such an interesting comment I ask him what he means.

"I like the way I look in the pictures you take of me."

"You want to be seen as possessing a formal abstract beauty, is that it?"

"It's more like I love being loved by your eyes," he says.

I stroke his dusky face. "Camus said: 'Death and colors are things we cannot discuss.' "

"He also said, and I like this very much: 'There is no fate that cannot be overcome by scorn.' "

I owe him so much: For introducing me to David Bohm's theory of the implicate order, without which I might never have sussed out what Maddy was doing. For an act of loving kindness I can never put out of my mind—how, on our first Christmas together, he gave me a painting of an Indian goddess which he photographed first in black and white, to make sure it would be pleasing to me even though I wouldn't be able to see it in color. Most of all for his gentleness as he helped me cope with the trauma of the gun room, urging me to draw what I could not face, helping me to unravel the mystery of the bee. He understood too why I needed to go back to the G.G.C. to watch Hank blow it up.

Two p.m.: The Warren Field House at Sonoma Valley Community College. Over two hundred martial artists from all over California have assembled here for a five-day intensive aikido retreat.

It's the last afternoon. Exams are about to begin. Six of us are going for our black belts, others for higher ranks. My fellow aikidoists, including Rita, sit in *seiza* position, suited up, in two long rows along the edge of the gigantic mat. Others—a good hundred guests in civilian clothes, among them Joel, Lucky, Sasha and Dad—sprawl at the far end.

Three judges, senior senseis from Japan, have come to administer the exams. They sit at a table off center from the *kamiza* where the photograph of O-Sensei hangs.

Those of us about to be tested are busy stretching and warming up on the mat edge.

The exams begin. I take my place in the front row. The first candidate's name is called. I watch as he moves to the mat, bows in, bows to the judges, then goes to his knees to take the first attacks from his *uke*.

I watch but do not watch. My eyes are turned inward, looking deeply into myself, seeking the warm center where the power lies, the power upon which I know I soon must draw. Nearly an hour passes. Three other candidates complete their tests. My name is called. I awake as if from a meditation and move onto the mat.

Ralph is my *uke*. He is ten years younger. Tall and graceful, he had been a black belt himself for only a year. We have trained well together ever since he joined Marina Aikido. His style is direct yet gentle, no-nonsense but not too tough. I want him to love me even as he attacks me, and I want to love him even as I throw him off.

I apply the first series of compulsory techniques, as required, from the kneeling position. Then, as the senior judge calls out further requirements, Ralph rises to attack me from full height. Next I rise so that we face one another, both of us on our feet. More techniques. More throws. I start feeling really good.

I don't look at the judges, nor at Rita, who I know is watching me intently. She has warned me not to mimic her techniques, but to perform in my own style according to my sense of my own power. I am here today for myself. I don't even look much at Ralph's face. Rather I look past him. I want to defeat his attacks without effort. Even when I throw him down I barely notice.

Everything feels "right" this afternoon. I have found my center. I own the place where I stand, and a good-sized area around me. Rita has counseled me many times: "When you step onto the mat, take possession, make it your own."

It is time now for the *randori*. For the first time in all

my years of aikido training, I don't tense in anticipation of
a multiple attack. A good ten aikidoists contend to go at
me. The first four in line ready themselves while the others
fade back to their positions in the rows. I give a quick
glance to my attackers. Two men, two women. All four are
familiar. We have all trained together during the retreat.

I stand ready to take them on, claiming my space,
drilling my legs down into the mat, preparing to blend.
And then, just as they come at me, I enter a trance state.
Even the bright sunlight that floods the field house doesn't
distract or blind me now.

I don't think about anything, don't calculate, don't prepare, simply take them on as they come, turning, blending,
wheeling as I throw them off. I float. Every move I make
seems faultless. I turn . . . and turn . . . and can do no
wrong. No gesture is wasted. I seem to have achieved the
miraculous state of mindless perfection which Rita calls
"pure flow."

Nothing can touch me unless I let it. No one can hurt
me, not these attackers, nor anyone else. I am not there
when they think they have reached me. They collide with
one another as I step between them or move back. There is
no resistance from them because I have defeated all resistance within. Everything is clear. Even the light seems to
change, to modulate to a darker tonality more gentle on my
eyes. Targets become larger, easier to see and find, the
light becomes sharper and, paradoxically, more mellow.
The squeak of bare feet on the mat. The sounds of heavy
breathing. I don't face my opponents, I face only myself as
I sweep them all aside.

I am the center of a whirlpool of energy, aware of
everything around me yet fazed by nothing. Time is
warped. Actions that appear to others as sudden are for me
orderly and slow. Shadows are elongated, becoming
deeper, textured like black velvet. Grunts, groans, cries
and pants turn into music. And I am at the center of it
all, she-who-harmonizes, she-who-*is*-the-music, blending

effortlessly, cleanly, in tune with the cosmic process, every breath clearly drawn, every move structured as in a dance.

The exam is over. I'm seized by an enormous sense of clarification. I pause, search the faces turned toward me, read admiration in hundreds of pairs of eyes.

I think: *I did it, and now I have regained my life. My time of mourning and anger is over. Once again my life belongs wholly to me.*

NOW AVAILABLE IN HARDCOVER

Lee Child

author of DIE TRYING

TRIPWIRE

PUTNAM

NOW AVAILABLE IN HARDCOVER
JUDITH KELMAN
A NOVEL OF SUSPENSE
AFTER THE FALL
PUTNAM